ALL OUR GHOSTS

JESSICA NORTON

Book Cover by Aurora McGaughey

Editing and Proof Reading by Becky Clapham & Aubrey Taylor

Illustrations by Aubrey Taylor

First Edition 2024

To the ones who are tired of choosing flight.
Fight like Hell.

CONTENT WARNINGS

<u>This book contains themes of the following:</u>

Domestic Violence Representation

(Not the MMC, minimally described both Physical and Verbal.)

Talks of Miscarriage and the trauma surrounding it.

Narcissism (not any of the main characters)

Violence (The Hell Hounds MMC are Morally grey characters)

Sex Work (Implied, never described)

Sex Trafficing (Implied, never described)

Open Door Smut

Death (Blood, gore, guns, knives)

Description of drowning, CPR, bruises etc.

Kidnapping

Be kind to yourself. Take breaks, get some water and remember you are loved.

OFFICIAL PLAYLIST

DOOMSDAY - LIZZY MCALPINE
DO I WANNA KNOW? - ARCTIC MONKEYS IT
WILL COME BACK - HOZIER
BONES - KOETHE
HEAVY IN YOUR ARMS - FLORENCE + THE MACHINE
I MELT WITH YOU - MODERN ENGLISH
I FELL - WICCA PHASE SPRINGS ETERNAL
SEVENTEEN GOING UNDER - SAM FENDER
SAY - RUEL
FEAR - BLUE OCTOBER
SLEEP DEPRIVATION - CHANCE PEÑA
BACK IN MY BODY - MAGGIE ROGERS
WILDFIRE - CAUTIOUS CLAY
AMEN - AMBER RUN
HILL THAT I'LL DIE ON - JONAH KAGEN
DEAR PATIENCE - NIALL HORAN
THREE LITTLE BIRDS - CLAY & KELSY, ELDER SISTER
UNTIL THE LEVEE - JOY WILLIAMS
BROTHER - EVAN HONER
THIS IS ME TRYING - TAYLOR SWIFT
CAN'T HELP FALLING IN LOVE - JAKE & SHELBY
THE CHAIN - FLEETWOOD MAC

Contents

PROLOGUE

So, what do you do when everything you planned your life to be, goes to absolute shit? God—if you believe in him—looks at the path you've carved out for yourself and laughs. A laugh like he's just seen the most hilarious comedy show ever. Though, it's not funny.

KADENCE

July | Miami, Florida

I feel numb. Staring out of the large pane windows of the hospital room, my hands have finally stopped shaking. I feel empty. Why me? The voices behind me are muffled by the slow thud of my heartbeat. I can't focus on the medical terms and prognosis of my stay here, so instead, I watch the clouds swirl and form together into soft pillows in a blue sky. My green eyes flicker down and onto a woman being pushed in a wheelchair, her arms wrapping tightly around a blanket, her fingers tracing along chubby cheeks. The man pushing her halts their journey, planting a kiss on top of her head followed by the infant's. I wince at the family, a haunting picture of what my future should have been.

The voices grow louder and, as if turning a knob on an old radio, they become clearer. "Kadie? Sweetie, are you listening?" My mother's voice. I wrap the deep gray knit cardigan further around my body like a shield as the new parents disappear from my view.

"*Kadie.*" I can hear the sternness in Janice's voice as I turn around, purposefully using the nickname she knows I hate.

Doctor Watkins clears his throat, crossing his arms over his chest. "It's very important that she rests for the next few days. Her body has been through a lot and needs to heal." His words drip with monotonous sympathy and his brows furrow with a pain he has no right to feel.

"When can I go home?" I ask, glancing between Watkins and my mother.

The doctor sighs, looking down at my chart. "We can discharge her now if you'd like—" He glances towards me once more before turning to Janice. "However, I would recommend that she stays overnight for observation."

I narrow my eyes as he addresses my mother as if I'm not in the room. Anger brews in my chest and my fingers curl tighter around the woven threads of my cardigan.

"*Doctor*, I would really appreciate you addressing *me*. I lost my child. I didn't lose my hearing," I bite.

"Kadence Marie Andrews," my mother snaps. My eyes never leave the Doctor. I wish I could take a picture of the look on his face, surprised by the sudden conviction in my voice.

"I would like to be discharged now."

"I don't think—" Janice begins, staring at me with silent heat in her eyes.

"Take me home or I'll find another way home." I cut her off before the gaslighting starts. Before it gives her the chance to convince me this was my fault more than I already feel like it is.

I can't stay in this hospital room for another night. Constantly being poked and prodded at, arms bruised from the constant IV drips, and exhaustion turning to irritation with every bright-eyed, bushy-tailed nurse that walks into my room.

"Fine. Gather your things." Janice sighs, pinching the bridge of her nose at my protest, her words laced with bitterness.

The doctor nods, his face twisting in obvious disapproval of my choice, though he doesn't push the matter. "Right this way, Mrs. Andrews. I'll have the nurses get the discharge paperwork filled out."

"Thank you, Doctor." Janice smiles, the bitterness quickly turning to sugar as she peers up at the man in his mid to late fifties, with salt-and-pepper hair and the perfect salary for my mother's liking.

My stomach had filled with dread the moment he walked through the door to my room. I knew my mother had spied the lack of a wedding ring on his left hand just by the elated smile that had crept across her face. His hand roams to the small of her back as he pushes her out the door with my mother grinning as another hook has been set.

I roll my eyes and move to sit on the edge of the bed, flinching at the jolt of pain that courses from my core and up through my spine. I hadn't known it was possible to give birth at 16 weeks, but nobody really expects to have a miscarriage. Nobody expects to be abused by the person they thought loved them, but this is my life now, alone, abused, and enraged, with any plan I had developed over the last few years suddenly up in flames.

The door clicks back open, Janice sauntering in behind it. "Are you ready to leave? I have an appointment—"

A date is what you really mean, I think.

My mother's dull brown eyes glance down at the knock-off Chanel watch on her wrist. I stand, grab my bag, and throw what few items I have into it. "—I'd really like to be on time and since Jeremy *obviously* can't pick you up and you refuse to stay, I'd like to go."

I stare at my mother as the unbelievable words fly from her mouth. Making it sound as if Jeremy, currently being held at the Miami-Dade County jail, is *my* fault. Not that I expect him to stay there long; being the Lieutenant of one of the biggest counties in Florida means you make a few friends. Most of them won't believe that an upstanding officer of the law would *ever* hurt the woman he claims to love so much. But I know differently. Jeremy Miles is a different person behind closed doors, one with an explosive temper and one that only I was unfortunate enough to meet.

"I'm so sorry my trauma has inconvenienced you, Mother," I mutter, doing a quick once-over of the room as a nurse walks in with a wheelchair.

"Don't be ridiculous, Kadie." My mother sneers.

Jeremy had quickly become my mother's favorite out of the two of us. Not that it was surprising. Janice is a mother only when she absolutely needs to be, and even then, her motives are questionable. Jeremy's silver tongue charmed his way into Janice's heart the first night I introduced them four years ago. Ever since then it's always been two against one.

The drive from the hospital should only take twenty minutes, but with my mother's incessant complaining, it feels like hours... I haven't moved fast enough from the wheelchair to the car seat, then it's the traffic and, as we pull into my driveway, it's the sloped concrete that she has to park her precious '08 Mercedes Benz onto. *"You know I hate this driveway, Kadie. You need to move."* I'm positive she's speaking about the speed I'm moving to get out of the vehicle and not the actual home itself.

Janice hands me the packet of care instructions and a bag of prescription meds and grins in the rear-view mirror, one hand waving out of the window as she drives off.

"As always, good to see you, Mom," I mutter, watching the car disappear down the road.

I turn around towards the two-story, white townhome. I dread walking through that blue door, not ready to face the reality of my life from here on out. People talk about skeletons being hidden behind closet doors. Those people are lucky. Closets are small, confined, and the skeletons contained. I have a whole townhome full of skeletons and secrets; so much so that it feels like they ooze from the walls at times.

I push open the door to be greeted by a mess only a tornado could make. Picture frames lie in pieces on the floor. Tiny shards of glass stick up from the thick carpet. The dinner I had made is splattered onto the wall and stains the carpet below. I set the items in my hands down on the table in the entryway. Tears sting my eyes.

It was never supposed to be like this.

Love is never supposed to be like this.

I make my way up the stairs, gripping tightly onto the wooden railing that clings to the narrow hallway. The grief slowly creeps in with every step. The hallway is dark, lit only by the small, blue-and-teal stained-glass window at the other end, its halo falling onto the only closed door to the room I'm terrified to walk into. One that I'm not allowed to be in without him.

Jeremy has controlled every aspect of my life except for the one thing I would not budge on. My home. The very first big purchase of my own and I refused to let him take it from me. I remember the fight we'd had about it. I also remember having to buy four different kinds of concealer to try and hide the bruise under my eye. When he'd apologized, if I can even call it that, he'd promised to let me keep the house. He reminded me every day after I found out I was pregnant that he did so, and to appease his incessant reminders, I told him he could choose the nursery theme. He'd ordered and bought everything you could think of that an infant could need, only letting me in the room when he was home, and for a while, the fighting and the temper had stopped.

I thought things had changed.

My fingers wrap around the metal doorknob, freezing for a moment, almost expecting an open palm to the back of my head for even thinking about touching it. It doesn't come so I twist the handle, pushing open the door and letting the stream of sunshine light up the pale blue and yellow features. It illuminates the small safari animals painted on the walls; their eyes watchful and full of disappointment.

I feel tears begin to stream down my cheeks as I pick up a small stuffed giraffe with button eyes. It's the only thing I had been allowed to pick out for the room. I hug it to my chest, setting myself down into the rocking chair housed in the corner. Every raging emotion I willed myself to hold in while in the hospital finally begins to spill over. It feels like someone turned on the faucet and set my cup under the tap to let it flow.

This isn't a home anymore and the longer I sit, the more I realize that it hasn't been a home for a while. It will never be my home again.

HOLDEN

July | Stockton State Prison, Stockton, CA

"It's your lucky day, Nash." Jones smirks, handing me the bag of belongings I came into this hell hole with. "Say, Jenkins, how long do you think before we see soldier boy back here again?" He jests, nudging the officer standing next to him.

Jenkins grins, shaking his head. "Shit, with his temper? I give it a week."

You've never seen my temper, dumbass, I think.

I fake a smile at them both. The two of them have been giving me shit for the past eighteen months, something I've had to bite my tongue on to keep my head low, for Cole's sake. I slip my rings onto my fingers, raising a brow at the two dipshits laughing in front of me. I spent ten years in the military, dealing with the God complexes of almost all of my commanding officers. These two were child's play compared to them and my tour in Iraq.

"As much as I'd love to stick around and watch the two of you fuck each other in the showers, I've got places to be," I taunt as I shrug into my sleeveless leather cut.

The two officers go quiet, both staring daggers at me. It seems like I've hit a sore spot, making me smirk.

"You think you're fucking funny, Nash?" Jones steps forward, nose to my...chin. It's kind of hard to intimidate a man who's a good six inches taller than you. I bite the inside of my cheek, holding back a laugh as Jones' shit-brown eyes glare at me.

"Nah, Jonesy. I think I'm adorable." My lips pucker and make little kissing noises at the officer.

"ALL RELEASEES PLEASE MAKE YOUR WAY TO THE FRONT GATE. ALL RELEASEES PLEASE MAKE YOUR WAY TO THE FRONT GATE."

I snort at the voice coming over the intercom. "Saved by the bell, Jonesy!" I pick up the rest of my belongings, clipping my wallet to the belt loop of my jeans and stuffing it into my pocket before turning and making my way down the long corridor.

"See you soon, Nash!" Jenkins laughs.

"Only in your dreams, asshole!"

I knock on the glass at the end of the hallway; the cute blonde-haired officer looks up for a moment before grinning. A loud buzz from above me sounds like freedom as I push the door open, throwing her a wink before letting the door slam behind me.

The scorching heat beats down on the back of my neck. I can already feel it turning the slightest bit pink following the long maze of chain-link fences and guard towers. The excitement and adrenaline begin rushing through me as I realize this is what going home feels like.

At the end of the fences another buzz sounds as the metal gate begins to slide against the pavement. Weathered black motorcycle boots take a step forward onto new ground, ground I haven't had the luxury of walking for over a year. A deep heavy breath leaves my lips and for the first time in forever the smell of sweat, body odor, and ass doesn't flood my nose. It almost makes me cry.

"Nash!"

My head snaps to the left, a grin spreading across my face as I see the source of the voice that calls my name. My best friend is leaning up against the unmistakable faded blue and white tow truck with the letters "O'Neil's Towing and Garage" written on the side. Cole runs the garage now after his father passed away. Along with the garage, he inherited the responsibility of the Hell Hounds Motorcycle Club; Pine River's best and worst kept secret. Cole has been President ever since his father passed away, a vote that took little to no discussion from any of the other members. I was voted in as Vice President shortly thereafter.

Cole pushes his sunglasses up onto the crown of his head, shoving the now grown-out hair out of his face. "Man, you look like shit."

I throw my head back and laugh, really laugh, the way only my best friend can make me do. "Yeah? And what's with the hair? You gettin' ready for the disco or somethin'?" I grin, stepping up to Cole, who just shakes his head.

"Fuck you," he chuckles, pulling me into a massive bear hug. "It's good to see ya, Pal."

"Yeah, you too," I mutter, clapping him on the back before pushing away. "Now, get me the fuck outta here," I smirk, walking around to the other side of the truck.

Cole climbs in, turning the ignition and blasting the air conditioning. It's easily almost ninety degrees outside and, no doubt, almost over a hundred in the truck. I relish in the missed luxury of the cold air and throw my bag of shit onto the floor by my feet as I jump in. Cole pulls out of the parking lot and heads towards the highway. One step closer to being where I belong.

It's a four-hour drive from the prison to Pine River, which gives just enough time for me to catch up on club business before being thrown back into it. When I was sentenced, it had been Cole's idea that I keep deaf ears on all club business while on the inside. I was less likely to get into any trouble being in the dark than I was knowing everything that was going on. Considering I have a way of getting myself into unsavory situations, it was a no-brainer. I'm a magnet for them. It's the reason I was in prison in the first place, but I don't regret what I did, just what it got me.

"So, guess I should tell ya now before ya find out from someone else..." Cole starts, glancing from the road to me. My jaw twitches as he shifts in his seat. "Trey is the new VP."

"Shut the fuck up. That dumbass?"

Cole sighs. "He's not a dumbass."

"He painted a fuckin' falcon on his bike." I roll my eyes. "Our mascot is a fuckin' wolf."

I watch my friend trying to hold back laughter, but his shaking shoulders give him away. "A bird! Cole, a fuckin' bird."

"Alright, alright. I get it. Not his brightest moment."

"He doesn't have many of those," I mutter, glancing out of the passenger window.

"Regardless, he's VP. So, let's be civil, huh?" Cole reaches over into the glove box, pulling something out and tossing it to me. I catch it, glancing down at the small piece of fabric. *SGT. at ARMS.* "That makes you our new Sarge..." Cole grins.

"How ironic."

"I thought it was fitting." Cole looks back out of the windshield with a shit-eating grin on his face.

I stuff the patch into the front breast pocket of my cut. "You're an asshole." I laugh.

"Yeah, well, you can blame the boys for that one. It was their idea and the vote was unanimous."

"'Course it was." I sigh, slouching down into the seat. "Anything else they voted in that I missed?"

Cole inhales, shaking his head. "We've got a meeting with Stokes tomorrow."

I roll my eyes at the name. Bradford Stokes, Pine River County Sheriff. A two-faced bastard who picks and chooses which side of the law he wants to be on. Stokes had been the first one to rat on me after the incident. Rat, meaning Stokes showed up at the garage and arrested me in broad daylight, no warning call, nothing. Showed up and cuffed me on the ground in front of fifteen members. *"Holden is an example,"* he'd claimed. I knew otherwise though. Stokes has disliked me ever since Cole and I were teenagers. How the hell was I supposed to know that the field I 'accidentally' set on fire was Stokes's cousin's?

"What the hell does Stokes want anyway?"

Cole shrugs. "Dunno. Probably just wants to make sure you aren't gonna kick his ass."

I laugh again. "He's gonna be lucky if I don't."

Cole sighs. "Look Nash, I'm glad you're home, but we need you at the garage and with the club. This past year was fuckin' rough without you." He glances over to me and a twinge of guilt fills my chest. "So don't go gettin' into any more shit."

"You mean don't get caught." I smirk, trying to ease the tension that was slowly filling the cab of the truck.

"Same fuckin' thing." Cole laughs.

KADENCE

Smoke billows from under the hood of my '63 Mercury Comet. I'm honestly surprised I've made it through 3,078 miles, countless tanks of gas, horrible fast-food stops, and plenty of traffic. My backseat is filled with what's left of my belongings after selling the townhome and most of its contents along with it. My entire life reduced down to two suitcases and this car.

"Shit," I mutter, carefully pulling to the side of the road and flipping on the hazard lights. I know that white smoke typically means the radiator needs water. This smoke isn't white and definitely doesn't smell good either.

I check the side mirror before climbing out of the vehicle and popping the hood. I walk around to the front of the vehicle, propping the hood up, only to be met with a dark cloud of smoke. I cough and wave my hand in front of my face stumbling back to catch a breath of fresh air.

"Goddamnit." Turning I look up and down the two-lane highway. There is nothing but desert and a few lone trees on either side of the road. It doesn't help that I don't remember the last time I'd seen a sign marking any sort of life in the future.

Slipping my phone from my pocket, I sigh. *No Service* stares back at me. We have electric cars, billionaires going to space, but shitty cell service in one of the most populated states in the US. Go figure.

I lean against the driver's door, hoping for someone to pass by. The heat is already creating small beads of sweat on my forehead. I pull open my door, leaning over the seat to grab a bottle of water. Climbing back out of the car, I twist the cap off, chugging half the bottle before tossing it back through the window, keeping my eye on the road for anyone willing to stop and help me.

Two hours go by without seeing more than a few cars. I try waving them down, but instead, I'm met with a glare and tail lights. Each dismissal only makes the pit in my stomach grow larger and it doesn't get any better when the sun starts to set. I won't be able to see shit in the pitch-black night.

There are bigger things for me to be scared of though. Darkness is only temporary, and if I had to sleep in my car on the side of the road in whatever hell hole I drove myself into, I would. Anything is better than staying in Miami.

I climb back into the Comet, stretching out across the seat. My stomach rumbles softly as I try to get even the tiniest bit comfortable. I reach onto the floorboard, rummaging through the sack of snacks I bought three hundred miles ago. Whatever I pull from this bag will have to do until I can figure out what to do, but as I lift my hand, I can't help but feel a little disappointed.

"Donuts for dinner it is then," I sigh, pulling open the wrapper and stuffing one in my mouth. Another car passes by. Hearing it at the last second, I sit up with a mouth full of donut, glancing out of the back window and groaning before plopping back down into the seat.

A gust of wind passes through the car and a slight breeze slips through the cracks of the doors and windows. I love this car, but it's old and a part of me is surprised that it even made it across country in the first place. The man I bought it from was old enough to be my grandfather and I got the impression he bought it brand new off the lot. It's definitely well taken care of other than whatever is going on with the engine, but even I can appreciate the amount of care he's put into it for sixty years.

I reach into the backseat, unzipping my bag to try and find something to keep me warm. As I move clothes around, my gaze lands on the ear of the stuffed giraffe. It's the only thing I took from the house other than my clothes and photographs from my childhood. Everything else I left. I have no interest in keeping any strings attached to my past life. It had been easy saying goodbye to that house. In fact, leaving that town was the easiest decision I ever made. The moment my eyes landed on that giraffe on my last walk through of the house, I couldn't leave it. Not to that house. I couldn't let it become another skeleton left to rot there alongside the painted safari animals.

I swallow the small lump growing in my throat as I grab my ratty University of Miami sweatshirt, quickly zipping the bag closed again. I shrug the sweatshirt over my head and shoulders. The black tank top and jeans I'm wearing do little to keep me warm as the night takes over. Settling into the seat I make sure the doors are locked, windows up, and the small, folded pocket knife I stole from Jeremy is tucked close by before curling back into the seat.

The stillness of the night starts to seep into the car around me in a shroud of fleeting comfort. The quiet, combined with knowing that he is thousands of miles away, unable to touch me, unable to convince everyone else I was the villain, had my eyes closing and soon the bucket seat of the Comet felt more safe than anything else right now.

I wake to what feels like sunshine beaming into the rear window of the car. My eyes peel open slightly and for a moment, I try to remember where I am and why it feels like God himself is pissing sunlight into my eyes.

Tap, tap, tap.

The noise coming from behind me makes me fly up out of my lying position to curl into the other side of the car. My breath catches in my throat as I grip the pocket knife in my hand. My eyes land on the source of the noise. A figure standing outside my window with hands up in mock surrender and wide eyes. Medium-length, sandy-blond locks brush over his cheeks as he leans down to my view.

We stare at each other for a moment before his hands come down to lean against the car.

"Ma'am, do you need help?" He asks, his voice muffled by the thin glass.

I glance around quickly, my eyes scanning the area, only to realize I had been asleep long enough for night to consume the land around me. I can't see anything past the glare of his headlights.

"Miss?" The man asks again, his voice laced with concern.

My eyes meet his, my fingers white-knuckling around the knife in my pocket. His thick brows are furrowed, mouth set in a firm line under the gray patched beard.

"My car broke down…" I say, watching as he nods, glancing toward my still-open hood. "It started smoking and won't crank over now," I say with a shrug to try to hide the anxiety clawing at my throat. Ocean-blue eyes peer back at me, glowing in the darkness.

"I got a call about a car abandoned on the highway... Guess no one actually checked to see if anyone was inside." He chuckles. "I can tow you into town if you want?"

I look back, realizing the lights my eyes are currently trying to battle are spotlights of a tow truck, its crane illuminated by the tail lights below it. My heart still races from him scaring me awake and my grip is still firm around the folded blade.

"How far is town?" I ask.

"About 30 miles, that direction," he says, pointing towards the direction I was headed in the first place. I follow the direction of his finger, glancing down the roadway again. "I won't hurt you, if that's what you're worried about."

I won't hurt you.

I've heard that before.

My gaze flicks back to his own. I can only imagine what I look like right now. Eyes wide, the vein in my neck pulsing with my heartbeat. I probably look like a caged wild animal. But even still, I don't miss the sincerity in his voice and the soft look he gives me makes me believe him.

I nod. My grip loosens on the knife but keeps it firmly in the pocket of my sweatshirt. I unlock the driver's side door opposite him, climbing out and stretching out my body for a moment as he watches me. As I turn, the blue tow truck comes into view. *O'Neil's Towing and Garage*. How convenient.

"What's your name?" The timbre of his voice almost scares me again as he slowly makes his way around the rear of the vehicle. I stiffen at the sound and turn towards him. He stops in his tracks, catching the slight movement.

"Uhm...Kadence," I say softly. "You said you got a call about my car?"

He smiles as I say my name and nods. "Yeah, people will call in abandoned vehicles to the sheriff's department and they call me."

I purse my lips together.

"Cole, by the way..." He takes another step towards me.

My hand finds my pocket, matching his step but backward. My fingers wrap around the handle of the pocket knife as he takes another step. I watch as his eyes flick down to the pocket of my sweatshirt; my heart begins to hammer again as he sighs.

"I'm just gonna get you hooked up if you wanna wait in the cab of the truck. I know it's cold." He offers and I realize he thought I was cold. I'll continue letting him think that. "You need anything from the car?"

"Y—yeah," I stammer as I open the door again. Grabbing my phone, wallet and keys. When I turn around, he's snuck his way around to my side of the vehicle, standing beside me by the rear door. "Jesus!" I gasp, almost dropping the items in my hand.

"Sorry! I didn't mean to freak you out." Cole takes a step back again, eyes narrowing in on me for a moment, assessing my skittishness.

I close my eyes and steady myself against the car with a deep breath.

"Are you sure you're okay?" He asks and I flash him a pointed look. He chuckles before tossing his head to the side towards the tow truck. "Door's unlocked and the heat's on. It'll only take a few minutes to get you loaded."

I nod. "Thank you..." I say softly as I step around him, heading towards the truck. When I see him follow me, I stop, turning my body around. "What—"

Cole stops again, furrowing his brow before realizing what him following me looks like. "Gotta flip the truck around to get you hooked up."

"Right."

"If you wanna wait by the car till I'm done... you're welcome to." He offers again, a gentle smile spread across his face.

For a moment, I feel bad. This man is trying to help me and I'm treating him like he's a serial killer. But that's what life as a woman has come to, right? Fearing the idea of leaving the house at night, walking down the street alone. Normal things that men don't even spare a second thought. But I can't afford not to. I've spent four years not fighting back against someone who laced his bitterness and evil with an all-addicting love. I'm not about to let my guard down now.

"Yeah, I'll do that..." I say, clutching my items closer to my chest as I lean against the car.

Cole smiles again. "No problem, Kadence."

He disappears into the cab of the truck, and I watch as he pulls it in front of the Comet. Once he's got it positioned the way he needs it, Cole hops out. His large frame climbs over the edge of the truck, lowering down the hook and chains to pick up the car.

"Door's unlocked if you wanna climb in," he yells over the rumble of his truck's engine.

I nod, heading towards the cab. My eyes inadvertently watch him as I pass. He flashes me a pearly-white smile and gives me a reassuring nod before getting back to work. The man is attractive, I can't deny that. I don't miss the ripple the muscles in his arm make as he pulls on the chains.

People thought Ted Bundy was attractive too.

My inner self scolds as I open the cab. A waft of what I can only describe as the scent of man, hits me. Spice, citrus, and motor oil fill my nose as I climb inside. Holding my belongings close to me, I pull out my phone, still no service and the battery slowly draining. I'll have to see if I can charge it when we get to town.

After a few minutes, Cole climbs back into the cab with a huff and flashes me another smile before putting the truck into drive.

"Shouldn't take us too long to get to town. I've got a garage there; I can take a look at the car in the morning," he says, checking over his shoulder as he pulls onto the desolate highway.

I subtly scoot my body closer to the door as he begins to drive. "Sounds great," I mutter. My tone is sharper than I intended, and my eyes slide shut. "Sorry, I'm sorry," I say, glancing over to him. "It's just been a long day."

Cole just nods and doesn't press me. "How long were you out there?"

I laugh. It's hollow and void of anything other than annoyance. "Since late afternoon?" I say and he sighs. "These roads aren't very popular, I take it?"

He laughs softly. "Well, that and it's small-town folk out here who are tired of tourists."

My mouth sets in a firm line and I nod. "Yeah, I can tell," I say, glancing back out the passenger window. A silence washes over us, filling the cab with unasked questions.

I glance over at him as he focuses on the road. It's the first time I've really looked at him. His hair is tucked back behind his ears, and it shows off the beard that's clearly hiding a chiseled jawline. Tattoos litter his body and arms, peeking out over the neck of his shirt. I notice a rather large tattoo of a wolf on his forearm; the lettering around it has faded slightly, and I can't quite make out what it says in the dimly lit cab.

"What brings you to California?" He asks, breaking me from my trance.

Other than running from my abusive ex-boyfriend who murdered my child?

"Road trip," I answer.

"You from around here?"

"Nope."

He chuckles again, getting the hint at my short answers. "Not much of a talker, are ya?" Cole glances over to me before looking back at the road. My body is pressed against the passenger door, my eyes glued to the window.

"Like I said, long day," I say softly.

He nods, not saying anything else.

It takes about twenty minutes for us to reach any sort of life. I see the brightly lit sign that reads *Welcome to Pine River, Population 5394.*

I never understood the point of population signs. They were littered all over Florida. The town I grew up in was about half the size of Pine River. The only thing population signs were good for was to show the life and death of a town.

"My shop isn't too far from here," Cole says, his voice cutting through the tension-filled silence in the cab.

I don't say anything, but as we pull up to the gate of the shop, Cole stops and hops out. I lean forward in the cab, watching him jog over and open the lot so he can pull in. O'Neil's Towing and Garage is painted on the side of one of the three buildings that are gated in the lot. The other one looks to have Hell Hounds painted on the side of it with a mural of the same wolf tattooed on his arm. My stomach flips for a moment until I see a line of motorcycles parked up against the building.

"Ready?" He asks, climbing back into the cab and pulling the truck in.

"You guys do vehicles too?" I ask, and it sounds stupid coming out of my mouth.

Cole nods. "Cars, trucks, motorcycles... if it's got an engine, we'll fix it." He pulls into one of the bays. "I'm gonna unload real quick and if you want to grab your things from the car, I'll take ya over to the motel."

"Thanks, Cole," I say. He smiles again and it feels comforting and not at all terrifying.

Without another word he jumps from the cab and starts to unload the car for me. I open my phone, feeling it begin to vibrate with messages and notifications.

> **[maria]**: *haven't heard from you. Just wanna know you're safe.*

> **[maria]**: *call me, Kade. Please.*

I sigh softly. Maria has been keeping track of where I've been throughout my trip. Just mainly wanting me to check in every state or so. Maria Santos has been the one person who hasn't condemned me for what Jeremy did. Never blamed me for the backlash he received, or lack thereof, but helped me stay safe. She's been the only friend I've had in years that didn't have to be approved by Jeremy.

> *just made it to California. I'm okay. I'll call you in the morning.*

I scroll through my other messages; there are a few from my mother. New photos of her and Dr. Watkins on their vacation to the Bahamas that simultaneously make my stomach sink and that familiar surge of anger brew. Two weeks. It took two weeks for Janice to sink her claws into him. I should be surprised. But I'm not. I'm sure I'll get a call in two months, and it'll be my mother sobbing on the other end about how it didn't work out. Looking for sympathy that I stopped giving years ago.

I tuck my phone into my pocket and sigh before climbing out, grabbing the suitcase from my car after Cole gives me the okay that it's safe to get near the Comet. I carry it over to the truck, climbing back in, Cole following suit.

The ride to the motel is quiet and I know he's curious about me. I can feel his questions and curiosity brewing. Instead, he drives straight to the motel like he said he would. My fingers occasionally wrap around the knife whenever he makes a quick movement or glances over at me.

The parking lot is barely vacant, with a few cars sporadically parked throughout. Cole stops the truck in front of the office and turns towards me. "You want me to wait till you get a room?" He asks, and my head snaps to him, my eyes wide, and I open my mouth, but before I can say anything, he shakes his head.

"No! I mean to make sure you make it in safely. Not for... that..." He waves his hand haphazardly.

"Oh!" I say, shaking my head with a small laugh. It's the first time I've laughed for real since meeting him and he notices. "Uhm... sure. Gimme just a sec."

I jump out of the truck, heading towards the office. The night receptionist is nice and sets me up with a room fairly quickly. Though more expensive than I would have liked, I don't plan on staying here long. Just long enough for the car to get fixed. He hands me the keys and smiles, pointing to my room along the row of doors. I thank him and head back outside.

Cole is still waiting, drumming along to some song he has turned up a little on the radio. I smile softly, opening the door. "I'm set up over there," I say grabbing my things. "Thanks again for the ride."

He smiles again at me. "No problem. Give me a little bit of time tomorrow to check out the car and I'll swing by and pick you up, say around noon?"

I nod. "Sounds good."

Cole taps the steering wheel and sighs. "Well, I guess I'll see you tomorrow then."

I watch the wolf flex over the ropes of muscles in his arms and nod.

"See you tomorrow."

I shut the truck door and step back, heading towards the room. I glance back, the truck still idling in the parking lot. As I get to the door though and step inside, I see the tail lights light up the building as he pulls out.

The door shuts behind me and I lock the deadbolt, followed by the top lock; I can't be too careful. I do a round throughout the room, checking the window is actually locked and close the curtains. After checking the closet and bathroom, I sit down on the edge of the bed.

The image of the wolf still dances around my mind. I'm not sure why I feel so drawn to it, but it feels familiar and safe. My mind races with my interaction with Cole.

I won't hurt you.

What he said replays in my mind and it's the first time in years that I trusted those words coming out of a man's mouth.

KADENCE

y eyes fly open. The room is still cloaked in darkness, and the only light is the soft glow around the curtains from the vacancy sign. I roll over to my side, glancing at the clock. 6:32 am. I sigh, not remembering the last time I've been able to sleep in. I hate that this is my new normal; that when I wake up like this, my body is covered in a thin sheen of sweat and my chest feels tight in a bittersweet indication of the anxiety dreams I can't ever remember in the morning. A part of me is glad that I can't remember them. Who knows what horror show my subconscious has cooked up to force my body to jolt awake in flight or fight mode.

I throw the scratchy sheets off myself. The smell in the room wafts through the air as I do. The smell doesn't bother me, it's not a wet musty smell, just a room that has been lived in by travelers and who knows what else. I'm not sure if that's any better, though, as my feet touch the stiff carpet. I take a few breaths to steady the rapid beating of my heart. I still haven't gotten used to having an entire bed to myself. No matter how toxic Jeremy was, it was one thing I loved; having someone next to me at night, filling that void that pillows can't.

An empty bed means I'm alone. Which then leads me down a path of what ifs and could-have-been. It was a vicious cycle of reminding myself that what happened wasn't my fault. Although, to an extent, I feel it is. I allowed myself to stay in that situation. I didn't leave—couldn't leave. The all-too-familiar feeling of guilt floods my chest as my fingers splay out over my stomach. Lingering there only to feel nothing.

With a shaky breath I reach over, tugging on the metal chain for the bedside lamp. The pale orange glow gives life to the dull room. My eyes scan the corners, ending on the deadbolt of the door. Still locked. Three thousand miles away and it still feels like he's on my heels.

I stand, walking towards the window and take a pleat of curtain between my fingers, pulling it back slightly. The sun has begun to rise over the horizon. The black mountains that sit off in the distance are backlit by a violet sky that is quickly turning to a pale blue.

I scan the parking lot, not seeing any vehicles that look strange or out of order to me. I recognize the ones that were parked in their spots last night but other than that it feels quiet. The tiniest sense of relief washes over me. I drop the curtain back, fixing it to make sure no one can see inside, before grabbing my things and heading to the bathroom.

The shower pressure is less than helpful as I try to wash the shampoo from my long, brunette hair. It takes me a lot longer than it normally would and the thought crosses my mind to chop it off. Shorter hair would make it harder for him to find me, but I like my hair just the way it is and I refuse to let him dictate my life any longer.

Once I've given up on the trickle that pretends to be water pressure and feel somewhat clean, I climb out of the shower and get myself ready for the day. Cole said he'd be by in the morning but I want to explore and get out of the mindset of running from my past. Even though I am.

I tug on a pair of jeans and a black t-shirt, brush out the locks of my hair and leave it to air dry. Shrugging on a black jacket, I open the door. The fresh morning chill hits my skin and covers my body in goosebumps. The air isn't humid but has a certain crispness to it that you can only get from being away from the city.

I double-check the lock on the door as I turn, glancing up and down the main road. It's early enough that the shops are still closed, and life hasn't begun to bustle about the streets. This is where I feel most comfortable. No one to question who I am or where I come from. Just the freedom to discover the town without the third degree.

Over the past two weeks, I've stopped at all the places I've wanted to go since I was a kid. My favorite of all the places was the Grand Canyon. I drove all night to find the best lookout over the vast trenches. Making it just as the sun was coming up, I parked and climbed out of the car. I felt my soul reset watching the terracotta and rust-colored rock dance with lavender and pink skies. Even as the watercolor skies melted together and I felt truly free for the first time, I screamed. Screamed into the vast canyons and crevices, letting the clay and rock soak up every ounce of pain it was willing to take. For a little while, I was happier.

I begin walking back in the direction we drove last night towards Cole's garage. Thankfully Cole didn't take too many turns and it'll be easy for me to find my way back. The less enclosed spaces that I have to be in with the male species, the better right now. His kindness wasn't lost on me but, in my experience, men aren't just kind for no reason. There are ultimatums and agendas that don't end up in my favor.

I whip my head to look behind me, hearing the first car of the morning. My breath catches in my throat as I watch the Pine River County Sheriff's squad car pull up to the curb next to me. *Great,* I think. The last thing I need is some small-town cop digging around into my past or, worse, making a curious call to Miami.

The window slowly rolls down as I continue to walk, the car creeping alongside me.

"Excuse me, Ma'am?" His voice breaks through the morning air and for some reason it causes a chill to run up my spine. I stop, closing my eyes for a moment before turning around to face him. My eyes meet his beady ones and I try to hide the unnerving feeling his toothy smile gives me. "I uh-haven't seen you around here before. You lost?"

"No, Sir. Just passing through," I say shortly.

The officer nods, his eyes trailing over my body from head to toe like a predator examining his prey. He sucks on his teeth before glancing down the main road. I hear him place the car into park before the door clicks open. I take a step further back on the sidewalk as he climbs out of the vehicle, giving myself space from him and crossing my arms over my chest to barricade my own personal bubble from his. He's tall, his frame lanky and dull blue eyes that make my skin crawl as he stands before me.

"What's your name, Sweetie?"

Bile rises in my throat, threatening to spill all over his cheap boots at the pet name. I shift on my heels, standing a little taller as he grips his belt.

"I'm sorry... Officer, have I done something wrong?"

The officer eyes me for another moment, the uncomfortable silence spilling onto the sidewalk around us before he chuckles.

"No, no, Ma'am. Like I said, never seen you around here before. Not many folks like to walk around the streets in the early morning. You caught my eye, just tryna be friendly is all. I'm Deputy Sheriff Jake Watson." He glances up and down the road again, and something about the way he moves and keeps peering up and down the road makes my gut twist. It feels like he's checking for other people and not in an *I'm here to protect the town,* kind of way.

"Kadence..." I say, reluctant to give my last name to him. "Kadence Smith."

Watson narrows his eyes at me for a moment, sensing the fact that I'm lying, but thankfully he decides not to press me on it.

"Well, *Kadence*, is there anywhere I can give you a ride to?" He emphasizes my name and the bile creeps up again.

"No, Sir. Just gonna take a walk."

"Where are you staying?" He blurts, ignoring my answer. "Girl like you shouldn't be wandering around alone. Do you have family here?"

His twenty questions are starting to irritate me. "No, Sir. Like I said," I repeat his own words back to him with a bite, "Just passing through."

A smirk spreads across his face. "Maybe I can show you around town a little tonight? Give you a proper Pine River welcome?" Watson asks it like a question, but I can see behind his eyes that it's not a request.

"I really don't think I'm going to be in town all that long. I'd rather just stick to my own if you don't mind," I say, trying not to sound so happy about giving him the rejection.

I watch his face twitch slightly before it turns back to a smile, a look I'm all too familiar with, and it only confirms the twist in my gut I've felt before.

Watson steps back towards his car. "Understood. Have a great day, Miss Smith."

I nod once. If this were a month ago, I would feel the urge to apologize, run after him, and give in to his disappointment. Now? The pure adrenaline from watching him walk away courses through my body, my feet firmly planted on the concrete as I hold my own ground. I can feel myself getting back to the person I was before Jeremy. It's a slow process but my light has started to shine through the hardened cracks around my soul, ready to one day, break through.

Watson gives me a tight-lipped smile through his window as he drives away, his squad car turning left after a few blocks. I let out the breath I didn't realize I was holding and continue down the sidewalk, trying not to let the uneasiness of his presence seep into me.

After a while of walking, I find a small diner. The baby blue paint on the outside of the building has faded from many years of the sun gleaming down onto it. Aluminum panels wrap around the bottom half making it look straight out of a fifties movie. As I step inside, there's a few older couples sitting in the various cherry red pleather booths. The old men scanning newspapers and their spouses chattering away into their eggs.

"Take a seat anywhere, baby, I'll be with ya in a sec!" I hear the soft raspy voice yell from behind the counter. The woman turns to flash me a smile before turning back to tend to whatever she's flipping on the grill top.

"Thanks," I reply, seating myself in one of the empty corner booths, furthest away from any of the patrons.

I set my things down into the booth next to me, between myself and the wall. From this spot I can see the mountains and clouds giving way to the blue sky. I also have a perfect view of the front door and anyone who walks through it. The vinyl menu is that same soft sky blue color with photos of everything they serve here and for some reason I feel comforted.

A few moments later the owner of the voice leans against the edge of the booth across from me and smiles. Her gray hair is pulled back into a French braid, face adorned with smile lines and crows' feet showing many years of laughter. A black shirt with a name tag that reads *Maggie* covers her short frame. "Morning, Baby. What can I get for ya?"

I glance up from the menu with a smile. "Morning," I say, a little exasperated. I've stared at the menu for the past few minutes, unable to pick from all of the options. My eyes flick back down to the breakfast side of the menu and the woman chuckles.

"Too many options right?" She asks, as if this is a normal problem. "I keep tellin' Lee he's gotta make the menu smaller." Maggie laughs softly. "How about a cup of coffee and the special?"

I chuckle. "You know what, that sounds great." We exchange a smile as Maggie nods, taking the menus from the table.

"I'll get that going for ya. There's cream and sugar on the table there," Maggie says, pointing to the small bowl on the edge of the table closest to the wall. "Lemme know if you need anything else."

"Thank you, Ma'am."

Maggie laughs. "Oh Sweetie, don't make me feel older than I already do. Call me Maggie." She winks, stepping back behind the counter.

I watch her move about the diner, putting in my order and pouring cups of coffee like it's a choreographed dance that she has practiced for years. A rhythm she knows by heart, bustling about the kitchen and laughing with a few of the other customers. It's beautiful and warm and something that I've not felt in a long time.

I lean over, grabbing the small notebook and pen from my bag, setting it down onto the tabletop and going through my list of stops and finances that I've burned through already. The sale from the townhouse did pretty well but my funds are quickly running low. I used it to pay off all my debt I had accrued in Miami and to buy the Comet. It looked just like the one my dad had when I was a kid before he passed, and before Janice sold it for a Coach handbag.

"Life's all about appearances, Kadie. That car was an eye sore in that driveway."

I remember the day it sold. My mother didn't know but I cried in my room for two days. The one last memory of my father was gone. I was only ten at the time but, as my mother began dating and living the social life she'd always wanted, I grew up faster than I should ever have needed to.

"Mornin', Cole!" Maggie's greeting suddenly breaks my staring contest with the lines of the notebook as my eyes flicker to the door. Cole's large frame leans over the edge of the counter, a smile plastered on his face. "The usual I take it?"

"Throw an extra Lee's special in there for Nash, would ya?"

I watch as Maggie nods, leaning over in close to Cole as they begin talking. The smile falls from Cole's face and soon so does Maggie's. Their voices are hushed as they speak and I see the somber look fall across them both. Maggie grabs his chin, lifting his gaze back to hers and says something that gets him to quirk his lips in a side smile before he sits down at the counter. Maggie goes back to work behind the counter, setting a cup of coffee down in front of him before heading over to me, sliding my cup across the table.

"Your food will be up shortly, love," Maggie says softly, her demeanor having lost a little bit of the sunshine she had before.

"Kadence..." I say softly, giving Maggie a reassuring smile.

Maggie smiles, it doesn't quite reach her eyes, but a glimpse of that warmth comes back. "It's nice to meet you Kadence." She taps the top of the booth once before stepping back to the counter.

I grab two packets of sugar and one creamer, stirring them into the dark liquid before taking a sip. It's definitely not the Cuban coffee I'm used to, but it's caffeine and my body desperately needs it. I set the mug back down, going back to my book as a shadow casts itself over my table.

"I see you found the only good place to eat here," Cole's voice teases as he leans against the pleather, the smile that was plastered on his face is now back. I laugh softly.

"Uh... Yeah, I guess you could say that." I smile up at him.

He nods, taking a sip of his coffee. We stare at each other for a moment before I gesture to the booth across from me.

"Would you like to sit?" I don't know why I offer, but now that it's daylight he doesn't seem so intimidating to me anymore. The sharp angles of his face are softer now, almost lighter and, though his frame still towers over me, his presence doesn't feel anything like Watson's.

He smiles and slides into the booth across from me as I slip my notebook back into my bag.

"How did you sleep? I hear the beds at the motel are questionable," Cole teases. He's walking on eggshells but I can sense the curiosity behind those ocean eyes.

"I slept alright. I've slept on worse," I laugh and it's a little hollow.

Cole notices and nods. "Well, hopefully we'll have ya back up and runnin'. Now that it's daylight, I'll be able to find the issue better."

I take a sip of my coffee as Maggie brings over a plate of food that is still steaming and the smell almost instantly causes me to drool. Fluffy scrambled eggs, two sausage links, two bacon strips and hashbrowns that look to be just the right amount of crispy.

"You two know each other?" Maggie asks with a smirk.

Cole rolls his eyes as I take a bite of my food, my own eyes rolling back into my head as the eggs practically melt in my mouth from all the butter.

"Kadence's car broke down on the highway last night, I just helped her get towed back into town. I'm looking at her car later this morning."

Maggie nods and leans into me. "Don't let those blue eyes fool ya. He's a rascal as much as the rest of them." She grins as I smirk with a bite full of hashbrowns in my mouth, cocking my head to the side as I glance at Cole. His cheeks are pink with embarrassment as he hides behind the mug in his hand.

"Good to know." I tease.

"Alright, alright. Since when is this *pick on Cole* time?" He says with a brow raised up at Maggie.

Maggie stands tall, patting him on the shoulder. "Sweetie, it's always *pick on Cole* time."

I bite back a laugh as his mouth drops slightly watching Maggie walk away, taking another sip of my coffee. Cole sighs, leaning back into the booth as he watches me. I go back to focusing on my food and when I feel his eyes on me again, I freeze. My eyes meet his, suddenly self-conscious eating in front of him. He notices and downs his coffee as Maggie sets his order onto the bartop.

"You finish up here, I have a stop I need to make but how about I swing back by and pick you up from here? We'll go back to the shop then."

I swallow the bite of food in my mouth and nod. "Y-Yeah that sounds good," I stammer slightly as he nods once before setting his mug on the counter for Maggie to take.

"See you in a bit," he says, grabbing the bags of food. "Maggie, tomorrow mornin'?"

"It's a date, handsome!" Maggie yells from somewhere in the back.

I watch as Cole heads out of the front door towards the tow truck. He climbs inside, tossing me a wave through the diner window as he pulls out of the parking lot. A tiny part of me feels like this place is gonna stick with me when I leave.

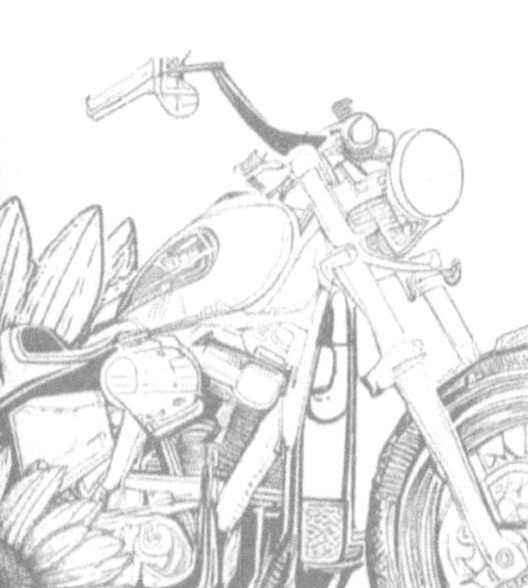

HOLDEN

y head is pounding, or is that the door? I'm not sure but whatever it is, needs to stop. I groan, the persistent banging getting louder as I tuck my head under the piece of cotton I claim is a pillow.

"Holden! You have about two seconds to get your ass up before I break this door down!" I hear Cole yell from behind the trailer door.

The cold, yellow, dingy linoleum feels sticky against my skin as I peel myself up off the floor. At least I remembered the pillow this time. Sitting up I sigh, rolling my left shoulder a few times. Wincing when it gets to the one sore spot that only shows up when I'm dumb enough to sleep on the floor again.

"Untwist your thong, O'Neil," I bellow, using the flimsy counter to pull myself up to my feet. With a hard yank, I pull the door open giving view to Cole's now furrowed brow.

"What took you so long?"

I roll my eyes, sitting on the edge of the bed I missed when I stumbled into the airstream last night. "I was planning your murder," I bite back. "Had to hide the evidence."

Cole mockingly laughs. "Ha. Ha. Ha. Funny."

He steps into the trailer and I know the smell of old beer, sweat and cigarette smoke floods his nostrils; his feet barely missing the maze of beer cans as he steps further inside. He does a once-over of the trailer before his eyes land on me.

"Jesus, Nash." He sets the bag of food on the small kitchenette, pushing a tower of beer cans and a pizza box out of the way. "When was the last time you took a shower? Or cleaned?"

I groan, knowing this conversation all too well.

My friend turns back towards me, brows still furrowed. The disappointed father look is adorned all over Cole's face. I hate that look. It makes me feel like a child again and I don't need another father. The one I had was shitty enough.

"What do you want Cole?" I grumble, running my fingers through my long hair.

Cole sighs. "Look, it's been a month, and everyone is torn up about Rebecca's death... Nash. But it wasn't your fault. You can't..."

"If you're about to tell me that I can't blame myself, save it. I don't want to fucking hear it, Cole," I snap. My fuse is much shorter these days.

"Well, you're gonna fuckin' hear it, Nash. You need to pull your shit together and get back to your life—" I go to open my mouth, but Cole stops me. "This isn't a fucking life, asshole. You're a fuckin' shell of who you used to be, man. You need to figure out how to crawl out of the hole you're in because if you don't, you're gonna end up six feet in the ground next to Becca."

I narrow my eyes on my best friend. Anger bubbles in my chest, fists clamped around the edge of the platform bed. "You fuckin' done?" I grit out.

Cole shakes his head, bending over, grabbing a shirt off the floor, and tossing it to me. I catch it with my left arm, wincing as the pain shoots through my shoulder down into my side.

"Get your ass back in therapy, Nash. The club needs you..." He pauses, his hands resting on his sides. "I need you," he says softly and it feels like a knife right through my heart hearing my best friend beg. "Maggie made up your favorite. Eat and meet me at the garage later. We got an older car to look at and I could use your expertise," he says, walking towards the trailer door. I haven't said a word, my fingers fumbling with the balled-up shirt in my hands. "Don't make me drag your ass back to the clubhouse."

The trailer door slams shut behind Cole and I let out a shaky breath. My head drops and my eyes slide shut to keep the tears brimming in them from falling. After a few deep breaths, I stand, undoing the knot on the bag of food, and open the carton, shoving a piece of bacon in my mouth before washing it down with the bottle of whiskey I keep on the milk crate I call a nightstand. It's gonna be a long fuckin' day.

KADENCE

Maggie watches as I push my eggs across my plate. It's not that I'm not hungry. I am. Starving in fact, but I remember the look Cole gave me when I started shoveling food into my mouth. It was almost the same as the one Jeremy used to give me before making some remark about my eating habits or weight; whatever he deemed fit that day. A part of me knows that Cole meant nothing by it, but it doesn't stop that tiny little asshole voice in my head.

"You all done, sweetie?" Maggie's voice cuts through the toxic thoughts. I smile up at her and, with a curt nod, let Maggie take the plate. Before she turns to walk away from my table she pauses. "Ya know, Sweetheart, it sounds like you're in for a long day. Why don't I whip you up a sandwich to go?" I get the feeling that Maggie can read all my deepest secrets. "Just in case you get hungry later, on the house of course."

"Oh, you don't—" I begin but am cut off by Maggie waving her hand.

"My treat." She smiles knowingly at me before heading back towards the counter.

My throat tightens as a swell of emotions begin to wash over me. I've only been here for twelve hours and already I've been met with more kindness than I've had in over two years. Between the fake smiles and speak-when-spoken-to attitudes, I'd almost forgotten what it felt like for someone to just be kind to me.

After a few minutes, Maggie waddles back over to me, setting down the check for my breakfast and a sandwich wrapped in paper. "No rush, Honey."

"Thank you," I say softly, my voice breaking slightly. Maggie glances down at me, brows knitting together for a moment.

"You sure you're okay, Sweetie?" She asks, stepping back to the table. "Because if you're in some sort of trouble or somethin'—" I shake my head, cutting Maggie off.

"No, I'm not. Just... thank you for being kind."

I glance up at Maggie and see the quiver of heartbreak flash over her features before a smile that doesn't quite reach her eyes spreads across her thin lips.

"You're welcome, Sweetie." Maggie turns to head back to the counter as the low rumble of the tow truck pulls back into the parking lot.

I can see Cole in the driver's seat. His face looks less warm than before, almost tired as he takes a moment to climb out of the truck. His shoulders have dropped slightly and he looks sad. He pulls open the door, and I down the last of my coffee as he makes a beeline straight to me. His features only look more sunken as he approaches and I wonder what in the hell happened in the last thirty minutes since I'd seen him.

His eyes meet mine and he tries to hide the gloom. "How was breakfast?" He asks with a forced smile.

I smile back at him for a moment before grabbing my things. "It was good."

Cole gestures to the sandwich still wrapped on the table. "Lunch?" He asks and I nod as he turns. "Hey Maggs, mind makin' two more of those for me?"

Maggie nods from behind the counter and starts working on them.

The air between us is awkward; it's not the same warm feeling I'd had around him before. His sunshine personality seems snubbed out by whatever happened while he was gone. "You okay?" I ask as his eyes flit back to me.

Cole slides into the booth opposite me with another forced smile. "Yeah, everything's okay."

I can tell he's lying and he knows he's not doing a very good job of hiding the pain written on his face but I don't push. It's not my place and I don't feel the need to get close.

"You ready to go?" He asks.

I don't say anything, only nod as I slide out of the booth, taking my bag and sandwich with me. He follows suit, his hand resting on the middle of my back to guide me to the door as Maggie hands him a bag, holding onto it for a moment.

"Tell Holden we miss him, yeah?" She says, her soft eyes glossing over with tears.

"Will do, Maggs."

We make our way out to the tow truck and I can feel the tension radiating from him. It's a stark difference from the man I met last night and shared coffee with this morning. He's rigid and almost defensive as he opens the door for me with a huff, letting me climb in before rounding to the driver's side and climbing in himself.

The truck comes to life and I glance over at him, "If it's too much trouble I can just wander the town a bit. You don't have to babysit me." I don't mean for it to sound as bitter as it comes out.

"Wha–No. I'm not—" He sighs, turning towards me. "You don't need a babysitter, Kadence. I just figured I'd take you to the shop to check out the car. If you don't want to, I can just call you with an update," Cole offers, his eyes scanning my features. I don't miss the slight hurt in his voice and I feel like an asshole.

"Sorry," I mutter softly. "I'll go with."

He watches me for a moment, slightly taken aback by how easily I gave in. The caged animal he found last night has begun to curl in on herself. My instincts kick in to keep me safe as I lean against the door, biting the inside of my cheek to keep myself calm.

Without another word, Cole pulls out of the parking lot onto the road. The town is livelier now than it was this morning. People have started to clutter the sidewalks and shopkeepers are flipping their signs to open. Pine River is a cute little town, big enough that there's plenty to do but small enough that I get the feeling everyone knows everyone, and that's what scares me.

Cole pulls into the lot for the garage; the line of motorcycles is still parked in front of the side building. A few men are standing outside of the garage, all wearing the same 'O'Neil's Garage' shirts. The mural of the white wolf painted on the side of the building shines bright in the early morning sunlight. It's beautifully done; details of its fur are etched into the wall, and its muzzle is pointed towards the sky as if it's howling for the moon.

The Comet is parked near the garage, and when I see it, my heart twists for a moment. I love that car. I couldn't believe it when I ran across the listing on Craigslist. It was like my father was reaching out, giving me a way to escape the hell I was in. They don't tell you how quiet the world becomes and how loud your mind gets when you're in the car on your own. Late nights on the road when I couldn't sleep were spent talking to his ghost as if he were a passenger in my front seat. Never judging, never interrupting, he just listened. If the car is dead, I know it's dramatic... but it would feel like losing my dad all over again.

"There's an office next to the garage. It's air-conditioned, and there's a coffee maker. You're welcome to help yourself," Cole rasps as he rolls into a parking spot and turns to me. "If anyone asks who or why you're here, you tell them you're with me, okay?"

"Cole..." I say softly, my stomach churning at whatever he means.

"You're safe here, okay? Just...stick to the office," he says as he climbs out of the truck. I follow him, crossing my arms over my chest in defense. Defense from what, I'm not sure, but the tone in his voice brought a familiar fear back.

As we head towards the office, I notice a group of men standing outside of one of the garage bays watching us. A few of them are puffing away on cigarettes, and the others are peering over their sunglasses to look at me. Suddenly that warm feeling I got in the diner completely dissipates. One of the men, who is taller than the rest of them, with curly brown hair and green eyes, smiles at me. It's crooked and makes my skin crawl.

"Quinn!" Cole yells just as we get to the office door and I watch as the crooked smile falls from the man's face as he stands to attention. "Take the Comet into the garage for me, will ya?" Quinn nods and takes one last drag of his cigarette before stomping it into the ground with his boot. I follow Cole into the office with Quinn following behind.

The room is barely big enough to be considered an office, almost like an afterthought. File cabinets line the wall and the small corner desk is covered in paperwork.

"Aye, O'Neil you got the keys?" Quinn asks over my shoulder.

I take a step to the side, letting him through the doorway and, truthfully, to get him out of my space. The only man so far that I've felt any sort of comfort with being close to me is the stranger currently rustling around in a stack of paper.

Cole stands up, glancing over at Quinn. "Shit, uhm..." He looks around for a moment, hands on his hips. I dig in my bag, pulling out my keys and holding them out to Quinn. He glances over at Cole who nods, like Quinn was waiting for permission to take them. "Thanks," he mutters.

"No problem." I smile, sitting down on one of the chairs.

He glances over at me before going back to the stacks of paper. A part of me cringes every time he swears under his breath, shoving papers aside, clearly frustrated with whatever it is he's trying to find. I have some experience managing an office, and the lack of organization in this room digs at my obsessive compulsiveness to keep things orderly.

"You need some help?" I ask before I even have time to realize my mouth has started to move.

"Huh? Oh–" He chuckles, carding his fingers through his hair. "The woman who used to run the office passed about a month ago. It's been hell in here since."

I wince, "I'm sorry..."

Cole lets out another sigh, shaking his head. "It's–" he pauses, "thanks." He stands staring at the empty chair for a moment before he shakes himself loose of whatever memories he got lost in. "Uhm–Help yourself to the coffee and tea. It might be a bit." I nod, getting comfortable in the chair as he heads back outside.

HOLDEN

The water from my shower stings against my tanned skin. I don't remember the last time I was actually fully awake enough to enjoy a shower. Today still isn't that day, and while my guilt drowns in the alcohol, I remember why I pray it knocks me on my ass. These days I'm just trying to find something to keep me distracted from the club, from Cole, and the ghost of my sister that haunts the compound.

Whiskey does that for me. And Layla. She keeps me company when the whiskey fails to do its job, and lately, it's been happening more and more that I find a brief solace in her. She doesn't ask questions or glare at me every time I pick up the bottle.

Reaching up, I turn off the water, not remembering how or why my knuckles have become bruised and swollen. My body bumps into the edges of the small shower, twisting and turning to make it out of the small trailer bathroom. I could just shower in the house, but since Becca's been gone, I haven't been inside. Cole told me buying a trailer and parking it on her front lawn was ridiculous. That my little sister would kick my ass knowing her only brother wasn't strong enough to walk through the front door. But I wanted to be close to her without actually being close. I don't deserve that yet.

Not after I failed her.

I make my way from the bathroom, kicking beer cans and stepping over the pillow I curled up with on the floor last night. I glance over at the half-eaten breakfast that Cole brought me. I hate when he tries to take care of me. It makes the guilt worse and only makes Cole the worry wart, well... worry. But I'm grateful that at least someone still gives a shit about me, especially since it's sure as shit not myself.

A long breath leaves me as I sit down on the edge of the shitty mattress. I know I should go to the shop, Cole asked me to be there, and I know he's right. I gotta pull myself out of this hell. The guilt starts to flood back in when I think of all the people I've shut out and pushed away over the past few weeks. People who only wanted to be there for me during the hardest time of my life.

Since Becca died I feel alone, which makes me sound like an idiot when I have a whole club standing behind me and know that if I called any time, night or day, they'd be there for me. Every time I think of her goofy smile and the stupid nicknames she used to call me, my heart shatters again and images of that night take over my mind like an old movie I can't seem to quit playing.

My breath hitches in my throat just thinking about her and my hand instinctively reaches for the bottle of whiskey, bringing it to my lips to wash down all the feelings currently swelling in my chest. Warmth fills my throat and spreads throughout my chest with the taste of the amber medicine. I take another swig, a shiver running through my bones as the warmth of the alcohol takes over.

I should go to the shop. I really should go to the shop and not disappoint the one person left in my life that depends on me. Then I remember the pitiful look he gave me this morning.

I reach for my phone, take a third swig, and dial the number that has given me peace for the last three weeks. I know Layla wants more from me. Being a part of the Hell Hounds has its perks, and one of them is being able to pick from any of the girls at Moon. Layla headlines there every Thursday night for the god-fearing pricks of this town who avoid spending time with their families. To her, I'm the meal ticket to go from being a dancer to Old Lady. To me, she's a way to keep my mind clear and dick warm. It rings once before I hear her voice on the other end.

"Holden?"

Hang up, I think.

"Yeah, Babe, it's me."

"Everything okay?"

"Need you."

I hear her sigh on the other end. "Holden... It's early."

Another swig. "Please, Layla." It comes out almost whispering and desperate as hell, but I don't care.

Silence comes through on the other line before I hear her suck in a breath. "Meet me at Moon in an hour."

"Okay." I hang up before she gets any ideas that this is more than what it is and lay back on the bed. I'm gonna regret this and I can already hear the shit storm Cole is going to lay on me. A month ago, I might have cared, but now?

Now all I want is not to think.

KADENCE

I t's been a few hours since we got back to the shop and I keep seeing Cole pace back and forth across the parking lot, dialing someone on the phone and then hanging up a few moments later. The sun starts to dip and the sky turns a deep shade of orange when he finally comes back into the office. He's stopped by a few times, making sure I'm okay and that I have a plate for my sandwich, but for the most part he's kept his distance. I appreciate it. The less hovering he does, the more my anxiety sits at a low thrum in my chest.

Cole lets out a huff as he leans against the desk. His face is covered in motor grease and his forehead is slick with sweat.

"So, you want the good news or the bad news?" He asks, and suddenly my worry doesn't seem so silly anymore.

"Good..." I answer without hesitation.

Cole nods. "Well, you need an entire new engine."

My mouth drops slightly. "That's the good news?" I ask in disbelief.

"Bad news is, these engines are hard to come by now. It's gonna take a little bit before we can get one and rebuild it."

My stomach twists. "How long?"

"Couple weeks, maybe?" He shrugs. "It might just be better to find a new car, Kadence."

"No," I blurt out and he furrows his brow as I shake my head. I swallow back the lump in my throat, "This car means too much."

"It's expensive to fix a car like this," he says gently.

My eyes meet his and I know exactly what he's saying but I can't give up on this car that easily. My father wouldn't. I did the math earlier in the diner, figuring out how much money I have left to my name, and I know it's not enough to cover the car. Cole doesn't even have to tell me. The pitiful look he's giving me says it all.

I run my hands over my face and sigh. I have disappointment and sadness radiating off of me like heat right now. He shifts on his feet like he can feel it.

"You really want to keep the car?" Cole asks, quirking a brow.

I look up at him, "I do...I just–I don't have the money for it." I admit and he glances around, putting his hands on his hips like he did before as if he's assessing everything around him.

Cole freezes for a moment and a flicker of light crosses his blue eyes. "This might be out of line, but I could offer you a job here. In exchange for work on the car."

I furrow my brow. "A job? Why would you do that?"

He smiles, and, for the first time since this morning, it reaches his eyes. "Think of it as a mutually beneficial business decision." Cole chuckles. "This place is a mess, as I'm sure you can see, and I could use all the help I can get right now."

I glance around the mess that is the office.

"There's a mother-in-law apartment upstairs." His chin lifts slightly. "You're welcome to stay there for the time being."

My eyes well with tears as I shake my head. "Why are you being so nice to me?" I say tightly, trying to keep the ball of emotions tangling in my throat at bay.

Cole's features go soft, his eyes drop slightly and a sadness washes over him, but it's not pity this time. "Because you look like you need someone to be nice to you."

The words shatter my heart and a sob slips from my lips. I bury my face in my hands as embarrassment floods me. Do I really look that broken? The floor creaks under Cole's weight as he takes a step and I feel his presence as he crouches down in front of me.

"Hey," his voice cuts through my pathetic cry, "Look at me, Kadence." Cole hesitates for a moment before gently pulling on my arms, getting me to look at him. He tilts his head slightly, catching my gaze. "I don't know who made you feel like kindness was a privilege you weren't worthy of, but I'll do what I can to get you back on the road."

I sniffle softly, my eyes searching his. I can tell he's being genuine, no hidden agenda that I can sense, and for the first time in a long time I feel safe with a man. It's a strange feeling. Not having the urge to pull away from the warmth of his calloused hands. He flashes me a crooked smile, it's a little awkward but, to be fair, I am currently staring at him with tears streaming down my face, inches from his.

"Okay."

"Okay," he whispers back before standing up with a nod. "I'll give you a minute, and then we can get your things from the motel if you want."

I nod, grateful not to have to sleep on those musty sheets again. Cole takes a step backwards from me shoving his hands into his pockets before he turns and leaves. My chest heaves with a deep shaky breath and I wipe away the tears from my cheeks before moving to follow him.

We climb into the tow truck and make it back to the motel. Cole helps me gather my things from the room I rented and I hand back the key to the kid behind the office counter with a smile. It doesn't take very long and soon we're headed back towards the garage.

"You said I was safe?" I ask looking over at him. "What did you mean by that?"

Cole looks over at me before glancing back to the road. "Well, I'm sure you've noticed that we're not just a garage. We're a motorcycle club as well."

I nod, "I figured that."

He looks over at me again, a look in his eye that tells me he's debating on how much to divulge. "We protect our own. Right now, that includes you if you're going to help out and live at the garage."

Cole clears his throat adjusting his grip on the steering wheel. "Some of the guys can be a little... much. So if you run into any problems, you come find me or Trey, our vice president, and if they get really out of line, you find Wolfe. He'll handle it."

"You get how that sounds awfully suspicious right?" I can't help but chuckle leaning back against the seat and swallowing the nervousness gathering in my throat.

This time he laughs, shaking his head. "Yeah, I can see where those red flags might pop up. Look, you're welcome to any part of the property. There's the clubhouse where the guys go to unwind. A few of them stay there, but if you need anything just ask the prospects, Quinn and West. You met Quinn earlier—"

The sound of Maria's ringtone fills the cab of the truck, interrupting Cole. "Sorry," I say, giving him an apologetic look.

"You can take that if you need to." He glances over at me with that same crooked smile.

"Thanks," I mumble softly before answering. "Hi, Maria."

"Jesus, Kade, where are you?"

"Uhm, Pine River. The Comet broke down last night. I had to get towed into town, and it looks like I'll be staying here for a while." I explain quickly, knowing she's going to have a million questions. I chance a look at Cole, who is trying his hardest to pretend like he's not listening.

"*What do you mean?*" Worry laces the question as Maria asks.

"It needs a new engine. There's a local mechanic who is gonna help me get it squared away."

"*You can afford that?*"

I keep my eyes on Cole. "He's giving me a job and a place to stay while I'm here." I see Cole smile slightly. "I promise, Maria, I'm okay."

"*This sounds like the start of a horror movie, Kade. What if he's actually a serial killer? You know small towns have those.*" She sighs.

I laugh and glance over at Cole, "You aren't going to murder me are you?"

He grins, "Yes, yes I am." He winks and turns back into the garage parking lot. I roll my eyes knowing that Maria heard him.

"*See!*" She bellows, "*Kade, I know you don't want to come home. I get it—*"

"I'm not talking about this right now, Maria. I'm fine. I'm safe. That's all that matters," I interject, knowing what's coming. I love Maria. She's one of the only people who didn't turn on me after I went public with the things Jeremy did. But she tries to fill the hole my mother left and I hate it.

"*Promise me you'll call me if things get too bad? If you need money—*"

"Maria—"

"*No, Kadence. If you need anything, please call me.*"

I sigh and close my eyes letting my head drop to the back of the seat. "Okay," I concede, "Okay, I will. I have to go Mar. I'll call you later, okay?"

Maria huffs on the other end. *"Alright."*

"Love you," I say softly.

"Love you too."

"You ready?" He asks as I hang up. I can tell he wants to ask who Maria is, and at this point I would probably tell him, but he doesn't say anything as he gets out of the truck and grabs my bags.

He leads me up a set of stairs on the side of the shop to the apartment. Cole pushes the door open and flips on the light. It's small and more of a studio apartment, but it smells recently cleaned, and I don't need much. A bed, a shower, and a place to put my things.

"Make yourself at home. There's a bathroom and a small kitchen around the corner, and if you want groceries, I can point you to the store that's a few blocks away." Cole sets my bags down on the bed, turning on his heel towards me.

I wrap my arms around myself, taking in the space. It feels weird to be in a place I can call home, even if it is temporary. If it was up to me I'd be back on the road by now but the more time I spend here the more I feel like the Comet broke down here for a reason. It made it over three thousand miles, just to break down outside of Pine River.

"I'll let you get some rest." he says, pulling out his phone. "Put your number in here and I'll text you so you have mine in case you need anything. I'll be at the club house tonight, if you want to stop in."

"Thanks, Cole." I take his phone from him and save my number before handing it back. He sends me a quick text before shoving his phone back into his pocket. "Really... for everything. Thank you."

"You're welcome," he says with that soft gentle smile that I have become accustomed to. "Have a good night Kadence." Cole gives me a nod, shifting around me, and moves to the door.

"You too."

He gives me one last smile before shutting the door behind him. The few things I had in my arms I set down on the small table before collapsing on the edge of the bed. I bounce a few times to test it out. It's soft and doesn't feel like it's going to kill my back by morning. Another thing I'm grateful for.

I do a check to make sure the door to the apartment is locked before changing and settling into the bed. It doesn't take long for my eyes to grow heavy. The combination of the warm blankets and the chilled air from the air conditioning has me giving into the sleep I need but am constantly in fear of.

I roll over onto my side, my eyes springing open. That tight feeling is back in my chest and it feels like my heart is going to burst. Reaching for my phone and almost blinding myself with the screen light I check the time. 12:23 am. With a groan I toss the phone onto the pillow next to me and roll onto my back. I hate this time of night. The in-between of being asleep and waking up from whatever horror my mind has already blocked out before I either fall asleep again or lie awake and make friends with the ceiling tiles.

I sit up and lean against the headboard, pulling my hair back into a bun, and try to calm my nerves. The door to the apartment swings open suddenly, slamming against the wall and startling me. A chorus of giggles and moans follow and I fly out of the bed, scrambling for my phone, as a man and woman fumble their way into the room.

"Hey!" I yell through the rushing sound of my heartbeat in my ears, just hoping to get their attention off of each other as pieces of clothing start getting tossed onto the floor.

The two jump and pull away from each other, the man pushing the already half-naked woman behind him. His long, dark chestnut hair is messy on one side giving light to the sharpness of his jawline in the glow of moonlight filtering through the window. Bright blue eyes connect with mine, and for a moment, I'm stunned by how light they actually are in the dark.

"Who the fuck are you?" His voice is harsh and smoky as it fills the room and his brows furrow. The woman behind him peeks around his shoulder, glaring at me with smoked-out eyes and a snarl adorned with red lipstick.

I narrow my eyes at him. Noticing the motorcycle cut I stand up a little straighter and the death grip I have on my phone eases briefly. "Don't be rude," I snap, and the corners of his mouth quirk up slightly. "Cole said I could stay here."

The man takes a step forward and instinctively I take a step back, pressing my body further into the corner. "Yeah? Well I know Cole and he doesn't let just anyone stay here. So I ask again, who the fuck are you?" He snarls, taking another step towards me.

"Nash, who is this bitch?" The woman speaks up, folding her arms over her chest like I've done something wrong.

"I don't know either of you, so back the fuck off."

"That's the problem, Sweetheart," he coos sarcastically. "We don't know who the fuck you are either."

I glance down at my phone quickly trying to find Cole's number but my fingers are trembling. A second passes and I find him, dialing the number just as my phone is ripped from my hand and tossed to the bed. "Who the fuck are you?" He barks.

My entire body freezes ready for whatever beating I'm about to receive from this man. I hate that my body starts to shrink in on itself as I stare at eyes made of blue fire.

"Holden!" The woman snaps and he turns so fast it makes my head spin and has me sinking to the floor. That familiar gut-wrenching fear creeps through me.

"Shut the fuck up, Layla, and go get Cole!"

Layla's face drops at the tone in his voice before she snatches her shirt off of the ground. "You're an asshole, Nash!" She screeches before stomping down the stairs.

When he turns back and realizes I'm on the floor, his eyes go wide, and he takes a step back from me. His chest is heaving with heavy breaths, and his fists are clenched. "What is your name?"

I don't answer. I can't. Tears are burning in my eyes and I feel myself slip into that same dark space I always did when Jeremy got loud.

"Kadence!" Cole's voice cuts through the tension and I can make out his footsteps as he barges into the apartment and shoves past Holden before kneeling in front of me. "You okay?"

I'm still frozen, and even when he tries to help me stand up, my legs feel like molasses.

"Who the fuck is she?" Holden snaps.

Cole turns on him, a firm grip on my arm. "What the fuck are you doing here, Nash?"

Holden... or Nash, I'm not even sure at the moment, is shooting a glare in my direction. Those blue eyes darken and his fists are balled at his sides. I recognize that dark look all too well.

"Was bringing Layla up here and found her." He tilts his head to the side with a wolfish grin forming across his lips while his eyes trail down my body. "I didn't realize you were taking in strays, O'Neil," he quips and any fear I had in me quickly dissipates with anger.

"I'm not a fucking stray," I bite, but it only makes him chuckle.

"Not so scared anymore when you've got O'Neil here, huh?" He taunts. "Who is she, Cole? Some new bitch for the club?"

Cole steps forward, shoving Holden back. "You're fuckin' drunk again aren't you?" He seethes, continuing to push him backward. "I asked you for one thing today and you couldn't even do that. Now you're here? Drunk off your ass and intimidating a woman? What the fuck is wrong with you?" He shoves him once more before Holden finally shoves back.

"Get off me, man. She fuckin' started it." His hand flies out pointing towards me.

The sudden movement makes me flinch but I try to hide it and cross my arms over my chest. The veins in his arm pop as he pushes towards Cole again. My heart is hammering in my chest and I'm trying my best to put on the bravest face I can manage even though I'm biting down on the inside of my cheek to keep the tears from falling. I haven't felt like this in a while and it makes me want to run again.

Cole steps back, shaking his head. "Get out Nash. Go home and sleep off whatever you drank today."

Holden scoffs, stumbling backward. "Fine." He goes to turn as Cole opens his mouth.

"Apologize." Holden scrunches his face like a child when they don't get their way and shakes his head. "Kadence is the new office girl. She's taking over for Becca, so *apologize*," Cole grits through clenched teeth.

I watch Holden's body tense at the new name, his face going pale, and it looks like he wants to throw up. Cole crosses his arms. I get the feeling that this happens more often than not and the worry returns as a heavy pit in my stomach. Just like that, Cole's promise of keeping me safe feels weak and fragile.

I watch as his face turns back into a snarl and he stumbles out of the room. "Fuck you, O'Neil," he slurs slamming the door behind him.

Cole stares at the door for a moment listening to the sound of Holden's large frame bouncing down the metal stairs before turning to me. "Are you sure you're okay?" He asks.

"Yeah, I just--wasn't expecting that to happen." I chuckle to break the tension that now invades my space, and even though the laugh is hollow, it makes me feel slightly better as he leads me over to the edge of the bed.

"Holden is... going through something right now." He runs a hand over his face. "Not that it's an excuse for his behavior." He sighs, "It's just complicated."

I laugh. Really laugh, and Cole looks at me like I'm fucking crazy. "I can understand complicated, Cole." If he only knew. "But that was something else." He glances over at me, a tired look washing over him.

Cole fixes his vest. "Get some rest, Kadence. I'll see you in the morning." He turns and heads out of the apartment.

It takes everything I have not to pack up my shit and just leave, but the car means too much to me and a small part of me is tired of running every time I get scared. Instead, I crawl back into bed. My mind starts to wander back to the darkened blue eyes that I can't seem to get out of my head. I recognized the look he had when he stepped towards me, madder than sin and locked on me. But when I recoiled, he looked almost terrified, like the idea that he was going to hurt me physically pained him, and that's the thing that makes me curious.

KADENCE

The sun shines through the window across from the bed, bringing light to the fact that I haven't slept a wink after Cole left. I can't get my mind off of Holden and the unmistakable sadness in his eyes that he tries to hide with anger and alcohol; not to mention the fact that they're the bluest eyes I've ever seen on man.

Around 7am I roll out of bed, dragging my exhausted body to the shower. Cole sent me a text earlier letting me know that there's coffee and plenty of "breakfast shit" in the clubhouse if I wanted to join. A pit of anxiety brews in my stomach when I think about getting close to a motorcycle gang, and it only reminds me of his comment last night about some of the men being too much. For the moment I push the feeling aside, turning on the shower and getting it to the right temperature before undressing and climbing in. A thousand questions run through my mind about the events of last night, all of them landing on one man I shouldn't feel this need to get to know.

Embarrassment floods me when I remember cowering in front of Holden. Everything happened so fast that I hadn't realized that he wasn't trying to hurt me. But I remember that look of darkness. I've seen it before, just not weaved with the sadness I'd felt seeping from Holden as Cole pulled me up off the floor. I know Cole is going to have questions too; he has to.

I don't realize that I've made it through the motions of my shower routine until the water starts to run cold, bringing me back from the depths of my mind's own picture show of the night before.

I step out of the shower, dry off and get ready for the day. I brush my hair, letting the wet locks flow down my back, which create little damp spots on the back of my black tank top, and slip into a pair of shorts. If today was anything like yesterday it was going to be hot and if I'm going to be in the cramped office all day, I want to be somewhat comfortable.

I take one look around, grab my phone, and shove it into my back pocket before leaving the apartment. It's still early enough that the garage hasn't opened yet, the big bay doors are still closed and the lot looks like a ghost town.

The row of motorcycles is gone, leaving only a few stragglers and one that I don't remember seeing from the day before. I don't really think anything of it as I head over to the clubhouse. As I pull the door open, a waft of stale alcohol and cigarette smoke floods my nostrils. I take a few steps down the hallway, where the room opens up into a large lounge area. To my left is a corner of couches and pool tables. A few men wearing cuts are curled up on the sofas; no doubt sleeping off last night.

I glance to my right, seeing a fully stocked bar, the counter a polished dark wood with dark green stools set underneath it. Behind the bar is another mural of the wolf, this time the words Hell Hounds are painted on either side of it. It's not howling this time. The wolf sits, its tail wrapped around his hind legs with bright glowing blue eyes that feel familiar to me.

"Mornin'." Cole's voice rasps from behind me, still littered with sleep.

I jump slightly at the sound, spinning around with my hand on my chest, laughing nervously. Cole raises a brow for a moment before chuckling.

"Morning." I respond.

"Are you usually this skittish?" He asks, taking a sip from the black coffee mug in his hand. He's leaning against the frame of what looks to be a small kitchen behind him. One arm is tucked across his chest, the fabric of his shirt pulling and stretching against his biceps. The fact the shirt is still clinging to his body surprises me.

I frown. "Are you usually this sneaky?" I quip back.

"Yes," he fires back, taking another sip, hiding the grin spread across his face.

"Maybe we should get you a bell." I tease, playfully narrowing my eyes at him, crossing my arms over my chest.

Cole laughs, his head tilting back slightly. "That would ruin my element of surprise, Kade." He smirks and flashes me a wink before standing straight, nudging his head behind him. "You want some coffee?"

I smile shyly, dipping my head down for a moment at the nickname before glancing back up at him. "Yeah, coffee would be great."

I follow him into the kitchen, sitting down at the table. "So, do you live here?" I ask, leaning back into the wooden chair.

The clubhouse from the outside doesn't look big, but on the inside, it's spacious with an entry hallway and another long hallway off of the kitchen that I noticed. A few closed doors and two double doors at the end of the hallway.

He nods as he moves throughout the kitchen, grabbing a mug for me from the cabinet above the sink. "I stay here when I need to," he confirms, and I get the feeling there's more to that. I don't have any right to push for information about him, so instead I hum softly.

Cole pours me a cup. "Two sugars and one creamer right?" He asks, glancing over his shoulder at me.

I tilt my head slightly. "How did you—?"

"Between Maggie's and the office yesterday, you had about ten cups. Hard not to notice after a while." He shrugs as he rips open two sugar packets and dumps them into the dark liquid.

"You were watching me?" I ask, the anxious pit forming in my lower stomach again as I sit forward in the chair, and as if he can hear the nervousness in my voice, he turns, glancing at me as he pours the cream.

"Not like that—" Cole reassures, setting the cup down in front of me on the table. "I was in the military–Holden and I both were–you learn to pick up on certain cues." He slides the chair opposite of me out from under the wooden table and sits down, leaning back.

The nervousness doesn't leave as he watches me try to hide the panic across my face. I don't want to tell him about what happened or that Jeremy is still a very real threat in my life, and a part of me doesn't want to admit it either because admitting it means my fears are real. But the longer he studies me, the more his gaze feels like a truth serum threatening its way into my veins.

"I see." I pick up the mug, taking a sip.

His gaze doesn't let up as he begins to drum his fingers against the ceramic. "What are you runnin' from, Kade?"

I freeze at the question, the lump in my throat making it difficult to swallow. My eyes meet his pleading for a silent pardon not to have to answer him.

"Nothing," I whisper, my eyes dropping to my coffee.

"Does nothin' have a name?" Cole asks gently.

I purse my lips, shaking my head. "Nope."

He nods, narrowing his eyes for just a moment. "I made you a promise, Kadence, but that's a hard promise to keep if I don't know what I might have to protect you from." Cole's fingers stop drumming. "Whatever it is, I don't need to know now. I don't even need to know today—" He tilts his head to catch my gaze, "—but I can't have anything threatening the club. You understand what I'm sayin'?"

I nod. "Yeah, Cole, I do." Sooner or later I know shit is gonna come out but I can't relive it today. "I don't want to ruin what you have here, so if it's better for me to just be a customer, I'll figure out a different way to get the money for the Comet."

His brows furrow. "I think you're a little more than just a customer now, don't ya think?" Cole takes another sip of his coffee.

I raise a brow. "You realize how kidnappy that sounds, right?"

Cole almost spits out his coffee, coughing once he finally gets a breath in. "I didn't, until now," he chokes out between coughs.

I grin, shaking my head softly as the tension begins to dissipate, not fully but enough that I don't feel the weight of my secrets as much anymore.

"I should get out to the office." I offer as I stand. "Gotta reorganize your mess." I tease, grabbing my coffee cup.

Cole grins as he runs his hand over his bearded chin. "You know, Kade. I think you're gonna fit in just fine here."

I scoff, leaning against the door frame. "After last night, I think you're the only one who believes that."

He winces. "About that..."

"It's okay, Cole," I say almost instinctively.

Cole stands so fast that I take a step backward into the hallway, causing him to stop, his face crumples for a moment, realizing just how jumpy I am.

"What Holden did isn't okay, Kade. His actions were not okay." He inches towards me, "You know that right?"

I instinctively take another step backward. "I–I know," I say, and the words don't even sound convincing to myself as I say them. "I know," I repeat, forcing the confidence past the lump growing in my throat. "I don't want to be a wedge, Cole, and last night..."

"Last night." He stops me. "Holden was drunk off his ass and being an even bigger one. That's not anything you should be apologizing for." Another fatherly sigh leaves his lips and his hands find that dip in his waist again. "I'm not excusing what he did. I'll talk to him."

"Cole, you don't—"

"Kadence, if you apologize for his behavior, I'll fire you." He threatens, his eyes softening with a hint of playfulness and it makes me laugh gently to hide the nervousness.

"Okay."

A door down the hallway swings open, making both Cole and me glance toward the noise. We watch as Holden stumbles his way out of the room, backwards, missing the shirt he was wearing last night and a smug grin plastered on his sleep-swollen face. His jeans hang low on his hips, giving view to the sharp V of his waist. I swallow again, and my eyes flicker up to his face. The stubble has grown a little thicker overnight, casting a shadow over the edges of his jawline, and even though he looks exhausted, I can still see how blue his eyes are from this distance.

Holden laughs, mumbling something as a short blonde leans against the doorway and I have to fight the urge to roll my eyes. It's not the same woman from last night, and even though I shouldn't be, a small thought passes my mind of what his adonis would feel like under the weight of my touch.

Cole clears his throat, standing next to me. "Holden." Dark brows furrow as bright eyes glance down the hallway. They briefly connect with mine and I hate that I can feel the heat creep up the back of my neck under the penance of his glare.

I watch as a flicker of darkness casts over his eyes before he smugly leans against the wall of the hallway. "Cole, you've met Jane?" The gravel of his voice carries down the hallway, hitting me like a sack of bricks.

Jane waves at the two of them with a soft morning smile. Annoyance begins to flood my chest, watching Holden smirk. He hasn't stopped staring at me, and even as Cole sighs, his eyes don't leave mine.

"Yeah, we've met. Hello, Jane."

"Hi, Cole," she mutters before disappearing back into the room.

Holden makes it a point to watch her walk back into the room, tilting his head to admire whatever body part his mind was objectifying. Before I can even stop myself, a small scoff leaves my lips, and I roll my eyes. Holden grins, his head tilting towards me.

"Mornin', Princess," he says, sarcasm dripping from the haunting pet name as he saunters towards me and Cole. "Sleep well?" He asks, leaning forward with narrowed eyes and a look that makes the hand at my side ball into a fist and white knuckle the mug in my hand.

I turn to Cole. "I'm gonna head out to the office," I say as he nods, eyeing the stupid grin on Holden's face.

"Yeah, alright. Let me know if you need anything."

"Will do," I say, glancing back at Holden once more before heading out of the clubhouse. It takes everything in me not to throw the mug against the ground as I let the wooden door slam behind me. Who the hell does he think he is and why does he go from looking like a sad lost puppy to the biggest ass I've met?

The rumble of a motorcycle sounds behind me as I head across the parking lot to the shop. I spin, seeing an older man with chin-length dark graying hair that looks like it hadn't been washed in a couple of days pull in next to the other bikes. I watch as he climbs off, peeling the dark black sunglasses from his face. He's got a few scars on his cheeks that I notice and try not to stare at. His cut is worn and looks like he's had it for years; the leather is dull and the Hell Hounds MC patches are faded.

"And who might you be darlin'?" He asks, the Scottish accent thick like he has a mouthful of molasses. The man struts toward me and I realize he's wearing an O'Neil's Towing and Garage shirt under his cut.

"I'm Kadence."

"Kadence…" My name rolls off his tongue and it makes me smile. "I've never seen you here before, love. You gettin' your car fixed?"

"Sorta, you could say that." I laugh. "My car broke down. Cole's helping me get it fixed and in return, I'm helping him out in the shop."

He nods, glancing back to the clubhouse before landing back on me. "Sounds like something that O'Neil would do." He grins. "I'm Scottie."

"Nice to meet you, Scottie. It looks like we're gonna be workin' together?" I ask, tilting my cup towards his shirt.

Scottie smiles again, the scars on his cheeks moving perfectly with the curvature of his mouth. "Looks like it, lass. If you need anything, just holler for me."

We both begin to walk towards the shop, he gives me an encouraging nod towards the office as he goes to open the bay doors.

"Thanks," I say, heading inside.

I glance around at the office again. The stacks of paper are all strewn about still, haphazardly, and as if they just get scattered or migrate about the room instead of actually filed. Something tells me that Cole's office management skills aren't his strong suit. I take a sip of my coffee before sitting down at the desk, finding a small empty spot to place my mug before starting to rifle through the paperwork. Separating bills and organizing old work orders.

The shop starts bustling, and I can hear music begin to play at one point. Men yelling and laughing from behind the closed shop door. I remember Cole dropping in to refill my coffee cup at one point, but my hyperfocus kicks in and I don't realize that two hours have passed until the sound of heavy boots hit the floor in front of me.

I glance up, seeing a more awake Holden and like a nervous tick, I feel the annoyance creeping back in. "Can I help you?" I bite through a forced smile.

Holden shakes his head, plopping down onto the small couch. His feet kick up onto the corner of the desk, narrowly missing knocking over the stack of paperwork I just organized. He purses his lips, shaking his head.

"No." He pauses. "Well, you can tell me how you somehow swindled my best friend into giving you a job and free housing," he muses, his tongue flicking over his bottom lip.

"Hmm," I hum. "See, I didn't swindle Cole out of anything. He offered. So you should probably get your facts straight before accusing me of whatever it is you're accusing me of."

I stand, taking a step forward to move from behind the desk and past him, but when he doesn't move his legs and just stares up at me with a smug smile, I huff and push his feet down. His boots land on the floor with a thud.

"You got a last name, Kadie?" He questions.

My body freezes at the name my mother always uses. I pull open the filing cabinet, wanting to ignore him, but he huffs and I hear him move behind me.

"It's Kadence," I grit through a clenched jaw, spinning around to see him leaning against the desk.

Holden narrows his eyes again "Okay," he drawls. "Kadence. You got a last name?"

I stare at him. I can feel the anger in myself beginning to bubble with every precise push of my buttons that he can do. "Not for you I don't. What do you want, Holden?"

"I want to know where you came from."

"Not gonna happen," I say shortly. "So unless you need keys for a car or a work order or something, I can't help you right now."

He laughs. *Laughs.* I know it's to piss me off, but the noise is sweet and I hate it. "Where did you come from?" Holden asks again with a raised brow. I can't tell if he's being sincere or not as I go to move around him.

"Why are you suddenly so interested in me?" I all but yell as I catch his gaze, my brows furrow and my neck is starting to get the splotchy red spots from me trying to keep my anger down. "You seemed pretty busy last night," I pause, "and this morning. So if you're looking to have a busy afternoon, Holden, I'm not it."

Holden just grins at me, his eyes narrowing again like he's studying me or carefully considering his next words. "You jealous, Darlin'?" He finally says and it comes out as smooth as smoke, kicking off the desk and taking a step towards me.

Normally, I'd flinch or shy away, but after last night, I can't let him win. I won't let him win or give him any ounce of satisfaction that he's gotten under my skin, although I'm pretty sure at this point I've failed at that.

He leans towards me, his hand resting against the file cabinet behind me. The heat of his body radiates against my own and I can smell the sandalwood and spice on his skin. He must have showered before coming to irritate me. Holden reaches up, and for a moment, I feel like he's about to touch me, and my body fills with anticipation. Instead, he pushes back the fallen strands of his own hair behind his ear.

"Because if you are, all you have to do is ask," he rasps.

I suck in a breath, which doesn't help because I just get another full-bodied smell of him, and my skin starts to tingle. A wave of confidence washes over me as I run the pad of my index finger along the middle of his chest, flattening my hand against the hard muscle there and narrowing my eyes back at him.

"Tell me, Holden, do you usually put your dick into anything or is it a whole, *oh woe is me* deal?" Up close his eyes are ice blue and turn colder with my words. I push him backward, just hard enough that he steps out of my space. A part of me is a little surprised that he lets me.

"Grow up, Holden," I mutter, moving past him and grabbing my mug. I have to get out of this room before either of us do or say something we both regret.

"You don't know what the fuck you're talking about," he spits, making me turn back towards him. I see the same anger and sadness from last night wash over his features.

"Neither do you." I agree, stepping out of the shop. Still feeling his heated gaze on my back, my eyes squeeze shut and I suck in the first steadying breath I've needed in a while.

HOLDEN

*G**row up, Holden.*

Her words cut through me like a dull knife and the fact that those words, coming from a woman I've known for less than 24 hours, hurt that much makes me angrier. Who is she? I watch as she walks back to the clubhouse, not missing the way the jeans shorts she's wearing hug the curve of her hips. My hands ball into fists at my sides and the urge to run courses through me.

"The lass has got a fire in her." The Scottish accent booms from behind me. I turn to see Scottie standing in the doorway that leads out into the shop. A smirk plastered over his face like he knows something that I don't.

"I don't trust her," I mumble, pushing past him. "There's no way Cole would just hire someone on the spot like that, let alone a stranger." I huff, sitting down on a stool in front of a pieced-together motorcycle.

Scottie drums his fingers along the empty gas tank, "Are you pissed because he hired someone who calls you on your shit? Or that he replaced Becs?" The name makes me freeze and my cold blue eyes glare up at him. Nobody mentions her name around me other than Cole and only when he wants to get under my skin. Scottie does it because he knows I'm better than the shell of the man who's been haunting the shop.

"This has got nothin' to do with Becca," I hiss, picking up a greased rag and twisting it between my fingers.

He nods. "You keep tellin' yourself that, Brother."

He rounds the bike and pats my shoulder a few times before heading back to whatever car he was working on before. My head dips forward, eyes sliding closed to suck in a breath. When they open, I catch the glow of her skin under the midday sun. The natural waves in her hair bouncing over her shoulders as she sips on her fifth cup of coffee this morning. Not that I'm counting, I just noticed that she clearly has a caffeine addiction.

"Nash, you keep starin' any longer, at some point she's gonna notice."

"Shut up, Scottie."

I hear the chuckle behind me and her eyes briefly meet my own. Even from this far I can see how green they are. I watch as her chest rises and falls with a heavy sigh, breaking eye contact and heading back into the shop. I remember the way she cowered from me last night, the way she shrunk in on herself to get away from me like I was going to hurt her. I wasn't. I was shocked at her reaction, and for a moment, it threw me back to a time I refuse to remember. I hate the feeling she gave me at that moment. I'm not my father.

I'm angry at the fact that Cole thought I was actually going to hurt her, I'm not that man, but I can only imagine what Cole saw when I barreled through the doorway. An image that definitely wasn't in my favor and I know that. It was just easier for me to stay the bad guy than try to explain.

Fuck. The glaring memory of me snatching her phone and throwing it invades me. That... I should never have done.

Still, there's something about Kadence that both draws me in and makes me cautious. It's like she has this invisible warning sign flashing above her head that I'm doing everything I can not to ignore but lures me to her like a siren call. I can't explain it.

I stand, tossing the rag onto the handlebars of the bike. I head out towards my bike, sliding my phone from my pocket.

"Oy! Where ya goin'?" Scottie asks from behind me.

"I didn't realize I had a babysitter," I bite, turning back to Scottie who raises his hands in mock surrender.

"No need to get touchy," he mutters.

I shake my head as I leave the shop, taking one last glance at Kadence as she moves about the office, this time unaware of my gaze. I watch as she pushes back the hair that's fallen over her shoulder, giving view to the crook of her neck, and suddenly I'm imagining what it would be like to bury myself into her soft skin, inhaling the vanilla and lavender that flooded me earlier when I had her up against the filing cabinet. Only to be reminded of the words she hissed at me like venom and the fact that I was now going to have to deal with a half-hard erection.

I glance down at my phone, scrolling through my contact list and sit on the seat of my bike, clicking the number I need. I bring the phone to my ear, glancing back at the shop's office. I'm acutely aware of the woman currently biting her lip as she sorts a stack of paper, with not a clue what she is doing to me.

"I didn't think I'd ever hear from you again."

I grin. "How ya doin' Fisher?"

"I'm old and tired, Holden. Livin' the dream." A chuckle came from the other line. "Now, I know you didn't call me to catch up. What do you want?"

"Always straight to the point, Hank." I run a hand through my hair, pushing it back behind my ear. "Do you still have contacts at the bureau?"

"Yeah, why?"

"I'm cashing in the Mosul favor."

"Jesus Christ, Nash. What's so important that you're cashing that in?" I can hear the hesitation in Fisher's voice. Mosul felt like a lifetime ago and yet not at the same time. Both he and I barely made it out alive that day. I carried Fisher through five miles of enemy territory before a rogue bullet ripped through my left shoulder. I was medically discharged a month later.

"I need information on someone."

My eyes flicker back up to Kadence, watching as she moves through the office with ease, cleaning up the mess the guys had made in there over the last month after Becca was killed.

"Who is so important that you're cashing in Mosul?"

I sigh, running a hand over my face to get myself to take my eyes off of her. "A woman. Showed up one night, somehow convinced Cole into giving her a job and a home, but there's something about her–"

I hear laughter echo through the other line.

"You're cashing in Mosul over a woman because 'there's something about her'?" I can tell Fisher is still trying to bite back laughter as he says the words.

"You're an asshole," I grumble. Fisher laughs even harder but I don't find it the least bit funny. "You done?" I snap.

I hear Fisher clear his throat on the other end of the line and sighs. "Yeah–Look, Nash, have you ever thought of just...I don't know, maybe getting to know her? Like a normal fucking person? Not re-questing a full FBI background on her?"

I know it sounds insane, but I also have a feeling that I'm never going to get the truth from her. I recognize the anger and sadness that she tries so hard to hide, but one look from her and it feels like I'm looking into a mirror.

"Fisher, you said any time, whatever I needed, no questions asked." I remind him.

The line goes quiet for a few moments before Fisher groans. "What's her name?"

My lips quirk into a grin, "Kadence. Won't give me her last name, but you can run her plate right?"

"Jesus Christ, Nash." Another sigh. "Yeah."

"Great." I stand, pulling the pack of cigarettes out of my cut pocket, lighting one and taking a long drag. "Papa-Tango-Charlie-4-6-2. You got that?"

"Yeah, I got it. Gimme a day or so and I'll have something."

"Thanks, Fisher."

"We're even after this, Holden," Fisher warns.

"I know." I take another pull off the cigarette, letting a stream of smoke flow from between my lips as I lean against my bike. The line goes quiet again and my brows furrow.

"I heard about Becca," Fisher says. His tone is softer and more cautious than before. "I'm sorry."

I swallow the lump quickly growing in my throat. I feel that unrelenting twist in my chest again but I don't know how to respond. Normal people say thank you and move on with the conversation. But saying thank you is accepting the grief for me and I'm not ready to do that yet.

"Call me when you have something." I manage.

"Alright."

I hang up the line, stuffing the phone back into my pocket and take another drag off of the cigarette before flicking it onto the asphalt, stubbing it out with the toe of my boot. The nicotine does nothing for the heavy ball of emotion currently sitting in my stomach. I hate the feeling more than anything I've had to deal with. I have a hard time focusing on the things around me when it gets too weighty; my body feels like it's going to shut down, and everything starts to feel catastrophic. There are only two things that make me feel better, alcohol or meaningless sex, and as my gaze lands back on Kadence for the umpteenth time, neither of them seems appetizing.

The door to the clubhouse slams closed catching my attention as Cole saunters toward me across the parking lot. *Great*, I think, seeing the ever-familiar furrow in Cole's brow.

"What games are you playing with her, Nash?" He fires off, Cole's chest heaving as he comes to a halt in front of me.

Anger flares in me as I shake my head. "I'm not playing any games, Cole." It's only a partial lie but I recognize the flicker of rage that flashes across Cole's face when I say it.

"Quit the bullshit. Kadence said—"

"For fuck's sake," I exhale, running a hand over my face, "Why do you care about her so fuckin' much? Huh?" I snap, pushing myself off of my motorcycle standing toe to toe with him. "Seems to me you got a little crush on the new girl, O'Neil." My words bite like venom through the heavy summer heat.

Cole's nostrils flare, "There's only one person I had feelings for, Nash and she's fucking gone." His tone is low and that weighty ball of grief in my stomach churns. I always had my suspicions about Cole and Becca and now they'd just been confirmed. All of her late 'work nights' suddenly started to make sense. "I'm not trying to replace her–I know that's what you're thinking. We needed someone in that office and she needed help. That's. It."

I search my best friend's eyes, taking a step back. It hits me that I haven't been the only one still dealing with Becca's death. We all grew up together, Becca being two years younger than us, but even so, she was glued to our hips, getting into the same trouble we were. Becca had a habit of being the 'brains' of our operations, meaning she'd give us stupid ideas and watch the two of us try to entertain whatever she'd concocted in that brilliant brain of hers. We always took the fall and never ratted on her to our parents or the cops. I should have known that it was only natural for her and Cole to grow close.

"I didn't–" I start but stop as Cole shakes his head.

"It doesn't matter now, Nash," he sighs. "We both need to deal with our grief. We can do it together or on our own. It really doesn't matter to me as long as you're doing it in a healthy way. Booze twenty-four hours a day and running through the roster of Moon girls, isn't it."

He isn't wrong. Moon is the one place where I don't have to worry about the brothers judging me for how much alcohol I consume or how many of the girls we call Lunas dance for me.

"I need to clean out the house, Cole. I just..." I swallow hard.

"The house will come with time. Get your mind right first. We'll deal with the house later."

I nod. This is why my friendship with Cole works. The two of us could be having a conversation out loud and a completely separate conversation just by the tone of our voices or the looks we share. We always understand each other and Cole calls me on my shit.

"I'm not playing a game with her," I blurt. "I just don't trust her."

"I think the feeling is mutual, Pal. Just go easy on her? I get the feeling she's running from something bad. I just can't figure out what," Cole says, glancing behind him towards the office. Kadence is still nursing the fifth cup of coffee she's had that day.

I think about telling Cole that I called Fisher but I know what he'll say and then most likely would call Fisher himself to tell him to quit searching. "She's skittish and that makes me nervous," I admit, remembering the night before.

"I'm thinkin' something is someone," Cole muses, glancing over to me again.

"Makes sense. The question is why though."

Cole shrugs, clearing his throat. "Abuse is my guess, but she won't talk about it. She's strong, I can tell that much, but whatever she went through has to be fuckin' bad."

I watch as Scottie heads into the office, leaning against the door frame as he chats with Kadence, her face lighting up for a split second when he makes her laugh. My temper flares at the idea of someone breaking her down, but the way she cowered from me and the way she shrinks in on herself is starting to make a whole lotta sense.

"Just be nice," Cole says, poking me in the arm with a pointed look.

"Chill, Cole. I'll be nice." I smirk, making Cole roll his eyes.

"Yeah, well, don't make me kick your ass, Holden. It was embarrassing the last time I did it." Cole grins, clapping me on the shoulder as I laugh.

"If I remember correctly, we decided it was a tie."

"*You* decided it was a tie," he jests, slowly backing away from me and back towards the clubhouse. "Oh, Wolfe, Blake, and Trey should be back from their run Friday, which means–"

"Family dinner," we both say in unison as I nod.

"I still can't believe you let them take Blake."

"I didn't let them do anything. Blake showed up at the first drop with her shit after I already told her no and forced them to let her ride along. Girl's persistent." Cole shakes his head. "Wolfe said something about 'If they don't take her with them, she'll draw dicks on Trey's falcon paintings and hide Wolfe's favorite knives while they're gone'."

I have to stop myself from laughing as I brace myself on my handlebars. "Never thought I'd see Wolfe afraid of a twenty-five-year-old."

"I think it was more so he didn't want to hear Trey bitch the whole time if they didn't take her."

"You still worried about patchin' her in?"

Cole shakes his head. "Nah, she can handle her own. I was thinking about doing it after they got back, but we'll wait to do it. Marlowe wants everyone at the house by seven Friday night and I'm gonna bring Kadence, get her acquainted with some of the women–Don't look at me like that." He sighs.

I chuckle, "I'm not looking at you like anything," I pause. "You think that's a good idea though? You know how Ma gets with new girls."

"She'll be fine."

"Ma or Kadence?"

Cole shrugs, "I'm hoping Blake can be a buffer."

I raise a brow at my friend, snorting a laugh. "I see."

"What?" Cole asks.

"Nothing. Just you punishing Blake by sticking her between Ma and fresh meat."

Cole tries to hide the smirk growing on his face but fails. "If she wants to be a member of the club, she'll learn to take orders like one and see what happens when you don't–and Kadence isn't fresh meat."

I grin, knowing full well the soft spot Cole has for Blake. "Yeah, okay, big guy."

"You know what?" Cole chuckles, turning to head back into the clubhouse, "Get your ass back to work and get a fuckin' haircut." He grins.

"I will after you do."

I watch as Cole tosses his head back and laughs, "Touché, Nash. Get back to work!"

"Yeah, yeah, yeah," I mutter, shaking my head and make my way back over to the shop.

KADENCE

The first few days I've been here have been weird. Some of the guys have made their presence known, introducing themselves and being polite for the most part. Cole checks on me every now and then but mostly leaves me to focus on the paperwork. Scottie pops his head in, making fun of the abundance of coffee I've had but still refills the coffee pot for me. I think we're in some sort of weird pissing contest of who can drink the most cups in the day and honestly? It's nice to have something so easy to focus on aside from Cole's files.

My eyes flicker up and out into the shop. From here at the desk, I have a good view of each bay, including where Holden sits hunched over a motorcycle frame. He's kept his distance and never comes into the office unless he has to, which hasn't been lately. He never asks for a work order or requests to order parts, but he's always working on that motorcycle.

I shouldn't care that we have this weird bubble between us, but every once in a while, our eyes will meet from across the shop, making it feel like I'm getting sucked into a black hole I can't look away from. I hate it and the exhaustion that lingers deep in my bones sucks.

Sleep still hasn't come easy. It's not for a lack of trying but I'm sure my coffee intake doesn't help. Neither does the sound of revving motorcycle engines long past midnight. I know I just have to get used to the noises of being in a new place even with the constant feeling of someone watching me. And the worst part of it all? I'm running out of clean clothes.

I glance up from the shop to look at the clock and see that it's about time to close up. Most of the guys have left to drink at the clubhouse, but not Holden. I stand with a deep breath and step out onto the shop floor. "Holden?"

His shoulders tense and it takes him a good moment to look up at me. There's a smear of grease on his cheek and it only brightens the blue in his eyes. It throws me off and I don't realize he hasn't said anything to me until his brow raises, expecting me to continue.

The fact that he doesn't say anything only digs at my nerves. "I'm closing the office."

"Good for you, Princess," he mutters and goes back to twisting whatever bolt is more important than having a normal conversation.

The frown on my face deepens as I smack the button next to the door, watching as the big bay doors start to creak and slide closed. He looks up at me with narrowed blue eyes.

"The hell do you think you're doing?"

"Closing. Like I said." I bite. "Have a good night."

Before he can protest or snap back, I shut the office door behind me and grab my phone to leave. I hear the clanging of metal and him cursing as I shut the door to the main building, grinning to myself at the small victory as I bound up the stairs towards the apartment.

Cole had said to reach out if I needed anything and, since I haven't seen him all day, I send him a quick text asking if I could use the clubhouse's washer and dryer. Once he gives me the okay, I gather my clothes in one of my suitcases and make my way back down to the clubhouse.

As soon as I open the door the smell of cigarettes and beer floods me, along with a musk I can't quite nail down. Motor oil? There's also various colognes and a tiny hint of body odor. I make my way through the group of men, smiling at Scottie as I pass by him.

"Oi! Lass, where you goin' with that suitcase?" He grins, the scars on his cheeks stretching with his smile.

"Need to do some laundry," I call back with a laugh.

"Join us for a drink!" Another man yells behind him, and when he leans around Scottie, I see that it's Quinn. He gives me a smile but it's not quite as warm as Scottie's. It makes my skin crawl with unease, almost like he's trying to force it past whatever thoughts he's having.

Scottie gives him a soft shove. "Leave the girl alone Quinn. She'll join us if she wants."

"Maybe when all this is done," I say, backing away from them with the best smile I can muster.

Scottie nods once but Quinn's eyes narrow as he takes a swig from his beer. I swallow down the nerves and turn to head down the hallway. I want to be able to ignore the unease, to not second guess every male that comes near me because I can't tell anymore who is who. Who is actually good and who is just putting a sticky sweet front on to cover their monsters. So far Cole and Scottie seem genuinely good. Holden... he's... I don't know what he is anymore.

I find the door that's labeled *Laundry* and push it open to find a small room barely big enough for the washer and dryer in it. I'm shocked to find actual soap and dryer sheets set neatly on a shelf, grateful for whoever put them there. I start to sort my clothes when footsteps thud down the hall. Not thinking much of it I focus on my task until a throat clears behind me.

When I turn my heart sinks and that unease creeps up my ankles in angry vines holding me in place. Quinn smirks back at me. His sandy brown hair and green eyes at first make him seem harmless, but there's something in that smirk I don't like and yet it feels familiar. The underlying threat that hides beneath the toothy grin.

"You find everything okay?" He asks, taking a step towards me.

Taking the same step back, I nod. "Yeah, uhm... I'm good."

Quinn nods and I don't miss the way his eyes drag down my body before they crawl back up to mine.

"You're real pretty, ya know that?" He chuckles lowly, moving to reach for a strand of my hair. Swallowing hard, I step back into the edge of the dryer, leaving his hand hanging in the air and that's when I see it. That flicker of annoyance and self-entitlement for something he's not owed flashes in his eyes before he recovers with that creepy smile. "You don't gotta be like that."

"The answer is no," I say through clenched teeth and a white-knuckled grip on the clothes in my hand.

"I didn't ask," he says, coming towards me again. The distance between us is eaten up by his frame and the amount of space I have to run is disappearing with the air from my lungs. "Ya know, if you want to be a Luna of this club you have to make yourself...useful." He pauses moving to touch me again. I can't go anywhere. He's got me cornered against the dryer and all I can do is lean away from him.

"Get away from me, Quinn."

He leans with me and the smell of whiskey and hops on his breath fans across my cheek. "No."

"Hey, Princess!" Holden's voice booms down the hallway, forcing Quinn back a step as Holden's frame fills the doorway. I couldn't care less about the pissed off look on his face as he glances between Quinn and I, but something shifts as his gaze settles on me. His head tilts slightly. "You good?"

It takes me a moment to realize he's actually asking me if I'm okay. "Actu—"

"She's fine," Quinn cuts in, stepping in front of me and squaring his shoulders. It's a little comical, considering Holden's a good four inches taller than him.

"I wasn't askin' you." His voice drops to a low warning but his eyes stay glued to me as he takes a step forward. "Kadence—"

"Hey!" Quinn barks, shoving Holden back a step. "I said she's fine."

A smirk spreads over Holden's face as his attention turns to Quinn, almost like he's been waiting for a moment to let out whatever pent-up aggression he has. Before I know it, he's throwing his fist into Quinn's cheekbone, crunching whatever bone he connects with and dropping Quinn to the ground.

"He touch you?" Holden looks up at me stretching out his fingers.

I hear him but I'm focused on Quinn's groans and the blood dripping down his face.

"Kadence," Holden says again firmly.

"I'm fine." The words come out but not even I'm convinced that I actually am. The tight grip I have on the clothes shakes as our gazes meet.

"Did. He. Touch. You?" He asks again each word punctuated with a clench of his fist.

"He tried to."

Holden searches my eyes for a moment before grabbing Quinn by the collar of his cut, effortlessly dragging him to his feet. "You piece of shit," he growls. "Get the fuck out of here and leave your cut at the door."

Quinn stumbles holding his face as Holden shoves him out into the hallway.

"Holden." I step forward, unsure why I feel the need to stop him.

"Grab your things," he snaps back at me, stopping me from moving another step. He's still watching Quinn wobble down the hallway but as he looks back at me, his gaze softens ever so slightly realizing his tone. "The washer broke a week ago, Cole half-assed the repair. Damn thing doesn't work."

"Great," I mumble, ignoring the way his softened tone warms me.

"There's a laundromat not far from here," he offers and picks up my suitcase from the ground, setting it on top of the washer for me. "I'll grab the keys to the truck."

"You don't—"

"Humor me?" The corner of his mouth turns upwards as he steps back, giving me space to make the decision.

"You're really going to sit around and wait for my laundry to get done?" I raise a brow, challenging him only because not twenty minutes ago I locked him in the garage out of spite. I don't trust that he isn't going to wait for me to pack all my clothes up and drop me off like an unwanted puppy.

This time his grin spreads. "You promise not to lock me in any more rooms if I do?"

I can't help but smile back and set my clothes into the suitcase. "To be fair, you deserved that."

HOLDEN

K adence leads the way into the common room of the clubhouse, towing her suitcase behind her. My eyes track down her curves, the way her hips sway as she walks with a newfound confidence after I tossed Quinn out. Truthfully, I wanted to do a hell of a lot more than just crush his cheekbone. I've never liked the guy. He preyed on the Lunas like they were food, and though the girls seemed always to say yes, they never went back for more. I'm glad he's gone.

She steps out into the lot and glances back at me. "You really don't have to take me. I can walk there if you have other plans."

"I don't," I say, walking past her towards the truck.

"Are you going to be a dick the whole time?"

I bark out a laugh and turn back to her, watching her march towards me, towing that stupid suitcase. "I'm trying to do you a favor, Darlin'."

"I don't need any favors from you," she snaps back at me as fire stokes in her green eyes, but she hasn't stopped heading towards me or the truck, which means I haven't lost her completely yet. She drives me insane with her whiplash of an attitude, but at the same time, it's addicting. She pushes back at me instead of folding against my own personality, but hell, if it lets me get to know her more, then I'll put up with it.

"Get in the truck, Kadence."

She winces before steeling her features as she stares at me but it's too late, I already see that lingering fear from the night we met. Her shoulders pin back, and her entire body becomes rigid. I can see her body fighting between challenging me and submitting to my command, but I don't know if it's because she wants to or if it's a knee-jerk reaction for survival.

"You need to do laundry, I truthfully could use a cigarette and a break from here so…" I tug the passenger door open as she tries to formulate a response. "Let me do this." My eyes find hers searching them and hoping she'll just get into the truck. "*Please.*"

She studies me for a moment, and just when I think she's going to tell me to go fuck myself, the tension in her shoulders uncoils. "Fine."

I nod and wait for her to climb inside the tow truck before shutting the door once she's all the way in. I climb in and already I can tell she's nervous about going somewhere with me and, honestly, I don't know how to relieve her nerves. All I can do is hope this night doesn't end in complete disaster and we're back to not speaking.

The laundromat is on the other side of town across from Lee's; I wonder if I can get her to eat something aside from the pretzels I saw her eating earlier in the office. When we get to the laundromat I pull up out front all ready with a plan. I get out and open the door for her before she can, but I pause at the entrance.

"You aren't staying?" She asks, looking up at me, and I can see we're both surprised by her question.

I shake my head. "I'm gonna grab some food but I'll be back."

"Okay…" She says and pushes past me into the shop.

I hate that she gives in so easily, that she doesn't ask for anything, and I hate that her perfume wafts past me. Vanilla and something floral that raises the hair on the back of my neck with how much I want to bury myself into the smell.

With a sigh, I jump back into the truck and drive over to Lee's, picking up two specials for us. Then, I head back to the laundromat. I'm thankful Maggie isn't working tonight, otherwise I would probably miss the window I have with Kadence.

I find Kadence tucked in the back corner, reading a magazine that looks to be from the eighties. She's pulled her long dark hair into a ponytail and, for once, looks somewhat relaxed. I'm almost mad at myself that I'm about to interrupt her peace. Still, I clear my throat and hold up the bag of food.

When she glances up her brows furrow. "What's that?"

"Dinner..."

I bite my lip to hide the smirk as her frown deepens with my answer.

"You bought dinner? For me?"

"Well for us—"

"I don't need you to take care of me Holden," she snaps as she sets the magazine down. "Why did you do this?"

My fists clench as she starts to reprimand me for being nice. For trying. "Because pretzels aren't a fucking meal, Kadence, and you drink way too much coffee not to have something substantial in your stomach."

Confusion rolls through me as she balks and then narrows her jade gaze at me. "What I consume isn't any of your business."

I set the bag down on a folding table. "What the hell happened in the twenty minutes that I was gone?"

"What?"

"Why, all of a sudden, are you pissed off at me for trying to be nice?" I ask, trying to hide the brewing anger.

"Because I don't need to be taken care of Holden!" She snaps again. "I don't need a babysitter and I don't need you to fight my battles for me!"

"Is that what this is about? Because I punched Quinn?"

"I didn't ask you to do that!" Her voice raises and I feel the other patrons' eyes on me. I've spent the last month hiding from this town, from all the whispers and doubts that I didn't have anything to do with my sister's death. Now, here I am fighting with a woman I barely know for everyone to see.

"You didn't have to!" I boom back. "But you know what? I don't need this and clearly you'd rather sit here alone and starve." I snatch one of the containers from the bag and leave it for her. "Eat it or don't, Princess, I don't give a shit."

"Whatever Holden."

"Yeah," I laugh bitterly. "Goddamn this was a mistake."

"Seems about right," she says, just as bitterly, and plops her ass back down in the chair.

Huffing, I turn and grab the sack of my food and leave. I don't care how she gets back. I do and I'll probably tell Cole I left her there, which will be another fight, but right now I couldn't give two fucks. I have no idea what has changed in the past twenty minutes and why she's so fucking scared, but it's irritating. I don't know if I came on too strong, hell, I don't know anything anymore apparently.

HOLDEN

I spend the rest of the week working on the 1947 Knucklehead that I inherited from Cole's father before he passed away. A project I've been trying to finish for years, but a good stint in prison put a delay on my plans.

Some days I miss prison. Three square, although horrible, meals a day, a bed that didn't reek of sweat and alcohol–I really need to clean my place up–and endless time to read whatever the library had to offer. I didn't have to sit with the constant ache in my chest that I have now or the idea that everything that has happened to me and Becca has been the result of my careless actions. I don't regret going to prison. I regret that I ever had any amount of trust in Stokes and that it took so much time away from Becca and the club. Not even twenty-four hours after getting out my life fell apart. It was supposed to be one meeting. One meeting with Stokes was all it took to lose the one person I loved more than anything in this world. I should have been there, I shouldn't have let her leave the compound, not while we were away. I feel a hand grasp my shoulder, pulling me back to reality.

"You okay, Holden?" West asks as he rounds the table. Wyatt West, the youngest prospect the Hounds currently have, and even though he is young, the kid is smart. I like to give him shit, but I do like the kid. I wouldn't have done prison time if I didn't.

I glance out at the parking lot, realizing that the sun has now turned the sky a deep shade of orange.

"Yeah, West. I'm good."

Wyatt nods, shoving his hands into the pockets of his cut. "You've just been really quiet today. Scottie told me not to bother you, but you look..." His voice trails off, making me furrow my brow.

"I look what?"

He shrugs. "Sad..."

Did I really look that pathetic? I think as I stand, wiping my hands against the already grease-covered rag. After the blow-up at the laundromat, I've kept to myself. I've avoided the office as much as I can because now, I have no idea where I stand with Kadence. I shouldn't care but there's something deep in my chest that does.

"I'm fine, West."

Wyatt shakes his head "Forget I said anything... Are you going to Marlowe's?"

"Yeah," I grumble, tossing the rag onto my workbench.

"Okay, well I'll see you there then." Wyatt flashes an awkward smile before jogging out of the shop.

I watch as Wyatt makes his way across the parking lot. West is a good kid and lives with his Aunt. Like me, Wyatt had to grow up fast in order to survive. I see the good parts of myself in him, I just hope that he doesn't share the bad ones.

"Shit."

I hear muttered from the office.

"Stupid thing, just work!" Another soft hiss.

Kadence must still be working. No one is left in the shop other than the two of us and I figure Cole would have told her to quit working once the guys did. I should have expected it though, I think every day she's been working here she never leaves early or before the sun goes down.

"Goddamnit."

I hear again, another slew of curse words behind it. I try to bite back a chuckle listening to her fight with whatever has pissed her off. In the back of my head I know I should just leave it and let her take out her frustration on whatever she's cursing, but my feet start to carry me to the door. I've done everything I can to keep my distance this week and now I can't help myself.

Kadence and I have been circling each other all week. I steal glances at her whenever I get a chance and it's not lost on me that this is the first time in weeks that I've spent more than ten minutes actually working in the garage. I tried to make a connection and it blew up in my face. I still have no clue what happened between dropping her off and going back to the laundromat. She tosses me looks whenever she catches me watching her, which unfortunately is often. I feel distracted *and* the most focused I have in a while.

I lean against the frame, watching her inspect the ancient air conditioning unit in the window of the office. Smacking it with the palm of her hand as it sputters and whines back at her.

"You were working not five minutes ago. What the hell..." She bends over, trying to look at the bottom of it, but as she does, my gaze falls to the curvature of her hips and the way her shorts ride up just enough to see the cusp of her ass. The sight makes my heart begin to hammer against my ribcage and the traitor in my jeans alert.

Get it together, Nash.

I clear my throat, causing her to stand upright, almost hitting her head on the unit.

"Everything okay?" I muse, trying to bite back the grin on my face as she looks back at me, her brows furrowed in the exact way I pictured and her cheeks pink from the heat.

Kadence rolls her eyes at me. "Clearly not," she grumbles. I know she's pissed, I can see it on her face and it doesn't help that I find it cute.

"AC go out again?"

"It was working five minutes ago!" Kadence smacks it again with her palm, wincing slightly as she hits the corner of it. I grimace, watching her. "Stupid thing just won't fucking work now," she mutters as she begins twisting and turning the knobs.

"Okay, Okay... Hey–" I say, stepping into the shop behind her.

My hand falls over hers to get her to stop before she breaks it even more. Kadence's entire body freezes under my touch, her gaze piercing my fingers that are currently wrapped around her own. I fully expect her to pull away from me, but she doesn't.

"You're gonna break it, tough guy," I whisper leaning into her slightly. Her skin is soft and my hand feels like it's on fire against hers, the heat of our bodies fighting for control.

She looks up at me through her lashes, each of our hands still lingering against the other. I flick my tongue over my bottom lip, catching her eyes as they dart down towards the movement and then back up to meet mine again.

My own gaze falls to the way she pulls her bottom lip between her teeth. It doesn't help the fire growing in my stomach as we stand here, almost in our own tormented game of chicken, each waiting for the other to break first.

Kadence slides her hand out from mine and takes a step back from me as she sucks in a deep breath. Disappointment floods me for a moment and I clear my throat again to shake it away.

"If you have any other ideas, be my guest," she says, plopping herself down onto the couch and resting her head back against the edge of it.

Her eyes slide closed and she takes in a few more deep breaths.

"You just have to–" I grunt softly, kneeling down to unplug the AC unit and plug it back in.

Her eyes slide open as I lean back, waiting for it to kick on. After a few seconds, we hear the fan start to whirr again, and I flash a grin her way. I stand up, holding my hand out in front of the vent feeling the cool air blow against my still-heated palm.

Kadence stands and quirks a brow as she holds her hand out next to my own. Her eyes going wide for a moment before looking back up at me. "That's it? Just unplug and replug it back in?" She says, her voice littered with skepticism.

I nod, taking a step back and leaning against the desk. "Been doing it for years. Cole refuses to buy a new one until this one goes to complete shit."

She glances back at the AC unit, folding her arms over her chest. "At least I know what to do now..." Kadence smiles softly, her eyes still on the appliance before they flicker to me. "Thanks."

I feel the blush creeping up my neck, hearing the honesty in her voice. The tension from last night has dissipated and has been replaced with something else, though I can't quite tell what it is.

"I should–" She starts, pointing back to the desk. I glance down at it, the stack of papers that was there before is now sorted into separate piles and there are boxes that she's organized with new folders.

"Right," I say, stepping away from the desk as she goes to move past me.

Kadence gives me a smile. It's small and doesn't quite reach her eyes, but it's an improvement from the coldness she gave me earlier so I'll take it. It's not until she turns away from me that I notice a scar on the back of her left shoulder. It's jagged and the edges are pink from where it's scarred over. It looks like the one I have, only mine is smaller and more round.

I hear footsteps behind me, causing me to break the stare I have and realize she's been watching me the whole time. I go to open my mouth when Cole brushes past me, taking a guarded stance between me and Kadence.

"Everything alright?" Cole asks, glancing between the two of us.

Kadence is quiet, her brows furrowed again but this time not in anger. She knows I'm staring and I know I've been caught.

"Everything is fine," she says, her eyes never leaving my own. "Holden was just fixing the AC."

"Yeah, Pal. I think it's time to get a new one." I agree, finally breaking our stare to look at my friend.

Cole shakes his head. "If you fixed it, then I don't need a new one." He smirks before turning to Kadence. "We have a few members coming back tonight and we do this dinner every time a member comes back from a ride." He smiles gently at her. "I'd like for you to come, if you want that is. You'll be able to meet a few of the other members."

Kadence glances at me again and I shrug. "I don't know, Cole..."

"No pressure, okay? I'm gonna head out in about an hour, so if you want to come, just meet me outside."

She nods. "Okay."

Cole smiles again at her and for some reason I feel like punching the smile right off of his face as he turns to leave. "Nash, you ridin' with?"

Our eyes meet again and I nod. "Yeah, I'll ride with."

Cole claps me on the shoulder. "Good," he says with a smile before heading out of the shop.

I watch my friend leave before turning back to Kadence, the air around us filling with thick silence.

"I don't have to go..." She says softly after a moment, glancing at me. "These are your people Holden.. I don't want to wedge between that and it's clear that you aren't my biggest fan."

I'm taken aback for a moment, it surprises me that she's giving me the option. My brows furrow at her words. "Do what you want, Princess." I shrug, "It's not gonna hurt my feelings either way." I lie.

Truth is I can't stop thinking about her. It makes me angry that a woman I've barely known for a full week has driven herself so far into my head that I can't even be in the same room with her without wondering how her skin feels. I'm treading in dangerous waters and I know it, especially now after my call to Fisher. He hasn't gotten back to me on her information, which makes me cautious of her and intrigued by her. What is she hiding that's so damn bad not even Fisher can find the info easily?

Kadence scoffs, shaking her head as an empty chuckle leaves her lips.

"Alright, Holden," she mutters, sitting back down in the desk chair, the cold demeanor that she only shows to me slowly icing her over again.

My stomach drops, watching the slight progress I made thinking that she might not fully hate me, completely escape the room.

I turn, heading towards the door before glancing back at her. "Just... don't work too late. This paper pile will still be here tomorrow mornin'." My voice trails off as she looks back at me, her eyes narrowed. I sigh, shaking my head before turning to leave. It's no use now trying to get on her good side again. I ruined that the minute I opened my mouth with Cole in earshot.

Guilt trickles through me like a tormented waterfall as I make my way over to my bike. I see Cole on the phone, his brows furrowed and shaking his head. I'm not quite close enough to hear the conversation, but when I reach earshot, Cole glances at me before hanging up.

"What was that about?" I ask, pulling the pack of cigarettes from my vest.

Cole lets out a sigh. "Stokes wants to meet. Says he wants a bigger cut from the club."

I snort. "'Course he does."

"Says that Wolfe got into some trouble on their run and in order for us not to be 'pulled into an investigation', he wants a bigger cut." Cole takes the pack from me, pulling one out and lighting it before handing the pack back. I watch with a raised brow. Cole only smokes when he's stressed, otherwise it's all greek yogurt and that birdseed he calls granola.

"Fuck," I sigh. "Well, if it's Wolfe, it's probably warranted–bad–but warranted."

Cole chuckles, taking a long drag. "Far as I can tell, no one is dead. It can't be that bad."

"I've seen that guy do unspeakable shit without killin' someone. Trust me, it's bad." I light my own, pulling the smoke into my lungs and relishing the burn.

The first few drags off a freshly lit cigarette are my favorite. Something about the feeling hitting my lungs for the first time in a while and the way it smells when I first light it. That's the addicting part to me. I remember the first cigarette I had after Mosul. I will never forget how good it felt to have something other than artillery smoke fill my lungs.

"Fuckin' hope not." Cole pats my arm. "You and Kadence seem to be getting along this afternoon." A slight grin spreads across his face as we watch her head up the steps to the apartment. "Don't think I didn't notice the staring contest."

I narrow my eyes at him. "What are you implying?"

"Nothing." Cole takes one last drag before stubbing his cigarette out onto the concrete. "For someone who says they don't trust her and has a piss poor attitude about new people, you sure were quick to help her. Even last night..."

"Don't." I warn with a look.

"What? All I'm saying is you threw a prospect out of the club for her." His hands find his hips as he shrugs.

"He deserved it. Kadence isn't the first girl Quinn pushed too far. It was time for him to go."

I see a flicker of anger in his eyes. It's no secret Quinn had made his way through the girls at Moon. None of them were ever brave enough to stand against the club and he kept his... indecensies behind closed doors. But we all knew the rumors, and catching him with Kadence last night was just an excuse for a long-overdue punishment. It had nothing to do with the burning rage in my chest seeing her with someone else.

"You did the club a favor...but Kadence..." He starts. I know what he's asking and I don't like it.

"That office turns into a sauna if it's remotely hot." I shrug, "I'm just saving you from a workers comp claim." I wink, pulling from my cigarette.

Cole cackles, shaking his head. "Whatever you say, Holden."

I grin at my friend. It's been a while since I've been able to see Cole laugh, really laugh at something I've said. The sound is a nice change compared to the scolding Cole has been doing recently. When we were kids, I could make him so mad that his entire face would turn bright red like the tomatoes from Marlowe's garden. Cole has a temper that he's tried hard to hide for years. But when I see that familiar shade of red begin to fall over his features, I start cracking jokes. Just something stupid enough to make him smile and that red fades away.

"You're coming!?" Cole suddenly yells, a wide smile spread across his features.

I follow his gaze, seeing Kadence walking towards us. She's traded in the shorts for a pair of jeans that look like they've been painted onto her and her tank top is now covered by a lived-in black denim jacket with random patches that I can't quite make out in the twilight. I watch as her bottom lip finds home between her teeth again, something I've noticed she does whenever she's anxious.

"Figured it was probably a hell of a lot more fun than a pile of papers," she remarks, throwing a quick pointed look at me and, in a split second, the fire in my belly is replaced with annoyance. *Two can play at this game,* I think, realizing that she's only going to piss me off.

Cole laughs, climbing onto his bike and holding out his helmet for her. "Well, your chariot awaits."

I follow suit, climbing onto my own bike and kicking up the kickstand as I watch the hesitation wash over her features. "What? Scared of messing up the hair, Princess?"

Kadence purses her lips together as her eyes meet mine. Her fingers wrap around the edge of the helmet. "Is that why you're not wearing one?" She quips, sliding the helmet over her head. "Too afraid of split ends?" She snarks, waving her index finger at my head.

I hear a snort come from Cole as he helps her buckle the chinstrap. I roll my eyes, the annoyance in me stacking like wood on a campfire as my bike roars to life. The rumble of the engine vibrates against my ribcage as I watch her climb behind Cole, gripping the leather of his cut, her hands resting at his hips as his own bike comes to life.

I push off the concrete, twisting the throttle enough to get me rolling and, like kerosene, my jealousy is lit on fire when I hear her laugh as Cole's bike lurches forward, pulling up next to me as we head out of the shop gate. I want to be the one to make her laugh. The smile she flashes me as she turns her head in my direction makes my stomach flutter and though I know it's not for me, I'd do anything to see it again.

I'm fucked and I know it.

KADENCE

My fingers grasped tightly around the edges of Cole's cut as he and Holden weave through the streets of Pine River. It's been years since I've been on the back of a motorcycle, and as he speeds up and the wind whips through my hair and the cold prickles at the skin of my cheeks, I remember why I loved it. The heat radiating from Cole's body seems to help for a bit until he makes a left turn and the chill spreads over me again.

I can hear the roar of Holden's bike trailing behind us and my mind wanders to the office, his hand on mine, and the way it felt like tiny fireworks exploded onto my skin as soon as he touched me. Not even in the beginning with Jeremy did I ever feel anything like that.

His bike pulls up next to Cole's as they hit a straight road and my eyes glance over to the man my mind has been running circles around all day. His hair is tucked behind his ears and, at some point in the ride, he's slipped a navy blue ball cap over his head. He looks different with his hair tucked back and not shrouded around his face. The three-day-old stubble that speckles his face creates shadows that sharpen his cheekbones and jawline under the moonlight.

He's gorgeous and I hate the fact that every time we spend more than five minutes together, it turns guarded. Well...I turn guarded. Last night I got scared when he showed up with dinner. I have spent the last month protecting myself from men, from getting close to anyone other than Maria. When Cole offered me the job, I swore to myself that I wouldn't get close to anyone, but with Holden, it feels almost inevitable and that's what terrifies me the most. From him protecting me to offering to help and then trying to feed me...to some, it might feel ridiculous. To me, it felt like a heavy boot named anxiety pressing against the back of my neck for trusting a man again. Still, the both of us put up walls to block any vulnerability. He is crass, moody, and seems like he hates everyone except for Cole but a part of me still feels drawn to him. A twinge of familiarity sparked between us and I was still figuring out what that meant.

Holden's bike speeds past us, making a sharp turn to the left onto a long-curved driveway. Cole follows behind, the road winding as we ride further beyond the tree line that hugs the main road. Soon I can see the faint glow of lights peeking through the branches.

I gasp softly, seeing the size of the house as it comes into view. It's massive and made of long, dark wooden logs with lighter wood trim. The glow from all the windows lights up the driveway, making the small solar-powered trail lights almost pointless.

Cole parks his bike next to Holden's, kicking down the stand before climbing off. He holds a hand out to me with a bright smile to help me down.

"Thanks."

"No problem," he almost whispers as my hand grips his.

I swing my leg over the seat, firmly planting my feet on the ground. My legs feel almost numb from the vibration of the motorcycle and it makes my heart race in my chest. The feeling is as addicting as leaning over the edge of a balcony on a tall building.

Cole lets my hand go, his brows furrowing for a moment, and as I glance up at him, it's like he's finally taking a moment to consider whether or not bringing me here was a good idea. I can read the doubt behind his eyes from a mile away, and it's something I'm all too familiar with. The question of being wanted.

"I'll introduce you to Marlowe," he finally says. "But before I do, she's a little..."

"Nosy? Abrasive? Bit of a hard ass?" Holden quips, climbing off his bike. Those bright blue eyes turn on me, heating my skin as if he had superpowers.

Cole winces slightly, throwing a pointed glance at Holden. "I was gonna say protective..."

"Yeah, you can add that." He sits back on the edge of his bike, crossing his arms over the expanse of his chest, "Real mama-bear type," he goads, narrowing his eyes, attempting to be playful. It only makes the pit in my stomach grow about four sizes as I turn to Cole.

"I should have stayed back at the shop."

He shakes his head as his hands fall on my shoulders and for the first time in a long time, I don't wince at a man's touch. "It's going to be fine! She's gonna love you and if she doesn't, I know Blake will."

"So, there's a chance she's gonna absolutely hate me." My voice whines softly as Holden scoffs out a laugh.

Holden stands from his bike, takes a step towards me, and leans in. The smell of motor oil and spice mixed with a faint hint of coffee surrounds me, swirling the butterflies in my stomach.

"Just turn on that shining personality, Princess. You'll be fine." He smirks, his voice low and graveled as he stands back up.

"I have a name, you know. Unless that brain of yours is too small to figure that out." I sneer, my face dropping as I stare pointedly at him. I'm tired of him getting in every little dig that he can. It's driving me insane, along with the fact that whenever he is near me, it's like there is an electric buzz between us.

Darkening blue eyes stare back at me, narrowing as his tongue drags across his bottom lip before bringing it between his teeth. My eyes track the movement. His lips are plush and pink from the cold but the more he gnaws on it the more I feel myself growing warm.

The corners of his mouth curl upwards slightly as Cole waves a hand between us, "Can you two get along for literally one night?"

"No." Both of us answer at the same time. Cole rolls his eyes, shaking his head as his hands fall on his hips.

"Well, try."

He storms off towards the giant wooden door at the front of the house leaving the two of us alone. I narrow my eyes at Holden for a moment as he leans in again.

"You have a staring problem." He muses softly, his voice warming my skin like the low heat of winter fire.

"I could say the same to you," I bite back, turning on my heel and heading towards the door. The soft thud of his boots follows behind me, making me extremely aware of the distance between us.

He was like a shadow to me, dark but inviting, making me feel like I wasn't alone. I'm not sure if that's a good thing or bad. Holden aggravates me. Even in the small moments I'd spent with him, he irked every nerve in my body. But there's a part of me that feels this pull towards him. A familiarity in the way we share our anger and the deep-seated pain I can already sense behind his silver eyes. I can see small parts of myself within him, mostly the ones that feel painful and ache when triggered.

Everything he did was to challenge me, make me give in and fold. I'm done folding for people. I'd been a victim in Miami. Everyone I knew turned on me when I tried to tell the truth about Jeremy. About what really happened that night. The threats started after I got home from the hospital, and even though I wanted nothing more than to stand my ground, I was alone.

So, I ran.

Holden never forces me into backing down. It's like he knows when to ebb and flow with me and how to push my buttons without actually hurting me. I'm thankful for that.

Cole waits for us at the entryway, holding open the wooden door and letting the aroma of freshly baked bread, spices, and something else I can't quite pinpoint waft around me. I step through the threshold taking in Marlowe's home. It's the epitome of warm and cozy. Soft brown leather furniture adorns the open living area, plants hang from various corners and litter tables like mini gardens. Warm lights glow from the modern chandelier above us, and candles flicker gently on the side tables.

I can't remember the last time I'd been in a place that felt this welcoming.

There are a few men scattered around the living room. Some I recognize from the shop. Scottie and Wyatt lounge back on the giant leather sofa, arguing and chastising each other about something I can't quite make out. Scottie catches my eyes from his seat, throwing me a soft wink. I smile, tossing one back as the man who sits across from him turns to see who Scottie's looking at.

Dark brown eyes study me for a moment with a tilt of his head before turning back to the men, seemingly uninterested. Which I'm completely fine with. The last thing I need is to draw any more attention to myself than I already have and I'm not ready to get the third degree from another member of the Hounds.

"Come on," Cole says softly, leaning into me, jutting his chin towards what I assume is the kitchen judging by the way the smells get stronger as we travel down a side hallway.

As we round the corner, I spot an older woman with long straw- berry blonde hair tied off in a loose braid cascading down her back. Her skin glows against the kitchen lights as she moves about, almost floating around the kitchen and tables.

"Let's get the table set," her voice commands gently as she stirs one of the pots on the giant stove. "Blake those don't– No, please stop rearranging the forks and spoons."

Cole chuckles as we stand in the door. Another woman, this time younger, steps up to the island separating Marlowe from the dining area. She can't be much older than twenty.

"Haven't you ever seen Titanic, Ma? The small forks go over here." Blake points to the edges of the place settings, rearranging the small utensils as she gnaws on her bottom lip. She has long dark hair that is pulled up into a loose bun, and dark tendrils have fallen around her face, but what surprises me the most is the Hell Hounds Prospect patches stitched to the black denim vest she's wearing.

I glance up at Cole who's watching the scene with a smirk playing across his lips. I recognize a glint in his eye that I used to see in my father's as he watches Blake. She means something to him and it transcends a normal friendship.

"Leave it, Blake," Marlowe warns with a slight raise of her brow, "and Cole, if you're going to lurk in the doorway at least make yourself useful and help her," she muses knowingly, even though her back has been turned from us.

Cole laughs this time, the corners of his eyes crinkling softly as he steps into the kitchen, planting a kiss on the side of Marlowe's head. "You got it, Ma."

"Why do we need so many utensils anyway?" Blake asks, throwing her hands up in dramatics, making me smile to myself. Her eyes light up seeing Cole in the kitchen, her eyes going wide as if a light bulb has gone off in her head, "OH! Do you have any sporks? The guys would love that."

Marlowe shakes her head, handing dishes full of food over to Cole to place on the table.

"Blake, no one uses sporks over the age of five," he says, shaking his head.

"That's what you think, old man." She grins, pointing the end of a butter knife at him before he playfully smacks it away, tugging her to his chest.

He pulls back from the girl, his hands resting on her shoulders as he inspects her. "Don't think we're not discussing your little field trip after dinner."

Blake winces, guilt dripping over her face like a mask before another smile threatens the corners of her lips. "Yeah, yeah,"

I linger in the doorway, turning back to see that Holden has disappeared from behind us. My heart sinks for a moment, almost expecting him to be lingering behind me, watching and waiting to irk me further. Instead, he'd left me alone. Why am I almost sad about that? Why do I even care that he isn't there in the first place?

I take a deep breath, stepping into the kitchen.

Marlowe glances at me out of the corner of her eye. "You don't have to hide in the shadows, sweetheart. We won't bite you," she coos, as if she's lulling a scared animal from the corner of the room. "Despite what Cole may have warned you about." She grins, continuing to busy herself with dinner.

"Ma, Blake, this is Kadence. She's gonna help out with the shop for a while," he says, stepping towards me. I don't miss the pointed look Marlowe flashes to him and it's then that I realize that it's her who runs the show. Cole may be President and boss, but she is in charge of them.

Blake practically skips over to me as if I'm a new plaything for her. She circles me with a sly grin across her face. "How did Cole convince you to work for him? He's a *horrible* boss," Blake jokes, crossing her arms over her chest.

"I am not–" Cole narrows his eyes as he shakes his head.

Blake grins at him, forcing a sigh to leave Cole's chest as he pinches the bridge of his nose.

I chuckle softly as I tuck my jacket further around me and arms across my chest. I can't help but shrink in on myself though the house feels warm, Marlowe's gaze on me is chilling. It doesn't leave me the entire time Blake goads Cole and I know I'm not going to be able to escape it.

As the night goes on, Marlowe ushers the men to the table, forcing them all to sit like one large happy family. There's a place set next to Cole for me. I'm thankful because it's currently where I feel the safest.

Holden sits across from me and the man from earlier is next to him. I keep my gaze focused on my food as Blake rambles on about anything and everything motorcycle related, she can think of. She jokes and laughs with the guys, tossing back insults and jabs right at them as they mess with her. It's obvious she can handle herself around them. Her personality lights up the room like Christmas lights and I envy that about her.

I push my food around my plate, picking at small bites here and there as I take in all the conversations happening around me. I can feel eyes on me, studying me and it only brews the anxiety in my stomach. The food becomes more and more unappetizing, not for the fact that it doesn't taste good, it's amazing, and it's the first time that I've eaten a home-cooked meal that isn't my own in years.

The longer I feel the stares on me, the more aware I become that despite having Cole next to me as a buffer, I'm still a stranger. These people don't know me and I don't know them. There isn't any trust here and suddenly I feel like I'm intruding on what I can only assume is one of their most intimate times.

The need to leave creeps into my veins and nerves like a virus. My leg bounces gently under the table as, one by one, the guys begin to leave. Plates and platters start to slowly disappear as Marlowe and Blake clear them.

"You good?" I hear Cole's voice cut through the tension building within me.

I turn toward him, my leg still bouncing and hands wringing together in my lap. "Yeah," I mutter softly, my lips pressing into a line to fake a smile.

"You sure? Because you look like you're about to run."

I suck in a breath as the room suddenly freezes. I glance up, watching as Holden steps into the hallway, disappearing into the dark corridor, and the man with dark hair, who sat next to him, leans back into his chair. The corner of his mouth quirks up slightly as if amused by my nervousness.

It's seeping out of me onto the table by this point. I watch as his fingers drum along the body of his beer bottle. "Where did you come from, Kiddo?" His voice gravels through me.

Cole shifts in his seat, knowing that I'm not going to give a straight answer, but his attention turns towards me expectantly. Is this his true intention? To bring me here knowing that I wouldn't be able to escape the prying eyes and probing questions his friends would have?

"I'm from the East Coast," I force out. It's not a lie, but it isn't the whole truth either.

The man's lips upturn as he nods, "East Coast, huh?"

Cole sits back in his chair like it's his turn to be amused and it's the first time in forty-eight hours that the small amount of comfort I had around him slinks away.

"Wolfe, leave the poor girl alone. She doesn't need you interrogating her." Marlowe's voice settles over the table as she grabs a few more plates. "Now, make yourself useful and help me with these dishes."

Wolfe.

I lock eyes with Marlowe's knowing gaze as if she can read every secret I have like they're written on my forehead.

Wolfe's eyes darken and he narrows them at me before standing. *Great*, I think. The empty and drafty apartment above the garage is starting to feel more welcoming the longer I sit here.

I stand, glancing down at Cole. "Where's the bathroom?" I ask softly.

"Down the hallway, third door on the left."

"Thanks," I mutter. It takes everything in me not to run out of the room.

I don't really need to use the bathroom. I just need a reason to leave and not have Cole hover over me.

I follow the long hallway until it opens up into the living room. I find Scottie sitting with a few of the other men along the couches and side chairs, looking as if they are discussing something I definitely am not privy to.

It only makes my chest tighten that much more, and the overwhelming feeling that I don't belong sinks further into my bones.

I slide the tall glass door open. A chilled breeze surrounds me as I step out onto an expansive concrete patio. I finally let out a breath I'm not aware I'm holding. The autumn air burns my lungs as I suck in another breath, trying anything I can to get my nerves to calm themselves.

My body vibrates with anxiety. Every atom is bouncing around my insides like they're trying to escape, and in a way, it makes sense. Everything is screaming at me to leave, to get away from the pack of men inside, to get out of this town and the more I stand here, taking in deep breaths, the more stuck I feel.

"Heat gettin' to ya, Princess?"

I slide my eyes closed, sucking in a breath through my nose as his voice drifts from my left.

"You won't be able to hide forever, ya know," he taunts. "One day all those little secrets you're keeping are going to spill out of you. Or worse..." He pauses and the soft thud of his boots once again surrounds me, encroaching on me as my eyes squeeze further shut, almost willing him to disappear. "...you'll get someone killed."

"Stop it," I whisper, having had enough.

I peel my eyes open, turning my head to see Holden standing next to me, facing me as he puffs on a cigarette. Taking one last long drag, letting it linger on his lips as his lungs fill with smoke.

The smug look on his face falls when our eyes connect and he must have finally caught a glimpse of the fear behind my green eyes.

He drops the cigarette and my eyes follow watching as the ash crackles against the ground into tiny little embers before the toe of his boot snubs it out.

"Why do you do that?" I ask, ignoring how small my voice sounds as my gaze returns to his.

Holden's brow furrows for a moment. "Because you aren't alone, Kadence." His voice drops like he's sharing a secret with me and no one else was supposed to know. "Everyone has secrets and yours aren't special."

I tug my bottom lip between my teeth, gnawing as he takes the smallest step towards me. He's close enough now that the heat of his body radiates off of him. I take a step backward, and he takes another step towards me.

I feel my back hit the cold logs of the house. He's testing me. Pushing to see just how far he can get under my skin.

I want to push back. To shove him away from me, but the closer he moves in on me the more the pull I feel towards him grows.

"Are you scared of me Kadence?" He asks, but it's not to be cruel. There is a hint of something in his voice that makes me wonder if he is worried that I actually am.

"No," I lie. I am scared of him. Not scared that he'd hurt me physically but scared that he is slowly destroying the wall I built around myself, around my heart.

The heat of his breath fans across my face sending a wave of goosebumps down my spine. I can see the blue in his eyes because of the moonlight shining between us; they're bluer than I remember, with tiny green flecks, and the small smattering of freckles across his nose and cheeks are more apparent now.

Holden leans in a little further to me, tilting his head to catch my gaze again under the brim of his baseball cap. I can hear the soft jingle of the dog tags around his neck as he moves.

"You don't have to lie to me," he whispers, his lips hovering just above my own.

It only takes a moment to realize that my fingers are now clutched around the buttons of the dark Henley he wears, tugging gently at the collar until they tangle in the chain of his tags. My mouth begins to feel like cotton as he gently nudges my nose with his own. Careful only to touch the parts of me he can see, his hands plant on either side of my head, caging me in.

"You scare me, but not in the way you think you do." My head goes foggy as our eyes meet again.

"You've been avoiding me," he rasps.

My lips part and his eyes catch the movement as I will myself to protest his comment but I can't. He isn't wrong and now a tiny part of me wishes I hadn't.

Holden's eyes dart over my face. "Tell me to stop," he breathes.

My fingers tighten around his chain, tugging as I shake my head softly.

He only hesitates for a moment before slotting his lips over mine, slow and tentative at first, but as I pull him closer, he gains a little more confidence that I'm not going to change my mind.

And I wouldn't.

The moment our lips meet an explosion of fireworks goes off in my stomach.

His tongue teases my bottom lip, silently asking permission to dance with my own. I whimper as his body presses against mine and I part my lips to let him in. He tastes like whiskey and smoke. It's addicting. *He* is addicting.

The more I lean into him, the less I want it to stop. Both of us fighting for control over the other makes my mind swim with the idea of what his hands would feel like gliding across my skin. Molding me to him.

I pull back slightly to catch my breath. My chest heaves as his eyes search my face again. The blue is only a small sliver now compared to before with how dark his pupils have gotten.

My free hand rises, grasping his wrist gently, squeezing and hoping that he'll understand my silent plea for more.

Holden trails his hand along the wood, his fingers dancing along the collar of my jacket as they slide behind my neck. Slowly and softly, they wrap around me, tangling into my hair. I let go of his wrist but reach for his lips, touching them so softly that if they weren't burning and kiss-bitten, it feels like I'm barely touching him at all.

"I don't want you to be scared of me," he says against my touch, surprising me.

The lust in his darkened eyes has been replaced with something else as I stare up at him, shaking my head, "I don't want to be either."

He dips his head again, pressing his lips against mine without hesitation. Holden tugs my body closer to his with a groan, his other hand dropping from my neck around to my lower back.

Everything he touches feels like it's on fire, burning with the heat building in my core. I feel his knee slide between my thighs, practically holding me up. A moan falls from my lips that he's quick to swallow.

My anxiety from tonight slowly begins to fade away with the slow and calculated movement of his lips. I still feel like running, I'm worried that now it's always going to be ingrained in my bones to want to run.

Holden pulls away this time, "I want to leave, and I want you to come with me."

"To where?"

He shrugs, the corners of his mouth tugging upwards. "Anywhere but here."

I smile softly. He's giving me the chance to run and at this moment I don't care that he's with me. I welcome it.

"Okay," I breathe.

The smile on his face grows as he releases his hold on me and it's the first time that the hardened soul behind his eyes disappears. His fingers lace with mine as he pulls me along the edge of the house as if he'd snuck out of these dinners a million times. I don't doubt that he has.

I feel my phone buzz in my pocket, making me stop with Holden turning back towards me. I haven't had any notifications all day. I figure it's just Maria checking in on me. Easy enough, I'll text her back, tell her I'm fine, and call her in the morning.

I pull my phone out, glancing down at the notification.

My heart drops at the name.

> **[Mom]:** *You'll never guess who I had lunch with today! Jeremy says he misses you.*

> **[Mom]:** *Kadie, when are you going to stop this foolishness and come home? What you're doing isn't fair to Jeremy or me.*

She had lunch with him? My stomach feels like it's in my throat. What's wrong with her? She had lunch with him like he's a friend. Like he isn't the one who had put me in the hospital. Like he isn't–

"What is it?" Holden asks, concern dripping from his words.

My phone buzzes again and this time I really feel like I'm going to vomit.

"Kadence," he says, taking a step towards me as tears prick at the corner of my eyes.

> **[Unknown Number]:** *I'll find you Princess. You can't run forever.*

KADENCE

"**K**adence?"

Holden's voice is muffled by the sound of my blood rushing in my ears. How can my mother do that to me? Act like Jeremy is her best fucking friend and enjoy a meal with him. I want to be shocked but a part of me knows I shouldn't be. Jeremy has a way with words around my mother and the more my mind begins to spiral the more my stomach churns at the thought of them breaking bread at my expense.

I can feel Holden moving in on me, doing what any normal person would do and trying to console whatever terrified look is plastered on my face. All I can feel is anger and betrayal brewing in my chest as I shove my phone back into my pocket.

Warm fingers graze along my cheekbone, causing me to flinch back slightly. When our eyes meet, I see his are wide and wild, a concerned look dripping from them. His brows are furrowed and looking deflated as I realize I've pulled away from him.

I part my lips, wanting to apologize, to explain my movement but instead my face crumples. There isn't any explaining this to him. My past is my past and it isn't something I want to relive over and over again. Or re-hash like some old war story.

I expect him to press me and question my reaction but instead, the concerned and slowly hardening look, softens.

He inches forward, taking the smallest step I've ever seen a six-foot-four man take. Slowly reaching his hand back out for me. The gooey man in front of me is a drastic comparison to the one taunting me in the office ans fighting with me in the middle of a laundromat. A tiny piece of me wonders what changed.

It doesn't stop me from stepping towards him, giving in to the pull I feel once again. His fingers gingerly wrap around my wrist, intertwining our fingers once more.

"I'm right here, Kadence," he whispers. "You don't have to say anything or tell me the truth but," his head tilts slightly, catching my gaze, "I'm here."

"We don't know each other," I whisper back as if to lull the night air.

The corners of his mouth turn upwards slightly again. "Maybe it's better that way."

First, he wants to know about me, and now he wants to be my stranger.

"Princess?"

I flinch again, my stomach turning. "Please don't call me that," I choke through a harsh breath.

My gaze drops, avoiding him as tears begin to pool in my eyes. The word stings more than he knows. Before it was a way for him to irk me, but hearing it now makes my skin crawl. Jeremy would call me that to appease me. Make me feel special after he tore me down with threats and cruel words.

I never want to hear the name again.

"Hey, hey, hey," his voice coos, dipping his head once again to catch my eyes. I can't look at him, I don't *want* to look at him. If I can see the pain and hurt in his eyes, I'm sure he can recognize it in mine. "I won't call you that."

The glass door behind me slides open, a soft gasp leaving my lips as his hands fall from my face. Holden's eyes fill with guilt as I turn away, wiping the remaining tears that stain my cheeks.

"You know, if you guys wanna kiss again, the tree around the gazebo is much more secluded." Blake's voice appears from behind me. "Scottie started explaining the birds and the bees to West and you should have seen how red his face got, Nash. It was hilar–"

"Blake." Holden interjects, his voice firm.

"I know, I know, I shouldn't have been watching, but you really know how to just–" She gestures with her hands as if taking something.

"Blake!" He says through a clenched jaw.

I can't help but laugh softly, turning back towards Blake even though I can feel the blush creeping up my neck.

The grin across Blake's face tells me everything I need to know. She gets enjoyment out of torturing the men in this Club and being the only other woman I've seen so far that has been treated as more than just a quick fuck, I respect that. Boys' clubs aren't easy to meld yourself into. They're crass, rude, and sometimes just plain mean. But even then it never compares to the cruelty of the men I know from home.

"Hey, your secret is safe with me." She holds up both hands in front of herself in defeat. "But if you two don't want the entire club knowing, then you should probably know that Cole is on his way to find you." Blake points at me.

Holden lets out something between a growl and a sigh as he glances over at me, "It's now or never darlin'." He holds out his hand for me.

I glance at Blake. The grin on her face turns proud as she nudges her chin towards Holden's hand. "What have you got to lose?"

My heart thuds in my chest. I can hear Cole's voice muffled against the glass and it's getting closer to us. As much as I appreciate everything he's doing for me, it doesn't change the fact that he handles me with kid gloves. At least until dinner. I know Cole's curious about me and he seems to understand when I avoid his questions. But tonight, letting Wolfe press me planted a tiny seed of doubt.

I'll find you.

The words replay in my mind like a broken record. Fast and warped like a nightmare as my eyes meet Holden's.

I hate myself for taking his hand and intertwining our fingers. I hate that I'm going to use him as a distraction tonight. But I need it and by the way he kissed me earlier, he seems to need it too.

A wide smile meets those ocean eyes, making me mirror it back to him as he tugs me towards the edge of the house.

"Hey Nash?" Blake's voice stops them once again as he spins around. "Scottie and West don't know."

I watch his brows furrow for a moment before realizing that Blake is messing with us. He tosses her a wink. "Thanks kid."

A laugh bubbles from my chest as he once again smiles down at me, bright and glowing. Flames lick the inside of my belly at the sight. He looks younger, his eyes crinkle and his nose scrunches up slightly. A part of me wonders how long it's been since he'd smiled like that.

Holden stops along the edge of the front of the house, peering around the corner, checking for other members I assume. Secrets seem like a far-fetched thing with these men. Though I'd have to explain to Cole how I got home in the morning, it's just that. A problem for the morning.

I want to focus on nothing more than the man in front of me. The way his lips feel against mine. The way the slightest touch from him lights my skin up with tiny bursts of fireworks. I relish the fact that even though he gets under my skin, he also makes me feel alive. More alive than I've felt in a long time.

"Do you always sneak out of these dinners?" I ask softly, pressing my body against his back as I try to peer around him.

He shakes his head. "I never used to." Holden glances down at me. "Come on."

Used to?

He leads me over to his bike, the black paint sparkling in the moonlight as he grabs Cole's helmet. A knowing smirk plays on the corner of his lips as he helps slide it over my ears. He dips his head as his fingers fumble with the chin strap and presses his lips to mine. So soft and sweet that I can feel the tears threatening to pool around my eyes again. The twist tie around my heart only tightens as he leans in slightly, closing the distance between us before pulling away, taking me with him.

He stands up straight, his tongue flicking over his bottom lip as his eyes search my face. Holden's testing the waters, dipping his toes into my pond to see just how far I'd let him wade and with the way he's beaming down at me, I'm ready to see just how far he's willing to go.

My fingers wrap around the lapel of his cut, pulling him back down to me as I kiss him again. This time forcing myself to take a step backwards away from him. Almost taunting him to reach for me.

"We're going to get caught," he chuckles.

I can feel my cheeks start to hurt with the way I smile at him. "You better get me outta here then, huh?"

The text messages still sit in my stomach like an iron ball. Even as I watch him swing a thick jean-covered thigh over his motorcycle and settle into his seat, I can feel it weighing on me. It's a stark contrast to the way I grin as I climb behind him. My fingers trail along his waist to his stomach.

I swear I feel him shudder as my fingers intertwine and my chest presses against his back.

He brings the bike to life, letting it roar beneath us, and the familiar vibration spreads through my body. My toes curl in my boots as he glances over his shoulder, a smile plastered across his pink lips.

"Hold on tight, Darlin'." Holden revs the throttle, swinging the bike around as he speeds through the trees.

A gasp escapes me at the movement causing me to tighten my grip around his waist. I can feel his shoulders shake with laughter as he follows the driveway out to the main road. Barely slowing down, he turns left away from the direction we had come.

"Where are we going?!" I ask, yelling over the sound of his engine.

Holden turns his head slightly, his lips curling. "Somewhere away from here!"

KADENCE

He drives us further out of the city, the roads become darker and somehow the chill is a bit colder. I'm not sure where we're going but for some reason I suddenly feel like I can trust him. Maybe it's the way he kisses me like he hadn't just been with two other women earlier this week - a thought I quickly push from my mind - or if it's the fact that when he rolls into a soft curve in the road, his hand finds my thigh, squeezing it gently as if holding me in place, or when the road straightens out, the same hand rests over my linked fingers over his stomach. Gentle touches that remind me what closeness feels like.

The treeline along both sides of the road becomes more dense, blinders of darkness that shroud us as we make our way further into the mountains.

I can't help but peer over his shoulder for most of the drive; trusting him but also curious as to where he's leading me. Soon, the chill becomes too much and I press my cheek to his shoulder, shielding myself from the frigid wind as it finally ceases to nip at my nose and cheeks.

Holden has to be freezing by this point.

After a while, he turns down a darkened dirt road. The only light around us radiates from the motorcycle and even that doesn't give visibility to the end of the road, which looks more like a trail.

He pulls off to the side, kicking down the stand and turning the engine off. The roar in my ears is suddenly silenced, letting the complete stillness of the forest surround me.

Holden slides off of the bike, turning to me and helping me off.

"Where are we?"

"State park." He smiles softly.

I watch as his fingers reach under my chin, undoing the strap to the helmet before gently pulling it from my head. I smooth out the flyaways and smile up at him.

"You aren't going to murder me are you?" I breathe, a semi-nervous laugh leaving me.

Holden grins, his eyes somehow glowing brighter in the darkness. "Believe it or not, the thought hadn't crossed my mind." He narrows his eyes playfully, leaning in to steal a kiss before resting the helmet on the handlebar.

He glances down at my boots, raising a brow slightly. "You gonna be able to walk in those? It's a little bit of a hike."

I look down at the fake combat boots on my feet. They aren't the most comfortable things I own, but they're better than the Converse I normally wear. I run my tongue over my bottom lip, glancing back up at him through thick lashes.

"I'll be fine, but it's really dark, Holden."

I peer down the trail that leads into a wall of pitch black. It isn't the walk that scares me or even the darkness. It's being alone with him. He throws me off like a magnet to a compass needle and whenever he's around my mind still swirls with trying to hate him and wanting to tear into the cloth of his t-shirt if only to get a glimpse at the adonis body hiding underneath.

But here I am, proving I trust him, at least for tonight.

Holden follows my line of sight, bringing his bottom lip between his teeth as he nods. "It is, I promise it's not far and once we get beyond the trees, the moonlight will guide us."

His voice clouds around me. He speaks so softly I can pick out the gravel in each word and I realize that it isn't just me giving into that trust tonight.

"Okay."

He takes my hand without another word but beams down at me as I give in, leading me toward the wall of darkness and away from the safety of my only escape route. His motorcycle.

I focus my eyes down on the ground, watching for rogue roots and hidden holes in the mud and dirt. The last thing I need is to fall and break an ankle, though knowing my luck it's extremely possible.

"I've got you," he says, as if reading my mind. "I won't let you fall."

I peer up at him and see he's staring down at me with no regard for his own safety as we walk. Blush creeps up my neck again as I glance down the trail, avoiding his eyes.

"Have you been here a lot?"

Holden chuckles, finally looking ahead of us. "You could say that."

"Do you always speak in vague responses?" I laugh, not trying to be cruel but almost every question I've asked him tonight has prompted vague and cryptic responses.

"Do you?" He retorts, glancing down at me. "East Coast is pretty vague."

I meet his gaze, not realizing he'd heard my response to Wolfe at the table. "You were listening?"

His eyes cast down to our feet, shaking his head. "You make me curious, Kade." Holden looks up ahead of us. "I don't know who made you want to hide yourself away from the world, but whoever it was deserves an asskicking."

I watch as he rubs the back of his neck with his free hand. He seems nervous, treading the eggshell trail he's following me on as we walk. However, he also hasn't been completely truthful with me either. Both of us circle each other like sharks and our prey is honesty.

"What if..." I start, gnawing on my bottom lip as I stop walking, feeling him drop my hand as he turns towards me. "What if we start over?" I smile. "Clean slate?"

Holden's brows knit together, his eyes meeting mine. This is my olive branch, a small hope that maybe we could go from antagonizing each other like school kids to being able to have normal conversations without trepidation.

He slowly begins to shake his head. "Not a chance darlin'." A smile begins to play on his lips as mine falls. "I don't want to forget how we met. You've got a fire burning in you that only comes out when you're mad, really mad, and you're the first person to call me on my shit other than Cole in a long time."

Confusion washes over my features as his hands come to rest on my arms.

"I don't want to wipe away the hate you felt for me last weekend and this week. I want you to use that against me when I step over the lines I'm bound to cross because something tells me..." He pauses, dipping his head so that he is at eye level with me. "You're not used to standing up for yourself, and not because you didn't want to but because you couldn't."

I stare at him, the blue in his eyes turns soft as if he tries to piece together the jigsaw puzzle I call life without the picture on my box. He isn't wrong and that's what scares me. He's catching on quickly to the pain I still feel inside and the years of abuse Jeremy put me through, not to mention the shit my mother pulled after my father passed. Holden wants to know me, but he isn't interested in vague answers and I'm not ready to give him the real ones.

Truth be told, I don't want to start over either. The embers he sparked inside of me this week were the first time I truly felt safe enough to stand up for myself. To take charge and not get pushed around by men.

This seems to be the difference between Jeremy and the men of the Hounds. Jeremy hides his fear with anger, lashing out at me whenever he gets the chance. But these men speak their truths and know when enough is enough.

I let out the breath I don't realize I'm holding in. "I've never heard of someone not wanting a clean slate." A quiet laugh escapes my lips and I realize he's taken a step towards me, pulling me just a little closer.

"Darlin', I gave up on clean slates a long time ago."

"That's a little ominous." I laugh as my hands find his chest, my fingers gripping the edges of his cut. "You hiding some big, dark secret I don't know about?" *Like I am?*

Holden grins, leaning down to brush his nose along my cheekbone before nudging my own, sending chills up my spine and causing my eyes to slide close. "Guess you'll have to follow me to find out."

Suddenly, the heat I feel from his body disappears. My eyes fly open to see him further down the dark trail, walking backward with a sly grin plastered on his lips.

I can't help the blush creeping up my neck as I make my way to him, taking the hand he holds out for me. Butterflies explode in my chest as the warmth I'm quickly becoming accustomed to spreads from the hand he's holding to my chest.

Holden continues to lead me down the path before cutting through a patch of trees. It's not until the moonlight begins to peek through the trees that I can see the clearing ahead of us. He pulls a branch back for me, letting me walk through first as the sound of rushing water surrounds me.

I feel his hand rest on my lower back as we push our way through the greenery. My gaze lifts upwards to a train bridge, large dark steel trusses are covered in moss and overgrown ivy. Below sits a river, rushing and beating against the rocks and logs.

"Holden..." I whisper. "This is beautiful."

I turn to him, noticing how his eyes glisten against the water and moonlight cascading around us. He almost looks...remorseful.

"Come on," he says softly, taking my hand again and leading me further onto the bridge until we get to a spot where the wood isn't as worn and doesn't creak as much under our footfalls.

Holden sits down on the edge, letting his legs hang over the side. I follow him, sitting next to him. The beams shift above us, whining with the soft autumn wind.

"When Cole and I were kids," he starts, "we used to ride our bikes out here to swim during the summertime. Jump off the ledge over there." Holden points to the edge where the middle of the bridge opens up slightly. "We would spend hours here until it got dark and we'd have to ride back, cold and wet."

He chuckles to himself, a smile tugging at the corner of his lips at the memory but as soon as it was there, his smile fades.

"After a few summers, my sis–" he pauses and I watch his Adam's apple bob in his throat, "my sister started taggin' along with us." A laugh bubbles from his throat as his face falls. "We spent every day here, just looking for some excuse to not be at home."

I glance down at the water rushing below us. My feet kick softly with the wind that ripples between us. When my father got sick, I prayed for siblings almost every day, just someone who would not make me feel so alone while my mother acted like he was already gone.

My stomach flips at the remembrance of the text messages sitting on my phone like ticking time bombs. I'd have to tell Cole and Holden soon enough. Cole warned me that if anything were to threaten the club, he would do anything to protect it and I knew Jeremy could easily rip away what they have.

I feel Holden shift next to me, my gaze moving from the glittering water to him. Had he been talking?

"Where is she now?" I ask, my voice almost a whisper.

He shakes his head, his fingers running along the wood between us. "She passed away about a month ago."

The words come out like they're shattered glass and his eyes drop to where his fingers were tracing. I glance down, seeing etchings in the planks.

BN

HN

CO

"I'm sorry–"

Holden shakes his head again. "Becca would have hated people feeling sorry for me," he chokes out in between a laugh. "She also would have kicked my ass for acting the way I did the other night."

Finally, crystal blue eyes land on me. He's being genuine, not looking for forgiveness, but I can see the guilt riddled on his features.

It's then realized that his actions are far more complicated than him being a general asshole. I knew I recognized the sadness behind his anger, but now I know where it stems from.

"I was angry at Cole because it felt like he was replacing Becs with you," he admits. "I wasn't angry with you, I just..." Holden shrugs.

"Wasn't ready to let her go yet?" I finish for him.

His jaw ticks for a moment. "Yeah," he breathes finally.

I smile for a second, my chest feeling tight, and want to give him something. Be honest with him about some tidbits of my life, but I know it's going to be more difficult to tell him the longer I wait.

I turn back to the water, watching as it fights against the rocks and logs, unsure of how deep it is or how cold it is, yet there's something exciting and mysterious about what lurks beneath the darkness.

His fingers find mine, intertwining them. I didn't realize how much I missed the softness that touches can have. That not all of them can be harsh and laced with a cruelness that I wouldn't wish on my worst enemies. I'm slowly getting used to it again and the fact that when he touches me, my body doesn't flinch or cower out of habit only makes me that much more willing to let his hands roam.

My phone buzzes again in my pocket and my stomach drops. Whether it's another threat from Jeremy, a passive-aggressive text from my mother, or Maria checking in, I don't want to deal with it. I should have turned off my phone and it's taking everything in me not to chuck it in the river below us.

"The text I got earlier was from my mother," I blurt through the silence, my stare fixed on the waters below.

I can feel Holden's eyes on me, his gaze lighting a fire against my skin. "She and I don't get along very well and I wasn't expecting her to message me."

It's not a total lie; I wasn't expecting any texts from my mother and I *really* wasn't expecting the text I got.

"Is everything okay?" He asks. "Back home I mean."

I huff a laugh, glancing down at our tangled fingers. "I don't have a home, especially not with her."

Tears sting the corners of my eyes at the realization. My mother has never been a safe place for me to fall. Not even when my father was alive. It took a long time for me to figure out that my mother's supposed love was littered with ultimatums and fueled with gaslighting.

Holden turns to me again, his hands finding my cheeks as he tilts my chin to look at him. "You don't have to talk about this," he whispers, his thumb wiping away a tear that falls as I blink up at him.

I sigh, shaking my head. I'm not ready. I already feel broken and alone; if I tell him everything I know he'd look at me like a kicked puppy and that's the last thing I want.

His eyes search mine as his thumb trails along my cheekbone. I feel it drag down to my bottom lip, running across my cool skin. A soft gasp falls from my lips as he tugs it gently down, letting the pad of his thumb flick over it.

My head begins to spin from the heat swirling in my stomach, trying to push away the anger and hurt I'm still feeling that had bubbled up. Holden's eyes soften and he stares back at me, every once in a while flitting down to my lips and back up.

"This is probably horrible timing," he gravels, "but I'm dying to kiss you again." He leans in, his nose nudging tenderly against mine causing me to suck in a breath. "Can I kiss you again?"

I feel his lips brush against mine, my body practically melting into his. I slowly nod my head, watching him lean towards me and to tease him I pull back slightly tugging my bottom lip between my teeth.

Holden lets out a low growl, smirking as his hand wrapped around the back of my neck to pull me to him. I let out a laugh that's soon swallowed by his mouth. Plush pink lips slot over mine carefully but with a fire that turns from embers to full flames the longer we're connected.

I cup my hands around his face, feeling him hiss against me at the coldness of my skin as I relish in the way his stubble prickles at my palm.

A moan floats between the two of us and I'm not sure which one of us it comes from. Right now I can't get enough of the way he tastes, the whiskey still lingers on his tongue and as it dances with mine I clench my thighs together hoping to soothe the aching between my legs.

I feel him pull away for a moment, tugging at my bottom lip with his teeth before soothing his bite with a soft kiss. I rest my forehead against his own, the heat from his body sending a chill down my spine.

"Tell me the truth," I breathe, my hands resting against the collar of his vest. "Was this the famous Holden Nash kissing spot?" I grin, still breathless as I lean to trail gentle kisses along his jawline.

He chuckles. "No, that was a boulder we passed on our way here."

I pull back, scoffing as he laughs again. I shove his chest playfully, pushing him back slightly as his hands wrap around my waist taking him with me. Holden pulls me into his lap, my thighs straddling him. My body tenses for a moment, realizing that his legs are still dangling over the edge of the bridge and just the slightest lean back could mean me falling into the water.

Holden's hands wrap around my waist, pulling me further into him as his nose runs along my jaw and behind my ear. "I've got you, Sunflower. I won't let you fall."

I look back at him, the nickname hitting me straight in my core, and tug the baseball cap off his head as I lean into him again. I drag my tongue along my bottom lip, my fingers tangling into his hair before pressing my lips against his again with a sigh. "You'd better not."

HOLDEN

God, she feels good under my touch.

The softness of her skin, the way her lips ghost around the stubble of my jaw, sending me into a fit of giggles like I'm a kid again being tickled. Her hips grind down into mine, firing a jolt of electricity up my spine, and if it wasn't for the cold wood beneath me keeping me grounded, I probably would give her everything I have right here and now.

Kissing her at Marlowe's was like a dam breaking. Every doubt, every slice of annoyance that I feel towards her washes away with the way she melts into me. Like she hasn't been touched or kissed this way—ever.

I wrap my hands around the backs of her thighs as she straddles me. My legs are still dangling off the edge of the bridge. I'm not lying when I say I've got her. What she doesn't know is that I want her in more ways than one, but for now, I'd hang on to any moment that she'll let me have.

We've been like this for a while, staring at each other, her fingers dancing along my chin, studying each freckle on my face while I watch the way the corners of her mouth upturn slightly when she discovers something new about me and soon the moon dips behind the clouds blanketing us in darkness.

"I need to get you back to the shop," I whisper, even though everything in me wants to stay here, in the bubble we've created in a place that means more to me than anything else now.

Kadence hums, burying her face in my neck in protest. The gesture makes me laugh. She's coming out of her shell and I'm beginning to see the light in her through the cracks in her mask.

"C'mon, pretty girl," I chuckle, nudging her up. "Let's get you back to the apartment and get you warm."

She lets out a soft whine, "but I'm warm right here." Finally she lifts her head, grinning down at me.

I sit up, wrapping my arms around her, careful not to let her lean backward over the edge of the bridge. "You'll be warmer in bed," I grin and lean in to nip at her jawline, "and it's a hell of a lot more comfortable to lay on than this wood."

"Who says you're laying in my bed tonight, Nash?" Her voice drops to a sultry whisper that makes my cock tense.

I lean back again, taking in the sight of her darkening eyes. The bright green now a small ring around the black.

"Do you want me to?" I ask with a raised brow.

She taps her chin like she's thinking. "We'll see," Kadence says after a moment, another grin forming across perfectly plump lips.

I narrow my eyes at her for a moment, nodding slowly, "We'll see, huh?"

"Mhm," she hums, leaning back into me so our lips are barely touching. I feel the tip of her tongue dart out, wetting her bottom lip before gently running over mine. Again, my cock twitches below her which only eggs her on as she rolls her hips.

A groan settles in my throat as my head tips forward, our foreheads resting against each other, "You're going to be the death of me, Kade."

"Maybe, but not tonight," she whispers as her hands cup my face, forcing my eyes back to her own. My hands fall to her hips, causing them to stop the gentle roll she had started,

"Take me home?" She presses her lips to mine, softly and so sweet it feels like my insides are turning into a puddle.

I pull back, both of us breathless. "Let's go."

Kadence climbs over me, careful not to lose her balance as she teeters on the edge of the bridge. She smooths out her clothes, wrapping her jacket further around her as the night air hits the exposed skin of her stomach from where her tank top has ridden up.

I can't help but stare for a moment before standing. Her skin is perfect and it looks soft. Right now I want nothing more than to get her back to the apartment and explore every inch of her body with my lips.

I wrap my hand around hers and lead her back through the forest, at one point using my phone flashlight to help guide us as the trees became thicker. I don't miss the six missed calls that flash on my screen from Cole.

I already know what that conversation is going to consist of. Cole will assume the worst, no matter what my so-called excuses are, and once again I'd feel like a child being reprimanded. Truth is, I'm sick of it. Cole always has a way of finding the worst in me, especially lately. Ever since I got out a month ago and even after Becca, things haven't been the same between us. No matter how much we force our normal relationship in front of the club.

Deep down, I want to be better. I know I'm better than the trailer I sleep in and the way I drink liquor like it's water at the slightest inconvenience. I know I have issues to work through. That's nothing new for me.

My gaze falls down to Kadence as she holds onto my hand, her grip tightening as the ground beneath us grows softer. At one point she holds on with both of her hands, resting her head against my arm as we walk back to the bike.

There's something about her that stirs up feelings within me I haven't ever felt. Her being around makes me want to be happier.

I hold the bushes back for her, letting her go first out into the clearing where my bike is still parked. I help her with the helmet before throwing my leg over and settling into the seat. I hold out my hand, helping to hold her steady as she climbed on. Chills race down my spine as she scoots in behind me, her hands finding their way under my shirt. Her nails trace along the contours of my abs and I suck in a breath at the feeling.

I hear her chuckle against my back, knowing full well she's doing it on purpose. Trying to get a rise out of me and it's working. She runs them around my waist, the tips of her fingers digging into the top of my jeans. I haven't even had a chance to get the bike started before she starts to terrorize me.

My hands fall over hers, stopping her from going any further to the hard length in my briefs. "Darlin', you keep touching me like that, we aren't making it back to the shop."

I glance over my shoulder, seeing a mischievous grin spreading across her cheeks that are quickly turning pink. Her bottom lip finds home between her teeth and the moonlight lights up her eyes again. It takes everything in me to not bend her over the leather seat of my bike and take her right here, but something tells me that she isn't ready for that yet.

There's something she's still hiding. Tonight was the first time I'd actually seen her. Felt her be anything other than nervous and small.

She looks alive and I want to be the one to keep her feeling that way because it looks gorgeous on her.

Her fingers lock over my abdomen under my shirt to keep her hands warm. For once I don't mind the frigid feeling of a woman's fingertips tracing my skin. Her touch leaves a trail of tingles that shoot up my spine and course through me, sparking something that feels foreign.

I rev up the motorcycle, letting it rumble beneath us. I can feel her hips wiggle behind me, the vibration proving to be too much for her.

Good, I think. I want nothing more than to trace every inch of her body and feel her tremble and writhe beneath me. Something in me knows that she's different. She isn't the same as the lunas who hang around the club. They're easy and I like to play with my food.

Kadence is something else. Something deeper and I'm just not sure what that means.

I pull out onto the road, heading back towards the shop. At some point I'll have to tell Cole where we were. The rule is to never share that spot outside the three of us but it's a silly rule we made up as kids. Cole would understand that...right?

Suddenly her hands on my body feel far away, the warmth from her touch disappears as the reality of letting someone other than Becca and Cole go to our spot sinks in. I'm not replacing Becca with Kadence and I'm not trying to plug the hole I have in my chest with her. There's something else about her that makes me want to be around her, to not be the shell I have been.

The road curves around a bend, the treeline blanketing the road in a shroud of darkness. I know of a few turn-offs in this area. The club's used them a few times for bonfires and switching off during runs.

Fuck. We have a meeting with Stokes tomorrow. It's the last thing I want to do and if it's up to me, I'll do everything I can to get out from under Stokes' hand. It's not worth the money or the women that flood in and out of the clubhouse.

I love Cole, love him like a brother, and will do anything for him but the deeper we get in with Stokes, the more I worry we won't be able to get out. Cole always says the club needs help. Needs to stay on the good side of law enforcement in town. To an extent, I agree. The Deputies usually leave us alone, but lately it's been one thing after another. Members getting tracked down at the county line, searched and provoked. It's getting bad and our runs are getting shorter and more dangerous. I want out of the deal with Stokes. I just need to find a way to get us out before telling Cole.

The lights from the town flicker in front of us. The neon red sign for Lee's Diner acts as a beacon to me in the night until the sound of a siren whoops behind us. I glance into my side mirror, seeing flashing red and blue lights dancing behind us. I grip the handlebars, knuckles turning white. I know that car. I also know that I hadn't done anything that would warrant pulling me over.

The thought crosses my mind to keep going, my bike is a hell of a lot faster than the sedan. If I had been alone, I would have done it, but with Kadence riding behind me, I pull over to the shoulder. It's too reckless, something I'm not willing to put her at risk for.

Her hands move from my abdomen as I kick down the stand and shut the bike off. I know the routine. This isn't new for me. Anger kicks at my chest as I peer back, watching Watson step out of the cop car.

"What's wrong?" Kadence's voice cuts through the night air.

I shake my head, "Not sure," my hand slides behind me, finding her thigh and squeezing gently, "It's gonna be fine."

"Nash!" Watson steps alongside us. "Off the bike."

"What do you want, Watson?" I ask, keeping my eyes straight ahead.

Watson plants himself in front of the two of us. Beady eyes flicker from me to Kadence, narrowing for a moment as if he recognizes her.

"Nice to see you again, Ma'am," Watson coos like they're best friends.

I feel her hand grip the back of my vest, tugging herself closer to me, and the anger in my chest begins to grow. I know how Watson is with women. Sure, I use them for my own pleasure, but I at least treat them with respect. Watson is a creep. More than once I've heard whispers from the girls about the offhand comments and sly remarks he's made to them. The man makes my skin crawl.

"Did we do something wrong, Officer?" I hear her ask. I don't miss the shakiness in her voice.

Watson's smug grin spreads across his face as he glances back over at me. "I said off the bike, Nash. You too, sweetheart." He points a long finger at Kadence, turning it to make a come hither motion as he steps back.

I growl at the nickname. He has no fucking right to call her that and I can feel her shrink behind me with the words. Everything about this feels off and I know she can feel it too. I turn back to her, forcing the most reassuring smile I can. "It's okay. I'm not going anywhere."

Her green eyes stare at me for a moment, her brows knitting together with a small shake of her head. I can see the fear in her eyes.

"I've got you," I whisper.

She brings her bottom lip between her teeth before giving me a soft nod. I help her off, catching the way Watson stares at her ass as she swings her leg over the back wheel. She slips the helmet off her head, sets it on her seat, and turns back towards Watson. Her hands fist at her sides. Even from this distance, I can feel the anxiety that radiates off of her. I follow suit, swinging my leg over the bike and digging my boots into the dirt next to her.

Watson rests his hands on his tac-belt, the palm of his right hand resting on the butt of his gun. A not-so-friendly reminder that I'm still a criminal and a shit attempt at proving his power. I can't help the smirk that forms on my face.

"What's funny, Nash?" Watson taunts, sucking on his teeth. "When was the last time you checked in with your parole officer?" He asks, glancing up and down the street.

Kadence quickly glances up at me. I can feel her gaze bore into me but I stare straight ahead. I'll have to tackle that later. Right now I'm more worried about anything else Watson might say.

"Last week," I answer.

Watson nods his head, humming as he looks back at me. "Well, since you are a parolee, I'm going to need to search you...and her." His eyes trail back over to Kadence, his head cocking to the side as they roam her body.

It's then I contemplate murder again. Only this time it won't be an accident.

"You're not searching her. Search me and the bike, Watson, you have no reason to search her and you know it." I take a step forward as I speak, holding out my arms for him and moving to the right to stand in front of her. Forcing his rat-like gaze towards me instead of Kadence.

Watson laughs, shaking his head. "Good thing you're on that side of the law. She's with you tonight and with that fake name she gave me, I'm curious to know more about her." He peers over my shoulder. "It's a fake name, isn't that right, sweetheart?"

"Call her sweetheart one more time…" This time I step forward, putting myself nose to nose with Watson. *What the fuck did he mean by fake name?*

"Or you'll what?" Watson chortles. "You hit me and it's back to Stockton for you, big boy."

I drag my tongue over my bottom lip, the corners of my mouth upturning. "Imagine what that would do to business," I whisper, low enough that only he hears me. "Face it, Watson, this arrangement only works with me in it."

"Be that as it may, Nash, Stokes wouldn't give two fucks if you ended up back in prison…" that smug smile returns, "or like your sister."

I feel my jaw tick and my teeth grind together as my hands fist at my side. Becca's death was ruled an accident. My glare narrows in on Watson and I can't tell if he's speaking truth or fucking with me.

"What the fuck did you do to her?"

"Nothing that wasn't deserved."

I growl, and before I can control myself, my hands twist into Watson's beige uniform, the two of us stumbling as we grapple with each other. "She didn't fucking deserve to end up in a ditch, you asshole," I rasp, the air in my chest depleting. "What did you do!?"

"Holden!" Kadence yelps from behind us, I can hear her boots crunch in the dirt and gravel.

"Stay put!" I yell, the crunch stopping behind me.

Watson seethes. "You better listen to your whore, she just might save your life."

"Holden, let him go!"

My chest heaves trying to force the air back into my lungs. My vision blurs slightly as tears sting the corners of my eyes. Becca didn't deserve anything that happened to her that night. Stokes had done me the great service of showboating the forensic photos during my interrogation because why wouldn't a convicted felon biker kill his own sister, right?

Those images will never leave my mind and now they're flooding back in to the point I can't stop. My body suddenly twists by my wrist as he drags me over and shoves me against the hood of his cop car. Watson grabs my other arm and twists it to restrain me. I feel the cuffs click into place and let my forehead rest against the metal of the car. *Shit.*

"I fucking warned you, Nash." Watson steps back, letting me spin around and lean against the cab of the sedan. I watch as he pulls out his phone to call whoever else was going to witness this shit.

I roll my head over to Kadence. God, she looks so fuckin scared. I hate it. She stares at me, gnawing on her bottom lip and her face pale. How am I supposed to explain this shit?

"Kade," I murmur, standing myself up straight, "baby."

Her glare catches me, green eyes shooting daggers in my direction. I don't blame her. I deserve worse than just daggers.

"Don't *baby* me," she bites, so quiet that I almost don't hear it. "Why didn't you just listen?" Her voice breaks into a plea.

I feel a pang in my chest as I stare at her for a moment before dropping my head. What a fucking way to end the night.

She lets out a sigh, walking over to me as her eyes flicker between me and Watson's back. Whoever he has on the phone is occupying him long enough for her to step up to me. Her hand lands on my chest, pausing there for a moment before resting on my cheek.

Her head dips down to catch my gaze. "What was that about?" She whispers, feeling me lean into her touch.

I search her eyes and still find the terror I've seen before but there's something else hidden behind it. Something stronger as she waits for my answer.

"I can't tell you right now," I admit. As much as I want to, I need time to explain, and being handcuffed with Watson six feet away is not the time. Her brows knit together. "I will, Kadence, I promise you I will explain, but I can't right now."

I don't recognize the plea in my own voice but I know that I'll tell her. Kadence is the one woman I don't want to lie to. So I'll tell her. Tonight, if she'll let me explain.

"Hey!" Watson screeches. "Back away from him!"

"He's handcuffed, you idiot, what's he going to do?" Kadence snaps, her hand falling from my face. Her patience with the evening is clearly gone.

"Watch it Kadence, or you'll end up cuffed like him." Watson rounds the back of the sedan. "Matter of fact, what *is* your real name?"

"Kadence," she bites.

Watson's right palm finds the butt of his gun again. "Last name?"

"Andrews," she bites again, this time her arms cross over her chest as she steps back into my right side.

Watson claps his hands together. "Well! Look at that! We'll see if that's real or not."

"You'll find it is," She retorts.

A swell of pride bubbles in my chest hearing her stand up against him. I know fear creeps below her surface, but I also know she's much stronger than she seems.

He laughs, shaking his head. "Well we will see but if I find out it's a fake name again, I'll be paying a visit to O'Neil's shop."

His eyes land on me again. "Stokes wants you present for the meeting tomorrow. He's granting you freedom for the night." Watson steps up. "I suggest you take advantage of that," his glare flickers to Kadence, "before you end up in a hole."

I clench my jaw again, spinning so that Watson can undo the handcuffs. Feeling them unlock from around my wrists I turn again, reaching out for Kadence behind me. "I told you to watch the way you talk about her." I feel her fingers lace into mine. "Watch your back when you're off duty, Deputy."

"I suggest you quit while you're ahead, Nash, and take Ms. Andrews home." Watson leans against the hood of his car, arms crossing over his chest. "Drive safe now," he says, sounding more like a threat than anything else.

I feel Kadence tug on my hand. "Holden, please, let's go."

I take a few steps backward, waving my fingers at Watson before turning and helping her back onto the bike. I slip the helmet over the top of her head, buckling it before climbing on in front of her.

HOLDEN

I drive back to the shop, leaving Watson behind on the side of the road and without her hands tracing shapes under my shirt against my skin. Instead they stay gripped onto my vest. I know the conversation I have to have with her when we get back. It's going to be a long night, and even though the adrenaline is wearing off and the exhaustion is seeping in, I'm willing to spend the next ten hours explaining the shit show that my life has turned into.

The minute we pull back into the shop parking lot, I clock Cole sitting at the top of the stairs that lead to Kadence's apartment. A sigh leaves me as I back my bike into my usual spot. Once again I help her off the bike and with the helmet as she glances over at the apartment.

"How mad do you think he is?" She asks softly, her hand slipping into mine.

I shrug. "With you? Probably not at all."

"And with you?"

I suck in a breath, "Cole has different... expectations for me." Which isn't too far from the truth. Cole does have different expectations for me and at times expects way too much from me.

"Where the hell were you?" Cole calls from the top of the stairs before descending them, "Blake said you both snuck off like a couple of teenagers. What the hell were you thinking?"

I scoff. "I was thinking we're both grown adults and needed a break from dinner."

"So you just... what? Decide to take off with the one person you haven't stopped bitching about since she got here?" Cole snaps.

"Cole–" Kadence steps forward, her hand still tucked into mine. It's then Cole realizes we're holding hands. His gaze flickers from our interlocked fingers to her and then to me.

A wild laugh escapes his lips. "You have to be fucking kidding me, Nash." His hands find his hips as he glances back down at Kadence. "So what lie did he tell you to get you alone, hmm?" His head cocks to the side, "because I know you're smarter than that."

"Brother, I love you but you better watch the way you're talking to her." I step up to him, her hand falling from mine. "I'm not in the fucking mood to deal with your holier-than-thou bullshit tonight."

"Welcome to my fuckin' world." Cole fumes. "Stokes called by the way, so thanks for that."

My face crumples into disgust as I step back from my friend. "I don't know when you started caring more about that asshole's opinion, but I won't warn you again. Watch the fuckin' tone."

"Or what?" Cole taunts pushing the little patience I have left tonight. "You'll take over the club? Because you can't even take care of yourself lately, what the fuck makes you think you'll be able to take care of a club?"

"Guess we'll have to find out, won't we?" I growl back, not meaning it at all, but if he's going to be taking low blows tonight, so am I.

I move to step around Cole, reaching out for Kadence again until I feel the crunch of a fist against my cheekbone. My body stumbles backward and to the side as I feel something warm drip from my cheek. I reach up, feeling the red sticky liquid leaking from the new gash.

"Cole!" Kadence yells, rushing to my side. "What the hell is wrong with you!"

"He's what's fuckin' wrong with me!" Cole yells back, shaking out his hand and flexing his fingers to ward off the pain.

I stand, glancing down at her. Shaking my head as she lifts her fingers to the broken skin. "I'm fine," I whisper, wrapping my hand gently around her wrists. My gaze lifts to Cole, "If you're expecting me to hit you back, you better not hold your breath."

Cole just stares back at me, anger fuming between us and long overdue unspoken words threatening to spill out. His eyes cast to Kadence, staring at her like he expects more from her.

"I hope you know what you're getting into with him."

"I can handle myself, Cole," she says, and I feel pride swell within me again, unable to help the way the corners of my mouth upturn slightly.

Cole just laughs at her, making my blood boil more than it already is. "Tell that to the scared little girl who's been occupying my office."

"I don't know who gave you the claim over me Cole, but it sure as hell wasn't me. I appreciate everything you've done for me, but you aren't my father." She steps up to him. "So I think it's best we go to bed and revisit whatever dick-measuring contest you two clearly need to have in the morning."

She turns back to me, "I'm going to bed. Join me or not, but we're still having that conversation either way."

I nod. "I'm right behind you."

Kadence nods in response, stepping around Cole's hulking frame, and makes her way up the stairs. I watch her, waiting until she's inside and the door is shut before I snatch Cole by the collar of his vest.

"Hit me again, O'Neil, and you'll find out just how easy it is to lose this club." I seeth at my friend, staring back at him without words. I'm not sure if the threat's real or not and I know Cole is questioning it but we both know that I've gotten us into shit that's going to be a fucking hell storm to get out of.

I release him before making my way up the stairs and knocking on the apartment door as Cole makes his way across the lot to the clubhouse. The door swings open, and Kadence meets me in her tank top and jeans. She gazes up at me. I can see the exhaustion in her face and though I want to tell her everything, she needs the rest.

She moves aside, letting me into the apartment. I step inside and turn back to her, watching as she shuts the door and locks it. *Good girl* I think, before taking a step towards her.

Her hand comes between us, stopping me before pointing to the bed. "Sit."

I do as I'm told, watching her carefully as she moves past me. Kadence begins searching the cupboards, opening and closing the doors until she stops. I can see her pull a rag from the shelf and close the door before taking it over to the sink and letting it run under the water.

After a moment she rings out the excess water and turns to me before moving to stand in front of me. I glance up at her, my eyes never leaving hers as I part my thighs letting her slide between them.

She gingerly grasps my chin, turning my gashed cheek to her. My hands find the backs of her thighs, squeezing them gently as she makes her assessment. I'm surprised when she doesn't flinch away from me, instead just runs her thumb gently over the bruised and red skin. With furrowed brows she inspects it before raising her other hand and swiping away the now thick and sticky blood from my cheek.

The towel is colder than I would like, making me wince as the water hits the particularly tender spots on my cheek. I stare up at her, making a mental roadmap of her features in case this is the last time I'll be able to see them.

"Thank you," I whisper as she nods, moving to sit next to me and tossing the rag into the small sink.

Her eyes meet mine. "What happened tonight?"

I turn cupping her face, tongue running along my bottom lip, "You became my first priority." I lean in pressing my forehead to hers, my eyes sliding closed. "Watson's threats weren't empty," I whisper. "I'll explain everything, but I need you to promise to help me keep you safe."

"Holden..."

"Please." There's that plea again. "Just promise me." Tonight is the first night I fully and completely believe that Becca's death was not an accident and it terrifies me to have so many unanswered questions.

I open my eyes to meet hers, praying that she'll just say the words. For once not fight me, but just...trust me.

Kadence slides her hand to the back of my neck and I feel myself once again lean into her. Her lips part and as she sucks in a breath she begins nodding softly.

"I promise."

KADENCE

Fear creeps into the deep blue of his eyes as his hands find my face. His warmth flows through my cheeks as he makes me promise him that I'll be safe. I have my questions, and even with the worry slowly clawing its way up my spine, I want nothing more than to feel more of him.

"I'll do whatever it takes to keep you safe." Holden's voice cuts through the million questions that have started to spiral in my mind.

I pull back from him, pushing the ball-cap off the top of his head to really get a good look at him. His cheek has already started to bruise but at least the bleeding has stopped. I comb my fingers through his hair, pressing my forehead to his.

"I don't even know what you're keeping me safe from," I whisper.

"Watson, for one," he admits, "and whatever else tries to come for us."

I pull back from him. "What did Watson mean earlier? About you seeing your parole officer?"

"Kade, it's late and–" Holden sighs as he tugs himself from my grip to stand from the bed, ready to run, ready to shut down on me.

"You told me you would tell me everything, so tell me." Our eyes meet and I'm fully ready for the pushback. My hands tense around the edge of the bed but my heart is calm because, even though hesitation rolls off of him now, I know I'd run too given the chance.

His eyes search mine. I need to know what the hell I've gotten myself into. Cole won't tell me the truth, especially after tonight. The look he flashed me earlier makes me want to crawl into a hole and a part of me wonders why he's so disgusted at the fact that I've spent the evening with Holden.

"Kadence."

"You *promised* me."

His head drops with his gaze and I can feel the air between us become thick with our warring secrets. Tired blue eyes lift and find mine again only this time there's a hint of vulnerability that wasn't there before. It makes me wonder how deep the pain is rooted within him.

"I don't want you to think of me differently," Holden rasps, strained and tight.

"I'm not going anywhere, Holden, no matter what you tell me I'm staying right here." I point at where my feet are planted in the carpet. He stares back at me like he's expecting me to change my mind. I won't because no matter how many red flags keep popping up in front of me, being with Holden makes me feel like a moth to a flame.

"I got out of prison a month ago." His tongue rolls over his bottom lip as he looks away and lets out a breath I didn't realize he was holding in. "And about two years ago I killed someone." Holden's voice trails off as he studies me for a reaction. I don't know what to feel.

"Killed?" I hear myself ask as my toes grip the carpet to keep myself steady.

He nods with a distant look in his eyes. "It was an accident. Wrong place, wrong time."

"How did it happen?"

"Kadence, it's not important how–"

I shake my head, holding out my hand to stop him. "It's important to me."

He takes a deep breath and clears his throat before nodding. "We were out on a run and had almost just made it back here, but it started storming." Holden pauses. "The group stopped at a bar and this guy just kept...fucking egging us on."

The more he explains, the more my body feels on fire and nausea rolls over me in waves.

"He started shoving West, playing it off like he was messing around, but the more the night went on and the more the bar kept feeding him drinks, it got worse." He pauses again and I can feel his eyes on me.

"Keep going," I choke out, looking up at him with tear-brimmed eyes. "Please."

I need to know. I need to know he's not the same kind of monster I've dealt with for years.

Holden nods once more as I close my eyes. The bed dips down next to me but there's a distance between us that I hate and need all at once.

"The guy was belligerent and didn't know his left hand from his right. At one point a punch was thrown, West was on the ground and the guy was getting dragged out by the bouncers. No one really fucks with us, especially when there's three or four with cuts on. But this guy...didn't care."

He sighs again. "When we left he tried to ambush us. He went straight for West as soon as we went outside. Cole pulled the guy off of West and then he turned on Cole, pulling out a knife."

I finally get the courage to glance up at him as his voice trails off again. "And that's when you stepped in."

Holden nods. "I tried to disarm him but the knife caught my thigh and I hit him in the nose to get him off of me." His voice starts to shake as he speaks, his chin trembles when he dips his head. "I didn't mean to hit him so hard."

"You were just defending yourself," I finally say after a moment of silence that falls between us, "defending Wyatt."

"That's not how the courts saw it," he states as he shakes his head. "I had only been out of the army for a year; they deemed my hand's weapons because of my combat training, and a flat palm to the nose is deadly."

I take a deep breath, wiping away the few tears that had begun to fall. I don't know why I'm crying. He hadn't meant to kill that person. He was defending himself and his family.

"I spent eighteen months at Stockton and the night I got back Cole and I had a meeting with Sheriff Stokes. Watson was supposed to be there." Holden sucks in another breath, pausing as I begin to put the puzzle pieces together.

"That was the night Becca died," I finished for him. The tick in his jaw tells me all I need to know. Watson is somehow responsible for Becca's death and Holden hasn't known for sure until his threats tonight.

He finally blinks, breaking his staring contest with the wall. The tears that find home in the corners of his eyes fall and streak down his cheeks. His hands wring together in his lap as he nods, confirming my guess.

"She didn't deserve to die," Holden chokes out through a sob, the wall he's keeping bricked around his emotions slowly starts to crumble, making my heart shatter. "She should still be here."

My gut wrenches and tears sting my eyes as the herculean man in front of me breaks. A month of pent-up grief and sadness begins to flood his surface, and the more he wrings his hands together, the more I can feel him turning into a ticking time bomb beside me.

I move and kneel in front of him, slotting myself between his thighs as I cup his face. A sob rips through him and I can't help the one that falls from my lips as well. Seeing him like this tears me to pieces.

"Holden," I whisper, trying to get him to look at me. His eyes squeeze closed as his head drops again. Tiny streaks of red fall onto my palm from where his cut has opened again, "Holden, please look at me."

He shakes his head. "She's dead because of me."

I grip his chin between my fingers, sucking in a breath to keep me steady between his legs. I can feel myself crumbling on the inside. The words hit me like a freight train as the emptiness in my womb aches, words I cried over and over again in the hospital that day and no one told me otherwise. No one told me it wasn't my fault.

Finally his eyes open, broken, blue, and devastated, they glint at me.

"You cannot blame yourself for her death," I say, running the pad of my thumb under his eyes, careful to miss the gash as I wipe away the tears. His hands wrap around my wrists, pulling them from his face as his eyes narrow at me. Every brick that had crumbled forms back into place like some sick magic trick.

"How can you say that?" He snaps, the sadness flipping to anger so fast it almost gives me whiplash. "It's just a coincidence that she ends up dead the night I get back?" He stands, stepping around me as I fall back onto my haunches, watching him pace the room.

"Holden, I didn't–"

"Of course you didn't! Because you don't know." That dangerous glare turns my way as I push myself up onto my feet.

I know where the anger is coming from but why he's taking it out on me, I'm not sure. I also know what the flip looks like. The moment where they go from sweet and soft to pure rage and anger. Even after seeing Jeremy for what he is, I've still never got used to his switch.

"I never said I did," I fire back at him, "but I know that taking on that kind of blame is only going to make you torture yourself." My voice raises as he scoffs. "I may not know you very well, Holden, but I recognize pain when I see it. I know what it's like to blame yourself for someone else's actions and that the anger feels like a deep-rooted tree that's just constantly on fire."

"Yeah? You know what it's like?" He steps towards me, making me step towards him. I'm not about to back down to another man, not this time. Not when I'm only trying to help him.

"Yeah, I do," I snap.

He narrows those dagger-throwing blue eyes again. "You know what it's like to feel completely fucking alone in a room full of people that are supposed to be your friends? Your brothers?" His chest heaves as he stares down at me. "You ever drown yourself in so much fucking pussy and alcohol that you forget who you are and wish for that feeling?"

Tears sting my eyes as he digs deeper at me.

"Stop it," I hiss, "you're pushing me away because it's easier than letting me in."

"No, *sweetheart*, you wanted to know me." He seethes, taking another step towards me, the space between us quickly disappearing.

I stare up at the man who just went from sobbing on my bed to dead angry in front of me. My heart hammers in my chest. Rage bubbles in me as his assumptions begin to sink in. He kept his promise. He told me about the things he did. But I also kept my promise. I didn't push him away or scream like this is some horrible eighties horror movie. I ball my fists at my side as the two of us standoff.

He's pushing me again and it's my turn to push back.

Before I can stop myself, my hands fly up, shoving him in the chest, watching as he stumbles backward towards the door. My control finally snapping.

"Of course I want to know you!" I yell, unable to help the tears that fall down my cheeks and shove him again. "I've been here for a fucking week, Holden and all I can think about is you!" Another shove. "Who you are! Why you feel more like home than where I came from!"

He stumbles again, catching himself on the wall.

I take a deep breath. "Because you've managed to dig yourself so deep into my bones that I don't–" The anger slips into choking back a sob as I pause. "I don't know how I'm ever going to be able to leave this place knowing that I'm leaving the one person who finally sees me." I dig a finger into my chest, angry that the tears have started again and that I can't read the wide-eyed look on his face.

With a deep breath I feel another sob get stuck behind the lump in my throat. The night finally felt like it was catching up to me. Between dinner, Watson, and now him standing in front of me, flipping emotions like a two-sided coin, I'm exhausted.

"Kadence, I–" Holden takes a step towards me but it only makes me recoil away from him, stopping him in his tracks.

"Don't," I breathe a laugh. "I don't think I can do much more emotional whiplash tonight." I glance up at him, hugging my arms over my chest. "Maybe Cole was right. Maybe this is a mistake."

Holden growls as he flies towards me cupping my face in his hands before smashing our lips together so forcefully it almost hurts. My hands tangle into the cotton of his shirt, a moan slipping from me as he pulls away, breathless and lips already bitten red. All of the tension melts away as we stare at each other.

"Cole is an idiot," he whispers. "You've injected yourself into my veins, Kadence, like some sort of drug I can't get enough of and I'll spend every day making you see it."

He dips his head once again, kissing me much softer this time. Butterflies swarm in my stomach as I pull back from him, needing a breath, needing...something just to stop for a moment.

"Why do you get so angry with me?" I ask against his mouth, sounding much more pathetic than I want.

Holden shakes his head. "I'm not angry with you." He brushes back the hair from my face, planting a soft peck on my forehead. "I'm angry with the world darlin' and I apologize I've taken it out on you." His finger hooks under my chin lifting my gaze to his.

"I need you to control your emotions," I whisper, fiddling with his shirt, twisting it in my fingers and wrapping around the chain of his dog tags. "Let me help you take on that anger. Don't take it out on me."

He nods after a moment. "Us against the world?" A smile forms across his lips. "I could get used to that."

My bottom lip finds home between my teeth, biting back the smile I so want to give him. "I think I could too."

Holden traces his thumb along my jaw before gently tugging my lip from between my teeth. His eyes darken as he studies my features and after a moment of silence he dips his head once again, taking my top lip between his. I can't help the whine that escapes my lips as I melt into him, my hand roaming under his cut and up to his shoulders to slide it off.

The leather creates a soft thud as it hits the floor at our feet. I claw at his shirt, the clothes between us proving to be too much as his hands roam under the hem of my shirt. The warmth of his skin ignites tiny little fires against my own.

"Holden," I breathe as he dips his head, nibbling a trail of kisses along my jaw and down to my neck.

He hums against my skin, moving his way down while licking and sucking the spot on my neck that sends tingles down to my toes. I moan again, laughing softly as his fingertips graze over the ticklish spot on my ribs. I've never felt anyone touch me the way he is or take the time to get to know the ins and outs of my body. But with Holden, my body reacts with the slightest of touches, as if he already knows my roadmap and has for years.

I press gently against his chest, taking a step back with a heaving breath. He narrows his eyes briefly at me as I grin.

"What are you doin', sweetheart?" He asks, his hair a mess and lips turning a bright red from kissing my skin.

I shrug softly before lifting the hem of my tank top, pulling it over my head, and revealing the blue lace bra that has quickly become my favorite since the first time I wore it. It fits perfectly and the teal against my tan skin makes me, for once, feel beautiful.

He watches me drop the tank top to the floor, his pupils going dark. I ignore the pit in my stomach that begins to grow at the reality of me letting him in. It's been a long time since I've been intimate with someone and now everything is happening so fast that my mind is screaming at me to stop but my body melts as his eyes roam my skin.

Holden takes a step toward me, sinking to his knees as his hands wrap around the backs of my thighs. He looks up at me through thick lashes before planting a trail of kisses along my stomach, lingering over each divot just above my hips.

"You're gorgeous," he whispers against the soft part of my belly that still holds scars and pain I don't think I'll ever get rid of.

Tears threaten the corners of my eyes again, tangling my fingers into his long chestnut locks. I feel myself growing closer to him, and every time his touch lingers on my skin for just a little bit longer than intended, I tumble down that rabbit hole even further.

"Let's get you out of these," he says softly, his fingers finding the button of my jeans and tugging them down my legs.

I feel his fingers grasp along my calf, lifting them to pull my jeans off. Leaving a trail of kisses along the inside of my leg before letting it back down to the floor. He repeats this with my other leg before dragging his fingertips up and along the backs of my calves then gripping them into my thighs. All the while sending waves of goosebumps along my skin.

"You have entirely way too many clothes on," I whisper down at him as my hands tangle into his hair, ignoring the gnawing feeling in my heart.

Holden smiles so sweetly that if he weren't holding my legs my shaking knees would have knocked me over. He places a kiss on the inside of my thigh, dragging the tip of his nose closer to my center. My chest begins to rise and fall with the quickness of my breaths. He's lighting my skin on fire and I didn't even realize it.

"Holden," I whisper, the sensation of his skin on mine, the way his fingers knead into the squishiness of my legs, it's all becoming too much. I need a step back. My hands press against his shoulders, trying to push myself away from him, "Holden, let me go."

He drops his hands, standing as I take a step back from him. I want to keep going, I almost need to keep going to prove to myself that I can let someone in other than a person who dictated everything I was allowed to do with my body.

"What's wrong?" Holden asks, pulling himself up onto his feet.

I avoid his gaze as I cover myself with my arms. How am I going to explain this? I'm not ready to tell him the truth. A part of me is ashamed of letting someone like Jeremy take control of almost every aspect of my life. Including when we would have sex. It was never on my terms, not even when our child was conceived was it by my choice. But it was safer than dealing with the repercussions of rejecting him.

His hands cup my face, forcing me to look at him. My eyes meet his, and the tears I've been forcing back cascade from me like tiny little traitors marching into the battle of my heart.

"Kade, talk to me," Holden pleads. The shudder in his voice and the way his chin trembles shatters my heart again for the umpteenth time. "Please?" his voice drops to a scared whisper. "I didn't mean to," he pauses, "I didn't hurt you did–"

I shake my head, realizing that he thinks it's him that's scaring me. That he's done something to push me away. "It's not you, Holden," I protest. I didn't mean for it to come out that way.

"Then what is it?"

"It's just–" I suck in a breath as the pad of his thumb wipes away the tears escaping my eyes, "it's been a long time since someone has made me feel the way you have. Touched me and meant it to feel good."

His brows furrow. "What do you mean?"

I stare up at him, eyes glassy and tired. This is not how I want to tell him and a part of me doesn't know if I actually can. It all seems too much and I don't want to be this broken toy that he would inevitably try to put back together.

"My last relationship wasn't the best," I admit, "he took what he wanted and that was that."

Holden stares back, his tongue flicking over his bottom lip as if an angry cat's tail. "He's a fucking idiot then."

I'm not sure what I'm expecting him to say, and even though it isn't the full truth, it feels like one or two bricks of this heavy wall that crushes me have been chipped away.

"You could say that."

He dips his head, pressing his forehead to mine. "We don't have to do anything you don't want to do, okay?" Holden's lips press to the tip of my nose. "You're the one in control." His voice dips to a whisper.

"I want to, Holden, I really do." I breathe, grasping his t-shirt in my fingers, a sob escaping my lips.

"Hey," he coos, pulling me into his chest, his hand tangling into my hair at the back of my head as I tuck my head under his chin, "it's okay"

I want the tears to stop, I need them to. Here I'm standing in front of him, in a bra and underwear, sobbing because he feels good. But it's still all too much.

Holden pulls back slightly. "Let's just get some sleep, yeah?"

I nod as he wipes away a few more tears before pressing his lips to mine in a soft sweet kiss. One that's just telling me that he's there, nothing more, nothing less. He's just...There for me.

He steps back from me, slipping out of his jeans and tugging his t-shirt over his head. Giving view to the ridges of his abs and the deep v that dips beneath the band of his briefs. We meet each other's gaze, his smile warm and calming as he holds out his t-shirt to me.

"You can wear this if you want," he offers.

I smile softly, the warmth returning to my chest and the remembrances of Jeremy slipping away from me. I reach out, taking the shirt from him and slipping it over my head before maneuvering to take off my bra under the shirt.

We climb into bed, Holden falling to his back as I find my way to being curled into his chest.

"Us against the world, right?" I whisper softly, knowing it's a big ask with both of our ghosts dancing around the room like a haunted house.

"Us against the world," he repeats softly, dipping his head to kiss me again.

HOLDEN

I don't remember falling asleep last night, but I know that when my eyes open this morning, it feels like the first real sleep I've had in a while. The first night of sleep that didn't consist of nightmares or phantoms of my past haunting me.

I slept.

Really *slept* and I know that it isn't a coincidence that the first time I've been able to is because she's next to me.

My head rolls to the side. Kadence is flat on her stomach, arm tucked under her pillow with the comforter pulled up to her chin. Part of me wishes that she's wrapped around me like a ribbon, but after last night, I know now I'm going to have to take a step back. Let her control the speed of whatever train we're riding on and knowing that she took everything I told her last night and didn't push me away only makes it that much easier.

Still, I've been staring up at the ceiling contemplating everything that happened. The million different ways I want to string Watson up by his feet and let him hang there until nothing is left. Even if he had nothing to do with Becca.

Deep down, I'm still pissed off at Cole. My cheek is fucking throbbing this morning, though it isn't anything I can't handle. Cole hit me like a bitch. I wasn't sure when Stokes crawled so far up my brother's ass but running the club based on Stokes's terms is getting old, and as much as I don't want to, I need to talk to Trey.

It's still early enough that the shop won't be open yet. I can sneak into the clubhouse and probably find Trey scarfing down the muffins that Marlowe keeps hidden in the cupboard above the fridge.

I scoff softly, freezing when feeling her shift next to me. *Sneak.* I'm thinking about sneaking into my clubhouse. My fucking home that the more I lay next to her, feels less and less like one. I didn't think in such a short amount of time, my world would shrink so far but something about her feels familiar and safe.

Before I can stop myself I roll onto my side, dragging my fingertips carefully through her hair, tucking it behind her ear. She hums softly, making me smile like fucking schoolboy.

"Morning," she whispers. It's full of rasp but soft enough that it sends chills up my spine.

My tongue runs over my bottom lip as I draw circles on her shoulder blade, slow and soft, scared that if I stop she'll vanish into thin air. "Morning."

Her eyes flutter open. Those jade green hues squint up at me, the sunbathing directly over her, letting the speckles of blue hidden within shine bright.

"You want some coffee?" I ask, forcing myself into a normal conversation and hiding the fact that blush is creeping up my neck at how she looks adorned in my t-shirt and sunlight that only gives light to every little perfectly imperfect freckle and line in her face.

A soft smile spreads across her lips as she rolls onto her side, groaning gently and stretching her limbs. "I could go for some coffee." Her lip finds home between her teeth as she stares up at me. "But not before this…"

I swear my stomach flips as her hand rests against my chest and she moves closer to me pressing her lips to mine. I melt into her like sugar in water. My mouth slots over hers pulling a moan from her as she arches into me, her chest presses against mine and hands tangle in my hair.

I pull back, hating myself as I do, "Darlin' if we keep going I'm not going to be able to stop," I all but whine, "and as much as I want to," I pause gauging her reaction as her nails trail along the expanse of my chest, making it difficult to stop, "are you sure you're ready?"

Her fingers stop, freezing as her eyes meet mine. *Fuck.* There's that look again.

"I'm a big girl, Holden," she says, rolling over onto her back. "Hey," I whisper, moving over the top of her, my hands planting on either side of her head. "I know you are," I reassure, dipping my head to kiss the tip of her nose.

When I pull back her eyes are searching mine as her fingers grasp at my dog tags. "Did you mean what you said last night?" She asks, worry filtering over her face.

Us against the world.

It's a big ask, a big promise that deep down I'm not sure I'd be able to fulfill but I'll spend my days trying for her.

"Did you?" I ask, nudging my nose against hers, my voice soft and low.

She tilts her head back into the pillow further to look at me and I lift my head to make it easier for her. I can tell she's contemplating the words threatening to drip from her tongue.

The confidence I once had in the woman laying below me slowly starts to fade. I can feel my face fall the longer the words hang between us.

"Holden–" she whispers as I start to roll off of her but her hand catches my bicep, stopping me.

My tongue flicks over my bottom lip. "It's okay… a lot was said last night and I don't–"

"I *did* mean it," she chokes out, green eyes glistening as she fights back tears. "I'm just…"

I suck in a breath, terrified of the words that she may say. If there's one thing I know it's that if she backs out, calling whatever this is a *mistake*, I'll be shattered. My fingertips trace along her hairline, tucking back the few loose strands behind her ear, forcing myself to focus on anything other than the inevitable heartbreak that's about to happen.

I can't be surprised, life always has a way of being really, really good for what feels like a second and then whatever good moment exists is torn away in the next.

Kade's face crumples gently. "…worried that this is all going to crash and burn.."

I nod softly to hide the disappointment tearing at me.

"It might," I say truthfully, "and I wish I could promise you that it won't but–" I pause, swallowing the lump in my throat. "I'm not making you any promises I can't keep." I run my fingers through her hair again, feeling her hands pressing against my bare chest.

Kadence stares up at me with something in her eyes that I'm not familiar with, adoration… Appreciation? I'm not sure but it soothes the cracks I felt only moments before expecting the worst from her.

"You promised to keep me safe…" she whispers. "You don't know that you can, not really anyway."

A smile flickers across my lips as I dip my head, ghosting my lips along her jawline, feeling her back arch up into me, only making my earlier refrain that much harder to keep.

"I know I'd die trying." I respond with as much confidence as I can muster. I lift my head to look at her again as she reaches up and pushes back the hair that has fallen in my face. I really need a haircut. As much as I don't mind the long hair it doesn't quite feel like me.

She worries her bottom lip between her teeth as she stares up at me. "We've known each other for a week."

I nod, "feels longer."

"Why is that?" She asks softly, the smile returning to her face. "I've never..." She stops herself, her eyes flickering from mine to my dog tags.

My eyes narrow for a moment before gently lifting her chin again. "Never what?" I ask in a whisper.

"I've never felt this way about someone before," she says after a moment. "It's terrifying."

Her brows knit together as she studies me. I can feel her reading and analyzing every twitch and emotion that masks my features. Unsaid words drift between us as I dip my head, pressing my lips to hers in a soft, long kiss. I feel her tongue dart from between her lips, wanting more from me. Everytime we touch I swear she melts into me. The feeling is addicting and the more my hands explore her body and sweet symphonies of sounds fall from her lips the more I want to stay right here. Next to her.

But I pull away, hating myself when a frustrated whine leaves her.

"We'll have plenty of time for that, Sunflower." I drag my index finger along her collar bone watching a wave of goosebumps roll across her skin, moving to draw a single line down into the collar of my shirt that she's wearing, "*that* I can promise you."

I smirk down at the frown she's flashing me.

"Are you as terrified as me?" She asks after a moment.

I chuckle. "Yeah, I am."

"Why are you laughing?" Kade's frown curls up softly as she tries to bite back a smile.

"Because if you would have told me a week ago I'd be spending every waking moment thinking about a woman and feeling things I don't think I've ever felt, I would have told you you're fucking crazy."

I smile again pressing my palm firmly over her heart. It's light flutter beating against my hand. I want to feel her, feel what ticks inside of her that makes her this addicting.

"Well you *are* crazy," Kade teases, gripping my chin gently with her fingers, the smile on her face falling for just a moment, "but I think I am too."

"Oh," I scoff playfully, "you're definitely crazy if you're with someone like me."

That beautiful glowy smile returns to her.

I duck my head, pressing featherlite kisses along her jawline, trailing them down to her neck just to hear the sounds that I hope will spill from those perfect lips. I feel myself grinning as she whimpers below me. I have to stop. Otherwise, we will never leave this bed, and even though I won't mind that the last thing I want to do is suffocate her with my shit.

"Coffee darlin," I hum against her skin before lifting my head, "before I trap you in this room."

"I wouldn't complain," she teases, tugging gently on the chain of my dog tags.

I laugh and shake my head, "Neither would I, Sunflower, but I should probably go talk to Cole as well."

Even if I don't want to. Cole is the last person I want to have a conversation with right now but if I don't I know that whatever fucked up tension is building between us would only separate the club more than it already is.

Kadence reaches up, running her fingers gingerly along the bruise under my eye. Her brows knit together as I search her eyes.

"It's not your fault," I say, moving to sit next to her, leaning against the headboard.

She follows, angling her body towards me and bringing her knees to her chest.

"Why was he so angry that I was with you last night?" She asks, her head tilting to lean against the wood. "He acted like you were Satan incarnate when we got back."

"Cole is protective of the things he cares about," I say plainly.

"Aren't you one of those things?"

I glance up at her, her face scrunching into a wince. She thinks she's pushing me too far, intruding on a relationship with Cole that by now is far too complicated for even myself to understand.

"He'll always be my brother," I start, my fingertips tap along the top of her knee mindlessly, "but things change, we've changed. I wasn't the same person that I was when he picked me up from Stockton. The club wasn't–isn't the same club that we left... That we built together after his dad passed."

I suck in a breath, shaking my head. "I don't know if we'll ever be back to what we were before everything went down."

"The bar fight?" She asks softly.

My head lolls to the side. "The bar fight, Becca... it all made every-thing too–" my voice trails off.

"Complicated?" Kadence finishes for me.

I feel a smile tug at the corner of my lips as I nod. "Yeah."

I watch as she leans into me, tucking her knees under her as she presses her hands into my chest before peppering my cheeks with soft sweet kisses. Her lips trail along the roughness of my stubble, pressing them gently to where the bruise tattoos my skin.

"Complicated feels like our middle names," she says softly before pulling away from me, brushing back the tangled hair from my face as her eyes trace over my features once again. I've never had someone be so... tender with me before. Not like this. Sure, I've spent plenty of time with the other girls that hang around the club, but it's never like this. There's something deeper, something meaningful in the way she looks at me. It terrifies me not to hide the cracks in the mask I put on for everyone else. That I've so easily let her in and so fast.

There's just something different in the way her fingertips linger on my skin, the trail of fireworks they leave behind with it. I want all of her.

"What's running through that head of yours?" I ask softly.

She smiles after a moment but I can tell there's something distant in her eyes. Kadence shakes her head.

"Coffee," she answers.

"Kade." My brows knit together as she tugs herself from my arms, climbing from the bed and moving to her suitcase. "What's wrong?"

She continues to dig through her bags, pulling out a pair of jean shorts and a ragged band t-shirt.

"Nothing is wrong." she glances over at me. "I just want a cup of coffee." Kadence slips into her shorts, grinning over at me before climbing back into the bed and pressing her lips to mine. "C'mon, don't make me face Cole alone."

I chuckle before letting out a sigh. "I'm gonna need that shirt back." I smirk, my finger slipping into the inside of the collar as she leans down to me and I tug gently pulling her lips back to me, "Please?" I whisper against her before kissing her one last time.

Kadence pulls back from me and slips off the edge of the bed, tugging the shirt over her head only to dangle it between her fingers and expose herself to me.

"You mean this t-shirt?" She teases.

I flick my tongue over my bottom lip, bringing it between my teeth as my eyes rake over her body, the curve of her hips, and how the jeans hug them perfectly. The perfect roundness of her breasts. If my friendship weren't at stake, I'd spend all day here with her.

"C'mon, Sergeant, come get it." Kadence bites on the nail of her thumb, looking at me through thick lashes.

I bolt from the bed, and the room erupts into giggles as I wrap my arms around her. I pick her up gently, swinging her in a circle as she grins and laughs, her head tilted back and her long hair cascading behind her.

"You're gonna be the death of me." I grin, pressing chaste kisses to her chest.

She laughs. "I hope not. Now put me down, you caveman."

Her hand playfully smacks my chest until I lower her feet to the floor. Kadence hands me the shirt before slipping hers over her head and putting her shoes on. I follow suit, slipping into my shirt and putting on my boots. I watch as she moves about, running her fingers through her hair and wiping the sleep from her eyes.

Standing, I glance over to her suitcases, catching a glimpse of something blue and soft. It looks like an ear to something. I can't quite tell under the pile of clothes, but as my eyes track back to her, she's made her way to the door.

"You comin'?"

I nod, stealing one last look at the ear and make my way to her. I want to ask but too much has already been said and I don't want to spook her. I take her hand, and the two of us make our way to the clubhouse.

HOLDEN

The sun is bright, and the pavement is already radiating from the heatwave. I scan the lot. Cole's bike is still in its spot next to mine. Anxiety creeps up my spine. I'm better than this. It's Cole, for christ's sake, I don't need to be afraid of my best friend. But I suppose it's much more than that. I'm afraid of losing the one person who's never left me behind.

As if she can feel the nervousness radiating off of me, she squeezes my hand as we approach the door to the clubhouse. I can't look at her and promise everything is going to be fine when we walk through that door. Not even I know what's waiting for us. There are two sides to Cole's anger. Quiet and calm like dark clouds before a storm and the other *is* the storm, the anger he hides so well, waiting and brewing under his skin until it's too late.

His resolve only goes so far and so does mine. I held back last night with empty threats and the promise to come to bed.

I push open the door to the clubhouse. Trey is sitting at the bar, sipping on a cup of coffee. His eyes widen when they land on me and Kade. It's the first time I've seen Trey in a while. The two of us avoid each other like the plague. I could never really figure out why. Trey is more political in the way he helps Cole run the club. More... level-headed than me.

Trey leads with the idea that the club could grow and dips his hands into the pockets of Town Hall to keep the peace between the big bad biker gang and the rest of the town. I lead with my heart and emotions. This place is the only family I have left and I don't want it to turn into some big political showboat race to ease the minds of the rest of the town.

"Nash, you sure you wanna be here right now?" Trey eases himself off of the stool, holding out his hand like he's trying to stop me from going any further. My gaze flickers down to his hand and with a raised brow lifts back to Trey, "What the fuck happened last night? Cole came through here like a goddamn tornado before locking himself in his room."

A soft scoff comes from my side.

Trey's eyes flicker over to Kadence. "You're the new office girl?"

I glance down at her, our eyes meeting for a brief moment before she nods. "Yeah, Kadence."

Falcone smirks as he looks back at me. I know exactly what he's thinking and even that thought makes me want to throttle him.

"Where is he?" I ask.

Trey sighs, nodding his head toward the Church. The room where too many of my brothers became comfortable with the idea of letting Stokes fund the club. "Been in there since I woke up. Dex is with him."

Ah, of course Dexter Wolfe is with him. Plotting whatever way they can to get me out of this club.

As if on cue the Church doors fly open, a blind rage plasters over Cole's features as his gaze lands on me. But it isn't me he's pissed at. His eyes flicker down to my side, to Kadence.

"What the hell did I tell you?" He marches towards the two of us. I take a step forward, guarding myself between the two of them. "I asked you if there was anything I should be worried about, and what did you say?" I don't miss the venom leaking from Cole's words.

Cole takes another step forward, forcing my hand to fly out.

"Hey!" I bark. "What the fuck are you talking about?"

I feel her grip tighten on my hand as she moves around them. Cole lets out a chilling laugh. "Your new conquest–"

I shove my hand into Cole's chest even before he can finish the sentence. "Watch it, O'Neil," I warn.

"Kadence is apparently a missing person," Cole says flatly, his eyes flickering back down to her. It's then Wolfe who rounds the edge of the door, clapping his hand over his shoulder, "And a fucking felon."

"I–" Kadence's soft voice filters through the powder keg threatening to go off between us. "What?"

My jaw ticks the longer Cole glares at her.

A missing person? What the hell is he talking about? Kadence sounds just as confused as I feel. Dex shoves Cole back a step, pulling his focus to him.

"You were supposed to *wait*, not storm out here like an asshole." Dex turns back to the three of us, his face exhausted, yet his brows pull together with the bulldog look he uses to intimidate people. It makes me laugh whenever he does it, though deep down I know Dex. Right now it's just a look, nothing murderous about it, at least not yet. "A news story from this morning, plastered all over Fox News, CNN, all that mainstream bullshit, says your girl here isn't who she says she is."

Kadence steps forward, her hand dropping from mine as she moves. "What news story?"

Cole shakes his head, steam practically rolling off his ears with the redness creeping up his neck. "Why don't you see for yourself?" He pushes his way past Dex, who shoots me a look.

I rest my hand on her lower back, guiding her towards the Church. Dex waits for us as Trey goes back to the bar. The door closes behind us. Cole's already standing in front of the TV hanging on the wall.

He unmutes the flashing photos and news junkets. Kadence takes a step towards the TV, her arms crossing over her chest. I can only watch her. Whatever is on the screen is bad, bad for her and bad for us. But I also know mainstream media is full of fucking bullshit stories flared for the masses to get views.

Now out of Miami-Dade County, Florida, we have Lieutenant Jeremy Miles, Lieutenant Miles what can you tell us about Kadence Andrews?

A man with short-cut hair appears on the screen. His face twists with what appears to be grief and he's dressed in some stupid fucking bandana wrapped around his neck. Kadence stumbles backward, her hands finding the table as she grips the edge, holding herself up.

We're investigating the disappearance of Kadence Andrews and an arson related to her disappearance. The man stated plainly. ***We have reason to believe that Ms. Andrews is under extreme duress and acting irrationally due to post-traumatic stress disorder.***

"That motherfucker." Her voice is only a whisper and only meant for herself to hear, but I catch it, and it fuels the rage within me as I try to figure out what the fuck is going on.

"What the fuck is this, Kadence?" I ask through gritted teeth.

The screen flashes to a townhome, completely burnt to the ground, pieces of a blue door still scattered across the screen.

Lieutenant, it's also stated that she's wanted for arson? Can you please tell the viewers more?

Certainly, Ms. Andrews, in a frenzy, set fire to the townhome that she and I shared.

"Shared?" My gaze flickers down to her again, confusion washing over me until it hit me like a fucking freight train. "Kadence, is this your ex?"

She tears her eyes away from the wood. Glistening jade green stares back at me tears well in her eyes as the white knuckle grip she has on the table only grows harder. She's going to hurt herself if she digs her nails into the wood anymore.

You and Miss Andrews shared this townhome we see on the screen?

That's right. Kadence and I have been together for almost four years. It was only until the last year that she started behaving strangely, and that was until she became pregnant with our first child.

You have a child with Miss Andrews?

The son of a bitches face scrunches like he's in pain, but even I can tell it's an act.

"Turn it off," she rasps, "Please."

Dex sits himself down in the chair on the opposite side of the table. His gaze never breaking from her. Cole's pacing back and forth in front of the TV.

I stare at her, watching her eyes slide close and tears trickle to the table, splashing against the wood. She has a kid?

As if she could feel the weight of all the questions running through my mind, she looks over at me. Those green eyes I'm unexpectedly falling for staring at me with grief and fear lacing through the flecks of gold. I can see her working out the lies in her head, working out whatever bullshit she's about to spew to me to spin it around into a sob story of her own.

I can't do this. I'm not going to sit here after so openly telling her every dark thing about myself, not when she took it in her stride and had every chance to tell me the same. I know she still holds a wall up around herself but she's broadcasted all over the goddamn country now.

Cole slams the remote onto the table, knocking over his chair and forcing her back a step. "Goddamnit Kadence! This is the last fucking thing the club needs. I *asked you–*"

"I know what you asked me, Cole!" Her voice raises whatever courage still left in her she's forcing out.

My fists flex at my side. She lied. Not to just me, but to Cole. I knew she was hiding something, but a fucking kid? Before I know what I'm doing, my feet are carrying me out of the room, shoving past Trey, who tries to grab me, and out the front door.

Us against the world.

The words run through my mind with a scoff as I climb onto my bike.

You're a fucking idiot.

KADENCE

*N**o, no, no, no. This isn't happening.*

Images of my old home, me and Jeremy flicker across the screen in front of me. Everything that I've been worrying of unfolding is right in front of my eyes. Lies. It's all lies. But the looks on the three men's faces tell me they don't care. I'm cornered.

I look at Holden. His eyes have gone cold, iced over and the warmth I found in them this morning completely snubbed out by everything that I've been running from. He shoves past Trey, leaving me in the lion's den.

"Holden!" I move towards the door but Trey has already filled the frame, "Move!"

Trey shakes his head, "he's gone. Took off on his bike."

I stumble back again, feeling everything crash down around me. I was going to tell him but the cocoon we made this morning, the promises... it just wasn't the right time. I should have told him. Goddamnit, I should have said something.

"I want answers." Cole suddenly fills my space, too close for my comfort, "is that true?"

"O'Neil," Dex's voice booms in the small room, "back off for a goddamn second!" I hear the chair he's in roll backward as he stands, rounding the table. "She's terrified, look at her."

Raging blue eyes rake over me before letting out a huff of air. I can feel the anger radiating off of him as he turns from me. "Start talking Kade." He bites and pushes for answers I'm not ready to give but because of his public display...Jeremy doesn't give me a choice. Dex is right, I'm plastered over the entire country right now as Jeremy spins up a web of disgusting lies and feeds them to the media on a silver fucking spoon.

"Sit," Dex urges, pulling out a chair for me, "Trey get her some water."

"But–" Trey protests until Dex shoots him a look, "Jesus Christ. Back for one fucking night and hell breaks loose." He mutters, turning from the doorway and disappearing down the hallway.

I sit down in the chair, doing everything I can to keep myself together though the tears stinging my eyes aren't from sadness. It's now anger rolling through me in waves. He left me. Left me here to deal with the aftermath of everything.

Holden is never going to believe me.

Dex slides the chair out next to me, sitting himself down in it. I can feel his dark eyes roaming my features. "O'Neil if you don't calm the fuck down, I'm kicking you out." Even Dex can feel the tension in the room crackling and splitting down the wood table like a fire.

I suck in a breath, my eyes falling closed at the idea of reliving everything. The last thing I want to do is go down fucked up memory lane with men I hardly know. I don't want any of them to look at me like some kicked puppy. I'm not that person anymore, or I hope I'm not.

"He's lying." I sigh, running my hands over my face.

Cole lets out a long breath and I hope it's to calm himself down. I need him calm. I need myself calm and the only thing grounding me right now is the man I've barely spoken more than a few words to sitting next to me.

"What do you mean?" his deep voice drops into a whisper.

A glass of water appears in front of me before the door clicks shut. Trey takes a chair across from us, leaning back and I can feel his glare boring into me. Cole leans against the window behind him, large arms crossing over his chest.

My eyes slide closed, images of that night bubbling just below the surface.

"Jeremy is my ex-fiance. That much was true." I say so quietly that I'm not even sure if they hear me. "But I never burned down that townhome. I loved–" I suck in a breath, my chin trembling as the words get stuck in my throat, "I sold it after everything happened."

"You *are* running." Cole speaks, shaking his head.

"Not for the reasons you think," I finally look up at him, "I *was* pregnant with his child."

Dex tilts his head as I glance over to him watching his brows pull together, his jaw ticking. "You don't have a child *now* do you?"

I shake my head. Tears bite at the corners of my eyes again as I breathe in, "I had a miscarriage after–" I want to be anywhere else right now. The crushing weight of the bottom of the ocean would be more comfortable than the suffocating memories flooding me.

None of them say anything, as if the weight of my words is finally sinking in.

"The man on the screen?" I nod my chin to the TV, "The grief-stricken, worried boyfriend? It's an act. It always has been."

"What did he do to you?" Dex asks. Only this time, I can hear his teeth grinding against each other as he speaks. Something within the way his jaw ticks and the dark flames flicker behind the dark brown in his eyes tell me he already knows.

A laugh bubbles from my throat as the night begins to replay in my head. "Everything... anything that he could that wasn't obvious. I made lasagna that night... he didn't want lasagna."

Dex's gaze flickers to the two men sitting and standing across from us. "I didn't fold his socks correctly. I ate way too much of the tiny portions he would only allow me to eat." It's like a different person is talking as I stare at the wolf engraved into the wooden table. "So I was punished."

"Punished?" he asks gently, my eyes flicker to his.

I nod, "A slap across the back of the head usually, that was his quickest and less cruel of punishments."

"What happened?" Cole asks, "To make you run?"

"What did I fucking tell you!" A loud crash echoes through the kitchen. I've backed myself into the same corner I always did. The one that allows the dining room table to separate me and the rage. "I said this goddamn morning that I wanted anything but fucking pasta!"

My eyes squeeze shut, his voice ringing through my ears.

"I ran from him that night instead of taking it like I usually did, but things were different. He hadn't been cruel since we found out about the baby. Well, not as cruel. But I was stuck and when he finally got a hold of me," my voice breaks but everything inside of me went numb, "it wasn't until I got to the hospital that I found out I had lost the baby."

Dex's head drops as the three of them stare at me. This is what I was afraid of, I don't want to be pitied or to be felt sorry for. I want to forget everything and just... live whatever resemblance of a life I have left.

"I'm sorry," the first apology comes from Cole and my eyes flicker to him. The rage is gone and replaced by the softest shade of blue in his eyes, "why didn't you just tell–"

"To complete strangers? Would you want to relive your worst nightmare?" I cut him off, "I just wanted to get away Cole. I wanted to live my life without the judgment and the lies that everyone was so quick to believe."

"What about your family?" He asks, his brows knitting together when I laugh.

"What family?" I shake my head, "Jeremy had my mother, if you can even call her that, wrapped around his finger the moment she laid eyes on him. She's dating the doctor who helped me that day. They're off on some island in the Bahamas. She hasn't been my mother for a very long time."

"So you're alone?" The question comes from Trey this time.

"Since I was ten." I confirm nodding as I glance at the men around me.

Trey shakes his head, "it doesn't make any sense, why the news junket then?"

I take a deep breath, "because he doesn't quit. He was put through what he deemed was hell after everything happened. He was arrested, but he's a Lieutenant in one of the largest counties in Florida. Embarrassments like that don't get taken lightly and when half of the force believed their so-called brother over his *dramatic girlfriend* and the other half wanted nothing to do with him anymore. He lost his fast track to Sheriff even if they did sweep everything under their rug."

Cole shakes his head as he rounds the table kneeling next to me, "You weren't being dramatic." He confirms for me. I know that deep down, but I stayed with him longer than I should have. Something I hated myself for, for longer than I want to admit.

"Tell that to the hundreds of death threats I got." I let out a shaky sigh, "people were more upset about the fact that he was put in a cell than the fact that he murdered his unborn child or at least caused it."

Dex huffs a breath, his fist slamming against the table, startling me. His gaze flickers back to me, "I'm sorry," he mutters.

"No," I shake my head, "I should have never let you pick me up that night or offer me a place here." My gaze trails over to Cole. He sucks in a breath, his eyes going softer than before, and shakes his head.

"Out of everywhere you could have ended up Kade," he reaches for me, his hand resting on my forearm, "this might have been the best of them. But..." his voice trailed off, "from now on, honesty." His head tilts to the side, "that's all I'm askin'."

I nod, "that's not all."

Cole shifts on the balls of his feet, his grip on my arm tightening for just a moment before releasing me. It's not meant to hurt me, it feels more like him trying to comfort me.

"I got a text from an unknown number last night before we left Marlowe's."

"From Jeremy?" He asks, his gaze flicking between the men as if they're all having a silent conversation I'm not privy to.

"Yeah," I sigh, "it's what drove Holden and me to leave last night, or rather me to go with him, among other things." I feel the blush creep up on the back of my neck at the remembrance of his lips on mine before the pit of guilt in my stomach becomes weighty.

Dex sighs, "gotta admit, he works fast."

I stand pulling myself from Cole's grasp, "I need to tell him. He needs to know that I wouldn't-" The lump in my throat returns at the idea of him believing Jeremy. As angry as I am that he left, I meant what I said to him. "Where would he go?"

The three men share a look, another part of the conversation I'm not privy to. "What?"

"He's at his house or the club." Dex says plainly, but the grimace that passes over Cole's features tells me there's more to that sentence.

Cole stands with a sigh, "are you sure you want to go after him?" he asks. There's something hidden behind the question.

I nod, "I have to. I can't let Jeremy ruin another good thing for me."

The words fall out of my mouth before I even realize it. Holden is good for me, he challenges me and has done so much more in the last week to show me he cares more than Jeremy ever has in the four years we were together.

"I'll take you to him, but..." Cole's voice trails off, "I can't promise he's going to want to speak to you. Holden is hard headed and stubborn, if he even has an inkling that what Jeremy said was true, he won't back down easily."

"I don't need him to back down," I say, "I just need him to listen to me."

He studies me for a moment as I square my shoulders. I'm not ready to give up on him, even if he's trying to give up on me. I know deep down he wouldn't have reacted the way he did if there weren't some sort of feelings there. I'm banking on it.

"Cole, we have that meeting with Stokes," Trey reminds, "he's not going to take kindly to you not being there."

I shoot him a look.

"I'll take her," Dex says from behind me, "you don't need me there if you take Trey and Stokes will be more receptive if Holden and I aren't there."

I turn to the man who had quickly protected me from Cole earlier. My gaze meets his and he gives me a brief nod. "Thank you." I say softly.

Dex shakes his head, "don't, Holden won't like that I'm with you but somethin' in those pretty green eyes tells me you'll have him handled." I try to hide the surprise on my face when the corners of his mouth quirk up.

I feel Cole's hand rest on my elbow, "can I talk to you? Alone."

"I'll wait for you outside," Dex confirms before leaving the room, Trey following behind him and letting the door click shut.

I'm not sure why the nervousness has returned to me as he leans against the edge of the table. His hands card through his hair, pushing it back behind his ears. I know he's still pissed, I can feel the heat radiating off of him like a screaming furnace. But I can't tell if it's now still directed at me or something else.

"What happened last night?" He asks suddenly, his gaze drifting to mine. His eyes are a piercing blue that only makes me feel that much more nervous. I knit my brows together, confused by his question. "With Watson?"

"Stokes didn't tell you?" I ask, unable to mask the annoyance in my voice.

His tongue flickers over his bottom lip, the corners of his mouth ghosting a grin, "He told me, but I don't trust Stokes."

"And you trust me?" I quip, knowing I'm pushing him. Cole has brought me into his circle and given me a home, and I've returned that by bringing Jeremy practically to their doorstep.

He shakes his head, "I do. I probably shouldn't, but I do." Cole cemented with a nod, "what happened?"

I study him for a moment, "Watson pulled Holden and I over, provoked Holden until he snapped and then cuffed him."

"That's all?" Cole pushes.

"He used Becca to get under his skin." I don't miss the tick in his jaw at the mention of her name. Something in his eyes turns dark and cold as I watch him. "I don't think he thought I could hear them but Watson made it sound like he was responsible for Becca's death."

Cole's silent for a moment and I figure that he's going over every scenario in his head, worst case, best case, either way I have a feeling none of them are good. Watson terrifies me, he has the same terrifying look in his eyes that Jeremy has. Laced with cruelty and a need for control. Even when he stopped me on the street, I could feel myself recoil away from him like he had a black cloud over his head that swarmed and swirled with darkness.

"He knows my real name, Cole." Knowing what the implications of that meant, his eyes focused back on me, "if he sees the news feed…" I pause, "There's nothing stopping him from bringing Jeremy to your doorstep."

"Watson is smart," Cole counters, "he won't show his cards right away."

"That's what scares me the most." He pushes himself up off the table, his hands resting firmly on my shoulders. Cole dips his head to catch my eyes and as our gazes meet, the darkness I see in them is replaced by something softer. He tugs me to his chest, his arms wrapping around me. I know he won't promise everything will be okay. We both know he can't guarantee it.

"The club will protect you." He says flatly and with about as much reassurance as he can muster.

I take it even if the words are hard to believe. Cole doesn't owe me anything, neither does the club. Believing that a group of men that I don't know will protect me sits uncomfortably in my chest.

"I'll protect you." He finally says as if he can feel my uneasiness seep into his chest. "Go find Holden, tell him what you told me, and bring him back."

Something else that sits heavy on my chest. I'm not entirely sure that he'll believe me or want to hear me out. I lied to him when he told me his darkest secrets, took me to a place that meant more to him than anything and gave me every chance to come clean… and I didn't. I hid behind the full truth of what happened to me and gave him just enough that it would quell that curious look he gets whenever his eyes find mine. He doesn't have to give me anything more now. If he wants out of whatever this is between us I just gave him the chance.

"I'll do my best," I whisper against him. He pulls back from me, giving me a weak knowing smile.

He walks me out into the main room of the clubhouse. Scottie and Dex are standing near the bar, speaking in hushed tones. Scottie's normal smile falters as soon as his dark eyes land on me. He tosses a quick nod in my direction and Dex turns to look at me. It's then that I know Scottie knows everything now, too.

"We'll talk later," Cole says leaning into me before leaving me to head out the door.

I make my way over to the men. I swallow the nervousness building in me, forcing the courage I have remaining to drag me across the room.

"You ready?" Dex asks, but my eyes are still on Scottie.

"You know?" I ask, ignoring Dex's question which from the huff he lets out, makes me acutely aware that he isn't used to it.

Scottie nods, his hand resting on my shoulder tentatively but when I don't flinch away from him as he probably expects me to he squeezes my shoulder gently. "We'll make this fucker pay if he comes after you."

I suck in a breath as my gaze flickers over to Dex, "I'm hoping he won't." I say, "but that's a child's wish."

"It's not a child's wish to want to be safe," Scottie says with a sad expression. Tears start prickling in my eyes again. Not because I'm sad or angry anymore. But he's looking at me the way someone who cares would and it's then that I realize I've only ever seen that look twice outside of the men in the club. Once with my father and the second when Maria helped me leave.

I should call Maria. By now the news junket has spread across the country; it's only a matter of time before I would get a slew of text messages and phone calls.

"We should get going," Dex suggests nodding his head towards the exit, dark eyes flickering back to Scottie, "keep your phone on, if O'Neil and Falcone need back up, you call me."

Dex steps back, giving me room to move towards the door before following behind me. My heart hammers against my chest the closer I get to the outside. What if he doesn't believe me? What if everything he promised last night *and* again this morning is just a ploy to get me in bed with him? But he had me in bed and stopped me from going faster than I knew I was ready for. Deep down I know that his promises aren't empty.

"Stop second guessing him," Dex mumbles as he holds the door open for me, "Nash is a lot of things, stubborn-headed, but not stupid."

I peer back at him until his steps match my own and he's walking with me, "what do you mean?"

"I saw the way he looked at you," the tips of his fingers reach out, pointing to his bike, "a man like Nash doesn't look at women like that very often. Whatever happened last night changed him."

I shake my head with a laugh, "I don't know if I–"

"Trust me sweetheart, I've seen him with the Lunas around the club. They ain't nothin' more than something for him to do." Dex lifts his helmet from the seat and holds it out for me, "and I sure as shit haven't seen him storm off the way he did with one of them either."

I slip the helmet over my hair before climbing onto the bike behind him, "you think I can get through to him?" I ask over his shoulder.

Dex peers back at me, "I think if anyone can it's you, just gotta find him first."

I nod as my hands grip the sides of his vest. I have to hold on to that hope that Holden will listen to me, just... give me the chance to tell him the truth because now, I'm not so sure if I can handle him not being around.

KADENCE

Riding with Dex feels different. His movements are swift, careful and cautious, whereas riding with Holden feels freeing. Up until Watson pulled us over, I had a moment of bliss with him. The anger that flows through me from my mother's constant betrayal, the worry that Jeremy will find me...all of it vanished in a fleeting moment of happiness. And as such is life, it was ripped from me at the hands of the man I fear the most.

Dex doesn't talk much to me on the drive. I'm fine with that. There isn't much else I can say that hasn't already been said and I can't bear another sad look from the men who have inadvertently sworn to protect me. Something I know I don't deserve.

"We're here," his voice booms over the sound of the engine as he pulls into a gravel parking lot.

I glance up at the flashing lights and neon sign that reads *Moon*. I can't help the chuckle as he cuts the engine and lets me climb off first. Of *course* the Hell Hounds have a strip club called Moon. It's a little on the nose, but I appreciate it.

He helps me unbuckle the helmet, setting it down on the seat as I take a few steps towards the door. Dex's fingers wrap around my elbow, stopping me from going any further as I turn to him.

"Marlowe should be in the back," he urges. "Find her first, don't go lookin' in any rooms."

My brows knit together. "Why?"

His hand drops to his side as the gravel crunches under his boots. "Because if you see something bad, I'm gonna have no choice but to drag you outta here and I really don't want to do that."

I stare at him for a moment before the realization hits me. He's talking about Holden, that if I see him with someone else, that it'll stir something up.

Dex nods at the apparent look on my face. "Go straight through, it's the last door on the left. I'll check the rooms and if—"

"If you find him, leave him," I say with conviction, squaring my shoulders.

It's his turn to furrow his brow as he stares back at me, "Kade..."

"Leave him Dex," I cement. "If this is the first place that he runs to... then he wasn't who I thought he was." It scares me how fast I've made the decision, but after everything, I need to find my worth, and it isn't in someone who runs from their problems into the arms of someone else.

"Then we'll both relish in the fact that we're wrong about him." He steps towards the doors, flicking his head towards the velvet paneled entry. "C'mon sweetheart."

I suck in a breath and nod, steeling myself for what I might or might not find. I follow him as he pushes through the door. The overwhelming stench of smoke, disinfectant, and overly floral perfume surrounds me as he leads me through the club. I recognize the blonde currently spinning around the center stage, her gaze landing on the two of us. Jane narrows her eyes when they focus on me before a vicious grin spreads across her lips. The nerves I forced down outside return as I cast my gaze forward, ignoring the laugh that bubbles through the club.

I feel the warmth of Dex's hand land on my back, "Ignore'm," he whispers before pointing down a long corridor. "That's where you'll find Marlowe. Ask her if she's seen Nash. If he's been here, she'll know."

I nod, trying my best to hear him over the music thumping around us. Dex nods once before moving down a second corridor, leaving me. I take another deep breath, pushing the nerves back down before making my way down the hallway. There are doors on either side and sounds that definitely prove the girls here are good.

I take another step before a door to my right opens, and a redhead stumbles out of the room, giggling and moving to wipe her mouth with dark-painted nails. I recognize this woman too. Our eyes meet as Layla shuts the door behind her, leaving whoever is in the room.

"What are *you* doing here?" She asks bitterly, straightening herself up.

"Just trying to find Marlowe," I say, attempting to move past the woman who had stumbled the same way into my apartment with Holden.

Layla lets out a venomous laugh. "Lookin' for a job? What? Cole already get tired of you being at the shop?"

I narrow my eyes at Layla. "No, he didn't. I'm looking for Marlowe and Holden."

That seems to pique her interest. Layla rolls her tongue over her bottom lip with a raised brow. "What do you want with Nash?"

"Why is that any of your business?" I fire back, again attempting to move past her just as Layla steps in front of me, "are you going to move?"

"I know where Nash is, but I don't think you'll like it very much." A wicked grin spreads across her lips as her eyes flit to the door. I follow her gaze, and a wave of nausea rolls over me. "What? You think you're special?" Layla spits with venom, "Nash is a man who has *needs* that—" she tilts her head, her eyes trailing down my body and back up to my gaze, "-clearly you can't meet."

"He's in there?" I ask, ignoring the jab. I have to know, it isn't something I want to believe is true but staring at Layla makes me second guess that.

Layla smirks. "Why don't you take that tiny little ass and march on outta here before you get hurt." Her arms cross over her chest, eyes raking over me again, "or you end up on the pole like the rest of us. Actually," she laughs as the music comes to a brief close, "if you want him then there's your ticket. Jane's set just ended. Hop on up, babydoll."

Anger begins to bubble in my chest the longer I stand outside the door and in front of a woman who is as vile as the words she's spewing. I know I should open the door and not trust a single word that Layla's saying. But a part of me can't. I can't face the fact that if Holden is on the other side of it, my heart will shatter. I should have never made those promises this morning.

She leans in, forcing me back slightly away from the smell of stale cigarettes and dick on Layla's breath, "He's not into scared little *good girls*. Go find someone else."

"Shut the fuck up Layla," Dex's voice booms from behind me, startling me out of my racing thoughts. He's *right* behind me, his face twisting in the anger that lurks beneath my own chest. Between the two of them the hallway feels crowded and slowly it closes in on me. I spin on my heel, pushing past the mass that is Dex, and bolt towards the door, hearing Layla's cackle echo after me.

"Kade!"

I ignore his call, pushing out of the front door into the hot sun that does nothing to soothe the tightening in my chest. This is it; I don't need confirmation or for him to come back now. I suck in the sweltering mid-day air, trying to force any amount of oxygen I can into my lungs.

The familiar sound of boots crunching behind me forces me to spin around again, kicking up dust as I do. Dex halts in front of me and I can only imagine how I look right now. Panicked, horrified, and disappointed, all rolled up into one furled look.

"Hey," his voice is softer than I've heard it before. "You can't believe anything that comes out of her mouth, okay?" Dex shakes his head. "Did you see Marlowe?"

I can only muster a quick shake of my head, the heat becoming unbearable with the crushing weight on my chest. He nods. "Holden's bike isn't here Kade, he's not here."

I toss him a pointed look. "You think he wouldn't hide his bike if he didn't want to be found?" I ask, the anger forcing itself out of me now. "Nothing is apparently a fucking secret in this town Dex, he's smarter than that."

He takes a step towards me, holding his hands in front of him as if he's trying to calm a rabid animal. Rightfully so, I feel like crawling out of my own skin at this point.

"All I'm sayin' is don't believe a bitch like Layla." His head tilts to catch my gaze. "She's got nothing better to do than suck dick and smoke."

A hollow laugh bubbles out of me, "that's exactly what I was worried about." I rake my fingers through my hair, gripping it at the root, and turn away from him to collect myself.

"If he wanted to hurt you, Kade, he'd make a show about being here."

I spin back around. "You can't be serious."

Dex shifts, pinning back his shoulders. "Deadly." He moves past me towards his own bike. "Let's check his house, if he's not there then you can go all thermonuclear on me, but for now, keep it under the surface."

I scoff as I follow him, ripping the helmet off the seat and shoving it over my hair. "Just take me back to the shop."

"No," Dex says firmly.

I turn to him, "No?" I ask with a raised brow. "What do you mean *no*?"

"You aren't giving up on him," he says, swinging his leg over his bike.

"Dex, just–"

He shakes his head. "Get your ass on the back of this bike. You aren't giving up on him yet, I won't let you." He raises a brow back at me when I refuse to move. "Get on the bike, Kadence, or I'll put you on it."

I roll my eyes. I'm a grown woman. There is no way– Dex starts to move off his bike, forcing me to take a step back. "Fine, Jesus," I mutter, climbing on behind him.

I hear him chuckle as I settle behind him again. "I'm glad you think this is funny."

"Oh, *mama*, you and Holden are more alike than you think."

I wonder what he means, but before I can ask, Dex starts his bike and peels out of the parking lot.

I start to recognize the area as he hits the highway, it looks like the route Holden took when we went to the bridge. It's not long until he makes a turn into a neighborhood I don't recognize and onto a side road. A small secluded home comes into view and, in front of it, a small travel trailer.

Dex kills the bike once again and climbs off, helping me in the uneven driveway. "This is his home?"

He lets out a breath, "it was Becca's home. It was the only thing left after..." Dex taps my helmet before tugging it gently off of my head. I move towards the house but his hand wraps around my forearm stopping me. "Nash won't be in there. He lives in the trailer and hasn't been in the house since she passed."

I knew the feeling. After the first night home from the hospital and the night I spent in the nursery, I couldn't bring myself to go back in there. Maria helped me pack the room and sell the furniture that took up the space. Every time I thought about going in there, I only felt anger and like I was a failure for what happened. Maria constantly reminded me that it wasn't my fault, but it did nothing to quiet the little voice in my head that screamed at me every time I passed the nursery door. My chest aches knowing that Holden has experienced the same.

"Hey, you comin'?" Dex asks. He had already made a few strides over to Holden's trailer while I was lost in thought. I take a deep breath and nod, not knowing what to expect.

"I don't see his bike, Dex, he's not here." I point out glancing around as we approach the door.

He looks down at me before knocking. "He sometimes parks his bike in the garage," Dex countered and I knew it was a lie only to make me feel better and to make me not lose hope that he ran home.

We wait for a few moments, listening for any sounds that might come from the inside of the trailer, but as Dex knocks again, the sound only bounces off of the emptiness inside. My shoulders slump. He isn't here and I'm still not entirely sure if he was at the club but after a third round of knocks I shake my head.

"Can we go back now?" I ask, the question coming out more pained than I wanted it to. Dex's gaze finds mine and reluctantly he nods.

"We'll find him." He reassures me by leading me back to his bike. Silence settles between us, uncomfortable and tight. I had been so sure before and now... now I don't know what to believe.

COLE

The warehouse is dark as usual when Trey and I pull up, the only noise around is the sound of our engines until we both shut off our bikes. I hate this place. Every time we come here, something gets even more fucked up than the last.

"Stokes's not even here yet," Trey sighs, climbing off his bike.

I shrug. "Probably waiting for us to arrive before he graces us with his presence."

Deep down, I'm grateful Stokes hasn't shown up yet. We need a break and something to hold over his head. Him not showing up to a meeting he called would give me the ammo to avoid him that much longer.

Trey nods. He's been suspiciously less chatty since we left the clubhouse, and even though I already know why, I enjoy the chatter. It keeps the nagging voice in my head at bay long enough for me to be able to think.

"You think Nash is good?" Trey asks, pulling open the metal door, the creak of it hard against my hearing.

"No," I say plainly. I know he's not. I've only seen that look in Holden's eyes twice and the first time, I lost my friend to grief and alcohol until recently.

Trey nods. "You wanna tell me why we're risking the club for this girl?"

"We aren't risking the club." It's a lie, and from the look Trey shoots me he knows it too.

"Right, so letting a random woman who apparently is now a fugitive and missing person live above the shop is not putting the club at risk?" He shakes his head. "Remind me, wasn't it you who said we keep our business in the inner circle? She's been here for a week, O'Neil and she already knows way too much about the shit we're in, more than any of the other Lunas that walk around the club."

I scoff. "If you think the Lunas don't know about the shit that happens at that table, you're clearly more oblivious than I thought." Trey never questions me unless warranted and even then I hate it. This is *my* club, *my* men. I have final say. "And since when do you question my decisions?" I ask, turning to my vice president.

"I'm only curious as to why Nash, you, and now Wolfe have a fascination with helping Kadence." He shrugs. "Especially after what happened to Becca."

My jaw clenches at her name. Becca is still a sore subject and Trey knows that. "I'm helping her *because* of what happened to Becca." Which isn't the total truth but Trey seems to believe me when he sighs. "If this asshole is truly after Kade then... we should help her."

"But why?" Trey questions again.

Why did I want to help her so bad? I could have treated her like any other customer, but instead I treat her like a bird with a broken wing and coddle her. Offered her a job, a place to stay. All because in those green eyes, I saw a familiar face. Scared, worried and terrified of the world around her.

"Look." Trey straightens himself. "I know you couldn't save Becca,"

"Falcone–" I growl in warning.

"No, Cole, you couldn't save her. None of us could. But I figured dragging some innocent chick into our shit would be the last thing that you'd do. You can't save them all."

I lunge at him, my hands fisting around the collar of his cut as I shove him against the closest wall. My chest heaves with the anger I'm failing more and more to keep hidden.

"I will rip that patch off your leather if you mention her name again." I seethe. My eyes flicker between Trey's wide, dark eyes. "I don't have to explain myself. You're my VP, but this is still my club."

The air between us becomes thick as Trey shoves me backward. I can't punch two members in two days but my fists clench at my side as I stare at my friend.

"Trouble in paradise?" Stokes' voice echoes through the warehouse as he crawls out of whatever darker corner he was hiding in, Watson on his heels.

"Shit," Trey mutters.

"Where's your lap dog?" Watson hisses. "Better not be hiding somewhere."

I chuckle, tugging on the ends of my vest to right myself, "Call Wolfe staying behind a peace offering."

Stokes narrows his eyes at me. "And Nash? I was hoping to be re-acquainted with him. It's been too long." He sneers. "I haven't seen him since--" Stokes pauses, alluding to Becca's death.

"Since you shoved him in an interrogation room and accused him of murdering his sister?" Trey questions.

Sheriff laughs. "Oh, that was fun."

"What the hell do you want, Stokes?" I snap. My hands clench at my side again when what Kadence told me earlier returns to the forefront of my mind. If Watson or Stokes had anything to do with Becca, I'll kill them both.

Stokes leans back on his heels, turning his chin up as his hand leisurely falls over the butt of his gun. I force back a grin. The fucker is really trying his hardest to intimidate me. It's going to take a lot more than a weak gesture to scare me.

"I want Wolfe," he states, so matter-of-factly that Trey shoots me a look. "And in exchange," he turns and begins pacing in front of them. A slow walk that only grates on my patience. "I'll leave your boys alone at the drop points."

"Why the fuck would I give you a club member?" I hiss.

"Because he put two of my officers in the hospital. Richards has a fucking breathing tube down his throat because your guy has a taste for blood." Stokes tilts his head. "I can't look weak to our town, O'Neil. You know what happens if they think I'm weak."

I narrow my eyes.

"The town will replace me," Watson stands up straight as if he's a fucking candidate, "and all of your lovely and seemingly above-board business ventures fall to pieces."

Trey turns his back to them, taking a step in front of me. My eyes never leave Stokes' even as Trey starts to speak.

"We can't risk it, man," Trey mutters, low enough only for me to hear.

My brows furrow at my VP, who so easily seems to be giving in to this asshole. "I'm not giving him a fucking club member, Falcone. Have you lost your damn mind?"

"Wolfe can handle it and we need a break. A distraction." He shifts.

"No," I cement. I wasn't giving up a fucking member for the sake of a few brief moments to breathe. "It's not happening." Trey sighs as he turns back around and a wicked grin spreads across Watson's face.

"So," Stokes' smug smile creeps across his features. "What's it gonna be?"

KADENCE

"**O**h come on, you can't possibly still be mad at Cole?" Blake asks, shoving another disco ball dress into her arms. "Stokes let Dex go. Like six hours later."

"That's not the point, Blake." I shake my head, hanging up the dress Blake has so graciously shoved at me. We've been moving from one boutique to the next trying to find something for me to wear on this 'girl's night' that she insists on us having. Something about me spending way too much time with the men.

Blake shakes her head and runs her hands over the rack once more, finding a few more dresses that I'm sure she is going to hurl at me. "Dex knew what was going to happen, Cole called him Kade, you can't be mad at him when Dex agreed to it."

I sigh. Blake's right. As soon as we left Holden's, Dex had gotten a phone call from Cole asking where we were. It was only after Dex told him that the hard-set line in his jaw had reformed as he stared off into space listening to Cole's instructions. Twenty minutes later Cole, Trey, and Watson pulled us over. I was fuming, not only at the fact that Holden was still missing but that Cole had freely given up Dex.

"It's for the best, Kade. I have to keep Stokes happy." Cole ushered me to his bike as I turned to watch Dex get shoved into the back of Watson's patrol car. "He'll be fine."

As soon as we had returned to the shop I went straight to the office, pissed off, confused, and in need of something to distract me from everything happening. Paperwork was easy for that. Working through the numbers and scheduling repairs. It was something I could do in my sleep. Scottie and Wyatt checked on me throughout the rest of that day but when it came time for them to convene around the table, I went to bed. Even with how exhausted I was, I stared at the ceiling for hours. Running through every worst case scenario, Holden hating me, Jeremy finding me—hurting me or any one of the guys.

I don't want that. I want fucking peace, but it's my own fault for not being honest the first time Cole asked me.

A little while later, I heard the sound of a bike pull into the parking lot. I had sprung from the bed to peek out of the window in hopes that Holden had come back but instead was met with Dex and Cole arguing outside the clubhouse.

"What about this one?" Blake's voice cuts through my mindless shopping as I turn to my new-found friend. She holds up a lilac satin dress. I have to admit, for a woman who mainly wears torn black denim and black tank tops and spends most of her day covered in motor grease, Blake has a sense of style.

I run my fingers along the hem of the dress, the satin is soft between my fingertips and I really do like the color.

"I don't know Blake..." I don't want to go back to *Moon*, let alone have a girl's night there, but she assures me that both Layla and Jane will be off that night. It's also the only place that Cole trusts us to go without bringing half the club with us. Even though I have a suspicion that we'd be around club members anyway.

"You're getting it," Blake shoves the dress in my hands, "because if you don't get it, I'm going to get it for you anyway."

"You know you really sound like Cole sometimes," I tease, folding the dress carefully over my arm.

Blake scrunches up her nose and narrows her eyes. "That was just mean."

I laugh as we begin moving through the store before going to purchase our items. I appreciate the time I'm getting to spend with her. She's a breath of fresh air compared to the testosterone-filled shop even if our outings were because Cole asked Blake to keep an eye on me.

"What the hell is he doing here?" Blake asks suddenly as we head towards the exit of the shop. I glance up from my bags, seeing Dex leaning against his bike just outside.

"That's a good question," I mutter, pushing the door open. Dark eyes find mine as I raise a brow at him. He raises one back and straightens himself, stepping up onto the sidewalk. "Did you come to find a dress too, Wolfe?"

Dex shakes his head, "Skirts aren't really my style kiddo." He grins folding his arms across his chest, "Sorry to cut the shopping spree short ladies, but I have something I want to show Kade."

I tilt my head regarding him with narrowed eyes.

"That seems very suspicious, Wolfe." Blake laughs as he shoots her a look. "Alright, fine. Here," Blake reaches for the bags I'm holding, "I'll take this back to the shop." I reluctantly hold onto them and glance back over to Dex.

"I don't have an option here, do I?" I ask.

He shrugs, "'fraid not, *mama*."

I let out a sigh and hand the bags to Blake. "Thank you, I'll see you later?"

Blake nods with a grin, "You bet your ass." She turns to Dex, pointing at him with narrowed eyes. "Have her back no later than six. We still have to get ready for tonight."

He chuckles and nods. "You got it, Porter."

With a satisfied grin, Blake spins on her heel and heads back towards the shop. I watch her for a moment before turning back to Dex, who's already on his bike leaning against the handlebars and holding out his helmet for me. I take a few steps towards him, glancing down at the helmet before looking back up at him.

"Do I even want to know what you have planned?"

"You'll find out." A mischievous grin spreads across his face as he tilts his head when I still haven't reached for the helmet. "C'mon, Andrews, live a little."

I shake my head unsure of what he has in store for me but still take the helmet and slip it over my head before climbing on his bike behind him. He waits till I'm situated before pulling away from the curb and heading to a part of the town I haven't been to yet. Run-down buildings and a train track separate us from the bustling sidewalks of Pine River.

Other than Blake, Dex has been around the shop more than I figure he has in the past. Even Scottie seemed shocked that he was doing 'actual work'. It makes me laugh, but every time I go quiet in the office or stare just a little bit too long at the air conditioning unit when it randomly goes out, he's there bringing me coffee or asking for something mundane that would pull me from my thoughts.

I feel fine being around people, around the guys and Blake, but those moments of quiet in the shop and at night are the hardest. The look on Holden's face just before he left haunts me. The sadness, the anger that had weaved through the speckles of silver and green in his eyes, tears me up. All I want is to see him, even if he hates me I have to know if Layla is lying and I need to know whether the promises we made are true.

Dex parks outside of a small building, the windows are boarded up but it still looks as if someone has been caring for the building. He climbs off the bike before helping me off. I slide the helmet from over my hair and set it on the handlebars.

"What are we doing here?" I ask following him to the door. He doesn't respond, only pushes the door open for me. The room is open with workout mats covering the floor. In one corner there are a few weight benches and in the other a punching bag hanging from the corner of the ceiling. I turn to him with a raised brow.

"You brought me to a gym?"

Dex locks the door behind us "Yeah."

I hold my arms out to my sides, shaking my head. "Why?"

He moves past me without a word and stops in front of a row of lockers. Dex opens the doors, pulling out a set of boxing gloves and a set of padded gloves. I huff, frustrated that once again he's ignoring me.

"Dex!" I all but yell. "Why are we here?"

Turning to look at me over his shoulder his eyes trail my features, narrowing for a split second before turning back to close the door to the locker he had opened. "Because that temper of yours is short-fused right now, Andrews, and it doesn't hurt to learn how to defend your-self."

I cock my head to the side. *Temper? What fucking temper?*

"I know how to defend myself," I say plainly, pinning back my shoulders and crossing my arms over my chest.

He turns to me, holding a roll of tape in his hands. "Humor me?"

I stare at him for a moment before dropping my hands and holding them out for him. I tried to take a few boxing classes back in Florida but the moment Jeremy found out I was forbidden from taking them again. He canceled my membership, which I didn't find out till I had tried to attend the next class. I still remember the embarrassment that flooded me as the coach walked me to the front door.

Dex takes my right hand and begins wrapping it in tape before moving to my left. "You might be fooling Blake and Cole, Kadence, but you're angry."

"I'm not angry," I mutter as he helps me slide the gloves over my hands. He glances up at me through thick dark lashes and shakes his head.

"Prove it." He challenges. "You've been sulking around the shop for a week. You haven't said more than a few words to Cole. *Prove it.*" Dex finishes tightening the gloves around my wrist before slipping the padded gloves over his hands and moves to step into the middle of the mats.

"Dex–" I stare, turning to him.

"What do you have to lose Kade? A wasted hour? C'mon, hit me." He grins.

"I'm not doing this."

"Why not?" He pushes as I try to pull the gloves off and miserably fail with the lack of my fingers.

"Because I'm not angry!" I snap at him, the frustration finally spilling from me.

His brows shoot upward towards his hairline as he cocks his head to the side again, "Then. Prove. It."

I give up on tearing off the gloves, wanting to prove my point. I'm not angry. At least I don't feel angry. Frustrated? Sad? Yeah. I gave up on anger a long time ago and learned to shove it deep down because it's easier than taking it out on people who don't deserve my anger.

I position myself in front of Dex and hold up my hands in front of me. He watches as I pose myself and shakes his head, tapping my elbows with the pads. "Tuck'em in and protect your chin." I adjust myself and glance up at him, waiting for more instructions but he only nods. "Now hit me."

He holds up the pads in front of him. I focus on them before laying a punch onto the one covering his right hand. My eyes flicker to his as he nods in approval.

"Again," he urges. I let out a huff and swung again, hitting his left hand. Dex stands straight again. "Turn your hips a little more–there you go, again."

I suck in a breath before swinging, landing one on his right hand letting out the breath I'm holding. He shifts on his feet before shaking out his hand with a pointed look.

"You can do better than that, Andrews," he taunts.

"I'm not going to hurt you, Dex," I huff, pushing the hair that has fallen into my face behind my ear with the glove, "this is pointless."

He chuckles. "Man, you are stubborn as hell, aren't ya?" Slowly he pulls the pads off of his hands and tossed them to the mat. "You wanna tell me why you're hellbent on ignoring O'Neil?"

I stare at him before shaking my head. "How can you not be pissed off at him?"

"Why are you?" He counters as he walks over to the punching bag in the corner of the room. Dex turns and crosses his arms over his chest.

I follow him and stand on one side of the bag as he rounds the other side, holding it in place with his hands. "He gave you up, Dex, isn't that some huge no-no for you guys?"

"A huge–?" He tilts his head back and laughs. "We can handle ourselves, Kadence. Stokes needed to showboat for the town to keep us in his good graces. I'm lucky I'm not sittin' in a cell over in Stockton right now," he nods towards the punching bag. "Now hit."

I glare at him for a moment before readying myself. "And what? You all just jump and don't ask how high?" I hit the bag once and then twice, shaking out my hand as he steadies the bag.

"It's the way things are." He confirms though the words are strained and through gritted teeth. I glance around the bag at him but he pushes on it, letting it swing towards me until I stop it with the fists of the gloves. "Again."

I let out a low growl and ready myself again. Clearly I'm not going to get an answer other than that. I hate the fact that they're tied to assholes like Stokes just as I'm tied to Jeremy. It seems like the people I'm *supposed* to run to are the ones to be scared of the most. Every cop I see sends a chill up my spine as if Jeremy's hold on the Sheriff's office in Florida is larger than I could have imagined. That one would stop me and shuck me in the back of a van and take me back to hell and now, with the new junket still making its rounds, the worry is further rooted into my nerves.

I throw a few more punches at the bag, the frustration climbing its way to the surface again as I focus on duct-taped 'x' in the middle of the bag.

"Why are you angry, Kadence?" He says from beside the bag, still holding it for me as I punch it over and over.

"I'm not angry," I bite again for the third time, "stop asking me."

"You are. You're angry." He shoves the bag at me again. "Why are you angry?"

A breath releases from my lips as I catch it and shove it back at him. "I'm not angry!"

Dex steadies the bag and nods at it again, silently urging me to keep going. At this point I should stop but it feels good, the release. I hit it again and he shoves it back at me.

"Why are you angry?" He repeats, though this time I miss stopping it as it smacks into my side, forcing me back a step. I glare at him with a snarl before moving to hit it again, punch after punch, I suck in breaths and let them out quickly. Now he's pissing me off.

"I'm not fucking angry."

Dex shoves the bag at me again, this time knocking me on my ass as it hits me.

"What the fuck is your problem!" I yell, shuffling to my feet with the stupid gloves still on my hands. He stares at me, not moving. "Fine!"

I march toward the bag and punch it again until my hands start to hurt. "I'm pissed off. I'm fucking angry that I tried to get away, I ran. I gave up my *entire* life in Florida to start new and somehow, even three thousand *fucking* miles away, Jeremy is still haunting me. Still trying to dig his fucking claws into me so I can't live a normal fucking life!" I stumble back when the pain starts to climb up my wrists, even more angry now that the tears have started to sting the corners of my eyes. *Fucking traitors,* I think as I wipe my upper lip clear of the sweat that's formed there.

"I'm angry he left," I finally say. "I'm angry that I didn't just tell him on the bridge that night. He asked. He gave me every fucking opportunity to tell him the truth and I didn't."

"Why?" Dex's voice finally cuts through the swirling tornado of thoughts that swarms me. I don't miss the flash of surprise in his eyes at the mention of the bridge and it only makes my heart ache that much more.

My gaze finds his, "because I was scared that he wouldn't want me." Dex takes a step towards me, shaking his head, but I hold up my hand to stop him. "I didn't want to be looked at the way you, Trey, and Cole looked at me when I told you what happened."

I let out a breath, that familiar tightening in my chest returning. I don't want to break down in front of him, I don't want to break down in front of *any of them* but yet, he's right. I know that there's still anger flowing through my veins like a sick poison.

I begin ripping at the gloves again, they feel suffocating, and I can feel the tremors start to worry my hands. He steps forward again, this time holding out his hand for me to give him. I hold them out so he can pull the gloves off of me. As soon as they hit the ground I spin from him, shaking out my hands.

"Kadence," Dex follows me as I work my way toward the door, remembering it's locked, I stop. "You're angry for good reason," he says after a moment of silence.

I turn to him. "I don't want to feel like this, Dex. I don't want to feel..." I pause, taking a deep breath, "weak."

He makes his way to me, his hands resting on my shoulders. "*Mama*, you aren't weak. If anything, you're probably stronger than half the club."

I shake my head as if his words don't carry any weight. He's only trying to make me feel better.

"Hey," Dex dips his head to catch my gaze. "You did what you had to do to survive. That don't make you weak. You could have run the moment that news report came out. Could've lied your way through it, and you didn't." His tongue runs over his bottom lip as his eyes search my features. It's difficult trying to keep the tears from falling under the weight of his gaze. "You know what you did instead? You stared at three men you didn't owe an explanation to and spoke your truth." He taps my nose with his index finger. "You are the *furthest* thing from weak, Kadence."

My eyes flicker between his own, searching for any sort of deception or lie but I find none.

"Use the anger you have to take back your life and quit being angry at O'Neil for club business, yeah?" His hands drop from my shoulders as he takes a step back. "The man feels like an asshole already for having to do it. He doesn't need you giving him the cold shoulder, even though he probably deserves it." He chuckles. "Let me handle that."

I stare at him. The shakiness in my hands has disappeared as he speaks. "Thank you." My voice is a whisper but he doesn't seem to mind it.

HOLDEN

It only takes me four days to get from Pine River to Huntsville. I fucking hate Alabama. It's hot and muggy and if I have to see another sign about *Jesus saving me*... I'm going to crash my bike on purpose. Aim straight for the guardrail. There's nothing about me that Jesus or any other deity would be able to save. I realized a long time ago that I'm doomed for hell.

Still, a thirty-six-hour ride doesn't stop me from needing to get the information I seek. I have to know and not from her. I want physical proof of what this dick is spewing across the country. Every shitty motel I stay at plays the same clips of that asshole's interview over and over again. Every time I watch the fake concern pass over his features my stomach churns because even Jeremy can't hide the dead look behind his eyes.

I've replayed the night I met Kadence over in my head every night since I left. How she cowered, how jumpy she is whenever someone other than Cole enters a room. It was like watching a caged animal at Marlowe's dinner, one that, for some reason, I wanted to corner and calm down. She had no reason to be scared and yet, being in a room—at a table full of people who she didn't know - was probably terrifying. I don't regret kissing her. I don't even regret the words I promised her.

But I have to know the truth, and right now, I can't trust anyone. Not even her.

I called Fisher two days into my ride and gave him a heads-up that I was coming. Fisher laughed and said he'll have a bottle waiting for me and hung up. I've been standing outside his house for twenty minutes debating whether this will be even worth it. Deep down, I know it is. I can't sleep without seeing her face; she's tormenting me from halfway across the country.

The front door swings open as Fisher takes a step out onto his porch, holding his glock in one hand. I raise a brow as I trail over the old man. His beard is thicker than the last time I saw him, though he's still suspicious as ever.

"Nash." He regards me before glancing up and down the street. "Almost didn't recognize ya with that mop on your head."

I chuckle and run my fingers through the long hair, tucking it back behind my ear. I really need to cut it. "That homeless look suits you well, Hank."

Fisher shifts on his feet, eyebrows raising as he relaxes the arm holding the gun. I make my way to the porch taking the steps slowly as I glance up at my friend. "You got mirrors in California?"

He chortles. "Get in here, you're letting the cool air out."

I shake my head as I follow Hank inside. He sets the gun down on the table before turning to me as I make sure the door clicks shut behind me. "You didn't drive this far to talk about my looks, Nash. What do you want to know?"

"I need all of the information you found on Kadence."

KADENCE

I stare at myself in the full-length mirror in Blake's room. The lilac dress hangs off my body like a dream. I've never worn anything like this before. The straps dig into my shoulders but not enough that it's uncomfortable and the slit that allows me to walk ends just high enough on my thigh that nothing will be exposed. I can't help but think of what Jeremy would say if he saw me like this, the slew of insults that would have spewed from his lips as he looked upon me in disgust. I run my fingers through my hair, combing out the dark curls that after fussing with for so long, I decide to keep down.

It's hard. Seeing myself like this. Dolled up. There's a ball of guilt that sits in my stomach for how I look. I actually think I look good, gorgeous even, and Blake reminds me every two seconds that I look *out of this world* as she puts it. But still, I can't help feeling like I don't deserve this. Don't deserve the happiness that tonight is meant to bring when Holden is still out there without the truth.

"You look beautiful."

I spin around, almost toppling over before catching myself on Blake's dresser. Cole stands in the doorway of the room, leaning against the frame with his arms folded over his chest. His eyes are glued to mine as I look up at him. I'd finally stopped giving him the cold shoulder after my session with Dex and things between us have been a little less tense.

"Thank you," I sigh, turning back to the mirror. "I'm not used to feeling like this…" I laugh softly. Cole moves behind me in the mirror.

"Like what?"

I pause, my eyes rake over my body in the mirror. The black combat boots I insist on wearing because heels are completely out of the question make me taller, but he still towers over me. "Beautiful."

Cole rests his hands on my shoulders, turning me to him. "You are though, Kadence." His brows furrow for a moment as our eyes meet again. He tilts his head. "Did he tell you that you weren't?"

I suck in a breath, dropping my gaze from his knowing that 'he' means Jeremy. I feel his finger under my chin, lifting my eyes back to his.

"He lied." Cole's eyes search mine. The words come out firm and hardened as if he's etching them into stone.

I study him, looking for any deception in his eyes. Anything that would tell me he's just saying this to make me feel better, but I find nothing. A smile grows on his lips, it's not his usual Cole grin but it's something and there's still this weird wall standing between us. He taps my chin with his knuckle before taking a step back.

"C'mon, Blake and Dex are waiting and I can't leave those two alone for long periods of time."

I laugh and pick my leather jacket up from the bed. "Something tells me it's not because of Dex."

He slings his arm over my shoulder as he leads me back to the center of the clubhouse. "No, it definitely isn't."

We make our way into the common room. Blake's already badgering Dex, who's doing his best to ignore her. His head turns in our direction and his eyes rake down my body and back up to my eyes. A smile spreads across his lips as Blake follows his eyeline.

"See!" Blake grins running up to me. "Told you that you clean up good, Andrews." She playfully nudges my side as Dex approaches us.

"That she does," Dex drawls.

Cole stands up a little straighter, clapping his hand over Dex's shoulder. "You'll keep an eye on them tonight?"

"I thought this was a girl's night?" I ask with a raised brow.

Dex grins down at me, his tongue flicking over his bottom lip. "It is."

Blake wraps her arm around my waist, leading me towards the door. "Marlowe won't be there tonight, and judging how your last encounter with Layla went...it's probably a good thing." I look over my shoulder to the men as they speak in hushed tones.

"He'll probably end up just sitting at the bar with his ever watchful eyes, it'll be fine." She reassures me.

I nod, slipping out of Blake's grasp, and shrug on my jacket. It doesn't bother me that Dex is coming. I was just curious. Spending the night babysitting us is probably the last thing he wants to do and knowing that he'll be there in case something happens is comforting but it feels like another reminder that I can't protect myself and that ball of grief in my stomach rolls.

When we finally reach Moon, the parking lot is already littered with a few cars and I can hear the music booming against the walls. My gut wrenches. I really, really hope that neither Layla nor Jane are here, but without Marlowe here, it's unlikely that would be the case.

The three of us climb from the tow truck and head inside.

Dex settles us into a booth in the corner, one that gives us enough room to dance after Blake insists on it and one that he can see from his perch at the bar as well after bringing us a few drinks to get us started.

I down my first one in the hope that it will calm my nerves and settle the uneasiness in my chest. *I can do this.* I can have one night where I can be happy and enjoy my time with Blake. I can't remember the last time that I drank, it's been months since my last one so it doesn't take long for it to go to my head and make my cheeks feel warm.

Music blares around us as Blake pulls me up to dance, and after one song bleeds into another, I feel myself smiling and laughing at the stupid moves Blake does to get me to dance. Dex refills our drinks once more and again I down it as Blake watches.

"You sure you're okay?" Blake asks over the music, her eyes tracking the empty glass as I set it back down. "Those are meant to be sipped on." Her brows furrow in worry. I shake my head.

"I'm fine." I smile at her, wrapping my arms around her neck as I sway with her. "Thank you!"

Blake pulls back as we move. "For what?"

"For wanting to be a friend, for caring." I lean into her, wanting to make sure she hears the words. Blake freezes for a moment before her arms wrap around my waist and she pulls me into a hug.

We pull back from each other and she rests her hands on either side of my face. "We all care about you, Kadence. We won't let anything happen to you." Dark eyes search mine. Blake's normally bubbly personality has turned to stone as she says the words. "And we will *find* Holden."

The pit in my stomach grows as Blake stares at me. I don't want them to get hurt protecting me. I'm not sure that's a promise I can make to them.

Things have been quiet over the last week. Watson has left us alone and Cole hasn't heard from Stokes. I turned my phone off after an hour-long conversation with Maria when she saw the news piece. It was her suggestion. She knows just as well as I do how conniving Jeremy can be and if he hasn't tracked my phone already it's probably on his list of ways to torment me.

I still have the urge to continue looking over my shoulder every time I'm not around Cole or Dex. I trust Blake, but if Jeremy finds us, I'm not sure even Blake would be able to fend him off.

I give her a small smile, my hands coming to rest over hers. I lean in and press a kiss on her cheek. "I don't deserve you Porter."

Blake smiles back before dropping her hands. My head starts to feel dizzy as I try to hide the guilt riddling my insides. I feel that familiar weight on my chest start to get heavier the longer I watch her and it doesn't help that I can feel Dex's gaze on us.

"I need water." I huff out a laugh, stepping back from Blake.

"I'll come with you!"

I shake my head. "No, stay and dance. I'll be right back!"

Blake's brows furrow again but I give her a reassuring smile and step back from her before turning and heading to the bar.

I suck in a deep breath, my eyes squeezing shut for a moment as I attempt to gather myself. *You can do this. You're stronger than this.* I try to remind myself.

I settle at the bar next to Dex. He's leaning against it, a beer in hand as he watches me. I raise my hand to the barmaid and ask for water. He leans closer not saying anything but I can feel his questioning gaze on me.

"I'm fine," I mutter, glancing over at him.

He grins, "Yeah. You look it." Dex lifts the bottle to his lips taking a swig.

"Why are you here Dex?" I ask, turning to him as the water appears in front of me. "Blake doesn't need babysitting and neither do I."

A thick brow raises as he studies me. "I'm not here to watch either of you." He takes another swig before turning towards me. "Men here tend to get grabby." Dex tilts his head. "Do you understand what I'm sayin'?"

I stare at him for a moment. "So you're here to watch everyone else?"

"I'm here to make sure the others know who not to put their hands on."

I nod and pick up the water to take a sip. The drink does nothing to ease the fuzziness in my brain and here I am once again questioning the person who's trying to protect me. "I'm sorry."

Dex shrugs. "You have every right to be jumpy, Andrews."

The hair on my neck stands up at the same time a chill runs down my spine. I glance around the bar quickly, feeling like I'm being watched. I know it's not Blake. She's busy dancing, whooping, and hollering at a girl on the pole I don't recognize. Dex lifts his hand and brushes the strands of hair from my shoulder. My body freezes for a moment, unsure how to take such an intimate gesture but as he leans into me I know it's only so he could speak freely to my ear.

"You have to start learnin' to trust me, kiddo."

He pulls back with a smile that quickly fades as his eyes flicker to something behind me. He stands up straight, setting his bottle down on the bar top. "Well, this night just got interesting."

I furrow my brows and turn to see what he's looking at. My heart stops as soon as I do and the ball in my stomach rolls again as a pair of blue eyes bore into me.

Even with the loud music I can hear the heaviness of his boots as he marches towards us. His hands have balled into fists at his sides and his scruff is longer than the last time I saw him. Dark strands of chestnut hair are soaked and stuck to his cheeks. At some point between us arriving and now it must have started raining, making the one man my chest has been aching for look that much more menacing.

"Holden," I whisper as he reaches us.

KADENCE

"**G**ood to see you, Nash." Dex mocks from behind me.

"I leave and you think that gives you a pass to push up on Kadence?" Holden's voice is low but booms between us. His eyes are dark with anger but he's *here*, in front of me, and that's all I care about.

Dex's laugh echoes against the music. "I think you need to take a breath, Nash."

"Oh I've done plenty of breathin'," he rumbles. "You wanna explain to me why you brought her here?"

I shake my head pulling myself from the daze his presence has put me in. I raise my hand to press to his chest but stop myself. "I'm here with Blake." I try, but he shoots me a look that forces the words to get stuck in my throat.

Holden shakes his head and takes a step backward, glancing between the two of us. "I know what I saw."

I raise a brow. "And what was that?"

"Him touching you!" His hand flies up, making me flinch back. I don't mean to but the movement is so quick that it would have startled anyone. Holden's eyes go wide, watching me as Dex takes a step forward.

"Hey! Take a breath, Nash, this isn't what it looks like," Dex booms.

Holden lets out a breathy, hollow laugh. "Un-fucking-believable. I hope you both will be *very* happy," he mutters before turning to the exit.

I shake my head. "Holden!" I yell after him but he's already marching away from us. I follow him as he pushes the front door of Moon open, making a beeline straight for his bike. The heavy pour of rain makes it hard to see as I burst through the door behind him. "Holden! Stop!"

He turns back to me as he climbs onto his bike. "Go back inside, Kadence."

I stop in front of his bike, shaking my head. "No."

Holden stands up. "Go!"

I stomp my foot. Actually stomp my foot like a child and shake my head. "I'm not going anywhere till you let me explain!"

He grabs a hold of his handlebars and leans over the front of his bike. "Explain what? That you've been getting cozy with *Wolfe* in my absence? Hmm? What lies are you about to tell me now?" He bites, venom in his voice.

"I never lied to you!" I yell back at him.

The door to the club slams behind me and I don't have to look back to know that it's Dex's boots crunching in the gravel. I never take my gaze off of Holden. *My* Holden who came back. *My* Holden who I'm about to lose, again.

"No," he agrees and sits back down on the seat of the bike. " You just didn't tell me the truth. Do you know how hard it was telling you everything? To be honest, for the first goddamn time in my life with someone?"

I suck in a breath as his words stab my chest in dagger form. His bike roars to life. The sound is more ominous than it ever has been before. "Holden, I wanted to tell you everything I just–"

Blue eyes peer back up at me, his gaze still angry as he stares at me through wet lashes, "Move," he warns over the engine.

"Where are you going to go?" I ask, my voice turning hoarse trying to yell over the rainfall and the sound of his bike, knowing how pitiful I sound but I don't care.

"Go. Back. Inside," he warns again. I round the bike, coming to his side.

"Let me explain."

He shakes his head, his gaze flickering to Dex, who's inched his way closer to us. "You had your chance to explain. You actually had a few chances."

I take a step back, stunned by his words. "I was protecting myself."

"Good luck with that." Holden kicks his bike stand and twists his hand, lurching the bike forward. His wheels spin in the mud and gravel before he takes off onto the road.

"God Damnit!" I scream watching him leave.

Dex rests a hand on my shoulder but I pull from his grasp, spinning to face him. I realize I'm drenched, my hair sticks to my face and the dress clings to my body but it doesn't stop me from thrusting my hand out at him.

"Give me the keys to the truck."

He shakes his head. "You've been drinking, Kade."

"I am not letting him run away *again*." I bite through a clenched jaw, forcing the tears stinging my eyes to stay put. "Give me the keys."

Dex tilts his head back and sighs just before I press my hands to his chest and shove him. "You told me not to give up on him! You told me to trust him! Give me the keys, Dex!"

He looks shocked at my attempt to move him, but my words must strike a cord because within a moment he's digging the keys from his pocket and holding them out to me. Hope blooms in my chest, only for a moment, and replaces the grief. I'm not letting him get away with running this time. If he wants me to prove to him that I care...that I want him, I have to do this.

I grab the keys and start marching toward the truck. The ground is slick beneath my boots and the rain is only getting worse. I'm not sure how or where I'm going to find him, but I have a pretty good idea where he'll hide now that he's back.

"Don't do anything stupid!" He yells behind me.

"I already am!" I scream over my shoulder, pulling the door open and forcing the truck to start. I throw it into drive and press my boot to the gas, slinging mud and gravel everywhere as I turn the truck to the road.

I glance in the rearview mirror. Dex has already gone back inside, no doubt to let Blake know what's happened. A part of me feels bad for leaving her there, but I know Blake will understand.

I head towards the only place I know I'll find him. The one place that other than the Hounds, only I know about. My heart hammers in my chest as a single taillight comes into view up ahead. Even in the rain, I can tell it's him, but he's so far ahead of me I'm afraid he'll make a turn, and I'll lose him.

I can't–won't lose him this time. I won't allow him to walk away from this. I won't let *myself* walk away from this. This is my chance to explain and if he doesn't want to hear me out then at least I can live with the fact that I tried.

Don't give up on him.

Dex's words replay in my mind, giving me fuel to keep my boot firmly pressed to the gas.

It only takes fifteen minutes for me to reach the turn-off Holden has taken me to. My teeth chatter and goosebumps rise on my skin as I make the turn off the road a little too fast that the back wheels fishtail. I tense, quickly correcting the wheel and take a deep breath as I glance towards the pullout. It's then, in the dim light and flashing clouds above. that I realize I forgot my jacket in the club.

Holden's bike is parked near the makeshift path that's been carved out by years of him and his family using it. I pull the tow truck next to the bike, parking it as fast as I can, and climb from the truck.

"Holden!" I yell through the storm, wrapping my arms around myself as the chill from the rain starts to spread through me. When I get no answer I start towards the trail, but with the rain and the trees being so thick I turn back, moving to the utility box on the truck and searching for a flashlight. My hands wrap around the handle. "Yes," I mutter, switching it on to make sure it works.

I shine the light over the trees, shutting the box and moving to the path. I follow the trail, keeping an eye on my footing as I step over the overturned logs. Saying a silent prayer for deciding against the heels Blake wanted me to wear.

"Holden!" I holler but again no response.

I curse and continue walking. The rain isn't as bad with the trees covering me but still my skin crawls with goosebumps. After a week and a half of sunshine and blistering hot weather, of course, tonight of all nights is when Mother Nature decides to grace Pine River with a flash flood.

I push through the bushes, my arms red and irritated from the branches scratching at my skin, hissing when one comes back behind me, smacking me on the center of my bare back. I stop for a moment, sucking in a breath as the pain radiates down my spine but force myself forward. Only a few more minutes and I'll be at the bridge. Even with the rain I can hear the river rushing nearby. The cracking of wood as the wind blows through the trees makes it even harder to hear anything.

As soon as the edge of the bridge comes into view I stop, taking a deep breath before yelling for him again. I wait until I hear something but it's useless with the white noise around me. I force myself forward until I see him.

"Holden!" I yell, stepping onto the slick wood as it creaks beneath my feet.

He turns toward me, finally hearing me yell. "What the hell are you doing!" He screams through the storm.

"I came to find you!" I yell back, moving toward him but stopping when the metal of the trusses moans around me.

Holden takes a step towards me but halts. "Go home, Kadence!"

"No!" I yell back, my voice hoarse and my throat becoming raw. I take another step towards him, "I'm not giving this up! I need–" I suck in a breath, "I need to explain!"

"There's nothing to explain! Go back to Wolfe!" He sneers, taking another step toward me. Even now I can see the red around his eyes only highlighting the blue as if his emotions are getting the better of him the same as mine are.

I follow, taking a step toward him feeling the wood shift beneath me before stopping again. "There's nothing going on, I don't want Wolfe! I want *you*!" This gets his attention as he freezes, his eyes trail my goosed skin as I wrap my arms around me again. "I don't want anyone but you, Holden!"

"You shouldn't be here!" He finally says, inching towards me.

I do the same, ignoring the cracking of wood. "Yes, I should because all my life I've given in. I ran from what scared me the most! I gave up on my life, Holden! I gave up on the things I loved, I gave up my self worth!" I take another step. "But I'm done running and I will be *damned* if I give up on *you*!"

Holden's head drops, his hands fist at his sides again like he's at war with himself. For a long while we stand in silence, nothing but the sound of rushing water and rain splashing against the wood and metal fill the air around us.

Just look at me. Please, I silently beg him, the tears returning but camouflaged by the rain.

His eyes lift to mine and my breath hitches in my throat. Those eyes I love so much, so full of the things that scare the both of us. The ones that see *me*. There's only a few feet in between us now but he's slowly closing the distance as he moves towards me, only making the sound of my heartbeat drum in my ears that much more.

"Why didn't you tell me?" He asks, his voice raising but the disdain from before almost gone.

My hands fall from around me and down to my sides as I stare back at him. "Because I was scared." He closes the distance between us again, he's close enough to reach and even though my hands are itching to do so, I keep them still. "Because I didn't want to feel weak anymore."

Holden shakes his head. "You should have told me."

I nod. He's right, I knew he was right the moment that he walked out of the clubhouse a week ago, and I've been regretting not telling him since. "I know."

He stumbles back like the words are a punch to his gut. His hands come to his waist as he stares out at the water for a long time. I take a step towards him, the wood beneath me shifting under my boot but I press on.

"Holden." I'm so close to him. I raise my hand to reach out to him. "Please."

Holden tilts his head to me and I know that he knows more than he has seen on the TV. Something tells me he knows deep down what happened. But he never says anything.

"No more secrets," he says, and I nod furiously in response before he even finishes.

"No more." I repeat.

His chest heaves as he watches me. A chill runs through my body again, craving the warmth of his as I take another step. The wood beneath me begins to crack louder than it has before and this time I feel the shift. I glance down just as the wood gives out.

"Holden!" I scream, reaching out for him.

He lunges at me, grasping at my fingers as the rain pours down around us. My hand slips from his as I fall through the broken wood, my arm scraping against the rotting bridge.

"Kadence!" He screams after me, his body dropping to his knees as I fall.

Everything around me becomes muffled as soon as I hit the frigid water. It stings my skin as I'm dragged further below the surface of the river.

My scream pierces the water, the flashlight ripping from my grip as my body hits the river bottom. Crashing and rolling against the rocks and submerged branches. I claw at anything I can grab onto, only to be sucked away by the current.

I break the surface, gasping for air until I'm pulled under again, my arms fighting for the surface again. The current only gets stronger and I try holding the small breath I'm able to get, but as my body slams into a log, the air in my lungs leaves me in response and I suck in water.

I scream again, my pleas muffled by the river. The glimpses of moonlight shining through the water go dark and the sounds of rushing water are replaced by the sound of my blood rushing to my ears.

My eyes close as the current carries me. I'm not going to survive this. I'm sure of it and everything I've been fighting for, the vision of a future I want with Holden has quickly been washed away with the current and my body slowly giving up on itself.

I tried. I *fought*.

Fought for him and if this is how I'm going to die, at least I know I tried and for once ran towards the thing I'm scared of.

Love. *His* love.

HOLDEN

"Kadence!" I scream after her. My body falls with hers, hitting the wood as she hits the water. "No! Kadence!" Everything in my chest feels tight. It heaves, watching the shine of the flashlight hit the water, the pitch-black water camouflaging her body below the surface.

She was so close. I had a fucking grip on her hand and the goddamn rain let her slip from my reach. I'm already soaked from the storm but I stand, tearing off my jacket and cut, tossing them to the ground. I stare down at the water, acutely aware of the quickly passing minutes I'm wasting. I know these waters, I know the bends and curves in the river, but with the storm and the water being higher than it normally is, it's going to be difficult for me to be able to find her.

I'll be damned if I give up on you.

Her words echo around me, taunting me. It only takes one flash of the look in her eyes to force me over the edge of the bridge. The air in my lungs dissipates as soon as the frigid water hits my skin. I fight for the surface, waiting until the current breaks enough that I can swim upwards.

I never thought I'd be thanking my military training until the moment my head breaks the surface and I gasp for air, filling my lungs.

"Kadence!" I yell again, a part of me knowing that she won't answer but on the off chance that she's okay, that she's just made it to the surface. I have to scream for her. The current has picked up again, sucking me under. I open my eyes, trying to see anything within the bubbles and spray.

I only need a pocket, a spot in the river that isn't as strong as the rest. That's where I'll find her. That's where I *hope* I'll find her. My body slams into a log, forcing the air from me. This is my chance. I quickly wrap my arms around the log, holding on to it with everything I can.

My eyes sting from the rushing water as I press my boot to the wood, pushing off with all my strength and forcing myself upwards, breaking the surface just for another gasp of air before the current takes me further downstream. I move with it, kicking and fighting to keep above the surface. My eyes quickly scan the water and the treeline. Until I see it.

Something light colored within the darkness on a sandbar ahead of me. My heart hammers against my ribcage. It's got to be her. I don't know what I'm going to do if it isn't. Why did I go to Alabama? Why the fuck did I leave her? Blinded by my anger, blinded by the mistrust I have in people. I couldn't stay. I did what I always do and ran. Ran to get answers instead of hearing her out. Instead of trusting her, instead of keeping my fucking promise, *I left*.

I push my way through the current, getting over to the sandbar. She's lying face down, her dress the only thing that caught my eye in the darkness. When I walked into Moon it was the first thing that caught my eye. My stubborn girl. In her purple dress and combat boots. I'm not sure if I wanted to kill her for wearing something like that in public or kill the men around her whose eyes she had been completely oblivious to. Now? Now I'm thanking the stars for a damn piece of fabric.

"Kadence!" I climb onto the sandbar, crawling to her body.

The tightening in my chest returns when I realize that she isn't breathing. Her back isn't rising and falling with her breath. My hands hover over her for a moment, scared to touch her. Scared to find out that this is it. "Kadence, baby–" My throat tightens as my hand falls on her back. She's cold. So fucking cold, but I hold it there for a moment pulling myself together before rolling her over.

Her lips are a terrifying shade of blue and her skin–I dip my head to her forehead. Her skin is so fucking pale. I feel that familiar sting in my eyes as I slide them closed. "Don't do this to me," I whisper to her. "Please, just–*fuck*, don't do this to me."

I lift my head to look at her again while the rain pelts against my back, stinging and unforgiving. My training takes over as my palms cross over each other in the center of her chest. Pain shoots from my wrist to my spine and it's only now I realize how fucking sore my left shoulder is from the jump. It takes everything in me to ignore the pain and start compressions. I focus on my hands, forcing myself to count instead of focusing on her pale frame. *One, two, three*– I continue until I reach thirty and tilt her head back, plugging her nose and pressing my lips to hers, blowing a few breaths into her and waiting.

"C'mon Sunflower," I plead, continuing compressions again, "I need you to come back to me." I start counting again, *sixteen, seventeen, eighteen*–tilting her head back, pressing my lips to her cold ones, blowing again.

I don't know how much time has passed but I repeat the process. Compressions, breaths, compressions, breaths. Pleading to her in every moment her chest doesn't move.

My heart stops the moment she finally splutters. Her eyes shoot open before she starts throwing up water and sand. I lift her shoulder, rolling her onto her side as I cradle her in my arms. "C'mon baby, get it out," I coax, my voice shaky and hoarse.

She finally coughs and lets out a pained groan. Her arms lift to mine wrapped around her holding on to me with whatever strength she has left. Her grip is weak and her fingers are barely a touch on my skin, doing nothing to quell the twisting ache in my heart.

"Cold," she whimpers as her green eyes slowly open to find mine. We're both shaking at this point but she buries against me stealing any warmth in my bones and right now I'd give her anything she needs. "It--hurts--" she rasps, her eyes fluttering closed again.

"No, baby, open your eyes for me. Please." I move my hand to her cheek, turning her face to mine. "Baby, please," I whine, kissing her forehead, her nose, her cheeks, "please open your eyes."

They flutter open again and I can't help but smile when her brows furrow and I get a glimpse of those green eyes again.

"Atta girl." My lips press to hers before moving to her cheeks again. "I need to get you outta here." I glance up looking around. "I'm gonna need you to work with me, baby, can you do that?"

My eyes find hers still glued to me though it felt like she was looking through me. Her expression blank. "Baby?" I slide my hand to her throat, feeling for her pulse as a whimper falls from her lips. My eyes close in brief relief, she was okay, at least for now. Her heartbeat is still weak but it was there and her chest was still moving as she sucked in shallow breaths. That's all I needed, just... for her to keep fighting.

"Alright, Sunflower, this is gonna hurt, baby, I'm sorry."

I shift my weight in the soft sand, the water still raging around us. The rain is still coming down in sheets making it hard to see but I can make out a clear line to the trees, shallow enough to trudge through. I slide an arm under her knees and the other under her arms before lifting her to my chest. She lets out a whine so sharp it pierces through me, tugging on what little strings I have left.

"I'm sorry," I whisper into her hair, holding her head to my chest. "I'm so fucking sorry."

I start carrying her towards the treeline. I can make out the dark shadow of the bridge in the distance even with the rain, thankful we didn't travel too far down the river. There aren't many trails on this side but I know of one. I just have to get there. I shifted my weight evenly on the sand, trying my best not to fall with her in my arms. Flashbacks of carrying Fisher through the desert filter through my mind. Everything felt at stake then.

When you're in a situation like that it's a miracle that you end up leaving alive. That walk was blistering, the sun beat down on us as I carried him through enemy territory. But this? There is more at stake here. It isn't just my life or Fisher's I have to worry about. Yeah, I wanted to get us both out alive, but even then it was expected for us to die. For us to end up on a quick fifteen-minute memorial on the news, which, knowing the government I worked for, would have never happened.

I fought then, but the fight I had in my heart was nothing compared to what I'm feeling now and a part of me hates myself for it. To hold her life in such high regard that this feels more important.

My chest is heavy, my legs ache, and my shoulder feels like it's on fire but I know it's nothing compared to what she is feeling. The further I get through the trees and towards the trail, the more promises I begin to make to myself. Never to let her go. Never to leave her again. I'm done running from the things that scare me.

I glance down at her. Her eyes are still closed but her chest is moving. *She's still breathing. Keep going. Do not fucking stop.* I warn myself. I won't ever forgive myself if I give up now.

The minute my feet hit solid ground I book it. Careful of the downed branches and mud-holes until I reach the pull-off. I'll have to

come back for my bike but right now I don't give two fucks about it.
I look through the windows of the tow truck, searching for the keys,
and see them sitting on the seat. *Good girl*, I think.

I pull open the door and carefully lay her on the seat before sprint-
ing to the driver's side. I know I should take her to the hospital but the
closest one is over an hour away and I don't have that kind of time. The
shitty truck heater is my only hope right now of getting any heat to her
body. I flip it on high, fix all the vents in her direction, and start down
the road, the tires digging into the mud and gravel. My teeth chatter
until town comes into view and my jaw clenches hard enough to stop
it. Determination burns in my veins as I fight through the weather to
get her back to the compound.

I quickly peel into the parking lot on squealing tires and park.
There's a group of prospects walking towards me with concerned
looks and brows raised. I throw the door open and bolt to the other
side of the truck. Wyatt pushes his way through to the front of the
group with wide eyes and my heart flickers seeing the kid. "Go get
Cole, West!"

"What happened?" He yells while jogging to the truck as I help
Kadence out. His eyes go wide as he looks through the window, seeing
her limp form. "Is that...?"

"Go, Wyatt. Now!" I bark and shift her body in my arms. Her
groans dig deep under my skin. "I know, baby, you're okay, you're
gonna be okay." I promise over and over again until Cole bursts
through the door of the clubhouse with Dex and Blake on his heels.

"What the hell happened?!" Cole yells, his eyes going wide upon
seeing her.

"She followed me to the bridge," I mutter, pushing my way past
Cole. "She needs the Doc."

"She doesn't need Lang, Nash. She needs a fuckin' hospital," Cole growls, following behind me. I hear a gasp come from Blake as we pass her and Dex.

"Open the fucking door, Cole!" I rumble turning to him. "She needs to get warm, the hospital's too fucking far away!"

Cole glares at me, shaking his head and pulls open the door. "Take her to my room."

"Fuck no," I spit, moving into the clubhouse. I can hear the parade of footsteps behind me while moving down the hallway, pushing into the room I use whenever I stay here.

"Nash!" Cole's voice echoes down the hallway after me.

I kick open the door to the bathroom and carefully set her in the tub. Ripping the shower curtain off the rod and tossing it aside, I lean over and turn on the water, making sure it isn't too hot and just warm enough that it won't send her further into shock.

"What the fuck happened?" Cole asks from behind me as the tub fills.

I push past him, tugging on the dresser drawers and tossing clothes onto the bed, not even sure what I'm pulling out. Anything at this point was better than the wet clothes we were both wearing. "Did you call Lang?"

"Dex is on the phone with him now. He'll be here." Cole moves back this time as I pass him and go back into the bathroom to kneel next to the tub and take her hands, rubbing them between my own. I push back the hair from her face. A whimper leaves her as she leans into my touch and her eyes flutter open again.

"You're safe," I whisper, trying to give her a comforting smile.

Kadence nods, her eyes flickering to Cole as she slips into the water a bit further. Her dress hugs her skin and I know I'm going to have to change her. It's only in the light of the bathroom that I'm able to

take in the full extent of the bruises and cuts on her body. Her arms
are torn up from the fall, bruises tattoo her arms and her chin.

"Nash," Cole pushes, "what *happened*?"

I lean into her, pressing my lips to her forehead. "I'll be right back,"
I whisper against her skin before standing and shooting Cole a look
that could kill.

It isn't his fault. None of this is Cole's fault. I have to remember that, but my anger needs somewhere to go. I walk back into the
bedroom tearing off my shirt and grabbing one of the ones I tossed
to the bed. "She followed me to the bridge." I answer like it explains
everything.

"You said that."

"The bridge gave out and she fell into the water. I had–" I pause,
sucking in a breath and squeezing my eyes closed as the image of
her falling flickers in my mind. The terror on her face, the way she
screamed my name. It would haunt me. "I had to go in after her," I
finally say.

"Why the fuck were you out there anyway? You were supposed to
go to the club and bring her back here!" Cole's voice raises as I pull the
shirt over my head and turn back to him.

"I did go to the club, Dex was–it looked like," I mutter, shaking my
head. I'm fucking stupid for thinking Dex had touched her that way.
I saw it, but I saw it through a haze of red.

Cole shakes his head. "So you ran. Again."

I stare at my best friend. *Again*. I'm tired of hearing the word. My
gaze flickers to Kadence. "Yeah, and I feel like a fucking asshole for it,
for all of it, so put away your high horse, O'Neil."

"You're lucky she's fucking alive, Nash! Do you know what happened to her? Before you ran off to god knows where?" He snarls,
taking a step towards me. "Do you?"

"I went to Fisher's," I say almost defeated, my gaze never leaving Kadence. "So yeah, I know."

"You drove to Alabama?"

I nod.

"You know what was in the reports, but you don't know what she experienced," Cole says as if he knows something I didn't. I saw the hospital records and the photos of her skin. I even read the police report from the night her world changed.

"Does she know you know?" He asks.

I shake my head. "No."

Cole lets out a hollow laugh, glancing back at Kadence. "This is on you. Everything that happened tonight is on fucking *you*." He turns back to me. "You don't leave. Again." He bites through a clenched jaw. "You make this fucking right and you *let* her tell you what happened."

"You don't think I know that?!" I boom, tired of his lecturing. "You don't think I know that the reason she's half dead in that bathtub right now is because of me? I don't need you to tell me that, Cole, I fucking *know it.* You didn't have to carry her lifeless body through the fucking forest to get her here!"

"Hey!" Wolfe's voice interrupts. "Cole, get the fuck out."

I glance over seeing him in the doorway. His face is stone and his jaw locked. "What the fuck do you want?" I sneer at him. "You wanna tell me how much of a fucking idiot I am too?"

Dex narrows his eyes at me before tossing a glare to Cole.

"Take a walk, Cole, *now,*" he growls, not warning him again.

Cole moves past me, smacking his shoulder into my own before leaving the room.

"You two need to get it the fuck together *tonight,*" Dex seethes. "Whatever the hell is going on with you two is damaging the club and it's going to get someone fucking killed."

"Tell that to him."

"I'm telling that to you, Nash," he counters. "Neither of you seem to have a coherent thought when you're having a pissin' contest about who is more high and mighty."

"I know I'm not high and mighty, Wolfe." I turn to him. "Do you?"

Dex tilts his head. "Who the fuck do you think gave her the keys to the truck?"

Guilt flickers in his eyes, and I feel it in my chest. "Why did you do it?"

Wolfe moves to the bathroom doorway, watching her in the tub for a few moments before turning back to me. "Because you two are the most stubborn fucking humans I've ever met and I'm the one who told her not to give up on you."

My brows furrow. "Why? Why not just move in on her yourself? You two looked pretty cozy at the club." I shake my head, regretting the words as soon as they fall from my mouth. When the fuck did I become so fucking insecure?

Dex shakes his head "Because I'm not the one she's in love with, Nash." He says it as if it should be so obvious to me but all it feels like is a punch to the gut. "You know she went searching for you after you left?" Wolfe crosses his arms over his chest, leaning against the door frame. "Took her to Moon thinkin' you might be there. She stood up to Layla for about five seconds before Layla started suggesting she work at the club to get your attention."

I card my fingers through my hair, gripping the root. "Why the fuck–"

"Because she loves you. I don't know why and I don't even think she realizes it. I don't know what happened between you two that you both are now tethered, but she does and she was ready to give that up because you ran." He pauses. "Kadence needs sturdy, Nash. She needs someone to stand by her when shit gets tough, not someone who runs away when a minor inconvenience shows up in his path. She had that and worse... and she *ran*."

My eyes find her again through the doorway. The water has probably cooled off by now and I know I need to get her out of there, but I'm frozen. She doesn't deserve this. Doesn't deserve the constant flip flop of emotions I deal with.

"When that car is fixed, what do you think she'll do?" He asks, getting my attention. I hadn't thought that far. I knew she wouldn't go back to Florida, but maybe she would leave all of this behind, and right now, I wouldn't blame her if she did. "If you want her to stay, you have to show her that. Quit runnin' because she never gave up on you and I have a feeling she won't wait around again for you to come back if you do."

I consider his words as Wolfe pushes off the frame and moves towards me. "Be that rock for her because I can't--" He pauses, forcing my gaze to his. Something in the way he says it sounds like Wolfe wants to be that for her. "I won't be your stand-in anymore, Nash."

Dex moves past me. "Get her changed, get yourself changed and get her in bed. Lang will be here soon."

I watch the door shut behind Dex. Was she in love with me? Better question: was I in love with her? I had never felt this conflicted over someone before. I never felt as angry as I did the day I left. I should have let her explain, should have stayed even if what she had to say hurt.

The moment I opened the folder Hank had, my world tilted on its axis. I spent the whole ride home going over every detail. Every mark ever left on her body that was hidden and the ones that weren't. I was going to tell her. I had planned to go to Moon, bring her back to the clubhouse and tell her that I knew. I needed her to know that weight was something she didn't have to carry alone anymore. That I was sorry for leaving, but what she didn't know was that I hadn't given up on her. I just needed the proof. I needed something other than her words to prove to myself that she is who she claims to be. But all I'm learning is I need to trust her. *I should have trusted her.*

A whimper from the bathroom gets my attention again as I race to her side. Her eyes are open again, giving me a soft smile that shatters me. Cracking my resolve as my emotions get the better of me. I try to hide it as I drain the tub and reach for a towel, wrapping it around her and lifting her into my arms. I get her to the bed, afraid of saying anything as I lay her down. Dex's words run through my mind over and over again.

Kadence went after me. She didn't have to and I half expected her to be gone when I got back to town but she was here. Her things still scattered over the small apartment, her scent still lingering in the office when I went to search for her. It was then I realized how much I missed her. How much I failed her by leaving.

I'll do whatever it takes to keep you safe.

The promises we made replay in my mind, echoing behind Wolfe's. I'm going to keep them. I failed tonight, forcing her to come after me. Instead of going to her on that bridge I let her come to me, almost needing her to come to me, and she did. Not once did Kadence back down from my warnings or threats for her to leave me. It should've been me in that water tonight. It should have never been her.

I carefully peel off the soaked boots from her feet before sliding the dress from her. Cradling her head in my hands.

"I'm sorry," I whisper when a soft whine leaves her. Those green eyes look up at me again. Not a trace of anger or sadness is weaved into those flecks of gray.

I take in the smattering of bruises and cuts her dress has hidden. There is a particularly nasty bruise that lines her ribs. Tears I was having a hard time holding back fall. Her body is mangled and almost every part of her has a cruel spatter of purple and red marks that litter her skin.

"*Fuck*," I breathe as my face crumbles. Kadence lifts her hand and rests it over mine. Using what little strength she has she links our fingers, her eyes never leaving mine. "Why did you do it? Why not just leave me?" I beg.

The corners of her mouth quirk up gently, her head lolls to the side towards me as I kneel down next to her on the floor. Her lips part trying to say something, and finally, with a pained breath, she says the words that completely crumble what little resolve I have left.

"Because it's us–against the world."

KADENCE

My eyes open as I suck in a breath forcing a searing pain to shoot up my side, causing me to gasp and tense.

"Fuck," I breathe tentatively and feel how sore my throat is.

My entire body feels like it's been hit by a freight train and my arms feel like lead weights as I try to push myself up. The room is still dark minus the small stream of light that pours through the crack in the curtains.

I roll my head to the side and give up on moving. Soft snores come from next to me, but the bed I'm in is empty. I take a pained breath in and slide my elbows up to my shoulders beneath me, doing everything I can to push myself up. Stopping every few moments as the fire shoots through me. When I'm finally lifted enough I carefully peer over the edge of the bed, only making out half of his face.

"Holden?" I whisper but he doesn't move.

He's tucked under another blanket, a pillow behind his head. He's been sleeping on the floor? My brows furrow as I do everything I can to roll onto my side, letting out a low whimper as my arm presses against my ribcage.

Suddenly he's up, staring at me. His hair is matted and stuck to his forehead, and his beard has grown thicker since I last saw him. *The day in the clubhouse? No. Moon.* He had come to Moon and found me. My head throbs as the memories start to flood back in. The storm, the creaking on the bridge.

My eyes meet his, the blue becoming glossy.

"Kadence," he rasps, moving to the edge of the bed and helping me lay back down. "Don't move too much," he says, pushing back my hair as another wave of pain rolls deep within my muscles. His tongue rolls over his bottom lip, bringing it between his teeth. His eyes are overwhelmed with sadness.

"I'm okay." I know I'm not, but I can't bear to see the pity on his face. I've seen enough of it over the past week.

He shakes his head. "No you aren't."

"Holden," I whisper, "what happened wasn't your fault."

I move to sit up but he stops me, his hands come to rest on my thighs gently and almost tentatively, as if he were to put any more pressure on me, I would break. Little does he know I already feel broken. There isn't anything he can do to me that would make me feel otherwise.

"Let me sit up, please."

His eyes search mine for a moment before he leans over the edge of the bed, grabbing the pillow he was using and sets it behind me. He helps me sit up against the headboard, adjusting the pillow. He's unusually quiet as if he's debating his words.

I reach for him as he sits down on the edge of the bed next to me, his body turned towards me, and his knee curled under him. I rest my hand on his cheek.

"It's not your fault," I say again.

Holden shakes his head. "I should have never left you." His voice is so soft that I barely hear him. I tangle my fingers into the short beard forcing him to look at me.

"No, you shouldn't have," I start and his brows furrow, "but I should have told you the truth sooner."

His head dips down as his fingers tangle with mine, bringing my hand to his lap. "Do you remember the bridge?" He asks in a shaky voice.

I nod. "I'm not giving up on you, Holden."

"You swore no more secrets," he says, looking back up at me. "I need to promise the same." He feels distant, even with our hands intertwined and feeling his warmth radiate through me.

"You jumped in after me," I ask, looking down at the bruises on his hands, "didn't you?"

His face crumbles for a moment before he sucks in a breath. "Of course I did."

I feel the emotions between us wash over me, tears stinging my eyes. *He went after me. He didn't give up on me.* I remember the water and how raging it was with the storm and yet we both survived.

"Thank you," I whimper.

He leans into me, pressing his forehead to mine. "I almost lost you." Holden shakes his head, still pressed to mine, our noses brushing the other's. "I can't lose you, Kade."

"You didn't–you won't," I whisper, pulling back from him, my free hand pushes back the long hair from his face. "Ever."

I search his eyes, tears have gathered in the corners of them, and I know he's doing his best to keep them at bay where mine have failed. His thumb comes up to brush them away before resting on my jaw.

"How much pain are you in?" He asks softly, his fingers tracing over my skin tenderly. It was then I realize from the small jolt of pain that my chin must have been bruised.

I shake my head. "Right now, not a lot." A smile graces the corners of my lips, trying to do anything to get rid of the look on his face. The one that makes me feel weak and fragile. "Why are you sleeping on the floor?" I ask.

"I didn't want to hurt you, the bed–"

I shake my head, letting go of the hand in his lap and cupping his cheeks, forcing his gaze to mine.

"No more floor." I want him close. I need him near me and a part of me didn't care if it hurt to have someone laying next to me. I crave his warmth, his touch, the way he smells. I need it.

Holden leans in, carefully pressing his lips to mine, taking my top lip between his own before pulling back quicker than I liked. "Okay, baby."

I smile again. It feels good to smile, to see the corners of his mouth quirk upwards from my movement. I want that smile back, the one that sends butterflies soaring in my stomach.

"What time is it?" I ask.

Holden turns his head in my hands, picking up his phone from the nightstand. "Six in the morning," he rasps again.

The phone light gives me a view of the dark circles under his eyes. He's exhausted. I can see it and hear it in his voice.

"Lay with me?" I whisper. "Please?"

He sets his phone down on the bed and lifts himself from the mattress, letting my hands drop.

"Lang will be here in a few hours to check on you," he says as he rounds the bed, pulling back the heavy blanket I've been under. "He's a doctor. Unofficially."

I raise my brow. "Unofficially?" I ask, smiling and feeling the bed dip next to me as he climbs in.

Holden smiles as he helps me lay back down, curling next to me, careful not to touch me too much. Something that I hate, but I know right now it will be too much and even if I had asked for him to wrap himself up into me, he wouldn't, only to refrain from hurting me. Instead I settle for him laying close by, feeling his fingertips trace the exposed areas of my skin. I missed his touch. It's been only a week, but I missed the way the roughness of his hands feel on me.

"He *was* a doctor. Had his own practice, but his license was taken away." Holden's eyes rake over my face as if he's taking me in and memorizing me.

"You want to elaborate on that?" I ask, my voice straining as I look over at him. His eyes shoot to mine, brows furrowing again.

"Your throat hurt?" He asks gently.

I nod. "Probably from the water. It's fine."

Holden watches me for a moment, that pained look on his face appearing again as he looks for the lie. Truth is, right now, the pain, the soreness, none of it matters. What matters is him lying next to me. Him being here, with me. I raise my hand, running the knuckle of my index finger over the crease in his brow to smooth it out before running it down the length of his nose. His face softens with the gesture, just as I'd hoped.

"I'm fine, Holden," I whisper.

He lifts his head and leans into me, watching me closely waiting for the whimper of pain to fall from my lips and even though it tweaks my side I hide it. My hand wraps around the back of his neck as I pull him to me, pressing his lips to mine. He's tentative still, careful not to put too much weight on me, but I need more of him.

"Kadence," he whispers against my lips when I try to deepen the kiss. I hum against him in response. "Baby," he whispers again, a low chuckle falling from his lips, pulling back from me. "You need to rest."

He dips his head and captures my lips in a quick, tender kiss before moving to my cheeks and my nose. The movements of his lips, tracing my face with his kisses and leaving them anywhere they can reach open a floodgate of sensations in my chest. I remember feeling the warmth of his lips burning through my cold skin. I realize now that he's tracing the bruises that litter my skin with his lips. Mapping and marking each one. The tenderness of it all forces the tears back to my eyes with the echoes of his pleas.

I can't help but whine, trying to hold everything back. He pulls back again, cupping my face.

"What's wrong?" he asks, kissing away the tears falling down my temple.

"I thought for sure..." I sigh, closing my eyes as my chest aches. "I didn't think I'd survive that," I rasp, looking back up at him. "I couldn't–"

He trails his thumb over my cheek, giving me the time to collect my words as his eyes trace my features. Never pressing or pushing for me to relive that night.

My gaze finds his. "I couldn't stop picturing your face," I finally say after a moment, "and how I would never see it again." I let out a strained sob as I tear my gaze from him. "I remember hitting a log, the little air I had got–"

"Sunflower, you don't..." Holden buries his face into my neck.

I shake my head. "No secrets, remember?" I feel his lips against my neck, urging me to continue. "The air got knocked from me and when everything went black…I knew if there was a chance that I survived that, I would be done running."

He lifts his head. "What do you mean?"

I tuck my fingers into his hair. "I don't care about the car, or it getting fixed. I just want to be with you." My voice trails off at the end, I'm not unsure. I know that I want to be with Holden but the car. It's still the last reminder I have of my father, and hearing the words come from my own mouth that I'm ready to give that up for him just solidifies what I already knew deep down.

I'm falling in love with Holden Nash.

"You don't want to leave?" He sounds shocked but I don't miss the tiny glimmer of hope that flickers in his eyes.

I shake my head. "No."

"What about your mom?" He asks, his fingers comb through my hair until his hand rests at the back of my head, bringing me closer. I lean into him, pressing my forehead to his and close my eyes.

"What I told you about my mother was the truth," I sigh, "She hasn't been my mother for a long time. Just…the woman who gave birth to me." I pull back from him. "My father used to say something about family not always being blood, I never knew what he meant until now."

The corners of his mouth lift gently as his eyes rake over my features. "I think I know what you mean."

I smile. "I thought you might." I shift on the mattress unable to help the twist of my face when the pain becomes apparent again. It feels like a thousand tiny pins and needles are stabbing me in every direction. His hand rests on my cheek again, bringing my eyes open to the pained expression on his face. "Please stop looking at me like that," I whisper brokenly.

"I'm sorry," Holden replies gently, his fingers combing through my hair again. Something in his voice brings my attention to him again. He sounds...guilty? "I'm so *fucking* sorry this happened," Holden continues, shaking his head. "I should've just listened to you at Moon."

"This wasn't your fault," I say with a soft shake of my head. "That bridge would have given out no matter who was standing on it. This would have ended up with someone getting hurt no matter where we fought." I smile.

"I don't want you getting hurt," he sighs, lying on his back. "That's the last thing I want."

"I don't want you getting hurt either."

He rolls his head to the side to look at me again. I'm already looking at him. The man who jumped into a river after me, the man who can make me go from happy and content to irritated in less than two seconds flat. The man that blames himself for a freak accident because he blames himself for every tragedy in his life. Something I can relate to.

"Please don't disappear on me again," I whisper, the emotions and pain slowly pulling me back towards their dark tides. "I don't know if I could handle it."

The muscle in his jaw clenches for just a moment before shaking his head. "I won't."

I search for any sign of deception in his features but find that he's being sincere. We're back to making promises I'm not sure we can keep but I would give my last breath trying. He rolls over onto his side again, slowly and careful not to jostle me too much.

"You need to sleep, Sunflower." the corner of his mouth turns upwards in a sad smile. "We can talk about everything later."

I know exactly what he means. Later I would relive everything, *again*, only this time I know it will be the hardest recollection. He'll have questions. He won't be able to hide the sadness in his gaze or the frown that freckles his face when he's upset. In spite of that, I'll do it if it means keeping Holden. I'll answer his questions, tell him everything. *No more secrets.*

He scooches closer to me on the bed, getting close enough that I can reach out to him without straining. Holden rests his hand over my cheek, trailing his thumb carefully over my cheekbone. His eyes rake over my features again but I can see the exhaustion take its toll on him. Through heavy lids and slow blinks, he soon closes his eyes and I follow suit. The warmth of his hand still resting on my cheek grounds me into sleep.

"She's sleeping, Lang, let her have this alright? You can come back later."

Holden's voice filters through the sounds of rushing water in my dream. His voice is muffled but clear as day. My eyes flutter open; the room is brighter now. The light streaming through the window has turned from an early dawn glow to mid-day sun.

Everything still feels stiff. My legs feel crampy and the pain in my side throbs with every breath I take. I roll my head gently to the side, seeing him standing at the door, talking in a low voice with someone on the other side. The sleeves of his henley are pushed up on his forearms, giving a view of the scattered tattoos on his skin. My eyes trail down to his backside. The gray sweats he wears hang off of his hips but strain against the muscles in his thighs. He's a sight to see after water-logged dreams.

"Lang, I swear to god–" He threatens, his voice rough from sleep.

"It's okay," I rasp. Holden's head whips around at the sound of my voice. The hard look he has softening in an instant. "The doc?" I ask and to his dismay and the frown that blesses his lips, he nods. I smile softly. "Let him in."

"You need to rest." His grip on the door falters just enough that a shorter dark-haired man pokes his head through the gap with a dopey smile.

"I've rested enough for now, baby. Let him in."

Holden crosses his arms over his chest, shooting me a look as if to say, *fine, but I'm not happy about it,* making me laugh softly and wince from the pain. The man grins up at him, pushing past the threshold and makes his way to me.

"You have ten minutes, Shawn."

"Yeah, yeah, yeah," Shawn mutters as he pulls a chair from the desk in the corner and sits it next to the bed. "Is he usually this cranky?" He asks me through a smirk.

My gaze flickers back to Holden, who's currently shooting daggers with his burning blue eyes into the back of Shawn's head.

"He means well." I smile at him. "So, Doc, tell me. How long do I have to live?"

Shawn's eyes go wide looking up from the leather bag. "You're–n ot...miss.." He stammers his nervous gaze flickering between me and Holden.

I grin, shaking my head. "That was too easy. I'm kidding."

Shawn lets out a shaky breath and begins pulling out medical supplies from his bag, setting it on the bed next to me.

"It wasn't funny," Holden grumbles, moving around to where he laid earlier and sits against the headboard. I glance over at him and instantly regret the joke. His eyes flare with something I can't pinpoint as he moves the pillow he used to sleep and sets it behind my head. "Up you get, c'mon," he mutters softly, helping me sit up.

I wince at the sharpness shooting up my side, my eyes never leaving Holden as he helps me get comfortable. I didn't mean anything by it, but even though his face is masked in a blank look, I know it has affected him. I glance over at Shawn as soon as I feel like I can sit without being in pain. "Sorry, if I don't joke about it I'll cry and I've done enough crying for now."

He nods with a smile. "Well, you aren't dying anytime soon. But you will be sore for a few days." Lang nods, checking the small cuts on my arms. His eyes rake over my features and lifts his hand to turn my chin but before he can touch me, a low growl comes from beside me.

I turn to look at Holden who again looks like he's cutting off Lang's hand with his glare as it hangs midair.

"Down, boy, he's only trying to help." My own hand moves to his arm, giving it a reassuring squeeze.

"Maybe it would be better if you stepped outside, Holden," Shawn says, lowering his hand. The air in the room crackles with tension. "Just for me to be able to inspect the bruises, five minutes tops."

Holden shakes his head. "Not a chance."

"Then let him do what he needs to do. He's only trying to help, not cop a feel," I say, resting my head against the headboard, "or I'll kick you out." My voice is firm as his eyes meet mine. "But," I start as he narrows his eyes. "I'd like to have you here for support, so let him do his job, *please*." The last word came out as a whisper.

The darkness in his eyes softens again as he lets out an exasperated breath. "One wrong move Lang–"

"And I'll lose a hand. I know." Shawn smirks as he stands. "Now the bruise on your chin will heal fine and you have just a few scratches that won't scar. You'll look like yourself in a couple of days." He stands up a little straighter and motions for the blanket I'm still under. "I'd like to check the bruising on your side and stomach. Without a hospital, we won't know if there's any internal bleeding but I do recommend that you get checked by someone soon. I can only do so much here at the clubhouse."

I nod and pull the blanket back, freezing when his words hit me. "*Wait*, internal bleeding?"

"With the extent of your injuries, Miss Andrews, it's a possibility. From what Holden explained you took quite the fall and we don't know what happened while under the water." His eyes soften with the tone of his voice. "You're truly lucky he found you when he did."

My brows furrow. "Call me Kade, please, and what do you mean?"

Holden sucks in a breath forcing my eyes to move to his. "You were unconscious when I found you... and not breathing."

It's my eyes that go wide this time. "So you..."

"You'd made it to a sandbar by the time I found you. I had to–" His hand finds mine and gives it a soft reassuring squeeze though I feel less than assured right now. Holden doesn't finish his words, but I know exactly what he means.

C'mon, Sunflower...I need you to come back to me.

His words in my head are faint, muffled and garbled by the sound of raging water and wind but I remember hearing him. Tears sting the corners of my eyes realizing the horror that he went through for us to end up here.

"Oh my god," I whisper.

"Maybe we should focus on your injuries for now," Shawn urges, his voice wavering for a moment as his gaze flicks between me and

Holden. "You two can talk after?" It's a question now, but I nod anyway. Holden moves across me carefully and pulls back the blanket.

"Baby," his voice is soft as he tugs on the bottom of my shirt when I'm still frozen, my eyes glued to the door ahead of me.

I glance over to him, coming back to the present. I move to grab the hem of my shirt only to realize I'm not wearing anything underneath. "I uh–I don't have a bra on."

Shawn shakes his head, "It's okay. Just uhm..." His eyes flicker to Holden, "I only need it high enough to see your ribcage."

I nod again, tugging my shirt up enough to tuck under my breasts with Holden's help. Shawn gives me a small tight-lipped smile as I lean back into the pillow. His eyes rake over my stomach, his fingers gentle on my skin as he pokes and prods at me. Holden's tense beside me, his gaze glued to my abdomen while mine are glued straight ahead and scared to look down. I don't want to see what a mess my body looks like.

"The bruise on your stomach has definitely darkened," he starts, his fingers moving gingerly down the side of my ribs, sending a shooting pain to my spine. My hand juts out, gripping Holden's forearm as my eyes fall closed. "Your ribs are tender, but nothing seems broken." Finally the torture his fingers inflict stops as he straightens again and sits back down in the chair. "As I said before, I really recommend that you get checked by the hospital for any internal injuries, but I assume you'll heal just fine."

"You assume a lot for a doctor," I say softly.

Shawn laughs. "Well, without the technology, I gotta use my hands and eyes. You'll be okay, Kade. Holden saved you from a lot of worst-case scenarios."

I look up at Shawn before glancing at Holden. His eyes have moved from my abdomen to the comforter. I lower my shirt and sigh gently, careful not to irritate my ribs. "Thanks, Doc."

He nods and begins packing his things back up. "Keep the cuts clean and ice the bruises often. Fifteen minutes on, fifteen off." Shawn gives me a smile and a curt nod to Holden before moving to the doorway. "I'm a call away if you need anything. Holden has my number."

I nod. "Thanks, Shawn."

He excuses himself and shuts the door behind him as he leaves. The room goes quiet as the reality of everything we've gone through begins to settle within me.

"How long?" I ask softly, still staring straight ahead but feeling his eyes move to me with the question.

"I don't know for sure..." he says softly, "two or three minutes maybe."

I close my eyes, feeling the tears gather in my lower lids again. I'm lucky all I got was a beating to my body. "Thank you," I whisper again.

"I wasn't going to leave you," he says, forcing me to look at him. "Not at the river, not in general..." Holden turns his body to me, picking at the tiny balls of fabric on his sweatpants. "I went to Alabama when I left you."

My brows furrow. "What?"

"I have an old military buddy. He owed me a favor," he starts. "He lives in Alabama and I had asked him–" Holden pauses and looks back up at me, "before Marlowe's, I had asked him to look into you. As a precaution for the club." I open my mouth but he shakes his head. "I shouldn't have done that, I know. I just was worried about someone we didn't know being around all the time and..."

"You wanted to protect the club." I offer and he nods.

"I know everything," he says after a moment of silence, letting the weight of his words sink in. "I know what was put into the reports, the ones that are public record *and* the ones that aren't."

"Holden," I say softly, gnawing on my bottom lip as the anxiety of having to explain everything suddenly seems to be too much, but he stops me before I can finish.

"I'm not asking you to tell me your side...I won't ask that of you, but I am here when you're ready to tell me." His tongue flicks over his bottom lip as he curls his hand around the back of my head, cradling it and tangling his fingers into my hair. "I at least owe you that."

I stare at him for a moment, wanting to tell him everything but scared at the same time. Scared to relive it, scared that he'll leave again, and scared that the nightmares I've been narrowly avoiding will come back. My mind flickers to the stuffed animal in my luggage. The one that I refuse to give up but haunts me every time my gaze lands on it. I want to talk about him, and I want to remind myself of the happy moments I've had learning the little things about him. It's funny how much you can miss someone you've never met.

Even though the fear lingers in the back of my mind, I know when I curl into Holden's side, ignoring the pain, that the only person I'll share those things with is him.

HOLDEN

"You know I can walk, right?" Kadence chuckles softly as I open the truck door, helping her out. My eyes scan her, something I'd started doing since the moment she woke up a week ago. Just searching for a wince or any form of discomfort I can help with and ignoring the pang in my chest every time I find any of it on her face.

My hand wraps around her forearm, the other curls around her waist. "I know you can, but..."

"But you'd rather be my own personal walking cane?" She laughs again. No winces this time as my eyes search her face. The last few days she's started to feel better. She's been able to get up and move around. Not a lot, but enough that she isn't stuck in bed.

I grin at her, pressing my lips to her temple. "I like to think of it more as your personal leaning post," I murmur against her skin.

She smiles, that beaming smile that I missed so much was back. At least during the day. Nights are still the hardest. She always wakes up in a jolt, her body trembling and teeth chattering as if she's still in that frigid water. It pains me to see her like this. The only thing I can do is pull her into me and hold her tight, keeping her warm with my own body heat and shushing the soft sobs that fall from her lips.

"I don't know why we needed to come all the way down here," she sighs. "I'm fine, Holden."

I flash her a pointed look as we walk through the hospital's automatic doors. "I just want to be sure, okay?"

Kadence looks up at me, her brows furrowed. "Are you still worried about what Shawn said?"

"Aren't you?" I ask, helping her towards the receptionist's desk. I rest my hands on her shoulders and move to stand in front of her. "Look, this is just a precaution. Something to put us both at ease. If nothing is wrong, then we get to spend some actual alone time together. But on the off chance that there is something else wrong..." I pause and my stomach drops with the implications of what *could* be. "Shawn's good, Sunflower, but he's limited."

I know worry litters my voice. It's something I can't help at this point. Cole and Dex have told me that she needs space and that I need to stop hovering over her, but Kadence doesn't seem to mind it, and I'm not about to let her out of my sight. I'd be lying if I said I'm not scared to leave her alone again.

She reaches up, her hand cupping my cheek as her fingers dig into the beard I still haven't shaved down yet. I feel myself lean into her touch and I feel her warmth as my eyes search hers.

"My sweet man," she whispers and gives in. "Okay." Kadence nods.

The corners of my mouth turn upwards as I turn my face and wrap my hand gently around her wrist, pressing my lips to her palm. My fingers rest along her pulse, feeling the light flutter of her heartbeat beneath them. "Good girl."

Her tongue pokes out from between her lips, wetting them as a beautiful blush creeps over her cheeks. The words have done something to her, that's clear and something in the look in her eye makes my cock twitch.

Forcing myself to ignore the warm sensation in my belly, I pull her hand from my cheek and link our fingers. I check in with the receptionist, who gives us directions to the doctor's office. We make our way through the maze of hallways and two elevator rides after getting lost the first time.

Over the past few days of us sleeping in the same bed, I feel myself going mad. She'll kiss me, egg me on for more but even I know that it's not the right time. It kills me every time I put a stop to our make-out sessions. Cursing under my breath every time she looks disappointed. I want her as much as she seems to want me, if not more but I can't risk hurting her. I *won't* risk hurting her. Though there is no denying the sexual tension building between the two of us is a ticking time bomb.

Her appointment feels like a blur after the words *everything looks fine*, fall out of the doctor's mouth. Even Kadence feels the long exhale I let out in relief when her eyes meet mine and that beautiful smile returns to her face as if to say *I told you so*.

We make our way back down to the tow truck. I help her inside and jog around to the other side, climbing in. As soon as my door shuts I sit for a moment before starting the truck. *Everything looks fine.* The words keep repeating in my head. My hands wrap around the steering wheel as my eyes close. Images of her in that purple dress, lying face down in the sand, flood me.

"Holden?" She whispers, the seat creaking underneath her as I feel her move closer to me.

I didn't think it would hit me this hard. Hearing she was fine when I was so close to losing her. Shawn had told me before, the same from Cole and Dex. Even Wyatt and Scottie tried to comfort me whilst all I got was dirty looks from Blake. I still don't blame her for being mad that I left. That, because of my actions, Kadence ended up in the water. Hell, I'll gladly sit in that blame because it seems like Blake is the only one willing to punish me.

Kade's fingers dig into my forearm just enough to force my eyes open again to find her looking at me. Her brows furrow and worry is written all over her face.

"Baby, what's wrong?" She asks softly.

I smile gently, shaking my head and the horrible images away. "Nothing," I lean into her, pressing my lips to hers. "Nothing at all."

She smiles against my lips for a moment until I pull away. "You want to try that again a little bit more convincingly this time?" Kadence says gently.

I chuckle at her ability to read me so easily. The only other person who could do that was Becca. Her free hand combs through my hair, pushing it back. Something so soft, so intimate that I didn't think I'd enjoy so much. The feel of her hands on me, tangling in my hair. I still want to cut it, but I'd be lying if I didn't say I'd miss it for this exact reason.

Neither of us have spoken about the accident since after Shawn left that day. I don't want to relive it and it's something I'm not going to force on her. I'm only going to bring it up when she's ready for it or asks questions. I won't force her to relive that nightmare like she did her others.

"I am alright, babe," I rasp as I release the vice-like grip I have on the steering wheel and tangle my fingers into her hair at the back of her head. "You're alive, *safe*. I'm more than alright."

Kadence presses her forehead to mine, shaking her head. "I am both of those things because of you, Holden."

"You were in this mess because of *me*."

She pulls back from me. "Is that what you think?" Her brows knit together again, "I chased you, I went after you because I lo-" she cuts herself off and something in my gut wants her to finish the sentence, "because I wanted to. Because I wanted *this*." Her hand falls from my arm and she presses her palm to my heart.

"You should run for the hills," I chuckle, "it would be easier."

Kadence smiles. "I already ran for the hills, Holden," she presses her lips to mine again, dragging out the kiss before pulling back. "Those hills led me to you."

I stare at her for a moment, the realization that this woman isn't going to leave me hit like a sack of bricks. And not in the way that makes me sick or anxious but almost...giddy? I'm a grown man. Grown men don't get giddy. But if that is the case, why does it feel like a seventy-five-degree sunshiny day every time I look at her? Why does seeing the flecks of gold in her green eyes make me feel like I'm the richest man on earth or the way her laugh makes me feel the same as when I'm flying down an empty highway with nothing but my bike and the feeling of her arms wrapped around me.

I feel my brows furrow gently. That last part is new, and suddenly, everything I knew before feels irrelevant.

"You look like you just saw a ghost," she laughs, combing her fingers through my hair. "Where did you go just now?"

I chuckle along with her, leaning my head back into her touch as her fingers curl around the back of my head. My eyes search hers for a moment before I dip my head and kiss her. "To a happy place." I mumble against her mouth.

She pulls back gently and a grin spreads across her features. "If that look is your happy place it makes me a little worried, baby."

This time I let myself laugh, really laugh. "I promise it was."

Kadence hums in response. Her tongue darts over her bottom lip and she drags it between her teeth as she watches me for a moment.

"Can we move back into the apartment when we get home?" Her eyes glaze over me for a moment before moving away. "I just...I want to have you to myself and I can't do that with the guys and Blake, as much as I love them, hovering around us all the time and I really think that it's time. I can walk pretty much on my own and it doesn't hurt as bad and the doctor–"

I press my lips to hers again, cutting off her cute rambling and earning myself a small gasp at the movement. I cup her face with my left hand turning my body into her before pulling back.

"You don't ever have to ask to have me to yourself and..." I pause, debating on the stairs being a good idea at all even with her semi-clean bill of health. Other than the few bruised ribs she's fine to move about on her own, as much as I hate the idea of leaving her side. I watch the light in her eyes fade with my pause before shaking my head. "I think it's a good idea."

She smiles again. "Really?"

"Really." I mirror her. "The clubhouse was never supposed to feel like a prison, Kade. I just worry about the stairs, but you're better than before, so I think it's a good idea."

"As much as I love wearing your clothes, I don't think I pull off Badass Biker chic," Kadence laughs, curling into my side as I turn the key to the truck, letting it come to life. "I'm keeping this sweatshirt though."

"I could have grabbed your clothes!" I laugh heading back to the shop. "I just figured comfy would be better." I shrug as she looks up at me.

I glance down at her, taking my eyes off the road for a moment to notice the freckles poking out from her cheeks that I hadn't seen before. I dip my head and kiss her nose before looking back at the road.

Once we get back to the shop, we make our way through the clubhouse, saying our hellos to everyone and giving them the news that everything is fine. Wyatt moves to hug Kadence with a huge sigh of relief before I move in front of him, tossing him a warning look and earning a smack to my ribs from Kadence who moves around me swiftly to hug the prospect.

We gather a few things from the room we've been staying in and make our way across the parking lot to the apartment. I help her get settled, watching her every move for any discomfort even though she's told me about twenty times since the front door shut that she's fine.

"I'm gonna shower," she says softly, carefully trying to pull my sweatshirt over her head. It only takes one soft whine for me to jump up and help her, pulling each arm out and helping it over her head as her hands trail along my sides. Kadence stares up at me for a moment, my body coming alive with each gentle touch she grants me. "Do you want to join me?"

I swear my heart stops. Eyes wide. I watch her. "Are you sure?" My hands run down her arms and when she smirks I narrow my eyes. "Are you trying to seduce me, Andrews?"

She raises a brow and tilts her head to the side, my back arching forward slightly at the feel of her index finger trailing along the middle of my chest.

"Is it working?"

HOLDEN

My cock jumps at the low sultry tone in her voice as she looked up at me through thick lashes. It's working. It really, really, is working. Kadence doesn't wait for me to answer. Instead, she takes my hand in hers and steps back, tugging me towards the small attached bathroom.

She leans into the shower, her eyes never leaving mine as she bites that plush pink bottom lip of hers between her teeth. I try to push back the images I saw of her in the file Fisher gave me. The bruises that littered her skin, the evidence of trauma no woman should have to go through. Now, here she is in front of me, covered in bruises. I know I didn't physically put them there but knowing I was partially responsible kills me.

I believe what Dex told me and a part of me knows that she loves me. The fact that she's still here, not running for the hills and wanting more of me proves it.

I step forward and grip the soft flesh around her hips, being mindful to avoid any of the dark splotches that litter her skin.

"You know I would never hurt you, right?" I whisper. My voice is rough with the swirling tornado of emotions working their way up my throat and threatening to spill. "I would never do... or force you to..."

Her brows knit together as she cranes her neck to look up at me. Her eyes become glossy the longer we sit in this weighted silence. It's killing me, but I need to hear her confirmation. To hear her confirm I'm not the same.

"I'm not a good man, Sunflower, but I would never--"

"Stop," she chokes out, silencing me so quickly that my head spins for a moment. "I know you wouldn't hurt me- where is this coming from?"

I drop my head slightly, shaking it to try and clear the thoughts sucking any sort of sexual tension between us out of the room. Her small hand cups under my chin, lifting it to force my gaze to hers.

"I've seen the file, Kade, I just... I don't want you to be scared of me."

Her features soften as the night we first kissed replays in my mind. Her words burning my soul.

Are you scared of me?

Not in the way you think I am.

"Holden, I wouldn't have run after you if I was. I wouldn't have let you kiss me and I sure as hell would not have made you move from sleeping on the floor to the bed." She steps towards me, wrapping her arms around my waist. "A bad man would not have jumped into a freezing cold river to save me."

With every word, my body starts to melt into hers and I wrap my own arms around her. Her cheek presses to my chest undoubtedly hearing the thundering within it. If she believes in me this much, it is time I start doing the same.

"Please stop second guessing this," she whispers so quietly that if I hadn't settled into the brief silence, I would have missed it. Kade lifts her head to look up at me, resting her chin where her cheek had just laid. "I want this. I want *you*. No one else." My gaze flickers down to the tiny tremble in her lip. "If you don't want this, tell me now because I don't know if I could handle the fallout later down the road."

I swear my heart cracks. The last bit of cement I had around it turning into shattered debris at her feet.

My hand slides to the nape of her neck, tangling into her hair there as my gaze finds hers. Seeing and feeling every bit of doubt that my words just gave her.

"I want this," I rasp firmly, with as much reassurance as I can muster.

A soft sob leaves her lips and a wave of relief crashes down over us both. I suck in a breath of my own before feeling her hands snake around my body again, moving frantically as she begins to tear at my clothes. She pushes my shirt up and over my chest as everything we've both been holding back comes crashing through each of our walls.

I help her with the rest of my shirt, tossing it aside before peppering her cheeks and nose with soft kisses as her fingers work my jeans. She tilts her head back giving me access to the soft column of her neck. Her fingers roll down the waistband of my pants, pushing them down past my ass and to the floor. Her fingers are featherlight against my skin, sending a shudder up my spine and forcing a chuckle out of me as I kick the article aside, freeing my legs.

"Are you laughing at me?" She asks and even though my face is still buried in the crook of her neck I can hear the playfulness in her words.

"I'd never laugh at you, Sunflower," I say, gliding my hands down to her sweats and tasting the sensitive spot just below her ear. I lift my head, seeing her narrowed eyes at the smirk planted on my features, as I tease her midriff with my fingertips. Slowly, I start to kneel in front of her and loop my fingers within the waistband of her sweats.

"Hold my shoulders," I demand softly, peering up at her through my lashes. Her hands slowly climb over the muscle forcing the smirk on my face to turn into something softer. "Good girl," I rasp.

She tilts her head back and groans. "You can't say things like that to me."

I raise a brow, slowly peeling the sweats down her legs and helping her out of them before standing again.

"Why's that?" I ask, pulling her impossibly close to me. The heat of her skin against mine is enough to send me into a frenzy but I know I have to be careful and in control of my own needs.

Her tongue flicks over her bottom lip. "Do I really have to say it?"

I smile, kissing the tip of her nose and back her into the shower letting her take the rainfall of warm water first. "You don't have to, sweetheart, and we don't have to do anything you aren't ready for."

Her head tilts back as she lets the warm water run through her hair before looking back at me again. Even with both of us standing here exposed to one another I could still sense the hesitation lingering off of her. Hell, her eyes haven't gone farther than my waist. It makes my heart flutter at the idea that she has this innocence still within her but it also angers me that she was shoved back into it by someone who never deserved any part of her.

I dip my head, ridding myself of the blooming rage, and kiss her, letting the water cascade over both of us. "You're in control here, Kadence," I whisper against her lips. "You say stop and we stop."

She swallows hard and I see her bottom lip tremble softly again. I know that giving her the power to stop this is a huge thing and one that I would never deny her. I pull back slightly and wait for her to work through whatever is going through her mind.

"I'm okay," she reassures with a shaky breath, "I've never had someone—" Kadence cuts herself off. I wrap around her again as she presses her cheek to my chest once more. "I've just never had the choice before." The words come out thready and strained and it takes everything in me to extinguish the hatred in my chest for the man that broke her.

Instead, I press my lips to the crown of her head and rock her gently under the waterfall. "You'll always have the choice with me."

"I'm sorry," she says against my skin. Leaning back I tilt her chin up with the crook of my finger and smile taking in the glowing jade green of her eyes.

"Don't you ever apologize for what he did," I say firmly. "What happened was not your fault and I will spend every day proving to you that what he did was not affection, it wasn't lust, and it sure as shit wasn't love."

Her eyes flicker between mine, the tears gathering in them quickly well up until she blinks and they spill over her cheeks. Gently, I swipe them away, caressing her cheek. "He doesn't deserve your tears, Sunflower. He never did."

Kadence lets out an exhale as if another weight is being lifted off of her and it kills me yet again to see another brick fall away from her walls. I meant it when I said I'd break them all down to make her feel safe. To wrap myself around the parts of her no one else sees, the parts that she hides away from everyone else to shield her from the bad in her world. If only she'll let me.

I move in to kiss her gently, tangling my hands into her hair. I'm tentative and careful as I press against her. I want her to know that she has access to every part of me. Every jagged edge I have, I'll help her around, and every soft part I hide from everyone. She breaks the kiss and takes another breath to look up at me.

"Tell me what you need, Sunflower, anything at all, and I'll give it to you."

She stares back at me, swallowing tightly with whatever she is working through in that beautiful mind of hers.

"I need you," She finally says after a moment.

The corners of my mouth turn upwards. "You have me," I counter and feel her shake her head as I nip at her jaw.

"I *need* you." Her hands came up to rest over my chest, her right palm planted over my heart. "*Please.*"

My only answer is a kiss as I pull our bodies closer. Slick from the water and just as warm. I hear her whimper as I swipe my tongue over her bottom lip and without hesitation they part, granting me access to delve into her the way I want. Keeping one hand tangled into her hair, I slide the other down her body, barely touching the sensitive area over her hips before gripping her hip, digging my fingers into the soft flesh. In one swift motion I press her against the cool tiled wall and drag my lips to nip at her jawline wrapping my hand around her thigh.

"Lift your foot here," I mumble against her skin and help steady her foot against the corner edge of the shower. She's pliable under my touch and it only makes me harder realizing that she's trusting me this much. Combined with the flutter in my chest, I know she's it.

My hand slides up her thigh, teasing her and watching the way her body shudders and arches towards my hand. My lips find her neck, sucking on the sensitive spot below her ear, only grinning when she moans and grinds against my hand. My cock twitches with every tiny movement and noise she makes.

My thumb slides over her clit, pressing gently and making her gasp. I can feel her nails dig into my back, and knowing that she's leaving small crescent moon-shaped marks stokes the fire in my stomach.

"Tell me if it's too much," I breathe against her ear, nipping at her lobe.

She manages to shake her head. "Keep going," she moans and nips at my collarbone. "Please don't stop." Her fingers tangle into my hair, tugging gently.

"Only if you tell me to," I groan, continuing to work her with my thumb while exploring her folds with my fingers.

She's so wet that carefully sliding my middle finger into her is easy. Kadence gasps as another shudder rolls through her, pebbling her nipples. I smile when she begins to rock against my hand, taking more of it each time and using me for her own pleasure.

I pull back to watch her lose herself. Her cheeks are flushed and her hair sticks against her cheeks from the water. She's addicting.

I add another finger, watching as she tenses and relaxes in my arms all within moments. I'm not a small man, and after everything she's been through, I want to make her savor this. I want to show her what sex should be.

My lips attach to her neck, marking every inch of skin I can while bringing her to the edge and enjoying every pretty little sound that she makes. All of it sends jolts of pleasure straight to my cock. I latch on to her nipple, swirling my tongue around it before moving to the other and showing it the same attention.

"Oh my," she breathes, clenching around my hand and forcing a smug grin over my features, against her skin. She's close and it's taking every ounce of my control to hold back. Her lips move to my neck as her hands explore every part of me.

"I can feel you, Kade," I groan. "Fuck." Her moans echo off of the shower walls as I curl my fingers against her, finding that soft spot within her that has her knees weak. My lips hover over hers, our breath mingling. "I've got you, Sunflower, let go."

"Hol-den," her voice is strained in response and her head tips back against the wall as she falls over the edge. I don't dare stop as she rolls through wave after wave of her orgasm.

Sweet mewls and praises fill the bathroom, floating through the steam as she comes down from her high. She might have needed me, but watching her in pure bliss only fuels the need I have for her. To mark every part of her as my own if she'll let me.

"You're so pretty when you come," I praise, kissing her again as her arms wrap around my neck. I pull back hearing her chuckle softly. I smirk at the blush that graces her skin. "Don't go gettin' shy on me now, I'm not done with you yet." My hand wraps around her thigh, wrapping it around my waist. My cock nudges against her already sensitive clit forcing another moan from her. I nip at her chin, sinking my teeth into her neck and wrap my other arm around her waist.

"Jesus," she breathes as the tip of my cock works through her folds.

I'm careful as I start to slide into her. Her mouth drops open and I can feel her tense around me again.

"Are you okay?" I ask, searching her eyes. She nods but it's not enough. Not now. "I need your words, Kadence. Nothing happens without your words."

She whimpers and buries her face against my shoulder. "Please, I'm okay. Just *please*, I need more."

I smile at the neediness in her voice only because it matches what I feel. The ache of wanting her sits heavy in my core like a weight I never want to get rid of.

"Keep telling me how much you need it, Sunflower," I rasp, pressing my lips to the shell of her ear, nipping at her earlobe as I push further inside of her.

Every muscle in her body tenses for a moment when I fill her completely. I know better than to move until she is used to the size of me. The last thing I want to do is hurt her while proving to her she's safe with me.

I wait until she slowly begins to melt against me, her body relaxes and clenches around me. The combination was deadly and addicting.

Her toes struggle against the wet floor of the tub while I start to move in long slow strokes teasing us both.

A ragged moan leaves her and her arms tighten around my neck until I can't hold back anymore and lift her fully. She doesn't hesitate to wrap her legs around my waist as I press her against the wall.

She kisses me this time, biting down on my bottom lip as my pace quickens. Those sweet moans fall from her again and I swallow each one, unable to hold back any longer.

"Such pretty noises," I rasp. "Show me how to make you sing, Sunflower."

Soft praises start to fall from her lips and I can't get enough of the sound of her falling apart under my touch. I pull almost all of the way from her before sliding fully in. A squeal of pleasure fills my ears before she starts to giggle. I can't help but chuckle with her while marking her skin with little red splotches.

She flutters around me and my pace falters. I want more of her, need more of her, but right now, watching the way she comes has me on the brink. The tip of my cock hits that soft spot within her and she gasps, her body tensing. I freeze and pull back to look at her.

"What's wrong?" I ask, trying not to panic on the off chance I hurt her.

Kadence shakes her head, moving her hips in a gentle wave against my pelvis, still chasing her release. "Nothing, that just felt new."

Her admission makes my brows furrow. I chase that spot once more and her body reacts the same way only this time her head falls back again and a sinful moan leaves her lips.

"Interesting," I grin.

The fact that no one has made her feel like this before only eggs me on and a smug smirk falls over my features as I drop my head to suck on the soft skin of her breasts. In time, I'll show her everything I can do with that perfect little spot. I only want to make her feel good, and right now, with the moans dripping from her and her cunt fluttering around me, it was only pushing me further and further over the edge and into my own pleasure.

My movements become erratic, my hips stuttering as I move to kiss her again letting our tongues tangle together. "Come with me," I command softly against her lips, "I can feel you, Sunflower, come over that edge with me."

I grunt as her nails claw at my back again, the pain adding a sickeningly sweet combination to the rubber band tightening in my belly.

Kadence lets out a moan that sounds every bit pornographic and bites down on my shoulder as her climax hits her, sending me hurtling over the edge. Her name leaves my lips against her skin. Our bodies shudder with release as I spill into her.

I brace us both on the wall. Her body is jelly in my arms as the water spraying us turns lukewarm. It didn't matter though, with the way her body fit perfectly around mine. It could turn cold and I'd hold her here for as long as she'll let me.

"That--" She breathes, completely wrecked with her head resting on my shoulder, "that was..."

"How it's supposed to be," I finished kissing her shoulder. I carefully let her down and make sure she's steady on her shaky legs before letting go of her and turning off the water. She doesn't respond to me, only stepping back and looking shy again. "We'll shower when the hot water is back."

"Okay," she whispers, and I can tell that she's retreating back into her head and into whatever dark memories are surfacing.

I wrap a towel around her, rubbing her arms gently. "We can talk about it, but we don't have to."

"No," she shakes her head, "it wasn't bad--fuck--it was more than good." A slightly awkward laugh leaves her lips. "I guess I'm just.. shellshocked."

I can't help the smug look that returns to my face. Determination floods me to show her everything this could be, what making love should be. I wrap around her again, peppering her cheeks with soft kisses, something I had grown to love only because it usually coaxed a stream of giggles to spill from her like it did now.

"It's only going to get better from here, Sunflower."

KADENCE

His arms wrap around my waist, tugging me against his chest.

"I'm never going to let anything hurt you." Holden's words become muffled as he buries his face into the crook of my neck. My cheeks flush feeling his growing erection press against my belly.

"I'm sure you and the rest of the three musketeers won't," I murmur against his still wet skin.

His chuckles fill the room as he walks me towards the edge of the bed. "The three musketeers?" Holden asks, his hands running up and down my arms, sending another trail of fireworks down my spine.

I giggle, the fire in my core starting to burn in a soft smolder once again. What we did in the shower... I never experienced anything like it. It was like my own out-of-body experience as he gracefully explored every inch of me. Giving me everything I need physically and showing me that sex isn't just all about being forceful. It can be beautiful, too, and that realization is what brings on the shock.

"You," I breathe as he turns me around in his arms and presses a kiss to my chest, "Cole and Dex." I glance up at him, the smile on his face falters for only a moment as he steps back from me and that instant feeling that I've done something wrong sinks in. "What?"

He shakes his head and moves around me. "Nothing," Holden murmurs as he searches for clothes in his bag.

"Holden," I urge, hugging the towel to myself. I step towards him, running my hand over his back, "are you jealous?" I ask carefully, wincing when I feel the muscles in his back tense up.

"No," he bites but even I can see his jaw working as he pulls out a pair of briefs.

"Hey," I say softly, stepping closer because even though I can feel the tension radiating off of him, I'm not going to let whatever this is slip between our closing cracks. "This only works if you talk to me. I don't know how to make you feel better if I don't know what's wrong."

Holden runs a hand over his face and lets out something between a sigh and growl, the frustration in his eyes evident as he finally looks at me. "It's not anything that you did," he pauses for a moment and stares at me before reaching out his hand and tugging me to him.

He sits on the edge of the bed, urging me to sit next to him. "Things between Wolfe, Cole, and I haven't been the same since you showed up." I move to pull my hands from him, my lips falling open slightly to protest that statement but I'm cut off with his lips against mine. "It's not your fault," he reassures, silencing me. "I wasn't–haven't been the most trustworthy since I got out. They're leery of me having something that I could very possibly ruin, especially when that something is you."

"You aren't going to ruin me, Holden." I reply with conviction, "Cole and Dex will need to realize that they aren't my keepers and they aren't my jailers. They're my friends and I am grateful that they want to protect me, but protecting me from *you* isn't an option I'll let them have." The corners of my mouth turn up as I take his face into my hands. "I won't let them and you shouldn't either."

Holden chuckles as his hands cover mine, intertwining our fingers and bringing my hands to his lips, kissing each finger. "Has anyone ever told you that you're a tiny bit stubborn?"

I laugh. "Maybe a few times."

He grins before leaning into me, capturing my lips in his, making the butterflies in my chest swarm and flutter. A feeling that I'm getting used to and at the same time, not. I never felt this way with Jeremy. It always felt like walking on broken glass. Painful and on edge. Being with Holden feels like floating on a cloud when we aren't arguing which, over the last few days, has been less and less.

I'm learning to speak my mind again. To not shut down at the first sign of trouble and sink into myself. I've noticed a change in Holden as well, usually with some urging and my hands calming his tense muscles. He's begun to open up to me and show me a softness that I haven't seen in a really long time.

His lips glide over my own and I pull back gently. He's given me space to tell him on my own what happened that night, and for the years prior, but I have to also live by the words that fell from my lips. If this is going to work, I have to be open and honest with him. *No More Secrets.*

"I want to show you something," I say softly, pulling from his grasp and moving to my suitcase, which is still packed, making a mental note to put things away later. I quickly step into a pair of underwear and tug a tank top over my body, ignoring the dull ache in my side.

Digging my hand into the bag I know my past is hidden in, I freeze as my fingers wrap around the plush stuffed animal. I slowly pull it from my bag, staring down at the bright gold eyes and light-colored blue spots that decorate the giraffe's body. It feels like my heart is stepping into another world, staring down at one of the only reminders of what I've lost. My stomach aches as I turn back to Holden. His brows furrow but his gorgeous worried blue eyes are glued on the animal in my hands.

I make my way back to the bed and climb onto the mattress, sitting cross-legged in front of him. My fingers fiddle with the small ear as I search for the right words to say. Painfully aware that I'm tugging at what feels like healing stitches when I start.

"I wanted to name him after my father, George," I say softly, sucking in a breath. "Jeremy hated it, said it was an old man's name."

Holden reaches for me, his fingers wrapping around my calf giving it a reassuring squeeze as my eyes flicker to his. I feel the familiar burn behind my eyes watching his own softening with my words. He hasn't said anything and before he can offer me any sentiments I shake my head,

"He had been so on edge that morning, I should've–" I sigh. "For a few weeks before that day, everything had been normal again. He was loving, came home at a decent time, and didn't question every little thing I did. I had my freedom back for the first time in months."

I set the giraffe between us, watching as Holden uses his free hand to pick it up and inspect it over. His eyes flicker to me and I can see the tornado of sadness and anger swirling in them but even more it feels like they're begging me to continue.

"It had to have been something at work that threw him back into his anger. It was always something with work. A bad bust, reprimand for excessive force, the list was long with Jeremy and yet they kept him around." I shake my head. "He wasn't a good cop." I glance up at him, the warning low in my voice "He did things off the books that he shouldn't have. He and his partners had their own form of justice that the department let slide because it was working to bring down some of the worst humans. They just ignored the fact that they had some of those worst beings working for them."

His hand squeezes my calf again. "How do you know all of that?" Holden gently asks.

"Like I said, he wasn't a good cop in any sense of the word." I shift on the bed, tucking my hair behind my ear. "He left paperwork lying around, took calls in front of me, and didn't try to hide what he and his buddies were doing." A harsh hollow chuckle leaves me, "I guess he figured I wouldn't say anything so long as he kept me in line."

"Jesus, Kade," Holden breathes, his hands unmoving on my skin.

I let my hands wrap around his. "That night, I don't know what happened. I know he blamed it on me making fucking lasagna for dinner." I feel the prickles on my skin as the memories start to overwhelm me. I take a deep breath, my eyes sliding closed, feeling Holden's eyes bore into me in anticipation of whatever I'm about to say. "I ran that night. I found myself sitting in the same corner of my dining room, huddled away from him when I knew that it was just more than myself I needed to protect."

My hand rests carefully over my stomach, the empty womb that should still be carrying my child today, haunting me. "I used to run, but as time went on, it was harder to get away from him and easier just to take it." My chin wobbles and I know Holden can hear the shakiness in my voice. "He threw the dinner plates at me, barely missing me which only pissed him off more. I don't remember what he was yelling at that point. I just remember that one moment I was reaching for the front door and the next he had me pinned against the shattered picture frames on the wall."

I blink away the tears and hold my eyes closed for a moment trying to get the images to leave. Holden's thumb swipes away the tears on my cheeks as he moves closer to me, the giraffe in his lap as I look up at him.

"It's how I got the scar on my shoulder, glass dug too deep under the skin, but it was nothing compared to the pain I felt hitting the corner of the coffee table when he tossed me, calling me useless."

He sucks in a breath, his free hand cupping my face. His eyes have turned glossy, and even though they feel soft, the muscle working in his jaw tells me he's everything but. "I'm sorry," Holden whispers.

I shake my head. "Don't."

"Sunflower," he whines as I lean into his touch and wrap a hand around his wrist.

"Please just–" I suck in a breath, "just let me get through this." I squeeze his wrist, pulling his hand from my face and tucking it in my lap. I need to feel him to keep me grounded and to avoid getting swallowed up by the memories I have been trying so desperately not to drown in.

With a deep breath, I steady myself. "A neighbor walking their dog heard the commotion." I let out a soft laugh as tears trickle from my eyes. "Thank god for Mr. Capecci and his annoying terrier. He called 9-1-1. I don't know how long it took for them to get there truthfully, but when Jeremy opened the door it was over."

Holden grabs me and pulls me into his lap, hugging me close to his body. I want to push away. I don't want to feel broken anymore. I don't want to see the pity on anyone else's face. Especially his. But he holds me tight and for once I let myself soak up his warmth and comfort. I bury my face into his chest, squeezing my eyes closed. "They told me the baby didn't survive like it was just any other diagnosis and now... My mother is dating the man."

"She's what?" He asks anger trickling into his words.

"The doctor who told me stitched me up–he was in the Bahamas with my mother."

He pulls back to look down at me, his brows furrow as if to ask if I'm serious. I sigh.

"When I told you my mother hasn't been my mother for a very long time, this was just the cherry on top. She chose Jeremy over me. She chose herself over my father after he died, forgetting the fact that I was twelve and still just a kid. Janice is not my family."

"Jesus, Kade," Holden breathes and his arms tighten around me. Silence washes over us for a few moments. "Why did you tell me this? Why now?"

I shift in his arms so that my legs straddle either side of his waist, wrapping my arms around his neck. "Because you should know that the scars I carry aren't just visible on my skin. They aren't marred flesh that can be hidden with clothes. They live deep within me and I don't know how to heal them." My voice trails off into a whisper. "And because they haven't made me feel as nearly as strong as I do when I'm with you."

"Baby, you've always been strong. You had to be to live through that shit," he whispers. His hands tangle in my still damp hair, pulling me into him. "I should kill him for what he did to you," Holden pauses, anger flaring behind his blue eyes, "what he continues to do to you."

I press my lips to his tasting the saltiness of my tears mixed with his usual sweetness and a hint of tobacco before pulling back. "I'm scared, Holden," My voice barely over a whisper. "I don't want him to come after me. I don't want to see him, and I'm scared that he'll find out where I am."

The idea has been weighing on me ever since the news junket and the brief stout with Holden had distracted me from the fear. But now that he's back and that Jeremy has been radio silent since that day, it feels like everything is still crashing down on me in slow motion. I haven't even turned on my phone since that day. I know Maria must be worried, but I can't risk putting everyone in danger for one phone call. I also know how naive it is to hope that Jeremy will just forget about me.

"He'll have to go through me before he gets to you again," he says firmly. "No one is touching a hair on this beautiful head without suffering the consequences." Holden dips his head to catch my eyes and wraps his fingers around the back of my neck. "You hear me?"

Warmth flutters in my belly at the conviction in his voice. His free arm twists around my waist, pulling me impossibly close to him. I relish the way he holds me and protects me. Even if over the last week he had been, what Cole called, 'obnoxiously guard doggish'. But I love it. It makes me feel safe and like for once I can breathe.

Despite the scars that live deep within me, Holden makes me want to heal. He makes me want to forget what it was like to feel broken and unprotected. Every promise he makes, I know he will do everything in his power to keep.

"I hear you," I whisper, grazing my lips against his.

"Good," he rumbles, clearly satisfied with my words.

My hips roll against his, teasing the hard length that's pressed against my core. He pulls back to look at me, really look at me. His eyes flicker between my own as he searches for any hesitation. My tongue rolls over my bottom lip before I tug it between my teeth and I see him smirk.

"What's going through that pretty head?" He asks.

The grip he has on my neck tightens just for a moment like he's trying to hold himself back from tossing me behind him on the bed. Normally the idea would scare the shit out of me. Now? I want nothing more than that.

I want my power back. I want to know what it would be like to be in control for once. So when he leans in to nip at my lip, I plant both hands firmly on his shoulders stopping him. "Will you let me be in control?" I ask softly.

Holden's brows furrow for a moment. "You'll always have the control."

I shake my head. "I don't mean with my words, baby." I grind my hips down on him again feeling him between the thin pieces of cotton that separate us.

KADENCE

One of his furrowed brows lifts as he studies me for a moment longer. His arm falls from around my waist before helping me off of his lap. I frown at the gesture until he moves to stand in front of me. He dips his head to graze his lips against my jaw sending fireworks shooting straight up my spine at the warmth of his breath against my ear.

"Then I'm all yours, Sunflower."

The sudden rasp in his voice hits every nerve-ending as he presses his lips to my cheek and takes a step back from me. Offering himself up on the platter I asked for.

I inhale sharply, dragging my gaze over his body. I feel nervous that he actually agreed to do this, something I hadn't fully expected, but I'm grateful he's willing to give this to me. Judging by the dark look in his eye... I bet he's willing to give me more.

"Take off your briefs," I demand in a shaky voice.

My eyes flick up to his own, silently asking if that's okay. The quick upturn of his lips lets me know that it was more than as his thumbs hook into the band of his underwear and he slides them down his legs. Again my eyes find every ridge and rope of muscle that works as he stands straight again, kicking the clothing to the side. From the litter of tattoos scattered on his arms I'm surprised he doesn't have as many on his chest.

I step towards him, running the tips of my fingers over the large plane of his chest. Memorizing the constellation of freckles that paint his skin under the soft smattering of his chest hair.

"Tell me what to do," he urges softly, keeping his hands to his side while I explore him. "I trust you."

My gaze finds his and I can see it written within the deep blue. The words we haven't said yet, his want for me even as the blue is eclipsed into a delicious darkness I want to fall into.

"Undress me," I breathe, dropping my hands to my side.

Holden smiles approvingly at me, giving back a little bit of the confidence I had when I asked him to do this but had wavered when he agreed.

His hands come to my sides, gripping them gently. Holden trails his fingertips along the hem of my shirt, teasing my already burning skin. Carefully he tugs on the end of it and pulls it over my head. I watch as his eyes dance around the fading bruises that litter my skin for just a moment before they flicker back to mine and force out the breath I didn't realize I was holding as he drops my shirt. For a brief moment I hesitate. Can I really do this?

The moment his fingers hook into the elastic of my underwear and he lowers himself to his knees in front of me the doubt dissipates. He helps me out of them, tosses them aside, and sits back on his haunches, waiting.

The sight makes my heart hammer against my ribcage almost painfully. "What are you doing?"

"Tell me what you want," he rasps. His hands are firmly planted on top of his muscular thighs and his cock stands tall against his belly. Weeping and ready. I gnaw on the inside of my cheek, unsure of what to tell him to do, even though my body itches to feel his hands on every inch of me.

"Do you want me to stay down here?"

It isn't brash or condescending and for a moment I pause. His fingers drum against his legs, impatient but I know it's not because I can't make a decision but because I haven't let him touch me.

I nod, answering his question. "Yes."

Holden's grin grows wider as he lifts his chin, his long hair falls against his forehead and cheeks. I reach out, pushing it back from his face and tangle my fingers into the still damp chestnut locks.

"Kiss me," I whisper, the ache between my legs becoming too much with the sight of him on his knees for me.

"As you wish," he breathes, igniting the spark in my belly.

His hands lift and wrap around the back of my thighs, pulling himself forward and closer to my core. His eyes are still glued to mine as he perches up slightly and presses soft chaste kisses to my hip bones, dragging them against my heated skin between each one leaving a wake of goosebumps.

His lips begin to move lower and his hands move higher up my thighs until they're cupping the underside of my ass. Every movement forces a moan to drip from my lips.

"Don't let go of me," Holden mumbles against my skin.

My brows kiss in confusion until he hooks his arm underneath my knee, lifting it to give him better access to my core. Suddenly he dips his head, pressing a kiss against my clit before sliding his tongue between my folds.

My head drops back as a sigh leaves me. My hand that's tangled in his hair tugs at the roots while the other holds onto his shoulder, my nails digging into his skin. His tongue flicks over my clit again and it sends a jolt of lightning spreading through my spine.

"Oh God," I breathe. He pulls back for a moment, nipping at my thigh hung over his arm with a wicked grin spread over his lips. I glance down at him, every bit of me is needy for the feeling of his tongue against me again. "Why did you stop?"

His eyes glisten up at me, sucking his bottom lip between his teeth.

"Because every sound that falls from those lips makes it harder to keep myself from throwing you on that bed and fucking you in every way you've never been fucked before."

I gasp as he slides his index finger through my cunt, catching my arousal and spreading it over my clit so slowly that my leg almost gives out. "You're the sweetest thing I've ever tasted."

My eyes go wide and I can't tell if I'm blushing or hot with desire. No one has ever spoken to me like that before. I was comfortable making advances, but my sexual experience usually consisted of grunts and silence. My body was never appreciated for more than just what it was. A body. Tears threaten the corners of my eyes at the thought of being worshiped and at this normally gruff man praising every inch of me that he can get a hold of.

"Keep going," I demand quietly. "Please." If only to keep the emotions at bay.

He grins again, planting another kiss on my thigh before dragging his lips back to my core. The rubber band in my belly tightens with every lick and nip he graces me with. Every move makes me shudder and my knee feels weaker the closer I get, that is until he slips his index finger through my entrance and curls it ever so slightly while his tongue lashes at me. I clench around him, my breaths becoming ragged and shaky. "Holden, don't--" I sob out between mewls and soft praises.

"Don't what?" He growls against my skin adding a second finger and forcing a louder moan from me. Everything feels fuzzy as he works me, warmth spreads from my fingertips down my toes as the room fills with a chorus of our sounds. I look down at him, eclipsed blue eyes meeting mine. I can feel myself teetering over the edge, my toes dangling off the cliff as if he was holding the back of my shirt, letting me experience the thrill of dangling but keeping me safe.

"That," I gasp as he pumps his fingers in and out of me. "Don't stop that."

He lets out a slew of gruff curses and I can feel my arousal drip down my thighs, over his hand and chin. I've never felt this before and, as his fingers curl over that spot within me, stars burst through my vision and a ragged moan falls from my lips. He lets me fall with his arms wrapped around me, diving straight over the cliff into waves of euphoria. My legs shake and my toes curl against the carpet as he works me through it all.

Holden sits back and we both catch our breath, slowly letting my leg down and holding onto my thighs to keep me steady. I release the grip I have on his hair and step back catching the sight of his cock, bobbing against his stomach with each heave of his chest. Our gazes meet with the intensity of his burning through my skin in such a way that I can feel the fire in my belly stoke.

I hold out my hand, ignoring the emotions bubbling inside me with everything he's done for me today. For once, I didn't feel broken. Even after reliving that night, giving him every detail. I feel... whole. He is doing that for me, and even looking down at him with his hair all mussed and pupils blown out, I would never be able to express to him how grateful I am.

His hand slips into mine as he stands. Assessing me as I step towards him and rest my palms against his chest. I raise up on my toes and press my lips to his in a fevered kiss that he returns with no question. I'm impressed he still has the control to keep his hands at his sides while still giving me the reins.

"Bed," I say softly against his mouth. His tongue flicks over his bottom lip catching mine. I smirk and press against his chest, pushing him a step backward until his knees catch the edge of the bed. "Sit against the headboard."

He raises a brow and moves to sit on the edge of the bed but not before setting the small giraffe on the nightstand. An overwhelming urge to cry at the tenderness floods me, but I swallow it down, glancing at the animal before landing on a splayed-out Holden. His broad shoulders rest against the headboard and I don't miss the way his hands are clenched into fists. Suddenly the urge to continue to have him keep his hands to himself flies out the window, taking every warring emotion with it.

HOLDEN

Not touching her is the hardest part of all of this. I have to bite back a moan as she climbs over the edge of the bed. The mattress dips with her sweat-sheened body as she crawls toward me. The image burning into the back of my brain for later. God, the sight of her above me, head tilted back, long hair cascading down her back as she comes. I could die here and now and will be happy. But this? Watching the confidence flow through her as something in her expression changes, her eyes still blown out, but unafraid to take what she needs from me... I'll do it over and over again.

She glances down at my cock, her tongue wetting her lips as she settles herself between my legs. As much as I want her mouth on me, I also need to be inside her so much that my dick aches. I'm trying so hard not to touch her or myself that when I glance down at it, it almost twitches with anger.

"Can't decide," Kadence's soft sweet voice filters through my thoughts.

I suck in a breath. "Baby, I'm not gonna last very much longer before I need to be inside you."

The admission earns me a shy smile, one that tugs directly on the little heartstrings I have left. She rests her hands on my thighs, digging her nails into my muscles just enough that the sensation goes straight to my balls. "Maybe I should make you wait then," she counters, biting that plump bottom lip.

I chuckle. "Give you an inch and you take a mile, darlin'."

Kadence laughs a real wholehearted laugh that bounces off the walls. "Oh, I plan on taking plenty of inches." As soon as the words register, she grimaces, scrunching her nose.

My fists unclench as I try to bite back my own laugh. "That was terrible." I lean forward, pressing my lips to hers.

She smiles knowingly at me, pressing her hand to my chest and pushing me back against the headboard once more.

"I didn't ask you to kiss me," she says in a breathy whisper. Her palm rests right over my heart and I know she can feel it racing against her touch.

"Don't make me wait," I whisper back, not above begging her at this point. It's only been an hour since I last felt her clenching and fluttering around me and I need it again.

Kadence smiles again, moving to straddle me as her legs settle on either side of my waist. She lines herself over me and rocks her hips letting her cunt stroke the underside of my cock. I groan, letting my eyes fall shut as my head slams back against the headboard. Her arms snake around my neck.

"Touch me," Kadence's whisper forces my eyes open, her eyes glued to mine.

I try to hide the tiny party going on in my chest as I ask, "Are you sure?"

She chuckles, dipping her head as her hands find mine.

"Am I still in control?" Kadence asks, grazing her lips against my pec. She laces her fingers with mine at the same time and drags her lips up my chest over my collarbone. Waves of goosebumps rush over my body as she nips at my skin.

"Always," I reply with a shaky breath.

Kadence smiles against my neck as she lifts our hands, rocking her hips again. She moans practically in my ear. "Then touch me."

I can tell her confidence is growing and it makes me proud. If spending all day in bed with her makes her feel powerful, letting her do whatever she wants to me, I'll do it. Kadence guides my hands over her breasts before unlacing our fingers and snaking her arms around my neck. They're heavy in my hands. Her soft skin burns underneath my touch and I can feel the heat from her cunt radiating over me. It's driving me crazy and the need to be inside her is only growing with every gentle roll of her hips.

She continues to trail her lips over my skin before tangling her fingers into the hair at the nape of my neck as I begin gently tugging on her pebbled nipples.

"This feels incredible." Lust drips from her words but I sense something else in them too. Something softer.

I admittedly never take things this slow. I'm all for foreplay, but it's usually me giving it, not receiving it. If I'm being completely honest with myself, I've never wanted to take sex slow with anyone before. I care if the other women got off, sure, but I've never wanted more than just one night with them. Not until Kade.

I nudge my nose against the side of her cheek, forcing her to look at me before I capture her lips with mine dragging out a slow kiss. Her tongue darts out, swiping along the seam of my lips and without argument I part them for her. I slide my hands down to her waist, gripping her hips and digging my fingers into her softness.

Kadence pulls back, her gaze burning into mine as our breaths mix. I'm not even inside her yet, and still, I can already feel the tightening of my balls and the muscles in my back straining as I hold off my orgasm.

As if she knows what I'm thinking, I feel her lift her hips and reach between us. I can't help myself when my knuckles graze her clit pulling a hiss from her lips. She's soaked, and in return, I'm soaked and covered in her slick.

"You can't help yourself can you?" She teases through pants, her chest already heaving. I let out a soft laugh as I line myself up with her entrance.

"When you look like this? And you're practically riding my cock driving me fucking crazy?" I ask, moving my hands back to her hips and guiding her down, slowly filling her. "No, Sunflower, I can't."

A grin spreads across my lips when her mouth drops into a soft 'o' shape. Her eyes flutter as I fully bottom out. I dip my head, nipping the top of her breasts, sucking at the soft skin as her moans fill the room.

"You feel so fucking good," I breathe and feel her body melt into mine.

"God, Holden," she moans, beginning to roll her hips against mine, dragging her clit across my groin. I tangle my hands into her hair, pulling her to me and kissing her again. She tastes so fucking good, like strawberries and mint.

Everything starts falling together. My hips piston into her, unable to keep control anymore. She still has the power to stop everything if she needs to but every time I look at her she's further gone. She clenches around me, her body trembling softly as the sounds between us grow louder.

"Come for me," I breathe, reaching for her clit and drawing fast, tight circles around her swollen nub. Kadence lets out a ragged moan as she falls over the edge, taking me with her. My hips stutter beneath her and my head slams back into the headboard again as I groan with my release. Spilling into her as she flutters around me.

Kadence buries her face into my neck, her breathing heavy and hot against my skin. Her body still trembles gently against me. I haven't felt this satiated in a long time. I run my fingers up and down her back with one hand and wrap my arm around her waist holding her to me.

"Thank you," she finally whispers after a few moments of quiet silence has settled between us. Kade lifts her head, smiling softly at me through thick lashes. Her hair is tangled from my hands, her lips bitten pink. She glows even more than she did before.

I can't help myself when I pull her back for another kiss. My lips pressing to hers with a contented sigh. "I'd do anything for you, Kadence," I whisper against her mouth. "You taking what you need from me when it's just the two of us is something I'll always do."

I notice the familiar glossiness that begins to take over her green eyes. Making them that bright green I love. Her bottom lip trembles and she only responds with a nod, but I'm not going to push her any further than she's pushed herself.

"We should shower now," I say softly, kissing the corner of her mouth.

Kadence shakes her head resting it against my shoulder. "Can we just stay like this for a while?" Her voice sounds so quiet with the question. So vulnerable, and my heart aches with the realization that this post-sex cuddling is something she's probably never experienced.

"Did he do this?" I ask before I can even stop the question from falling from my lips as my hands run up and down her back.

"Do what?" She hums tightly.

I suck in a breath. "Did he hold you after sex?"

I don't miss the way her body tenses when I clarify, but I give her the space to answer if she wants to. After a few beats of silence, she shakes her head. My hand falls from her back, clenching in frustration before pushing back the annoyance. "I'm sorry," I offer.

"Don't be," She counters, adjusting herself so she can look up at me still resting against my chest, "I'm glad it was you and not him."

I nod but don't respond. Instead I settle back into the bed, holding her to me. I need to talk to Cole tomorrow. We have to figure out a plan if Jeremy decides to grow balls and come after her. I was serious when I promised that the prick would have to go through me to get to her. Hell, my trigger finger itches at the idea of putting a bullet between the fucker's eyes. But I'll never admit that to Kadence.

She has already had too much pain and death in her life, and if I can help it, I'll make sure she never has to go through shit like that ever again. Kadence is stronger than she gives herself credit for. She has said multiple times that she doesn't want anyone to pity her or look at her like she's a kicked puppy. What she fails to realize is that whenever I look at her, all I see is a survivor, a *fighter*. Someone stronger than I ever was.

The sound of a cell phone buzzing breaks through the comfortable silence that fell over us. She picks up her head, glancing at me, and her brows furrow.

"Mine's been dead," Kadence says softly.

I groan, knowing that it's one of the guys blowing up my phone. I'm reluctant to leave this spot and lose the warmth that radiates from her body. But I know that if I don't answer it now, at some point one of them will come bang down her door.

Kadence presses a kiss to my chest before pressing her lips to mine. "You should get that," she whispers softly. "I'm going to go shower."

The vibrating stops and a grin spreads across my face as I glance down at her, kissing her again and humming.

"Or," I dip my head, kissing the column of her throat, "we could ignore it and stay here for a few more quiet minutes." I circle my hips, feeling myself already getting hard again. She moans, rolling her hips with mine.

"How are you already good to go again?" She laughs softly, a sound I swallow quickly with my lips as I pull her back down to me.

"Well darlin," I rasp against her mouth, "when I've got a very pretty woman straddling my lap who I happen to still be buried in, it makes second" I pause, "no–third rounds that much easier."

She smirks, sending fireworks up my spine once again. I trail my fingers along her hairline, pushing back the shorter tendrils that frame her face. Just as I move to kiss her again, my phone starts vibrating.

She lets out a sigh dropping her forehead to my chest. "They're just going to keep calling."

"I know," I groan, running my hands down her back before giving her ass a soft smack. "Go shower, I'll see what they need."

Kadence lifts her head, giving me one last kiss before she climbs off the bed. I watch her walk into the bathroom, groaning again at the sight of her naked body before she closes the bathroom door.

I'm definitely ready for another round with her but the insistent buzzing of my phone needs to stop before I can take her again. The last thing I want is something to distract me from giving her all of the attention she deserves.

I climb off the bed, sliding into my boxers as quickly as I can before the call ends again. Plucking my phone from my jeans, I glance down at the name flashing across the screen. *O'Neil*. Sucking in a breath I press the answer sign. "Yeah?"

"*Nash?*"

I make my way back to the bed, sitting down on the edge of it. "Yeah, man, what's up?"

Cole lets out an exhale on the other end. It had been days since we actually had a conversation between just the two of us. Everything with Kadence has put a strain on our relationship and it hasn't been from anything that she did.

"*Ma's calling a family dinner.*" My friend's voice is tight and low, doing nothing to temper down the worry crawling across my nerves.

"Okay, Friday?" I ask.

"*Yeah,*" Cole pauses on the other end, "*She says we need a 'come to Jesus' moment and figure this shit out between us before we show up.*"

I chuckle, not entirely surprised. The last thing Marlowe wants is the club falling apart, and right now, Cole and I are at the helm of two passing ships ready to collide. She is right, as she usually is. We need to get over our shit in order to protect the club. To protect Kadence. Stokes is making more moves against the other members. Nothing major, just small annoyances that put us in difficult situations. When I found out that Cole had given up Dex for a pointless fucking arrest, I was pissed at how easily he gave up a member. But it was either that or worse.

"What are you doing now?" I ask before I can stop myself.

My eyes flicker to the closed bathroom door, picturing a very naked Kadence covered in bright white bubbles. I hate the idea of leaving her right now, but I want my friendship back and I want Cole's trust back.

"*Nothin', man. I've been fucking pacing the clubhouse since you both got back. Falcone's ready to throw me out. Meet me at Lee's in thirty?*"

"Who's on watch tonight?" I don't miss the sigh of relief on the other end of the line when I ask instead of denying him.

"*Wolfe and West. But...*" Cole pauses, "*Maybe it's good if you bring Kade. I think I owe her an apology as well.*"

I pull the phone from my ear, checking to make sure that I was still talking with Cole on the other end. Cole doesn't apologize usually. His hard-headedness gets him into bullshit, but that stupid fucking charm usually gets him out of it. "She's showering, but we'll be there."

"Good, man. I'll see you in thirty."

"Yeah."

The call ends and I stand, tossing the phone onto the mattress before moving to the bathroom door. I knock twice, hearing a soft *come in*, before a grin spreads across my lips and I step inside to bury myself in the one person who's taken the time to understand me.

HOLDEN

"Holden Nash! It's been *ages*!" Maggie coos, coming around the counter to toss her arms around my neck.

I can't help but smile wrapping my free arm around her. Maggie has always been kind of like a second mother. Aside from Marlowe, she's the only other person who never gave up on Cole and I.

"Quit sending those poor prospects to get food for you." She pulls back and smacks my chest with a playful scold. I grin and glance down at Kadence.

"Sorry, Mags," I say sheepishly, looking back at the older woman and feeling like a teenager again. "I've been... preoccupied."

Maggie's eyes glide to Kadence with a bright smile. "It's good to see you again sweetie." Her brow raises knowingly as she notices our connected hands. "Well, well, well.." Maggie giggles, looking back up at Kade. "I had my money on Cole, but you two fit."

Kadence chuckles and I feel like I'm completely out of the loop.

"Cole?" I ask, looking down at Kadence.

"He picked me up from here... the second day I was in town." She smiles looking back at Maggie.

"I'm glad you decided to stick around," she says with a knowing look between the two of us. "Alright, go! Go sit down. Cole already ordered three Lee Specials for you all."

I smile and nod. "Thanks, Mags."

She pats my arm, squeezing it gently and getting that same sorrow-ful look in her eye that people usually do after I come out of hiding. One that says *I'm sorry your sister was brutally murdered, she was a good kid*. I hate it but for Maggie, I know she means well. "Don't be a stranger, Holden."

I feel that same twinge in my heart again and nod. "Yes Ma'am."

She moves over to another set of patrons and I tug Kadence towards the table Cole picked. That lightness I felt from seeing Maggie quickly dissipates at the sight of Cole's grim look. Not quite grim, but regret-ful, maybe? I let Kade slide into the booth first, my eyes never leaving Cole's.

"Are you both sure you want me here for this?" Kade's voice breaks through our glare as she shrugs out of her jacket and sets it on the bench between herself and the wall.

I'm simultaneously focused on Cole and her. Making sure she's fine and that Cole knows better than to help her when I'm around.

I slide in next to her, leaning back in the booth. Her thigh brushes against my leg and it's a quiet reminder she spoke to us. "Yeah, Sun-flower. You should be here."

"He's right," Cole says, glancing over at her. "I uh.. I ordered al-ready."

"Maggie said you did," I reply with a little more bitterness in my voice than I meant to.

I can feel Kade's gaze flickering between the two of us. She's just as nervous to witness whatever this sit down brings as I am. My hand slides over her thigh under the table giving her a soft squeeze of reassurance. In an instant I feel her hand over mine, tangling her fingers with my own and giving me her own soft squeeze. I didn't just bring her here for Cole's apology. Kadence grounds me more than she realizes, and as her thumb runs over my index finger in a soothing motion, I know that whatever we have is more than just two broken people finding solace in each other.

Cole clears his throat, folding his hands together on the table as he glances between the two of us.

"I owe you both an apology," he starts and I narrow my eyes. "Kadence, I have no right to tell you who you should be spending your time with. I also know that you witnessed Wolfe getting arrested because of me... I know that things don't make sense right now but I'm sorry that I brought you into it." He leans back into the booth shaking his head. "I've been trying to hold shit together for so long and now it feels like it's unraveling at the seams."

I shake my head. "It's not–"

Cole stops me with his own shake. "I've had the string in my hand more often than not, Pal."

He stares at me and I can't help but feel remorseful. We were supposed to be a team, running the club together, and all I've done is fuck it up and leave it on his shoulders but still my best friend blames himself. "I let you down. I've let this club down more times than not in the past month and a half. Stokes wants all of us. The club gone, and full control of Moon."

"How can he do that?" Kadence asks the same question that burned the tip of my tongue.

Deep down I knew though. The girls that inhabited Moon came to us because they had no other choice and needed a safe place to stay fed and clothed...not all of them were strays in a bad place. Hell, even Layla had a family that loved her, she just chose this life, chose a new identity for whatever reason. I was sure the girls that Stokes brought to us sometimes weren't just lost women. They had families too, ones that cared about them. We never forced the women he brought to stay. If they ever wanted to leave they could but most of the time they don't. Whether they're too content to care or that this is a better life for them... We never know whether they're missing daughters or sisters... We never could prove it and the idea made my stomach roll. We were helping him feed his addiction and the women never complained.

"He has a lot built up on the club. Transactions, ledgers of the runs we've done for him and the ones we haven't. Handguns are easy to move when they're packed into bedrolls." Cole admits more freely than I would have.

I haven't told Kadence everything that the club does outside of running the garage. Guns were just a small portion. Moon brings in most of our income with the shop coming in second. We mostly transport weapons for other clubs. A middle man between MC's that don't feel the need to know each other face to face.

"They take the guns just over the border into Nevada, from there we don't know. They get distributed by the other MC's." I say glancing down at her.

If she was pissed, I wasn't going to let Cole take the brunt of her anger. I also had a hand in making the deal with the other clubs back when I was VP. Now, that's Falcone's territory. Her features are blank and I realize that I'm just as corrupt as her ex. Pulling her back into shit that she shouldn't be in.

"Stokes found out," she states, furrowing her brows and filling in her own blanks.

Cole nods in the full transparency that I'm still working on. "They let us move across the border without problems and in return they get girls at Moon."

"Until Becca died," I finish. "After we stopped letting Watson and his crew into the club. Girls started getting hurt and—" The words catch in my throat, and I feel her hand squeeze mine again.

"You didn't want them to suffer the same way Becca did," she says softly.

I nod curtly glancing back at Cole. "Watson had something to do with Bec's death. I know he did."

Cole bristles at the mention of my sister and Watson in the same sentence. He was silent for a moment before speaking. "Then we find the evidence, and then we kill him."

That was fine with me but when I look down at Kadence her features have stoned over. Her eyes are glued to Cole. "You loved her... didn't you?" She asks.

"More than I care to admit," he answers immediately.

It doesn't shock me how I thought it would. Cole is a hothead with a big heart and a love for Becca that I'll never be able to relate to. My gaze slides to Kadence. Or used to be able to relate to.

She glances up at me and nods. "How can I help?"

"No. Baby," I say, turning towards her. "You aren't helping with this. I'm not putting a target on your back bigger than the one already there." I look to Cole for help. "We're not involving Kade."

"Then why bring me today?" She asks with a hint of bitterness laced within her words. "After everything, you can't expect me to sit here and play the innocent girlfriend."

My eyes widen for a moment looking down at the woman next to me. Girlfriend. I know deep down that's what she is but hearing her call herself that sends a jolt of mixed emotions through me. I must have made a face because she rolls her eyes at me and I can't help the small upturn of my lips at her attitude.

"Watson already knows something is up with me. By now, with the news junket circulating, I'm sure he and Stokes both know more than we want them to know about who I am and why I'm here." She tugs her hand out of mine and sets it on the table. "It's only a matter of time before they make a phone call to Jeremy's office and Miami-Dade is crawling all over the shop, not to mention Stokes having everything he needs to take down the club. So, before that happens and I fuck things up around here even more, we stop them." She glances between us. "We stop them both."

"You want to kill Stokes?" Cole's brows shoot to his forehead, his shock matching mine.

I was beside myself staring at the woman who not two hours ago was moaning my name. I want her to be strong, to be this firecracker of a woman instead of the meek one she thinks herself to be but I don't want that at the cost of her life and dealing with Stokes and Jeremy at the same time was a death sentence.

"Don't you?"

"So, we kill Watson and Stokes, then what? There's just going to be some other asshole who will replace Stokes and pull the same shit or shut us down completely," I argue. "Killing them both won't work."

A throat clears to the side of us and we all look up to see Maggie standing there, arms full of our plates before she begins dishing them out. "Anything else I can get ya?" She asks, glancing between the three of us with a raised brow.

"No, Mags, thank you." Cole glares at me as she nods and walks away. "Keep your damn voice down."

Kadence picks up her fork, pushing around the hashbrowns on her plate before scooping up a bite. "It'll work," she mumbles. Her eyes bounce between us. "Hand pick someone. Use what you have already on Stokes, release it to the town and show them he's not the upstanding Sheriff he claims to be. Throw your hat in the ring for whoever you choose. It's best if it's a friend of the club's." She pauses. "And get the town eating out of your hands."

She shrugs like the master plan she just spewed wasn't more than a grocery list. I watch her take another bite and then another before the corners of my mouth turn up. A combination of pride and the fact that she's eating more now than she has in weeks.

I look at Cole, who is still staring at her with the same amount of curiosity and awe that I feel. "It's not a bad plan," I mutter and Cole's eyes collide with mine.

"It worked for Jeremy, well until..." her voice trails off, "his office pulled shit like this all the time. I'm not entirely sure about the whole murdering part but it wouldn't surprise me." She glances up at me. "Innocent girlfriend, remember?"

I'm thrown back to our earlier conversation of how Jeremy never hid anything he did. She flashes a grin at me before looking at Cole. "I heard things I wasn't supposed to, doesn't mean I forgot them and didn't catalog them for later as a backup plan."

I huff out a laugh, throwing my arm over her shoulders and press a kiss to her temple. The woman sitting next to me feels different than the woman I barged in on the first night I met her and fuck I'm proud of her.

"You're really something, Sunflower." I press my nose into her hair, taking in the lavender and vanilla that I love so much before dipping my head to her ear. "And you aren't my *girlfriend*," I rasp lowly pulling back as she furrows her brows at me.

"You're my *old lady*." I smirk.

KADENCE

"**B**aby?" I groan, slipping the straps of my light blue sundress over my shoulders.

I start buttoning up the front of it as I glance at the bathroom door. He's been in there for a while now and I'm sure he's finished showering. "You know," I tease as I fasten the last button on the bust of my dress. "We're gonna have to have a chat about the fact that you're taking longer than me to get ready for a party."

A chuckle comes through the door that makes me smile and a soft blush creeps up my cheeks. I'll never get tired of hearing him laugh. It's quickly becoming one of my favorite sounds.

"Sunflower, you don't need time to get ready when you're already so damn pretty," he says through the door, his voice muffled but doing nothing to tamper down the charm flowing from him. "I need time to fix this ugly mug."

I make my way to the bed, sitting on the edge to pull on my boots. "Holden, you are not–" The bathroom door opens, and my gaze trails down his body, taking in the more than worn-in jeans that hug his muscular thighs, the white t-shirt that stretches across the broadness of his shoulders, doing nothing to hide the strong muscles there. But it's when I finally look at his face that my mouth drops open and my eyes go wide.

He turns towards me, raising a brow. "What?"

I stare at the now clean shaven stubble that peppers his skin, a little thicker around his chin and mouth but not much. It makes the lines of his face look sharper, yet stronger somehow and his hair is cropped shorter. No longer the long chestnut locks that I love to tangle my fingers in, but now buzzed on the sides and cropped up top.

Holden laughs softly. "You like it?" he asks, rubbing one hand on the back of his neck in a nervous motion. My eyes flit to his bicep straining against the sleeve of his t-shirt as I stand.

"Are you sure we have to show up tonight?" I ask, the corners of my mouth turning upwards as I slide my hands up and over his shoulders. Holden's hands drop to my waist, wrapping me in his arms as a wicked smile grows on his lips.

"Yes, sweetheart, we do." He dips his head, his lips latching onto the spot between my collarbone and neck that sends shivers down my spine. A whimper falls from me as my hands continue up the back of his neck, the short hairs there prickling at my fingertips. Holden groans against my skin before pulling back from me and planting a quick kiss on my lips. "We have to quit it," he rasps, "otherwise we'll never leave this room."

I smirk softly. "That still doesn't sound so bad."

Holden grins and shakes his head as he grabs his own boots and takes my spot on the bed. His eyes rove down my body as I wait for him. "Be careful Kade, keep talkin' like that and I'll have no choice to tear that dress off you later and it's a really good lookin' dress."

I cross my arms over my chest. "Is that a challenge?"

He finishes slipping into his own boots and stands to tuck a strand of hair behind my ear. "It's a promise, Sunflower." Holden smirks.

He drags his index finger down my skin slowly, barely touching me but leaving goosebumps in his wake. He hooks his finger into the top button of my dress just above the swell of my breasts. A wicked smile grows on his lips and with a quick flick of his hand, the top button pops open.

I let out a small gasp, my fingers itching to touch him. To push him back against the bed and keep him here. Something tells me that he won't mind, but I know that we have to make an appearance downstairs. My newfound need to explore my desires would have to wait.

"Leave it open," he rasps, "I want to be able to see you."

My gaze flicks down to my chest. Not much more of my cleavage is showing, just enough that the blue lace bra I have on barely pokes out from between my breasts. "You're playing with fire, Holden."

He throws his arm around my shoulders, tugging me with him to the door. "Baby, you should know by now I like to get burned."

A laugh escapes my lips, shaking my head. "You're crazy."

"Only for you," he mumbles against the side of my head as he leads me down the stairs.

The parking lot is already full of members, some I recognize and others that I haven't met yet. The wolf mural seems to glow in the afternoon light and glints of chrome glitter off the wall with the long row of motorcycles that line up underneath it. Grill smoke fills the air around them and the sounds of boisterous laughter echo through the compound.

The gate that normally stays open during the day is closed and I can see a couple of members standing on either side of it, holding their ground as if they were guards watching over a fortress. I glance up at Holden. His eyes flicker left and right with his jaw ticking in overtime, taking in our surroundings and I don't miss the way his body tenses the further we get to the bottom.

Pulling from his grasp, I spin in front of him as we step off the last stair. His arm falls from around my shoulders and I quickly take his hand, intertwining our fingers. "What's wrong?"

Deep blue eyes glance down at me. "I'm second guessing this."

"Why?" I ask gently, knowing it takes a lot for him to open up.

"Because as much as I want to watch you walk around in this dress, tits on display for me..." He pauses, eyes flicking up to the sound of heavy boots on pavement behind us. I lift my hand cupping his cheek to catch his gaze again, "If anyone but me touches you, I'll take their hands." His voice is low and raspy with the warning that sends a shooting tingle up my spine.

I suck in a breath before standing on my tip-toes, dragging my lips over his. "Then you show them who I am."

A low rumble vibrates in his chest as his hands tangle into my hair and he closes the breath of a distance between the two of us. His lips crash down hard against mine, sending a thrill of goosebumps up my skin even in the high afternoon heat. I melt into him, holding onto the lapels of his cut with my hands trapped between us.

Holden pulls away, his lips bitten red and mine tingling from his newly shaved stubble.

"Wherever this spitfire came from," he breathes, running his thumb along my bottom lip shaking his head. "I owe it a thank you."

I grin and tug on his leather cut. "I think you'll need a mirror for that."

A low whistle echoes behind us as I spin around. Scottie stands in front of us, a wide grin spread over his face, highlighting the scars that adorn his cheeks under the peppered scruff. "You finally decided to cut off that mop?" He asks, jerking his chin at Holden.

"It was time," Holden rumbles behind me. His hands drift to my waist as he steps behind me. "Everythin' cool?"

"Anythin' was better than that shag you had goin'," Scottie chuck-les. "I hate to break you two love birds up but Cole needs Nash behind the grill before we lose al'our dinner."

I tuck myself under Holden's arm as he wraps it around my shoul-ders again and laugh when he tilts his head back to groan. "Who the fuck gave O'Neil the tongs?"

Scottie chuckles, clapping a hand on Holden's shoulder. "You have Marlowe to thank for that." Another groan leaves him as we head towards the clubhouse. Scottie leans over Holden, catching my gaze. "How you feelin' lass?"

"Way better," I smile.

"I knew you were a tough one." He grins down at me before glanc-ing between us. "And you two are okay?"

I laugh. "If I knew any better, Scottie, I'd think you were looking for some gossip."

Holden shakes his head. "Don't entertain him. He'll just keep askin'."

Scottie huffs out a laugh. "No, brother, I'm just making sure you don't fuck up and let this one go." He points a finger in my direction.

A flush grows over my cheeks as the two men glare at each other. A part of me loves that Holden has become so protective over me but I'm feeling like I don't need it. I feel stronger than I have in a long time. My body still aches in places and some nights I can still feel the cold water hit my skin like daggers but for the most part the nightmares of that night have subsided. I know that I've woken Holden up more than once with the chattering of my teeth at the memory. Still he never leaves me; instead he wraps his arms around me and holds me tight against him until the warmth of his body calms me.

I feel Holden's eyes on me and when I look up they're practically twinkling. Aside from the hard set of his jaw and the way his hand tenses on my shoulder, I see nothing but awe in his eyes.

"I don't plan to," he says softly, pressing a kiss to my temple.

Once again that warm fuzzy feeling in my stomach flutters and I know that the more time I spend with him, the further I fall.

"Nash!" Cole's voice hollers across the parking lot dragging our gazes to him.

His tanned skin glistens under the sun and the blue and white *O'Neil's Towing* trucker's hat he has covers his eyes, but even he looks happier than he has been in awhile. After we met at the diner things have been lighter around the three of us. Even with the feeling of Stokes and Watson lurking around.

I meet Cole's eyes as he grins at me. There is nothing malicious or hard behind the smile. He just seems normal. Holden turns and presses a kiss to my forehead.

"Go with Scottie and find the girls. Blake's been dying to have some alone time with you."

He cups my cheeks, dipping his head as his lips hover over mine just enough for the embers in my core to burn before he finally presses them to my lips. I hum softly, tangling my fingers into his shirt.

"A'ight you two love birds, break it up."

I giggle against his lips, taking a step back from him. "See ya later?"

"You can count on it, Sunflower." Holden smirks before spinning on his heel and jogging over to where Cole is currently fanning the grill with a pot holder. A few choice curse words fly from Holden's mouth as soon as he steps up to the grill assessing the damage Cole has apparently already done.

Scottie nudges me gently with his elbow, getting my attention. "How are you *really*?" He asks, low enough that only I can hear him. I hook my arm into his as he begins to lead us into the clubhouse.

"I am better." I smile, "things are..." I toss a glance over my shoulder at Holden, unable to help the smile that forms over my lips, seeing him and Cole grinning and shoving each other away from the grill, "Good."

He nods, a knowing smile plastered over his hardened face. "About the other thing, you uh... haven't heard anything from dick face have you?"

My brows furrow as he holds open the door to the compound for me. "Jeremy?" I shake my head when he nods again. "No. To be honest I haven't turned my phone back on since before the news junket."

"It might be time to do that, sweetheart," Scottie urges gently. "See if he's reached out. If he has, let us know. The more we know about whatever he's planning the better."

This is the last thing I want to think about today. My impending nuclear bomb that lurks in the shadows of my life. I'm sure that if I turn my phone back on, I'll have text messages from the bastard.

"Hey," he rests a hand on my shoulder. "Doesn't have to be today. Just soon."

I smile, though it doesn't quite reach my eyes. A sense of dread fills me thinking about the danger that's to come but it's quickly snubbed out by the sound of my name screeching out of Blake's mouth.

I spin, seeing the brunette basically charge right at me. A wide smile on her face and slender arms held out wide as she pulls me into her. I feel Blake's hand wrap around the back of my head in a death grip of a hug. I've seen Blake a few times over the past few weeks, bringing me clothes and food. Checking in on me when Holden needs his own change of clothes and has to leave for a bit. All fleeting moments that never lasted longer than an hour or so.

"It's so good seeing you up and about," she mutters into my hair. "I thought Holden would keep you locked up in that tower forever."

I pull back with a laugh. "If it were up to him, I'd probably be wrapped up in bubble wrap."

"Oh trust me, the man wanted to safety-proof the clubhouse. Cole had to convince him that you weren't a toddler and could walk just fine." She grins, "Dex almost agreed with Holden."

"Why does none of that surprise me." I laugh, wrapping my arm around Blake's waist. "I'm almost shocked that Cole didn't agree with them."

Blake flashes me a warm smile. "Because I told him I'd slash his tires if he didn't convince them otherwise."

I stare at her in shock and my mouth drops open as Blake laughs. "Blake, you didn't!"

"You can take care of yourself, Kade. You don't need these men turning cavemen around you, as much as they'd probably enjoy it way too much. They need to let you breathe, and the three of them were buzzing around you like bees to honey."

Blake leads me over to the bar where Marlowe is already passing out drinks to a group of women standing at the other end.

"They don't have to do that." I glance up to see Layla staring straight at me. Her dark eyes narrow and painted lips pursed together. "I don't want to be treated differently."

"But you are different," Blake says, stopping us just out of earshot of the rest of the group. "Holden and Cole hadn't said more than a few words to each other before you came along, and he and Dex sure as shit never agreed on anything before you. You're healing Holden as much as he's helping heal you."

I swallow thickly as my eyes meet Blake's.

"Look," Blake sighs, resting her hands over her arms. "After Becca died, the club fractured. Holden wanted nothing to do with the shop. He practically lived at Moon with the few exceptions where he'd show up here plastered and looking for another easy lay." She grimaces slightly with her own words but it's not anything that I didn't already assume. "Since you showed up, Holden has actually come to work. He's on speaking terms with Dex again and whatever happened the other night at the diner has had Cole in a better mood. None of this started happening until you."

"Why weren't Dex and Holden on speaking terms?" I ask, her brows furrow. It's not something that either of them ever mentioned before.

Blake's eyes flicker over me. "You don't know?"

I shake my head.

"Dex was on watch the night Becca died...no one was supposed to leave the compound and Becca snuck past the guys."

"I...I didn't know that," I mutter. It explains a lot of the tension between the two of them. Why Holden seems pissed at Dex most of the time. I sigh, shaking my head, "I don't want to be the peacekeeper between the three of them."

"I don't think you are," Blake says. "For what it's worth, I think you're just helping them find peace with the past and uniting them for the future."

I look at her with confusion. "What do you mean?"

"If this shit with Stokes and Watson gets worse, the three of them will need to work together not against each other, because if Stokes even senses any sort of tension within the club, we're doomed."

My eyes widen. "That's a lot of pressure Blake. I can't–I can't be that bandaid for them."

"You already are, my love." Blake flashes me a winning smile. "So deal with it because you, Kadence, are truly the missing piece for all of this."

"Jesus, Blake," I breathe. "How do you figure that?"

She hooks her arm around me and shrugs. "Just a feeling. C'mon, no more heavy talk though, yeah? Let's just have a good time tonight."

I nod, not protesting that. Everything has felt so heavy the last few weeks that tonight I just want a break. Something to keep my mind off of Jeremy, off of whatever the guys planned for Stokes and Watson. I want to feel normal.

I follow Blake to the bar and get to work helping fill shot glasses with whiskey and tequila. I smile and joke around with members as they pass by to grab a glass.

Cackles erupt in the corner where the group of women stand. I glance over at them, Layla and Jane are grinning at whatever one of the other girls are saying. My eyes roam over the group. All of them are wearing skin-tight dresses, heels that would make my ankles sore, and enough makeup to supply ten drag queens. I glance down at the light blue dress I'm wearing. It is speckled with white daisies and hits just above my knees. Compared to all of them, I feel like I'm dressed for a Sunday Service.

Aside from the silk lavender dress that was destroyed in my fall, I never wear anything like that. My normal makeup is *maybe* a little concealer and mascara. There was never time to sit in front of a mirror and take care of myself. It was always about Jeremy. But now, staring at the giggling group of women, I start to understand more and more why Sandy wanted a makeover in Grease. Men like Holden don't want women like me. They want the sex appeal. Something I've never had.

I suck in a breath and get back to pouring shots, shaking my head as I try to get rid of the doubt lingering in my head. Nothing Holden has said or done has made me feel like he doesn't want me. Hell, spending the last two days locked in the apartment exploring each other should be my first clue. But I can't help but feel that icky bubbling in my gut that makes me wonder if I am truly enough for him.

KADENCE

"**Y**ou've gone to the clouds there, sweetheart."

I look up to see Marlowe leaning against the bar top, smiling softly at me. Her long blonde hair is pulled back into a low pony. She's wearing jeans and a white tank top with the club's logo printed on the front of it and still doesn't look old enough to be anyone's mother.

"Sorry," I say softly, my eyes catching the glare Layla has tossed my way.

"Ignore them," Marlowe says plainly, pushing herself off the bar.

I let out a soft chuckle as I clear off a few of the empty beer bottles that litter the wooden counter. "That's easier said than done."

"You know the difference between you and those girls?" Marlowe says with a raised brow. She busies herself pouring more beers as she speaks. "You're here helping, keeping the guys happy."

"I'm not better than them, Marlowe." I shake my head. "They keep the guys happy in their own way. Ways I'm not willing to. I can't fault them for that."

"That." Marlowe points a finger at me. "*That* is what separates you from them."

I raise a brow at the older woman, confusion written on my features. "I don't understand."

"Because even as an old lady, you don't see them differently and that," she grins, filling a tray with beers, "is what makes you club material darlin'. It's what makes you a good fit for Nash."

I look up at Marlowe who smiles as she picks up the tray. "How do you–"

"I see and hear everything sweetie, you're healing this club and don't even realize it. You're gonna make a great old lady."

Tears prick at the corners of my eyes as I watch Marlowe move around the edge of the bar and over to a table full of members. Some I haven't met before and a couple I have. I recognize Quinn. West is sitting with him, laughing with a few of the guys, but when Quinn catches my eye he grins at me. Something in his smile crawls up my spine, turning the hairs on the back of my neck to stand straight. It doesn't feel like just a friendly grin. There's something off about it.

I tear my gaze from him, turning back to the bar where Layla stands with an empty drink in her hand and waves it in front of me.

"Since you've turned bar bitch," she sneers in a sickly sweet tone, "you can get me a drink."

A laugh huffs from me. "I'm not your servant, Layla. Get it your-self."

"Aw, but sweetie, here's the thing." Layla moves around the edge of the bar, leaning over it and pushing her breasts against the wood. "You're standing behind the bar, slinging drinks to the men. I'm just as important as them, *Kadie*. So, do us all a favor and act like the little wench you are and get me a fucking drink."

I glance around in disbelief. My last run-in with Layla didn't go the best, but this? This is straight catty bullshit that belongs in high schools. Blake's nowhere to be found and Marlowe is busy talking with a few of the other girls.

"Are you fucking deaf?" Layla hisses, "I told you–"

"I heard what you said Layla," I bite. "Doesn't mean I have to listen to it."

A bitter cackle leaves her as she stands up straight again. "I can't wait for the day Holden decides to leave your ass. Sends you back to whatever hole you crawled from."

"I'm sorry, did I miss the requirement of total bitch when I showed up today?" I cross my arms over my chest. "I suggest you walk away from me now."

Layla steps forward once more, a wicked grin spreading across her face. "Or what?"

I drop my arms, my fists clenching at my sides. She is testing my patience, and right about now those boxing tips Dex gave me seem very nifty. "Walk away from me, Layla."

The sneer on her face somehow grows, and her dark lipstick pulls tight against her lips. Layla raises her hand and it takes everything in me not to move. Not to give her the satisfaction of getting under my skin. Instead of whatever she has planned, Layla snags a bottle of tequila off the wall, dragging it down to her side.

"Watch your back, bitch," she warns as she turns and walks away.

I let out a breath I don't realize I'm holding just as the guys push through the main door, plates of food in their hands. I press a hand to my forehead as I turn towards the back wall behind the bar, at least to try and catch a breath.

"Hey," Holden's voice catches me off guard as his hand wraps around my waist, "you okay?"

I glance up at him, forcing a smile as I nod. "Yeah, fine."

He raises a brow down at me. "You sure?"

Just then the group of women erupt in laughter again. This time it's so loud it carries over the sounds of the clubhouse. I glance over my shoulder where Layla raises the tequila bottle in the air, her eyes glued on the two of us.

Holden tugs me to his chest, dipping his head so he catches my gaze. "Layla givin' you shit?"

I sigh and press my hands to his chest. "It's fine." I look over my shoulder again at the women but it's Holden's fingers that gently grip my chin, tugging my gaze back to his.

"We don't lie to each other," he says firmly, but the soft look in his eyes soothes my racing heartbeat. "If she's causing issues, she's out." A coy smile tugs at the corner of his lips. "No one disrespects my old lady." He teases pressing his lips to my temple.

"Holden, it's fine."

He studies me for a moment longer. "I'll tell Cole to get her out."

I shake my head as he moves to pull away from me. "No–" I blurt, tugging on his shirt, "don't. Please, it'll just cause more issues and I really would just like to have one day without shit hitting the fan."

Holden sets down the plate of food he has in his free hand and wraps both arms around me. "Okay, alright," he breathes into my hair. "You'll tell me if it gets worse?"

I nod against him. "I will. She's pissed because you don't give her attention anymore."

"And I won't again," he says pulling back from me slightly. "I'm done with all that shit. *You* are what I want." Holden smiles and kisses my forehead. "What did you tell me earlier? Show them who I am to you?"

I smile, already feeling better as the irritation and tension melts from my body with some sort of magic power that he suddenly has over me. One touch from him and I'm goo. My worries seemed to drift away in the wind and right now it's exactly what I need.

"Hey," he says gently as he releases his grip from around me and takes my face in his hands, those bright blue eyes boring into me with nothing but adoration behind them, "everything will be alright." Holden smiles. "Just have some fun tonight, okay? The guys and I have to meet later after all this but when we're done..." His voice drops into a low rasp. "I want to peel this dress off of you with my teeth."

Heat rushes to my cheeks as my tongue flicks over my bottom lip. "You can't say things like that to me." I breathe, curling my fingers into the front of his shirt again.

"Why's that?" He counters, that smoldering grin plastered to his face again.

"Because I'll drag you upstairs myself." I laugh trying to ease the ache growing between my thighs.

Holden tips his head back and chuckles. "Don't tempt me, Sunflower."

"Don't tempt *me*," I grin.

He dips his head, capturing my lips with his. "I brought you food," he whispers against my lips. "Figured you might be hungry."

My heart swells as I glance down at the plate of food. At the same time my stomach seems to rumble at the sight of potato salad, ribs and two slices of watermelon. All piled on the plate and way more food than I'll probably eat, but still, the idea that he thought about what I needed and took care of it himself is making it a hell of a lot harder to stand here and not drag him back to our bed.

"You're making me hungry for a lot more than food right now," I mutter, earning another light laugh from him.

A laugh rings out from behind us as Blake tosses a few empty bottles in the bin. "I saved you guys once from being caught doing nefarious things," she grins as we both turn to look at her. "But see, now I'm torn on stopping this."

"Blake!" I laugh.

The brunette shrugs. "You're both hot, what can I say?"

"Jesus," Holden sighs, tugging me closer to his chest in a brief embrace. "I'm escaping this conversation."

"Oh C'mon, Nash! Let me watch." Blake all but whines, though the grin on her face lets me know she's only screwing with us.

"Absolutely not." Holden shakes his head as he plants a quick kiss on my forehead once again and backs away from me. Something more than adoration flickers in his gaze as his pupils eat away at the blue in his eyes. "Eat, Sunflower. You're gonna need all the energy. For *later*." He tosses a pointed look at Blake before moving around the bar and turning to find the rest of the guys.

"What a boner killer," Blake teases, holding out a beer for me.

I take it with a laugh, taking a long swig. The hoppiness of it is bitter to my tongue but I relish in the warmth that blooms in my throat. I turn to watch Holden and Cole gather around one of the tables with a few of the guys.

Blake steps up next to me, leaning against the bar. "How you holdin' up?"

I glance at her, taking another swig from my bottle and shrug. "I don't know if I'm ever going to get used to this world." My gaze trails over to Layla and Jane. The two of them have floated over to where Holden and Cole stand. "Or that shit." I tip my bottle toward them.

"Don't worry about them," Blake urges, nudging me. "Layla's just throwing her weight around but it means nothing and Jane," she scoffs out a laugh. "Jane is harmless."

I glance at Blake. "You're right. I've dealt with worse things than Layla's pettiness."

A wince crosses over Blake's face. "if anyone can deal with her bullshit, it's you."

I wrap my arm around Blake's waist, smiling softly as my eyes land on Holden's. He smiles at me as Cole says something to get his attention back. Layla steps closer to Holden, her hand dragging up his arm until the flat of her palm lands over the rank patch on his cut. I stiffen, my eyes narrowing as that familiar anger bubbles up in my chest. Is it anger? It feels like my skin is crawling with the urge to shove Layla's face through a window the longer her hand lingers on him.

"You want me to shoot her?" Blake asks, apparently also seeing the display Layla's pulling.

"No," I bite, setting the bottle down onto the bartop with a thud and pull out of my embrace around Blake.

"Where are you going?" She asks as I make my way around the bar.

I turn back to Blake with a sickly sweet grin. "To show that bitch who he belongs to."

Blake's eyes grow wide before a laugh erupts from her. "Keep the hair pulling at a minimum."

I turn and glance over my shoulder. "I won't need to pull her hair."

Holden's eyes find mine again, his brows furrow and his head cocks to the side questioning me all while Layla's fingers languidly trace the patches on his cut, only fueling my need. I round the table dragging my hand along his back as I move to the opposite side between him and Cole. My eyes flicker to the snake-like look in Layla's eyes before dragging my gaze up to Holden.

My lips part to speak when Layla leans over the table, grinning. "Sweetheart, the men are talking, so–"

"Layla," Cole warns.

I glance at Layla. "See, Layla, the difference between you and me?" I feel Holden take a step towards me in the small space. "The men actually care about what I have to say. So I suggest you take your hands off of *my* old man before you lose them."

Layla's mouth drops open, her lips moving like a fish trying to gasp in air. "You're going to let her talk to me like that?" She squeals, looking between Holden and Cole.

"Oh," I tsk, "*sweetheart*, they don't control me. I guess that's another difference between you and me." I know I'm stooping to her level but if the only language Layla understands is petty bitch, then that's where I'll meet her.

Cole stares down at me in disbelief as Holden covers his mouth, biting back a laugh. He moves around me this time, standing behind me as I stare at the wide-eyed look on her face. Satisfaction rolls through me even as my heart hammers against my chest. I don't even realize my hands are shaking until I feel Holden's fingers intertwine with mine.

"I think it's time for you to leave, Layla." Cole finally says, breaking the stare between us.

"But-" Layla starts when Cole lets out a low rumble.

"Leave, Layla," he warns.

She scoffs and crosses her arms over her chest, staring directly at me. If looks could kill, I would be a pile of ashes on the floor at Holden's feet right about now. My body vibrates over the slight win as I step back into his chest. The grin on my face grows as I feel Holden shift behind me and as his warm breath fans over my neck, the embers that burn in my belly turn to flames. Holding Layla's stare, I tilt my head ever so slightly giving my neck to him. I feel the upward curve of his lips as he grazes them along my skin.

Layla's eyes go wide before turning to dark slits, daggers shooting from them as she lets out a frustrated screech and spins on her heel. The loud clacking of the cheap shoes echoes through the clubhouse as she makes her way to the door. Too distracted to care about the eyes on us I melt into Holden, still with my back pressed to his chest.

"What was that about?" He rasps, his lips barely touching the shell of my ear.

I turn my head to the side to look up at him. "She was touching you." I didn't mean for the words to come out with as much bitterness as they do but my body is still buzzing after that. It took a lot for me to stand up for myself, but I'm doing it little by little and Holden isn't something that I want to lose to someone like Layla.

"Was she?" Never once have I wanted to smack the smug smirk off his face until this moment. My brows furrow as I scowl and step away from his chest, pulling my hand from his. "Hey," he chuckles, attempting to grab me again but I move out of his reach. Holden raises a brow at me. "Cole, which room is empty right now?"

I hear him ask though those ocean blue eyes bore into mine. Out of the corner of my eyes, I see Cole shift.

"The one the girls use."

"Make sure they know it'll be occupied."

I feel my stomach flip as he steps towards me, this time taking my hand whether I want him to or not. He pulls me with him down the hallway, my eyes connecting with Blake's as we march. Blake grins, giving me a thumbs up, clearly hearing everything that had happened and once again fulfilling the feeling of triumph radiating through me. Though the small green monster on my back still rages, the need for him is quickly taking over.

He kicks open the door, tugging me inside in front of him before kicking it shut. "What was that about?"

I cross my arms over my chest. "Which part?"

"You pulling away from me."

"Oh, I'm sorry... I didn't realize that would hurt your feelings so much. Maybe Layla will comfort you."

Holden chuckles and shakes his head. "Layla is–"

"Doing everything she can to put a wedge between us," I interrupt. "How do you not see that?"

"She's no one, Kade."

"She doesn't seem to think so." I drop my arms to my side. "So while you're letting her put her hands on you, I'm supposed to what? Not care?" I shake my head. "If the men you call brothers can't even *look* in my direction without a death glare from you, how do you think a woman you used to *fuck* touching you makes me feel?"

Holden stares at me for a moment before holding his hands up in front of him in mock surrender. "Alright." he nods. "You're right. I should have told her to fuck off."

I let out the breath I'm holding as he takes a step towards me. "Yeah, you should have," I mutter as he plants himself in front of me with little space between us. He cranes my neck to look up at him. "You're an asshole," I bite, but can't help the upward tick on my lips.

He grins down at me. "I know."

"She better not touch you again."

"Or she'll lose her hands?" He curls his fingers around the base of my throat, a playfulness in his voice I'm not ready for yet.

I press my palms to his chest and shove him backward. He must not have been expecting it because his back hits the door with a thud. "That," I confirm with tension radiating from me. I step up to him and press my chest against his, gripping his jaw with my fingers, "and because you're *mine*, as much as I am yours."

HOLDEN

"You can't say stuff like that to me," I growl as I rest my hands on her hips and tug her impossibly closer to me. I watch as the corners of her mouth turn upwards in a mischievous grin.

"And why's that?" Kade purrs, digging her fingers into my jaw a little deeper before she slides her hand around the back of my neck.

I dip my head, nipping at her lips as my hands slide down the backs of her thighs. "Because when you tell me you're mine," in one swift movement, I lift her, letting her legs wrap around my waist, "it does things."

I feel her lips quirk against mine, "*things*?" She coos, and I swear the warmth from her breath fanning against my skin sends a jolt straight to my cock.

This woman. Soft and quiet when she wants to be but for me? For me all of that confidence her dipshit of an ex shattered is back tenfold. I know that what she did tonight to Layla had to have been hard. But hell, she fought for me, for *us*.

I shift her in my arms, my lips dragging down her neck as I hum my response. I swipe my arm across the dresser, knocking off whatever bullshit is in my way, and set her down on the wood. "So, so many things," I rasp against her skin as I slide my hands up her warm, bare thighs until my fingers graze her core. She gasps and digs her fingernails into my shoulders as I delve into her, easily sliding two fingers straight to the spot that has her seeing stars.

"You're soaked," I groan, "is this for me?"

Kadence begins to slowly rock her hips, chasing her release as I work her over. A soft moan is my only response and right now, I need words. Need to hear her say it. My free hand wraps around the back of her neck, fingers tangling into her hair as I tip her head back.

"Say it," I growl, "tell me that this is all," I gently bite down on the junction between her neck and collarbone earning myself another moan from her, "for *me*."

"Oh God," Kadence croaks as I soothe my bite with my tongue, "only you."

"Good girl," I grin, pressing my thumb to her clit and crushing my lips against hers, stealing every breath and moan that falls from her as I push her closer to her orgasm. I know she's close. Her core clenches and flutters around me. "Let go, Sunflower, I've got you."

Kadence whines, tipping her head back as her body shudders in a release. Her arms squeeze tightly around my neck pulling me closer to her which I gladly take advantage of and lick the column of her neck. Assaulting her skin with my lips as I work her through her release.

My cock strains against my jeans, angry and ready for her. Watching her come undone for me is quickly becoming my favorite thing in the world. The flush that adorns her cheeks, the soft mewls and moans she tries to keep in her throat but fails every time, and the way the darkness of her pupils eats away at the jade green whenever she looks at me. Kadence is my drug and I have been addicted ever since my lips first tasted hers.

I slip my hand from her, sliding it between my lips and savoring just how sweet she truly is. She watches me carefully, her chest moving in rapid succession and soon her hands have slipped from my neck to find the buckle of my jeans. She fumbles for a moment though her eyes never leave mine.

"I need you," she rasps. "Now."

I smirk and tilt my hips to give her a better angle as she shoves the waistband past my ass. Kade grips my length, sending a jolt of lightning up my spine. I dip my head forward, pressing it to her sweat-slick chest and groan as she strokes me.

"Jesus, Kade," I huff.

"Just Kade," she whispers against my ear but I can hear the playfulness in her voice and I have no doubt she's grinning ear to ear right now. My hand wraps around the wrist of the hand currently wrapped around me and I find her gaze.

I stare at her for another moment before capturing her lips again, tracing my tongue over the seam of her lips until she parts them for me. She lets go of my length and I pull her to the edge of the dresser, shoving her dress up until she's exposed to me. I line myself up and in one quick movement I slide into her.

My groan is met with a soft curse that falls from her as she pulls back. God she's so warm and soft and feels like coming home every time I bury myself into her. The room fills with the sounds of us, my groans and her moans, creating a symphony of the words I know we both feel but are still too scared to say.

I can feel them though, sitting on the tip of my tongue as she unravels for me but now isn't the time. When I finally say the words, I want it to mean something to her. I want it to be perfect. *Fuck,* when did I turn into a chick flick? I shake away the thoughts with punishing thrusts into her. Holding her close to me as she claws at my body, grabbing any part of me she can hold on to. Soft thuds of the dresser hitting the wall mix with our moans, and I swear I hear a soft click at one point.

Kadence's body tenses for a moment, but it isn't from her release. I know what that feels like when she comes and she isn't clenching me with a death grip like she normally would be, instead I hear a soft laugh and look up at her. Her eyes are focused on something to our right and as I turn my head Layla's bright red hair comes into view. I can't help the growl that leaves my throat as her beady eyes meet mine.

"You're not invited," Kadence rasps, the sound cutting off as I hit that soft spot within her. "Get out."

My eyes never leave Layla's. She stares at me, anger and something akin to hurt swirling in them. One of my brows lifts as Kadence's lips find my throat, her moans drowning out the sound of the dresser hitting the wall as I continue my thrusts.

"You heard her," I bite with a wicked smile growing on my lips. "Get. Out." I say punctuating each word with a thrust. Layla huffs and spins to leave. "Oh, and Layla?" I say, stopping her in her tracks and waiting until her eyes find mine. "You put your hands on me or even speak a word to *my* old lady, I'll throw you out myself."

Her features go stone. I know she's pissed at me but she's taking it out on Kadence and I won't let that happen. Kadence refuses to tell me any of the shit Layla has spewed her way but after seeing it tonight, I'm sick of it. What we had was nothing more than her using me for attention in the club and myself using her as a distraction. None of it held weight.

"You can leave now," Kadence moans against my neck and fuck if that isn't enough to push me over the edge, the way she flutters around me as she says the words make it close.

The door slams as Layla storms off, leaving us to our euphoria. Her hands cup my face and bring my gaze back to hers.

"Don't ever," she starts, a moan slipping from her as she bites down on her bottom lip hard enough to draw blood, "say another woman's name while you're buried in me."

I chuckle breathlessly. "Yes, ma'am."

She smiles sweetly, so sweet that my balls tighten. "Good boy."

"Oh, fuck," I groan at the praise, something I haven't ever felt, but the words tumbling from her send me flying over that cliff and taking her with me.

My hips stutter until my entire body goes stiff, releasing inside of her as she quivers and shudders with her own release. She collapses against me, breathing heavily as her face tucks into the crook of my neck.

This. This is what I've been chasing. A woman I never expected but one that with the simplest of touches turns my insides to mush. I'm so fucking in love with her, it almost hurts and seeing her claim me just as I have claimed her...I haven't ever felt anything like it before.

"I can't believe that just happened," she whispers against my neck.

"I can. This fucking dress you have on is a walking wet dream," I huff with a laugh, wincing as she softly rolls her hips with me still buried in her.

Kadence giggles though the sound is sultry and sated. "I meant her, but thank you."

I pull back, cupping her face in my hands and press my lips to hers softly. I refrain from dipping my tongue into her mouth and pull back. "I'm yours, Sunflower. Ain't no one gonna tell me differently and you," I pause searching her eyes.

"And I'm yours," she whispers.

A smile spreads and the feelings I have for her tangle around my soul like the most beautiful ivy. "You're fucking incredible."

"You getting emotional on me, Nash?" Kade smiles, tracing my bottom lip with the tip of her index finger. It forces the corner of my mouth to lift as I take in every inch of her in that post-sex glow. Her skin is still flushed and the green in her eyes is slowly starting to come back giving light to those tiny gold flecks woven in the vibrant color.

"No." I smile. "Maybe."

"Since when are you the sappy one in this relationship?" She asks, dragging that same soft finger down my chin.

"Since my girlfriend turned into this badass who takes no shit from anyone." I press my lips to her forehead and wrap my arms around her.

Kade snakes her own arms around me, tucking her head just under my chin. "I thought I was your old lady."

I smile again. "Sunflower, you're so much more than that."

She pulls back slightly, lifting her head with a smile and teases, "Sap."

I laugh and kiss her, dragging out the moment for as long as I can until a knock on the door forces us apart.

"Hey, Nash, we got Church, man!" Trey's voice filters through the wood before the thud of his footsteps disappear down the hallway.

Kadence presses her hands to my chest. "Go," she says softly with a smile.

"You'll wait up?" I ask, knowing just how pathetic and pleading I sound, but she nods, pecking my lips once more.

"Always."

I grin and pull back from her, tucking myself back into my jeans and help her down and into the attached bathroom to get cleaned up. As soon as we both looked presentable again, I lead her back out to the main room with my arm around her shoulders and her giggling into my chest. I catch Blake's gaze from behind the bar and shake my head when she raises a brow at me with the same Blake shit-eating grin on her face.

"I'll see you later," I mumble, pulling back from her.

She smiles up at me, nods and walks back towards the bar. I can't help but watch her for a moment with a stupid lovesick smile spread across my face when she turns to glance back at me. Blake wraps an arm around her shoulders and drags her outside holding a couple of beers in her free hand and no doubt to watch whatever is left of the sun.

HOLDEN

Church is already buzzing with the guys when I walk in. A few of them stand in a group by the end of the table, laughing and clinking beers together. Wolfe, Trey and Cole are all gathered around the head of the table though for a barbeque that seemed to be going well, even Wolfe's normal scowl looks deeper.

That unsettling feeling returns to my gut as I make my way over to the three men. We need to figure out a way to protect our runs from Stokes but we also need to figure out a way to protect the club from him as well.

I plant a hand on Cole's shoulder, pulling my brother's attention from the group. He glances at me with that worrisome look only I know the meaning of while Wolfe and Trey argue.

"Splitting up the club right now is dangerous, Falcone. How do you not see that?" Wolfe growls low enough that only the three of us can hear him.

Trey shakes his head, folding his arms across his chest. "It's the only shot we have to make sure we keep our deal with the Skulls."

I raise a brow and glance over at Cole. "Rollin' Skulls? They reached out?"

Cole sighs with a nod. "Yeah, while you were taking care of Kade." A knowing glint in his eye has me grinning for a brief moment, remembering the feel of her coming undone around me just minutes before.

"Layla left pretty pissed," he trails off, "wouldn't have anything to do with what she found in the girl's room is it?"

I shrug. "She should have knocked."

Cole huffs out a laugh and shakes his head. "You're evil."

"Trust me, it was worth it."

His face screws up in disgust as he pushes past me. "Gross." He pulls out his chair at the head of the table and bellows across the room. "Sit your asses down so we can figure this shit out."

Just like every other gathering at Church, Cole lifts the gavel sitting just to the right of him and pounds it against the table. The high-pitched thud rings through the room, letting the new recruits know it's time to sit down and shut the fuck up. In here you don't speak unless spoken to and you only spoke freely if you were at the end of this table.

I glance across the wood, my gaze catching Trey's. His brows are furrowed and that tick in his jaw is back. Wolfe huffs next to me, shaking his head. The two of them rarely go at it, but when they do it always has to do with the safety of the club. Trey doesn't mind being devil's advocate. He doesn't seem to give a shit that when the two of them are split on decisions, it affects the whole group.

It came with the responsibility of being club VP. He has to keep Cole level-headed when his anger, which he fully denies having a problem with, takes control. It's a hard job. I know that. I was that person for ten-plus years, standing with Cole in these leather cuts. Though they used to hang off of us when we were teenagers, now our vests were road-worn and like a second skin.

"Havoc called," Cole states, his voice level but even I notice the white around his knuckles from his tight grip on the gavel's handle. "He wants to meet and discuss the terms of our agreement with the Skulls."

"You think they're gonna back out?" I ask.

Cole shrugs and works his jaw. "I highly doubt it, but Havoc hasn't been the most sane club pres to deal with."

"Why call a meeting in person? The RS don't typically deal with club business in person unless it's serious," Wolfe states. "This has trap written on it."

"Oh would you shut up?" Trey barks. "Not everything is out to get us, Wolfe."

"Tell me to shut up again, Falcone," Wolfe leans forward, his forearms resting on the table while his voice drops to his *I'll kill you where you stand* voice. "I dare you."

The sound of the gavel echoes through the room again as Cole attempts to wrangle the two idiots. "Both of you shut the fuck up. We're taking the meeting. Havoc didn't say anything about Stokes, but he's gonna have questions on why you assholes keep getting picked up and why our runs keep getting intercepted. We owe him an explanation, one that we haven't given before."

"This is a bad fucking idea, man," Wolfe groans leaning back into his seat.

"It's either that or we lose the money coming in from the runs. We don't know what Havoc wants. If meeting him will show that we still have interest in the deal that we have with his crew, then so be it. We can't afford to lose the income that comes from running for them."

I glance over at him. "Cole's right. Now more than ever, we need other crews with us, not against us. If appeasing the Skulls means meeting with them, then why not do a show of good faith."

Cole gives me an approving nod, glancing around the room at the men sitting at the table. "Stokes has to go," he finally says after a moment of silence, "and we need every ally we can get when shit hits the fan."

"When is the meeting?" Wyatt asks from the back corner. "Blake's going to want to go and so will I."

The corner of my mouth turns upwards at his words. I had seen Wyatt's longing glances at Blake while the girl rambled on about bullshit that half of the time doesn't make sense at all. Still I knew the look.

"Nash, Wolfe, and I will head the meeting with him. Falcone will stay here to keep an eye on the club and the women."

"I'm bringing Kade," I say firmly, leaving no room for argument. "No offense to Falcone, but with the silence from Jeremy, I'm not giving him an opportunity to strike when I'm not here to protect her."

Trey shakes his head and holds up his hands in front of himself. "No offense taken, man, it's the right call."

"So," Cole starts. "Kade's with you. Wolfe and I will lead, and Wyatt," his eyes glance over to the kid. "Grab Blake. I want you both in the van following us." He raises the gavel giving every one of us one last look. "We leave in two days." The gavel sounds through the room again as he stands followed along with the rest of us.

I stand and wait for Cole as the others filter out of the room. The chorus of *I Wanna Dance with Somebody* blares through the Church every time the door opens. We give each other the same questioning look and head out into the main room. My eyes land on my girl. Dancing with a beer bottle makeshift microphone in one hand and Blake's arm wrapped around her shoulder as they sing off-key to each other.

A warm feeling spreads through me while I watch her. Laughing, singing, as if the shit we've had to deal with still isn't lurking in every corner of our relationship. Kadence is more resilient than she gives herself credit for, and it shows every time a genuine smile spreads across her face and when she still looks at me with that glint of adoration in her eyes. I half expected her to run by now, leaving the car, leaving me and yet, here she is weaving her way into the only family I've ever known. An ache spreads through my chest knowing that she would never get the chance to meet Becca. That my sister would have loved her.

A hand wraps around my shoulder pulling my attention away from Kade. Cole holds out another beer for me and we settle into the closest table. The one tucked back in the corner of the room that allows us to watch over everyone. The men are laughing, drinking, and looking happier than I've seen in a while. Marlowe was right, we needed this. We all needed the reminder that no matter what shit we got pulled into, this club is still a family.

"Thanks," I mutter as my gaze finds her again. They move on to a Queen song but are still laughing and dancing together. I can't help but smile watching her.

"She seems like she's doing better," Cole says from beside me.

I lift the bottle to my lips, taking a swig of the cool liquid. The soft burn spreads down my throat and it isn't lost on me that this is the first night I let myself drink without pain. Hell, it was the first time I drank any alcohol since Kade had shown up. I couldn't remember the last time I had drunk myself into a blackout.

"The bruises are mostly gone now," I say softly glancing over at Cole, "but I know she's still freaked out about Jeremy. She hasn't turned her phone on for weeks."

"Maybe that's for the best." Cole shrugs. "She's lived in fear of this asshole for too long."

I nod in agreement as my gaze catches hers. A soft drunken smile spreads across her lips before Blake pulls her back into singing. "We'll need to turn it on at some point to see if he's contacted her again."

"Wolfe's already getting her a new phone," He says with a nod, "and we will. But," I glance over when he pauses, "she needs some happiness first."

"I second that," I say, tapping the neck of my beer bottle against his.

We both drink to the idea but I know something else is bothering him. I knew Cole. On the outside he looks relaxed, the baseball cap he wears does a good job of hiding his furrowed brows but even I can see the way his jaw ticks every so often.

"What?" I finally ask.

"You're in love with her," Cole states after a moment.

The words hang in the air between us. I have no idea what it feels like to be in love but I also never gave myself the chance. I was always so wrapped up in my career in the military and, when I got home, the club. Making sure Becca had everything she needed and giving myself over to the deals the club had made with other crews. I lived and breathed this life. At least until Becca's death and at that point I turned into a shell. Numbed with whiskey and secluding myself from everyone that cared about me.

My eyes drift over to Kade again, always searching for her. I always know when she's near. Like some magnetic pull gravitates me towards her. I never want to know what it would feel like not having her in my life. She makes me never want to go back to what I was before.

I knew one thing. I would kill anyone that tries to take her from me.

"Yeah," I mumble. "Yeah, I am."

Cole chuckles. "At least you finally admit it."

I look over at O'Neil. "What the hell does that mean?"

"C'mon man, you've been glued to that woman since the night you met her." Cole grins. "I've never seen you go caveman with any of the other girls. Kade spends two days here and you're pulling her pigtails any chance you get." He nudges me when I don't respond. "You serious about her?"

"Fuck man," I groan, "it's been a little over a month." I trail off and then sigh knowing Cole is right.

"What happens when her car is fixed?" He asks.

"She said she doesn't want to leave." I grin. "And I don't want her to go."

He nods. "Right, so what's your endgame with her?"

"Why does there have to be an endgame now?" I ask.

"Because a girl like Kadence deserves a happy ending, Pal, and you do too."

I look back over to Cole who shoots me a pointed look. I never imagined myself with a happy ending, let alone settling down into a white picket life with a woman I loved. But as the music swells and I glance back at my girl, my Sunflower, the clearer that picture becomes. I can start over with her. Be the man my father never was and have my own family, one that I grow with the love of a good woman.

"Maybe it's time I clean up Becca's house," I blurt before I can stop myself.

"Nash, it was always your house too," Cole reminds me. "And as much as that place is haunted with the reminders of Becs..." he lets out a long, heavy breath, "whatever you need help with, I'll be there. The real question is are you doing it because it's time for you or because you want to give her something more?"

I consider his question. "Both."

"Don't fuck it up then," Cole chuckles.

I reach over and squeeze his shoulder, realizing that he is also still dealing with the loss just as much as I was.

"Kade was right." I chuckle. "She called me a sap earlier but, man, I think you're right there with me."

He shrugs me off, throwing his head back to laugh. "Jesus, we are fuckin' sappy tonight."

KADENCE

Holden trails his fingers along my bare back, leaving a trail of goosebumps in their wake despite the fact that I'm wrapped around his warm body. If someone had told me that I would enjoy waking up naked next to a man again, I would've laughed in their face. This though? Listening to the sound of his heartbeat, no pressure to do anything I don't want to, just... intimacy.

We've only been awake for a little while, the sun barely peeks through the slightly parted curtains, and yet there isn't another place I'd rather be. After the barbeque two days ago, we had gone back to our regular routine, no longer holed up in this room. I spent time working in the office while Holden worked on his bike. He told me about their meeting with another club and the idea of it weighed on me. I feel safe at the compound and I don't want to leave the little haven but just as Holden said, I knew it was safer with them than spending my time here worried sick.

"When do we leave?" I ask quietly, curling my fingers against his chest.

Holden lets out a soft groan. "In a few hours. Cole wants to get to Santa Barbara before dark."

I nod at his response, trying hard to ignore the worry that seems to still sit like a heavy ball in my stomach.

"It'll be fine," he says, pressing his lips to the crown of my head. "Meetings like this are normal."

I tilt my head to look up at him seeing that he's already watching me. His stubble has grown in a bit creating a dark shadow along his jawline and it reminds me of the soft burn on my inner thighs. My hand slides to his cheek, the hair there tickling my palm. "I can't imagine they're going to like having someone's girl hanging around."

"Hey," he rasps, curling his thumb and forefinger around my chin. "You aren't just someone's girl." That smug smile I've grown to love a little too much spreads across his features. "You're my girl and that is reason enough for you to be there." Holden leans down pressing his lips to mine. "Besides, getting some time with you outside of the compound will be nice."

"Oh yeah?" I ask, propping myself up on my elbow while his hand trailing down my back moves to tangle in my hair. "We're trading one compound for another." I grin.

"You assume I don't have plans for you."

"And what might those plans be?"

He shrugs. "Well, we're staying for a few days over there but I may have thought of a couple things to do."

I smile, shifting my leg over his waist and move to straddle him, biting back a moan when I feel his length brush against my inner thigh. "Do these plans have anything to do with us and a bed?"

He chuckles, wrapping his hand around the back of my neck and pulls me to him. "Mmm, are you going to be disappointed if I say no?"

I pout. "Maybe."

Holden shifts his hips, pressing himself against me. "It'll be worth it. I promise."

"I mean if you're denying me," I whine nipping at his bottom lip, "it better be."

He tilts his head back and laughs. "Sunflower, I'd never deny you."

Feigning a pondering look and nodding softly I narrow my eyes. "Pretty sure you are." The hold he has in my hair tightens as he pulls me back to him crashing our lips together in a kiss that does nothing to put out the fire in my belly. He gently sinks his teeth into my bottom lip, returning the nip I'd given him earlier.

"Baby, we won't ever leave this room if one of us doesn't force us out of this bed." He grins.

I shrug. "I fail to see the problem."

He laughs again. Every time the sound tightens my chest. I love his laugh, the soft giggle that he hides from the guys that's only meant for me. Holden swats my ass playfully. "C'mon, Sunflower, get up. You still need to pack."

I glance over my shoulder as he sits up, holding me in his arms. My suitcase is overflowing with all the things I took from Florida. With everything we have been through I still haven't unpacked yet and the sight of it makes a twinge of guilt spread through me. The idea of leaving this place, leaving Holden, was not a near feeling anymore. It's the last thing I want to do. Pine River was becoming my home and I wasn't planning on leaving it anytime soon.

"Maybe I need to unpack," I mutter looking up at him.

Holden raises a brow. "Kade," his voice trails off, "we talked about this. It's safer for you to come—"

I shake my head wrapping my arms around his neck. "No, baby, for good." A ball of anxiety forms in my throat as his eyes search mine. "When we get back, I think maybe I should unpack everything for good."

A small smile grows on his lips when my words ring true. "You sure you wanna be stuck with me?" He asks and I know he's teasing by the tone in his voice but it doesn't stop me from cupping his cheeks and running my thumbs over his stubble.

"That depends," I smirk, "are you okay with that?"

"Being stuck with you?" He asks, gripping my hips as I nod. "I guess I would be."

I scoff and he smirks as I push against his chest playfully to climb off of him but his hands tighten around my waist. He's laughing as he pulls me back to him and it sends butterflies through my chest. "Hey," he rasps, "I wouldn't want to be stuck with anyone else."

I can't help the smile on my face as I try to glare at him. "You're pushing it, Nash."

Holden nods with a hum as he tugs me closer and plants the softest kiss on my lips. He forces a whimper from me and I settle into his arms, leaning into him. Every time he kisses me it feels like he can't get enough and I relate to the feeling. I've never wanted to lose myself in someone as much as I do with him.

He is the first to pull back as his hands run up my sides. "You pack. I'll get us some breakfast."

This makes my smile grow. Food and I haven't been the best of friends since Jeremy but Holden always makes sure I'm fed. It doesn't matter if it's a bagel from the cafe down the road or a Lee's special, the fact he encourages me to eat is enough.

"Good," I groan softly, rolling my hips and ignoring the emotions swirling in my chest to tease him. "I'm famished."

Holden lets out a low growl from somewhere deep in his throat and rests his forehead on my shoulder. I don't miss the way his cock twitches under me. "You're killing me," he rasps against my skin.

"We wouldn't want that," I whisper, running my nails down his back and teasing him just enough to make him shudder before I push back and climb off of him. This time he lets me go, falling back against the mattress with a dramatic groan.

"You evil, evil woman," he chuckles, watching me push open the bathroom door.

I flash him a cunning smile. "You should have waited to offer me food then," I tease before closing the bathroom door behind me, ignoring the overwhelming need to crawl back into bed with him.

KADENCE

"Why are you packing a tent?" I ask, stepping up to Holden's bike as he finishes strapping down a pack behind my seat. He reaches for my backpack and tucks it into one of his saddlebags before answering me with a mischievous grin.

"I told you I had plans." Holden shrugs as he reaches for me and wraps his arms around my shoulders. "Now stop asking questions. I'm a steel vault, baby." He smirks.

I laugh. "Alright, alright, I'll quit asking...if you let me drive the bike."

His head tilts back letting out a laugh as his hand falls to his pec. "Sweetheart, it's backpack life for you until I can find an empty lot to teach you."

I raise a brow and step out of his embrace. "What makes you think I can't ride?"

He waggles his brows. "Baby, I know you can *ride*." My mouth gapes open with a gasp as I shove him playfully, forcing him to wince away with a shit-eating grin. The gall of this man. "It's a long drive, Sunflower." He relents with a sigh.

"Fine," I huff. His finger hooks into my belt loop as he pulls me back to him.

"How about this?" He cups my cheeks, dipping his head to catch my gaze. "When we get to Santa Barbara, I'll find us an empty lot and teach you."

My chest flutters with excitement. "Promise?"

Without hesitation he holds up his pinky with a sly crooked grin. "Promise."

I smile linking our pinkies together.

"Hey, Andrews!" Wolfe calls out across the compound. He jogs towards us, waving what looks like a phone in his hand. My brows furrow as he stops in front of us and holds it out. "Got you a new phone," he says with a nod. "Programmed Nash, Cole, and myself in there."

My fingers wrap around the device, taking it from him. I know exactly why they did it but I never expected them to actually take care of this for me. "Thank you," I mutter. "Blake?"

Wolfe raises a brow and laughs shaking his head. "She caught me five minutes into setting it up. You think I got away without putting her number in there?"

That makes me laugh as Holden's arms wrap around me from behind. "Thanks, Dex."

He nods, tossing a glance to Holden over my shoulder. "When we get back, we should turn your phone back on."

"Hey," Holden's low voice rumbles behind me. "Give it a rest, yeah? At least for the next few days."

"We've given it a rest for a while now, Nash. We need to know–"

"Wolfe," Holden's voice booms, forcing me to tense in his arms. He must have sensed this because, for a moment, his arms tighten around my waist before loosening again. "Please brother, one good weekend away from this shit, that's all I'm askin'."

Wolfe's eyes flicker between us and I force a small smile onto my lips, wishing that the tension that spreads between the two of them wasn't always down to my safety. The last thing I want to do is to have the guys fight over how to handle me. It wasn't the way to keep the club safe and focused if they were constantly pitted against one another.

"When we get back." I confirm with a nod before holding the phone back out to him. "Do me a favor? Take our picture?"

Holden dips his head, burying his nose into the crook of my neck. I feel his lips curl against my skin before he presses a gentle kiss to the spot just below my ear. "Why the photo?"

"I need a new phone background for that phone don't I?" I mutter, leaning back into his chest grinning as he nuzzles further against my neck.

"Mmm," he hums, and the vibrations send chills down my spine, my smile growing. I nudge him as Wolfe holds up the phone, his brows scrunched together as he focuses on taking the picture.

"Nash, don't be an animal. Look at the camera."

I glance up at him over my shoulder feeling his fingers dig into the softness of my belly where he holds me. His eyes flicker down to my own as he smiles softly. Nothing but adoration glints back but I knew something else was hidden beneath that. Something deeper and something I feel in my own soul.

I'm in love with him and I had no doubt that, no matter what the world was about to throw at us, I would pick Holden every damn time.

"There," Wolfe says gruffly, holding my phone back out. "Now if you two are done honeymooning, we should start heading out."

With a sigh, Holden drops his arms from around me but not before planting a kiss on the top of my head. "You gonna be warm enough?"

He asks with his eyes roaming down my body. A flicker of heat ignites in my core as those bright blue eyes meet mine.

I glance down at my outfit, tearing my gaze away from him in fear that if I stare too long, we will never get out of here on time. I wasn't going to miss the chance of getting actual alone time with him without the club constantly around. My black jeans are snug against my legs with just enough stretch that the long drive on the back of his bike shouldn't be too bad. As usual, I'm wearing my favorite pair of combat boots combined with an old band tee. Holden's hoodie sits on my seat waiting for me.

"I'll be fine." I smile and reach for his hoodie to slip it on.

Even though it's warm I know as soon as we get on the road, I'll be wind chilled within minutes. Holden's large frame helps block out the wind for the most part, but there is no way in hell I am going to be the one to make them all stop because I'm cold.

Once I'm situated and swimming in his hoodie, he hands me an extra helmet. I smile seeing the newly painted sunflower on the back of it and look up at him. "What's this?"

Holden smiles sheepishly and shrugs. "I might have asked Falcone to paint it on there."

Butterflies explode in my stomach as I run my finger along the flower. It might just be a small painted symbol but to me it feels like a promise.

I can't answer him with the emotions stuck in my throat. The realization that Holden isn't going anywhere and even more he doesn't want *me* to go anywhere.

He must sense that words are hard to come by because he reaches for me, wrapping an arm around my shoulders, and tugs me to his chest pressing his lips in my hair. "You don't have to say anything, Sunflower. It's just a helmet."

I let out a soft teary laugh and shake my head. "It's not just a helmet, Nash."

He pulls back and smiles down at me. "No, it's not." Holden gently takes the helmet from my hands and slips it over my head. His fingers drag down my jaw and to my chin to buckle it with a smile and a look in his eyes I can't quite place but I know it's only for me.

"Have you seen Cole this morning?" I ask, realizing he hadn't been on the lot when we came down and his bike was still in its spot.

Holden nods tugging on my chinstrap. "He's giving Trey a run-down of security before we head out."

"You think Stokes or Watson are going to do something while we're gone?"

"I'd bet on it, but the plan is to lay low."

I worry my bottom lip between my teeth. Even if the guys lay low at the compound, the six of us on the road were still open targets. It isn't a matter of whether or not I feel unsafe with the three men that I know would protect me. It's a matter of those men doing whatever it takes to protect me and their family that scares me. That familiar weight in my stomach starts to grow in heaviness again and extinguishes any ember his touch had ignited within me.

"Baby." His hands frame my face. "You start thinkin' any harder, I'm gonna be able to hear those thoughts." Holden's eyes flicker between mine, searching them and I know I'm not going to be able to hide from him. I never have been.

"What if something happens?"

His brows knit together and he shakes his head. "Trey has strict orders to keep everyone in the compound. The guys are here to work, no runs, and Marlowe is closing Moon for the weekend. Everyone is holding up here." His thumbs gently stroke over my cheekbones. "Stokes can't do shit if everyone is here."

"Or he'll be shooting fish in a barrel," I mutter softly, causing the corners of his mouth to twitch up.

"They're gonna be fine, Sunflower." He brushes his lips against mine before fully kissing me softly, doing everything he can to ease away my anxiety. "Stokes knows better than to stop us when we leave if he wants to keep his cash flow coming in."

"You'll be safe with all of us." His head drops a little to catch my gaze. "Okay? I won't let anything happen to you but you need to stay close to me."

The warning at the end of his words makes me shift on my feet. "I'll be glued to your side." I tease trying to ease the tension growing up my spine but he shakes his head.

"I'm serious, Kade, not all clubhouses are like ours. These men know better than to touch what isn't theirs. The Rollin' Skulls are a harsher club, so unless you are not with me, you'll be with Blake."

I nod as the rest of the crew begins to gather around us, all suiting up for the drive. It won't take us more than a few hours to arrive at the other clubhouse but it's a few hours of the low simmering anxiety in my stomach I'm not looking forward to. The one saving grace I'm banking on is being able to hold him the whole time. Being able to wrap around him has a way of bringing a sense of calm to me. I need it right now as I fight to hold onto the confidence I had this morning the closer we are to leaving.

"Everything will be fine," he reassures again, kissing my forehead as if he can read my mind. His lips graze my skin down to the tip of my nose where he leaves another kiss and then another soft one to my lips.

"You guys ready?" Cole asks, making his way to his bike.

Holden takes one last glance at me waiting for an answer. I barely nod but it's enough that he responds to Cole. "Yeah."

Everyone climbs onto their bikes. Wyatt and Blake joke and push each other around while Wolfe sits thoughtfully on his bike, slipping his helmet over his head until the hardened look in his eyes is disguised under his visor. Holden throws his leg over his own bike, settling onto it before holding a hand out for me. I swallow hard and take his hand climbing on behind him. I scoot as close as I can get to him and wrap my arms around his waist.

Out of the corner of my eye I see Cole glance in our direction. Something in his gaze catches my attention as I turn to fully look at him. He flashes me a weak smile, his eyes flickering between myself and Holden with something deeper hidden under his blue gaze. Something akin to want and regret.

Cole starts his bike, setting off the chorus of engines roaring to life around me and within minutes we're filtering out of the main compound gate and onto the road. Cole rides up front with Holden and Wolfe riding side by side behind him. Blake and Wyatt flank us in the van, all making sure we're safe and not followed. I settle against Holden's back, resting my cheek on his shoulder while I watch Pine River rip by us in a flash.

Town turns to trees and soon the trees turn into long winding roads of open fields. I recognize the spot I broke down over a month ago, and it only makes me realize how much things have changed. How one month feels like a year. It's crazy to me that only a short time ago I felt lost. I had no plans of where I was going, where my last stop would take me but now? Now I can't picture being anywhere else. That sense of being lost has faded and the foreboding hold I had in my heart has slowly started to fill to the brim.

Images of Holden and I in bed over the last few mornings and nights start to surface. The two of us tangled together, talking and laughing about little things. I never experienced that with Jeremy.

He never took the time to ask me questions, not even when we first started dating. Holden wants to know everything, and even as I told him about my dad, my car and a million other little things, I knew what we have is different. Holden wants me for *me*. He doesn't care whether I'm the perfect girlfriend, a trophy wrapped in floral dresses and drinking one glass of wine at events I had no interest in.

Holden wants me for the mess I am. The girl who wears ratty old band t-shirts and shorts, once called too slutty by a small man, were now Holden's favorite. He wants the girl who prefers combat boots over heels. The one that finally stands up for herself.

My arms tighten around him as the thoughts swirl through my mind. I know I'm in love with him. I also know that if whatever we had would end up in heartbreak, that the cracks I would feel would kill me. I feel his hand rest over mine as he drives and soon his fingers interlock with my own, resting comfortably over his abdomen.

We ride like this for a while until the roads deem it necessary to have both his hands on the handles. Every once in a while he reaches back, resting a hand on my knee and giving it a soft squeeze before trailing it down my calf. A silent form of comfort that sends butterflies tornado-ing through my chest and one I was quickly becoming addicted to.

As the sun begins to set over the horizon, we reach Santa Barbara. I peer over his shoulder as we ride down the 101, glimpses of the ocean flicker through the palm trees and buildings. The lights from the wharf burn bright even during the evening sun and a pang of excitement runs through me at the idea of spending a day with him there. I still have no idea what he has planned for our day together but whatever it is I have no doubt I'll enjoy it.

I see Cole signal to our left before turning onto a side street towards the marina. After another few moments we pull into a compound similar to our own. A large fenced gate blocked by black slats shoved between the fence rungs to block out any unwanted witnesses. The compound back home had the same, only the slats were blue. The gate slides open with a whine as we pull through finding a row of empty spots to park.

I notice over my shoulder a group of men loitering by what I assume is the clubhouse door. Gazes flicker between the six of us, some with grins and others with hardened glares too stoney to read.

I feel a tap on my thigh that signals me to hop off his bike as Holden kicks down the stand. My hands roam to his shoulders and I throw my leg over the side for the first time in hours, planting my feet steady on the asphalt.

He looks up at me, giving me a soft side smile as I steady myself. He helps me with my helmet, and despite having my arms wrapped around him for the past few hours, I step to him, wrap my arms around his shoulders, and move to my tiptoes to kiss him.

His lips are still a little cold from being wind bitten but I don't mind. Ultimately they were his and even if they felt like ice cubes I'd spend hours warming them up on my own if I had to. A low rumble forms in his throat as he kisses me back, his hands grip my hips and tug me closer.

"What was that for?" He asks, a sly grin spreading over his features.

I shake my head, not ready to spill every feeling I have for him right now. "No reason."

Holden smiles as if knowing there is more, but instead of pressing, he takes my hand and leads me over to the rest of our group. Wolfe is already peering around us, his eyes scanning each person in the lot, assessing any potential dangers while Cole rolls his shoulders, tilting his head from side to side to stretch out his stiff muscles.

"There's a lot fewer members here than I would have expected," Cole observes. "I figured he'd have a whole army lined up outside."

"Yeah, well we haven't been inside yet," Wolfe growls, tension rolling through him.

"He won't want attention, man," Holden counters, squeezing my hand. "Having a whole club here at once brings a lot of eyes to an area like this."

The clubhouse isn't far from the main drag, just tucked off into a small industrial fishing area next to the marina but still enough of it was out in the open that people knew it was here and if I had to guess, that was purposeful.

All of our eyes flicker over to the clubhouse as the hum of voices slowly quiets down, and the main door creaks open. A man steps out, his dreads are pulled back into a loose knot on the top of his head, he's got markings on his face I have never seen on anyone else. Not quite tattoos and not quite scars, but raised skin marked there for purpose. His caramel skin almost glows under the sunset as he makes his way towards us.

I stand firmly at Holden's side, hands still intertwined as a quiet nervousness begins to twist its way up my legs, holding me in place. The man approaches with the same stoic look as the men that flank him. A more than uncomfortable silence falls between both groups, each assessing and sizing the other up.

After what seems like minutes the man's stoney gaze cracks and a smile forms over his face. I glance over at Cole who stands toe to toe with the man. His own smile creeps across his features until the new man finally speaks.

"O'Neil." He breathes out a laugh as he pulls Cole into an embrace, thumping his back a few times.

"Havoc," Cole replies, returning the masculine hug and pushing him back slightly, holding onto his shoulders. "Been too long, brother."

"Far too long." Havoc steps back from him as he glances at all of us standing behind Cole. His eyes land on me for far longer than I like and, assuming from the way Holden tugs me further into his side, it was far longer than he liked as well. "Good to see you all."

Holden only nods his reply while the rest offer a smile or, in Wolfe's case a curt nod and a scowl.

"We've got a lot to talk about but tonight we relax. Leave business for the morning," Havoc speaks, his voice an octave higher, catching the attention of all the other members surrounding us. "O'Neil, Nash, a word first?"

Cole nods, moving to follow Havoc as they make their way back to the clubhouse. Holden turns to me pressing a kiss to the side of my hair before motioning to Blake. "She doesn't leave your side," he says firmly.

"Stuck on me like glue," Blake replies with a nod.

It's the first time I've ever seen her without a smirk on her face or her normal teasing of Holden being too protective. It was with that nod that I knew this place was different, that the men aren't the same as the ones from home and that, even with the semi-warm welcome we had received, everyone needed to watch our backs.

Holden nods again, reluctant to let go of me. I kiss him again trying to reassure him I'll be fine but it's unconvincing as I tug my hand from his. "Go," I say softly. "I'll be here when you're done."

A smile flickers over his features though it doesn't reach his eyes. The stress radiates off of him in waves as he takes a step back from me and moves to catch up with the guys. Leaving Blake and I on our own in the lot surrounded by bikers neither of us knew.

HOLDEN

Havoc's crew follows behind us, creating a wall of Skulls that do nothing but raise the hair on the back of my neck. I peer behind us, catching a glimpse of a nervous looking Kadence and a wide eyed Blake who looks ready for a fight.

"That your girl?" Havoc's voice brings my attention back to the men surrounding us.

"Old lady," I correct, crossing my arms over my chest. Ignoring the ache in them from riding all day. I catch Cole's gaze for a moment before turning back to Havoc.

A hollow laugh booms between the group as Havoc shakes his head. "Never thought I'd hear those words outta your mouth there, Nash."

I shoot Havoc a glare, unamused by what he's alluding to.

"Guess I didn't need to bring all the girls out tonight right?" Havoc goads, clapping his hand over my shoulder. "That's alright, more for the rest of us."

"What's the word?" Cole asks, undoubtedly sensing the slow rolling anger forming around me like a cloud.

This is one place I can't let the notches on my bedpost get to me. Not while we're away from home and not where Kadence can realize just how fucked up I am. We'd just gotten over my line of conquests back in Pine River, the last thing I need is having them brought back here.

I shrug out of Havoc's grasp, turning my body to keep an eye on the men around us as well as Kadence in my peripheral. I clench my fists open and closed a few times trying to get the unwavering need to protect her and her feelings to tamper down.

"Just wanted to give a warm welcome outside of the women's ears," he said, tipping his chin towards Kadence and Blake. "Though I have to say Porter sure has a mouth on her. I'm surprised she still got that Prospect patch."

I narrow my eyes at him. Something in the way he says it doesn't sit right with me and soon that uneasy feeling churns in my stomach. I open my mouth to question it but before I can Cole squares his shoulders.

"She'll make a fine member," Cole solidifies, "pretty sure she proved that the last time she went on a run with your crew." His own arms cross over his chest as the smirk plays on his lips. "How's Chauncey's nose?"

"Still healing, or so he claims." Havoc chuckles. "Your girl did a number on him."

I watch as Cole's hackles rise ever so slightly. Anyone else would have missed it but I know my friend and Blake's a sensitive subject for him.

"If memory serves correctly, he deserved a lot more than a broken nose." Cole bites, narrowing his eyes at the other club president. I grab his shoulder, holding him in place as Havoc once again laughs.

"Probably. Let's not dwell on the past, yeah? All I wanted was to give a proper welcome. We can argue tomorrow."

Cole nods. "Probably a good idea."

"C'mon, man." I pull back on his shoulder.

The last thing we need is a brawl in the middle of a crew who are already on shaky ground with us. It doesn't matter if the bullshit

Havoc spews about Blake makes my temper flare. I'm thankful that Cole actually breaks away from the group.

"Guy's still an asshole," Cole mutters as we head back towards the women.

"Yeah, nothing's changed there. You think this meeting tomorrow is gonna work out?"

Cole shrugs. "We can't walk away with them as our enemy. So it's going to have to."

"And if they ask for something we can't give?"

"Then we figure out how to give it to them."

Before we get back to where the girls have been standing I step in front of him, putting a hand to his chest.

"Dex's right, man, something about this meeting doesn't feel right."

The devil himself, Dex, steps up to us with West on his heels. "I fucking told you," he growls.

"We can't afford to take on Stokes *and* these guys." Cole glances between the two of us, his eyes landing on me. "We have to figure it out."

"Tomorrow," I say. "I'm sick of club shit tonight."

I turn from my brothers and make my way to Kadence. Her brows furrow as soon as her gaze catches mine. I shake my head before wrapping her in my arms, holding her to my chest as I bury my nose into her hair. Without hesitation her arms wrap around my waist making that stupid grin form on my face again.

"Everything okay?" She asks softly, only loud enough for me to hear.

"I don't know yet," I answer honestly.

Kadence lifts her head to look up at me. Those green eyes I love so much search mine.

"Will it be?" She asks and I know I can't lie to her. Not that I want to, but sugarcoating things would have been a hell of a lot easier than staring into her eyes and still uttering, "I don't know yet."

The next morning everyone gathers back at the Skull's compound. I glance around at everyone, including my girl. None of them look like they got a lick of sleep. Kadence looks more exhausted than normal and a part of me wants to run away with her. To let Cole and Dex deal with the bullshit here and spend my time burying myself in her but I know I have to wait until tomorrow and a part of me feels like shit for even bringing her on this trip. Even if it's the safest place for her to be.

"You ready for this?" Cole says as he steps up to the two of us.

"You heard from Trey?" I ask, glancing at Cole.

"Everything is fine, no one's left the compound even though the girls tried to sneak out." He sighs. "Fuckin' Jane and Layla apparently tried to go back to the club. For what reason I have no fucking clue because it's closed."

"Probably to do what they do best," Kadence mutters next to me.

I roll my tongue over my bottom lip before biting it to stifle the laugh that wants to burst out of me. Instead I turn to her and press a chaste kiss to her lips.

She melts into me, just as she always does when I kiss her. I groan before pulling away, eyeing her with a mocking glare. "You're making it real hard to do my job right now, Sunflower," I whisper against her lips.

Kadence brushes her lips against mine and sighs. "Well then I suggest you hurry this up so you have me all to yourself."

With that she kisses me once more, pulling back before I can deepen it and links arms with Blake, a shit-eating grin on her face as she watches just how the kiss affects me as much as it did her.

"I really don't need to see that shit," Cole mutters.

"Too fuckin' bad," I mumble back. I turn my attention to the girls. "Blake–"

"Yeah, yeah, don't let her out of my sight, I know, Nash," She chastises. "Go play with the big dogs, Kadence and I have some shopping to do."

"You know, for a mechanic, you like to shop a lot." Cole raises a brow.

"Just cause I'm a mechanic, *O'Neil* doesn't mean I don't enjoy shopping." Blake bites back. "Besides, these guys give me the fucking heebie jeebies, I'm not sticking around for longer than I have to. Go do your thing, we'll be back."

"You have your phone?" I ask, my eyes back on Kadence. She pulls it from her back pocket and waves it at me. "Good, use it if you need anything."

"Yes, sir." She mocks a salute and grins.

I roll my eyes and watch as the two of them climb into the van. As soon as they pull through the gate onto the street, I turn to Cole. "She's going to be the death of me."

Cole's gaze is still on the gate while he nods in response. His jaw ticks and though he looks fine, I see something deeper in his eyes.

"You okay, man?" I ask, nudging him.

Finally his eyes meet mine. "Yeah, why?"

"You were miles away just now," I say, raising a brow.

He frowns. "I'm fine."

I hold up my hands and shrug. "Just want to make sure your head is clear before we go in there, that's all."

"It's fuckin' clear," He grinds out before marching toward the clubhouse door.

I know he isn't just from that, but now isn't the time to push it. Dex and West are already inside as I follow Cole in. Both nursing black cups of coffee as they eye the men around them.

"Should we do this then?" Havoc's voice booms through the room as he stands in the doorway of their own version of Church. Another room with a large wooden table in the middle, chairs surrounding it just like back at home.

"Guess we're skipping the niceties this morning," Dex grumbles as everyone filters into the room.

Everyone takes their seats. The Hounds take one end of the table while the Skulls take the other half. All of Havoc's higher ranks sit before us. Cole sits at the head of one end, and Havoc sits at the other. The tension in the room begins to build the longer we all sit in silence, each crew observing the other one. Taking stock of what's to come.

"We'll just get into it, yeah?" Havoc states. "Nevada is getting nervous with how many hits you've been taking lately." He pauses as if that's supposed to scare us. It's not anything we didn't already suspect but still I glance at Cole who has turned stoic.

"Since when do you deliver messages for Nevada?" Cole finally says.

"Since your men keep getting picked up by backwoods cops," Havoc fires back. "Three runs in a row, O'Neil. You're haulin' my product to *my* customers."

"Then say what the real issue is," Cole challenges. His voice is strained and low in the way I know is only asking for trouble. This is exactly what I didn't want to happen. Lately, Cole's temper has been a powder keg hoping for a match and I'm worried Havoc just lit it.

"*You're* worried. Don't blame that shit on Nevada."

Havoc leans back in the large leather chair and taps his fingers along the edge of the arm. Assessing the anger that's brewing deep between the two sides. "Word is that these cops are connected to you. Local assholes that run your club."

"*I* run my club," Cole booms. "Nobody else."

"Then you better start fucking proving it," Havoc says in a murderously calm tone that, if there were anybody else sitting at the table, it would only *scare*. To us, it's another challenge. "We're holding off on shipments until your shit gets figured out. Prove that it is, and we continue business as always."

"That's not going to work for us," Dex cuts in.

"Was I speaking to you?" Havoc asks, turning his attention to a tightly wound Wolfe. "Keep your enforcer on a leash, O'Neil."

I lean forward, clasping my hands over the table, trying to break up the current of frustration between the men. I'm already having a hard time holding it back myself and want nothing more than to shove my foot through Havoc's jaw, but one of us needs to have a level head and West isn't equipped to deal with men like this yet.

"What do you need from us to get shipping back on track?" I say in the most level voice I can muster.

Havoc's gaze swings to me before landing back on Cole. "Get rid of your Five-O issues."

"Done," I interject. "What else?"

I can see Cole's fist clench on the table next to me.

"We double the shipments each month once your little problem is handled." One of the men next to Havoc finally speaks up. I recognize him as Piper, the vice president, who prefers the sharp edge of a blade over a bullet to do his dirty work.

"We'll need more manpower," Cole grits out. My eyes slide shut before I turn to look at my prez.

"Then I suggest you start patchin' in more prospects, O'Neil. That shit ain't my problem," Havoc states, reading my mind.

Cole nods. "One more run. I'll head it myself with Nash. Then you can pause it."

A laugh booms from across the table as Havoc loses his shit. "You want what? A second chance?"

"No," Cole states. "One more run, which we're overdue already, and then you hold off on shipments." He leans back in the chair as I stare at him.

"What the fuck are you doing?" I hiss at Cole. This isn't the pres that I knew, this is some bullshit dick measuring contest that Cole's trying to win. Still he doesn't answer me, doesn't even spare me a glance as Havoc's laughter dies.

"One more run. You get stopped, you're done."

"Deal."

"Cole," I hiss again and this time my eyes catch his. "This is a club vote."

"Problem?" Havoc asks as I turn to look at him.

"Nope," Cole says. "Are we done here?"

"For now." Havoc nods.

His eyes linger on me before his men stand, signaling that the meeting is over. With fucked stipulations. Cole stands with the rest of them and waits for Dex and me to do the same. I glance over at Dex, who looks like he's about to rip Cole's head off. A part of me doesn't blame him.

We begin following the Skulls out of the room, a hell of a lot further from diffusing the powder keg that is Cole. Once again we're going to have to figure out a way to keep the compound secure for days. Falcone can only do so much, and having fewer men at the clubhouse, along with leaving Kadence there, already has me on edge.

"Should've offered up Porter too," one of the Skulls chuckles. "Woulda loved to see that sweet piece of pussy walk around here again." He shoves his buddy next to him as Cole and I follow behind them.

"He should've put her on the pole, that ass looks too good to be covered up," The other member says with a howling laugh.

Before I can even register what's happening, Cole's on the member. His hand wraps around the nape of his neck as he slams him into a neighboring table.

"What the fuck man!" The first guy yells, catching the attention of the rest of the crew.

"You fuckin' speak about her like that again," Cole growls into the man's ear, "I'll let her castrate you my fucking self."

"O'Neil," Havoc yells, "you're outnumbered brother, think about your men before you start threatening mine."

"Tell your men to have some respect for my crew then, Havoc," he bites out, keeping the murderous gaze on the side of the pinned man's face. "Patched or not, she's a Hound. You treat her as such."

"Think you've proved your point, Pal," I say, grabbing the back of Cole's cut and hauling him off of the guy. With a shove I push him towards the door. Ignoring the fuming Skulls that surround us I turn back to Dex. "Clean this shit up."

Dex gives me a curt nod as I shove Cole again, forcing him out of the door.

As soon as it slams behind me, I throw my hands up. "What the fuck, man?"

Cole's hands fist at his side until they find his hips. He paces back and forth like a cornered animal.

"What the hell has gotten into you?" I bark. "Because that was not the fucking plan, Cole!"

"I'm fucking done, man," Cole says under his breath.

"What the fuck do you mean you're done?" I ask, watching Cole pace back and forth across the pavement.

"You've got your fucking happy man!" He halts pointing into the air.

My brows furrow. "What the hell are you talking about?"

Cole blows out a shaky breath and it's then I know this has nothing to do with the meeting or proving the size of his dick to Havoc. His ego took over because something else has been bothering him. I saw it the other night and I saw it this morning.

"I don't even know anymore," Cole breathes. "It fucking hurts, man." He huffs out a laugh and shakes his head letting it drop. "I'm happy for you," he says after a moment of silence between the two of us. "I really am, but watching you and Kadence have what–" His voice cracks and he swallows hard.

"Ah, hell, man," I say, taking a step towards my friend.

Cole shoots his hand out stopping me. "I failed your sister. Why are you even still here?"

"What?" I ask.

"Why the hell didn't you leave after she died man? I'd deserve it. Hell, I wouldn't even blame you if you were pissed at me."

"Cole, you told me Becca's death wasn't my fault. So how the hell was it yours?" This is an argument we've never had before. It feels strange to be on the other side of it, but I know where the guilt stems from. I may have been her brother but Cole was in love with her, and from the hurt littering his features, he still is.

"I was supposed to protect her!" He yells. "And I couldn't even do that and now I'm not even sure I can protect this fucking club."

"We were all supposed to protect her. It wasn't one person's fucking job, man. We all fucking failed Becca."

"You don't get it," he says incredulously, "She was–" Cole's voice breaks off again as he shakes his head. "She was supposed to meet me that night. Dex was on watch, but she was coming to see me."

Pain shoots through my chest as my heart begins to beat rapidly. "What?" I hiss. This is new fucking information. "No," I say shaking my head. "We were with Stokes, why the fuck–"

"We planned to meet after the meeting. She snuck out earlier than she should have."

His admission feels like a dagger to my chest as I spin around sucking in a breath. "You never fucking told me."

"Because no one knew about us," he says, "and when she died it didn't feel important–"
"Don't you fucking dare say what I think you're going to." I turn on my heel pointing at him. "*Don't.*" I stare at my friend who's slowly turning into a stranger. The realization hits me like a sack of bricks and it feels like all of the air in my lungs is suddenly sucked from me. "That's why she was on Highway Two," I say glaring at him. "She was going to the bridge."

Cole stares back at me before nodding.

"She was on Watson's route that night," I state as the puzzle pieces start to fall into place. "No one fucking knew why she was out there," I say, "no one except you."

Cole's eyes gloss over, pain etches into his features as he stares back at me. How the fuck am I supposed to sit here, standing across from him when he's the reason my sister ended up on that highway that night. Ended up dead in a ditch. Rage clouds my vision as I shove passed Cole.

"Where are you going?" Cole yells.

"To find my girl and fucking leave this shit hole!" I yell back. I hear Cole's boots behind me and shake my head, "Fuck off, O'Neil. I'll do this run for the club and then–"

"Then what? You'll actually be out this time?" He bites.

I throw on my helmet and shake my head. "For a whole month, you told me shit wasn't my fault. You watched me drink myself blacked out, you watched me lose my fucking self and you still couldn't tell me the fucking truth. I don't owe you shit right now." I start my bike. "We aren't coming back with you guys, figure out how to protect this club on your own, Cole. You said you were done." I curl my lips and shake my head. "I'm fucking done."

I rev my bike lurching forward and riding to the gate, leaving my best friend behind me. There's only one person in this world I need, and right now, she's the only thing that's keeping me from killing the only other person who I thought I had.

My hands grip the handlebars harder than I need to and it does nothing to ease the ache and anger spreading through my body. I know Blake and Kadence wouldn't go far from the Skull's compound and it doesn't take long for me to spot the van parked outside of a row of boutiques.

I park next to it just as they stumble out of a small leather shop. Kadence is now wearing a dark green worn leather jacket. If it weren't for the sun beaming down on them, I wouldn't have noticed it isn't black. My presence catches Blake's attention first. She nudges Kadence and points to where I'm parked.

She smiles at me, bright and wide, just like I figured she would, but as they draw closer to me, her smile fades. It's like no matter what's going on we're always able to sense the other one. Always aware of how the other is feeling. Fuck, she looks happy coming out of that store and I'm determined to keep her happy. For as long as she'll let me.

"Everything cool?" Blake asks, shoving the bags into the van. I shake my head. "Fuck." She curses.

"The others are headed back. I'll go with you back to the compound, make sure you get there and then I'm taking Kadence out of here." My gaze flickers to my girl as she steps up to me. Her fingers wrap around my chin as she searches my eyes.

"What the hell happened?" Blake asks.

"O'Neil can fill you in," I say, not breaking my gaze from Kadence.

"That bad?" She whispers, assessing my reaction as she usually does.

"Worse." Is all I can say before handing her her helmet. My eyes meet hers again and I know the emotions I'm swallowing are hiding in my eyes. "Just get on the bike," I say softly, whispering, *"please."*

She searches my eyes one last time and nods, pressing her lips to mine. "Whatever you need."

"Thank you."

Kadence takes the helmet from my hands and shifts it over her hair before climbing on the back behind me. Her arms circle my waist as we wait for Blake to climb into the van and I follow her back to the compound. We watch her drive through the gate and as soon as it closes I flip my bike around and drive. I'm not sure where I'm going or how long I'll ride to get there, but as soon as she squeezes my torso gently, my hand finds hers, covering them.

She intertwines our fingers and rests her chin on my shoulder. I don't give a fuck where I go. As long as she's riding behind me I have everything I need, right here in my grasp.

COLE

Holden's exhaust fills my nostrils as I watch him peel through the gate. I wasn't planning on telling him the truth. Ever. It was a secret that was meant to die with me. Even if it kills me every time he calls me brother. I don't deserve the title. I haven't since that night.

Watching him with Kadence grows harder and harder each day. Reliving every fucking haunted memory I have of Becca while watching them grow closer. I'm not angry that they're together. I'm angry that I don't have that anymore. That picking Becca up in my arms isn't an option. No matter how much her touch haunts me or how her peach and cinnamon scent still lingers in my bedroom.

Everything is falling apart and no matter how much I'm told it's not my fault, I know it is. Everyone is relying on me. Everyone looks to me for answers. I never asked for that. I never asked to be President of a motorcycle club at twenty. Barely a kid myself and still falling for a girl who was forbidden to me. I don't know if I can handle the pressure anymore.

"Will you quit it?" Her laugh echoes through the shop. "We're going to get caught."

Becca's arms wrap around my neck after failing to shove me off of her. I laugh and bury my face into her neck, nipping at her collarbone. "I thought you weren't going to wear these dresses to work anymore," I mutter against her skin, taking in her scent. Peaches mixed with motor oil from being in the office all day.

"I don't remember making such a deal," she says in a breathy voice as my lips graze the column of her neck. "I do remember you telling me that if I wore one again, you'd murder every man that looked at me."

I growl. "I haven't done enough murdering today then."

Becca shoves my shoulder, pulling back from me with a frown. "You'd never murder your brothers."

"If they stare at your ass in these dresses I will," I say, capturing her lips.

Slotting myself between her legs, I tug at the hem of her dress. As soon as the garage doors shut, I had her back against my toolbox. With the lid flipped closed it took me two seconds to plant her there and kiss her how I've been wanting to do all fucking day.

My favorite smile grows on her lips as my hands roam up her thighs, sliding further to where I knew she wanted me. "We have to tell them sometime, Cole."

I hum, dropping my head to her chest and kissing along the swell of her breasts. Becca pulls back again leaning against the wall behind her and digs her fingers into my beard as she cups my face. "I'm serious. We've been secretive for long enough."

Sighing, I relent on my attack on her skin. We've had this conversation a million times and it's always the same. "Your brother is going to kill me."

"My brother is in prison," she says, nipping at my bottom lip, making it harder to focus on what she's saying.

"He also gets out today," I counter. "If he knew what I've been doing to his sister, he'd kill me."

She lets out a soft whine as my hand cups her breast. "I need you to tell him the truth. I can't lie worth shit to Holden, you know that."

"Baby, I really don't want to be having this conversation with my hand practically in you and the other around your tit," I huff against her skin again and pull back. I cage her in with my hands on either side of her hips on the toolbox. "You really want to tell him?" I ask, searching her eyes.

Becca nods as she combs her fingers through my hair. "Tomorrow though. Tonight, after your meeting, I want you all to myself before shit hits the fan."

"That's a great vote of confidence," I laugh. "You mean you want one more roll around the sheets before I'm a dead man."

She grins and I swear it lights up the entire shop despite the fluorescent bulbs still lit above us. "Better make it worth it then."

I groan, pulling her into my arms and nuzzle against her neck again. "Fine, but I'm haunting this perfect ass if I die."

"Deal." She giggles as I dig my fingers into her ribs.

The meeting went far longer than I fucking expected. Stokes droned on about getting new girls at Moon. I wasn't interested. I was pretty sure where the girls were coming from and I wanted nothing to fucking do with it but I didn't have a choice because I couldn't prove it.

More than once, I checked the time on my phone and each time after the first I hadn't missed the way Holden watched me. I knew I needed to chill but all I could think about was getting back to her. For years, Becca invaded my mind. Her laugh, her smile. Everything about her felt like sunshine on the cloudiest days and I want nothing more than for my darkness to be swallowed whole by her light.

Once Holden was picked up by Stokes, we grew closer until one night I couldn't take it anymore. That kiss was still burned in my mind and since then she had rooted herself so deep in my veins I never wanted her to leave.

As soon as the meeting finished, I climbed on my bike and headed towards our spot. The bridge we'd go to as kids and one that Becca and I claimed over the last year and a half while Holden was away. More than once we've snuck out during the day or at night to get a few moments of peace. Which usually leads to us crawling into her bed at an ungodly hour and spending our time lost in each other until the sun comes up.

Flashing lights flicker on the road ahead of me. Odd for Highway Two. I know the patrols only come out here at night for animals or straggling hitchhikers, but the ambulance and firetruck that come into view make my stomach roll. I pull off behind Watson's squad car and climb off my bike, hanging my helmet over the handlebar and move towards the lights.

"Sir you can't be–" An EMT starts but as soon as her tail lights come into view, I push past them.

"Becca!" I yell, shoving past the young man.

Watson spins around, his eyes wide as I round the edge of her car. Her door is wide open, the dome light still lit, and her keys still in the ignition.

"Becca!" Frantically I look through the windows, hoping to see her sitting there and that this is just a misunderstanding but as soon as Watson's arm stops me, holding me back I know it isn't.

"O'Neil, you can't be here," he shakily says.

"Where is she, Watson?" I yell. "Becca!"

He shakes his head. "We got a call about an abandoned vehicle..." he starts but stops and swallows tightly. "I'm sorry."

"Don't! Don't fucking apologize, Where is she?!" I shove Watson back, pushing my way through the row of firefighters and EMTs that stand surrounding her.

Her foot comes into view first and my stomach drops. My entire world tilts on its axis as the rest of her body comes into view. "No, no, no, no," I whine, "Becca?"

"O'Neil!" I hear Watson yell behind me but everything begins to fade. The lights of the trucks and cars turn dim and the only thing I see is her. The bruises on her face make her almost unrecognizable. The dress I teased her about earlier was ripped, exposing the rest of her legs that have their own smattering of dark bruises.

My legs give out and I collapse to the ground next to her, tears stinging my eyes as I move to touch her. Barely a centimeter away but she already feels cold to me. I choke back a sob, my head dropping as I cradle her face. "What happened, baby?" I cry.

My forehead presses to hers as my shoulders shake and I lose it. "No," I whine, "don't do this."

"Cole," Watson's voice is right behind me, "this is a crime scene, I can't--"

"WHAT HAPPENED?" I yell, picking my head up from her to glare back at the man I've hated for years.

"We don't know yet," he answers solemnly, "but you have to let us do our job."

I shake my head, falling back into the grass, and carefully cradle her against my body. "Who did this to you?" I whisper into her hair. No longer did it smell like peaches and motor oil like it had before. Now, she smelt like a mixture of grass, dirt, and iron.

Tears drop down onto her cheeks as I hold her, running my thumb along her swollen and broken cheekbone. It's then I notice the handprints around her throat and look at Watson. "you find out who did this."

"Cole," Watson starts but I silence him with a shake of my head.

"You find out who did this, or I will," I warn. "I'll fucking kill them if I do, Watson. I promise you that."

"Sir," a soft voice filters from the other side of me, "we need to take her now."

I look up to find a younger female EMT looking down at me with glossy eyes. I shake my head but when I glance back down to the woman I've loved for years, my eyes slide closed. I'm going to have to tell Holden. I'll have to tell everyone.

"I can't," I sob into her hair again, "I can't do this without you."

Minutes pass while I hold her still body. Sobbing into her cold skin.

"Sir," the woman tries again.

"Just give me a fucking minute!" I boom, holding her tighter to me until I couldn't any longer.

I stare down at her, taking in everything that this fucker had done. Not understanding any of it or why they would choose her. Shit like this doesn't happen in Pine River. So why did it have to be her? My sunshine snubbed out. For what?

I cup her face again, pressing my lips to hers for the last time and whisper the one thing I know I never said enough.

"I love you."

Everything became a blur as I lay her back down and watch the EMT's zip her into a body bag and carry her away from me, taking my heart along with her. Slowly I stand, running a hand over my face and turning to Watson.

"Find them," I say through clenched teeth as I pass him, "or I fucking will."

My heart is still with her. Six feet under the earth and I know that's exactly where it will stay. I've failed everyone I know and the guilt I had from that day had sunk so far into my bones that I deserve everything that was being thrown at me and most of all, I know I deserve to lose Holden too.

KADENCE

He's been quiet the whole ride. I still have no idea where he's taking me and, at this point I don't think he even knows where he's going. Whatever happened during that meeting has fucked with the man I said goodbye to that morning. I've tried everything to swallow down the anxiety that has built itself a home in my stomach and nothing has worked.

Holden pulls off onto an outlook from the highway and kicks his stand down so I can climb off. As soon as I do, I pull the helmet off and turn to him. His eyes are cast out across the water that crashes below against the cliffside we're parked on and his brows are furrowed. Even with the passing cars, the silence radiating from him is deafening.

"Baby," I say softly moving into his side. "What happened?"

"I-" he starts, but his voice cracks and that's when my heart dips. Holden sucks in a shaky breath and shakes his head letting it fall forward with the weight of whatever's on his mind.

"Hey," I whisper, taking his cheeks in my hands and moving to stand in front of him.

I maneuver my fingers under his chin to undo the chin strap of his helmet before pulling it off of his head. I make quick work of hanging it on the handlebar only to move my hands back to his features. He looks like he is on the verge of breaking and it's killing me that I can't do anything to help it. His eyes focus on the water again, unable to look at me.

"Holden," I whisper again, hoping to get his attention.

"He lied." Is all he says before his arms wrap around me. He tugs me as close as he can to him, still on his bike. My arms instinctively snake around his neck as he buries his face into the crook of mine.

"What do you mean? Who lied?" I ask gently, trailing my fingers along the nape of his neck. His arms tighten around me like if he were to let go I would float away from him. Confusion wracks through me as I try to piece together what he was saying.

Holden lifts his head to look at me with tears welling in his eyes. I hate that he's shattering in front of me, piece by piece and I can't stop it.

"Cole lied about Becca's death."

"What?" I breathe out, my eyes wide as the words settle between us in a toxic cloud.

"He knew why she was on the road that night. Why she snuck out." He chokes out the words and drops his head again. "She was fucking going to meet him. He knew this whole time that I blamed myself for not being there to protect her that night. I spent–" Holden sucks in a breath but it sounds strained as if breathing was painful, "I spent the night staring at photos of her beaten body and he fucking knew."

My hands move to cup his face as a sob takes over the last few of his words. "Holden," I whisper, tracing my thumbs over his cheekbones and wiping away his tears as the grief of his sister's death washes over him again.

"Fuck," he curses shaking his head. "Fuck!"

Holden launches into a ramble about what happened at their meeting. How Cole had exploded over the tiniest of things. How nothing had gone to plan and how he found out about Becca. He holds nothing back as his words fall from his lips between small gasps of air and the slight raises in his voice when his anger takes over. I wipe his cheeks as he speaks whenever he lifts his head to look at me. All I can do is listen to him.

Truth be told, I don't know how to handle this with him. I don't know how to help him protect the club and I don't know how to help him protect his heart from breaking even more than it already was as he talks about Cole. All I want to do is wrap around him and be his shield.

He finally climbs from his bike and leads me over to the rock wall separating us from the cliffside below.

"How do I go back?" His voice is small and quiet as he turns to me.

"You have to." I hate saying that to him and I hate the look he gives me even more. His brows are furrowed and his lips are turned down into a frown. "I know that you're hurting and you have every right to be," I say as he starts to pull away from me. I know how he operates, Holden runs when things get tough, he hides behind his anger and grief the same way I do.

"I'm not your enemy, Holden," I say carefully. "And neither is Cole."

He spins so fast on me that it makes me dizzy. His eyes go wide, "You think I shouldn't blame him?" He asks, his words laced with hurt.

"That's not what I said," I sigh." You can hurt, you can grieve again. You're allowed to but don't let that get in between you and your brothers."

"How?" His whisper is almost a whine and it shatters what's left of my heart. "How do I look him in the face again knowing that he's responsible."

I wince knowing that I don't agree with him. "He wasn't the one that killed her, Holden."

That familiar darkness flickers in his eyes as he pulls away from my touch. "What the hell does that mean?" As soon as the words leave his lips it's like I can see his defenses build up around him and I'm desperate to stop it.

"It means just that. Cole didn't kill Becca just like I didn't kill my baby." The words feel like broken glass falling from my lips. I don't want to hurt him but he needs to hear this. Holden moves to pull further away from me, I don't let him this time. My fingers wrap around his hands and hold them to my chest. "You *know* who killed her. That's who you should be angry with. Cole should not have lied, he should have told you. But making him your enemy won't help anyone."

I know he's barely listening to me at this point but a part of me hopes the words ring true. His gaze has moved past me, back out at the water and his hands are clenched in mine. "Take the anger and hurt that you feel and direct it at the people who've hurt the ones you love. Use it against Stokes, Watson, hell even the Skulls if that's what you need, but don't weigh the club down with this."

"I'm tired of having it all on my shoulders," he whispers into the setting sun.

"I know," I reply just as softly. "Give me some of that weight."

Finally those cerulean eyes land on mine. Searching them for answers I don't have. This weekend was supposed to make things easier for us and yet somehow things feel even more heavy than they were a month ago. I know whatever we have to face is going to test us even more than we already have been but I also know that deep down we were so rooted within each other that we'd get through it.

Holden tucks my hands against his chest and leans into me slightly, tilting his head to the side as he studies my face. Taking in my features like it's the last time.

"Do you love me?" He whispers, keeping his eyes on mine.

Even if I try to deny it, I can't lie to him. My feelings for him are written in everything I do.

"More than you know."

For the first time since that morning, he smiles. It's soft but it still sends a flutter of butterflies through me as he leans further into me, capturing my lips with his. He tugs his hands from mine and tangles his fingers into my hair, kissing me with everything he has. When he pulls back, it feels like he takes the air in my lungs with him and when my eyes finally open he's watching me with something akin to adoration in his eyes.

"Ask me," he says breathlessly, sliding his hands to frame my face.

"Do you love me?" I whisper back without hesitation.

The corners of his mouth curve upwards again, lighting that small fire in my belly.

"More than you know," he rasps, pulling me to him and pressing his lips to mine. I melt into his chest, my fingers wrap around the lapels of his vest while his hands wrap around the small of my back, practically hugging me to his chest.

I pull back just enough to see his eyes, my breath fanning across his flushed cheeks. "Are we crazy?" My voice is barely a whisper. "It's been what? A little over a month?"

"Sixty-two days." He grins. It's so bright that it sends an ache straight through my chest. Holden trails his hands up my back and though he looks relaxed, when I move my hands down his chest I can feel the tension radiating through him along with the hammering of his heart against my palm.

"You've been counting?" I ask softly.

He nods as sadness flickers in his eyes. A sigh leaves him as he pushes back the fallen tendrils of hair from my face, tucking them behind my ear. He doesn't say anything for a moment but he trails his fingers down my jaw and on instinct I lean into his touch when they curl around the side of my neck.

"Good things don't happen to men like me," he starts while holding my gaze. "So when a good thing like you comes into my life, you bet your ass I'm counting the days."

Warmth blooms in my chest as a wistful sigh leaves my lips. No one has ever said such sweet words to me and actually meant them. Holden does it every time even if he doesn't mean to. With no expectation of anything other than just my love. "You really have a way with words, Nash."

"Only for you," he whispers, pulling me close and brushing his lips against mine. He takes them for his own once more before patting my thighs and pulling back, cutting off the kiss I so desperately want more of. "This is supposed to be our day," he says with a soft frown. "I'm sorry that it was spoiled."

I grin, glancing back down at the ocean. The sun is still above the horizon, the glow of it glistens off the water below. "The day isn't over yet," I say looking back at him. "We can still make the most of it before we go back tomorrow."

The furrow in his brow deepens. "We don't have to go back tomorrow."

I raise a brow with a smile tugging on my lips. "We don't?"

He shakes his head. "I'm not ready to go back and deal with the bullshit waiting for me. I want time with you and I'm milking every minute I can get of it."

I can't help but laugh. "How romantic."

"Hey." His fingers find my ribs, tickling me gently as I burst into a fit of giggles. My hands shoot out to his wrists to try and pull away from him until he finally grants some mercy, "I'll show you how romantic I can be."

He buries his face into the crook of my neck, nipping at the junction between my throat and collarbone. It's the one spot he knows that has my heart going from zero to sixty in an instant.

"Mauling me on the side of the highway isn't romantic," I pant, unable to hide that even the slight fan of his breath against my skin is hitting me straight in my core.

The corners of his lips turn upwards against my skin as he trails them to the other side of my neck. "I beg to differ, Sunflower." His breath is hot against my skin now, "I've never needed someone more than I do you."

"Oh God, Holden," I groan pulling back from him. "You have to stop." Laughing softly I cup his face, capturing his lips with mine.

He instantly takes control of the kiss, forcing a whimper from me as his tongue runs along the seam of my lips. As soon as I part them, he delves in. The kiss turns needy and almost impatient as his hands skate down my back and up the hem of my shirt. The warmth of his skin against mine is all I need to ignite that fire in my belly and turn every logical thought I have into mush.

I move to stand between his legs while he sits on the wall, never breaking the kiss. His hard length presses against my abdomen as my hands rest against his thighs. I break the kiss this time, glancing around us to find anything that could seclude us from passing cars. The only thing near is the wall and peering over the side of it, there is still a good six feet before the ground drops off the edge of the cliff. A wicked thought crosses my mind as I grin at him.

"Do you trust me?" I ask, peering into his curious blue eyes that I love so much.

Holden raises a brow. "With my life."

I suck in a breath not expecting that response and swallow the emotions bubbling in my throat in order not to ruin the lust burning through me. I climb over the rock wall, shoving back the nerves running through me with his statement. They wrap around my veins like roots knowing he trusts me that much. I don't know what the future holds for us but Jeremy is still out there and still gunning for me. Having him trust me with his life is a terrifying thought when I know that the man who almost killed me would do just about anything to get me back.

"What are you doing?" He asks with amusement in his voice. The question melts away the thoughts running through me as he turns around to see me standing near the edge of the cliff. It's still a few feet away but seeing the drop up close makes my heart thunder. Adrenaline courses through me as I look back at him.

"Mauling you," I chuckle to even out the sound of my voice.

I take two steps towards him, settling between his thighs and wrapping my fingers around his belt. With a tug, I pull him off the wall.

"Is that so?" He asks, watching me with curiosity laced with the fire burning in his eyes.

I hum my response and begin to work his buckle undoing his belt before moving to his jeans and making quick work of the button and zipper. A groan falls from his lips as I slide my hand beneath the waistband of his briefs, lifting to my toes to trail my lips along his jaw.

"Baby, you don't have to do this," he breathes. The shake in his voice tells me that this is exactly what I should be doing.

"I want to," I all but moan as my fingers wrap around him. Already hard and wanting, I trail my thumb over his head, spreading the soft bead of precum over his tip.

Before he can protest further I drop to my knees, tugging his jeans and briefs down just far enough that he's now exposed to me. His length bobs heavily and I realize it's been a long time since I've done anything like this to a man but I trust Holden just as much as he trusts me.

With slow purposeful strokes, I glance up at him through my lashes. Those blue eyes are glued to me and darkening while he watches my hand move against him. His jaw ticks as I quicken my pace, twisting my wrist gently to work him in a corkscrew motion.

"I'm in control," I rasp firmly. "Hands on the wall."

A growl escapes him, but still he does what he's told. Holden leans back against the rocks, his ass resting against them forces his hips to jut against my grip and he rests his hands on either side of him.

"Thank you," I whisper.

His nod is strained, but his eyes are full of the love I now know he feels for me. The same love that runs through me in waves every time he is near.

My tongue darts from between my lips as I lick his head, forcing a hiss from his lips. I can't help the smile that forms on my face as I begin to take him in my mouth. bobbing my head softly and using my hands for whatever I'm not able to take.

Not even the rocks and dirt digging into my knees can distract me from the man falling apart in front of me and at my mercy. Something about the idea of a man his size crumbling under my touch makes me feel powerful. Makes me feel like everything that was taken from me, stolen from me, was just within reach again.

"Christ, Kade," he groans as his head drops back and his eyes slide closed with a shudder as my tongue swirls around his tip again.

With the adrenaline and newfound power surging through me, I hollow out my cheeks, taking him as far as I can until I feel him at the back of my throat. Satisfaction rolls through me with a soft gag and I back off giving myself room to breathe as his hips roll gently between my lips.

"You have no idea what you're doing to me," he growls, bringing his head forward and finding my eyes again. "How beautiful you look right now."

Tears prick at the edges of my eyes. They're not from his intrusion in my mouth but his words. Everything that I have wanted to hear for years is falling from his lips with ease and spearing my heart. Doing nothing but carving his name over the scars that had hardened there.

I move faster, taking him however I want and Holden lets me. He's giving me everything in this moment while I give him the release he desperately needs. I lift my free hand, wrapping it around his thigh to hold myself up. My core is soaked and aching for my own release but right now this is for him. It's about him and I know that he will make good on giving me what I need later.

"Baby," he groans. "If you don't stop now, I'm going to come down that pretty throat of yours." Every word is strained and hoarse but still his eyes never leave mine and I refuse to back down. "*Sunflower,*" he growls and my eyes flicker to his hands where the whites of his knuckles shine against the sunset as he grips the stone below him.

With a hoarse moan, I feel him swell between my lips and his hips stutter until he is doing just that. Spilling down my throat as I hold him there, moaning with him until he exhales and his shoulders slump.

Releasing him with a soft pop, I run my tongue over my bottom lip relishing the salty and bitter taste of him. In an instant, his hands are on me, pulling me up off of my knees and to my feet. His lips crash into mine while one hand slides to the back of my neck, holding me firmly to him and the other wraps around my waist. I nip at his bottom lip, forcing a chuckle to form deep in his chest.

"I love you," I whisper softly against his mouth. His breath fans across my cheeks with an intoxicating heat that does nothing to tamper my own needs. My body feels so sensitive the slightest of his touches sends sparks down my spine.

His smile is beautiful as the sun sets behind me. "I love you too, Sunflower."

With another soft peck to my lips, he releases me and tucks himself back within his jeans. He climbs over the wall and turns back to me, holding out his hand to help me over. "C'mon, I think it's time we focus on ourselves for a bit."

I know that there's still that lingering sadness under the smile he reserves only for me. The weight of his club, of his relationship with his brothers, all of it hangs around us like a dense cloud but, for now, I'll take every moment of happiness I can with him before we go back to the mess waiting for us.

HOLDEN

I ride for longer than I probably should have. The sun has already dipped behind the horizon by the time I stop again. This time I find a small beach park we can camp at. Once I find a spot, I stick some cash into the little box at the park gate for our time here and we pick out a spot to spend the night.

"I didn't realize you were an avid camper," Kadence teases as she climbs off the bike.

Her voice is hoarse and a part of me feels bad, but it's a small, *small* part of me. Still she looks beautiful in the moonlight, her hair is messy from the wind and there's a small flush on her cheeks from the chill in the air.

"I'm not, well.." I pause. "I haven't been for a while." I flash her a grin as I unpack the tent from the back of the bike.

She glances at me, grabbing our bedrolls and setting them on the small wooden picnic table. "You used to be?"

I nod and start to put the tent together. "In the Army, we camped a lot when we were on mission but as a kid Cole--" I pause again and the memory of the two of us crammed into a small, one person tent in Cole's backyard sends a pang through my chest. Clearing my throat I choke out the words as I kneel to fix the tent poles into their holes. "We would camp in his backyard, just the two of us piled into this small ass tent."

The crunch of her boots on the gravel behind me has my shoulders tense for a moment until I feel her fingers run along the top of my head down to the nape of my neck and into my shirt.

"You guys will get through this," she says so softly that I almost miss it. "It may not be this week or the next, but it'll happen."

I stand, forcing her hand to fall to my back. "You have a lot of faith in our friendship. More than I do right now."

She smiles and it lights up my world for a brief moment. "Because I know you and, as angry as you are and as betrayed as you feel, you'll forgive him."

"How can you be so sure?" I ask. It's not that I don't want Cole to be out of my life. In fact, it's the last thing I want but right now it feels impossible.

"Because you forgave me and I didn't give you a reason to but you did it because you love me." Kadence steps towards me, almost melting into my body the way she does when she wants to be close to me. Instinctively I wrap my arms around her, abandoning the tent for the moment. "And you love him."

"When did you get so wise?" I chuckle, pushing back tiny tendrils of hair from her face and tucking it behind her ear.

She grins, pressing a kiss to my jaw. "I've always been wise, my love. You're just stuck in that head of yours."

"That may be true," I say with a rasp. "But I can't forgive him yet."

Kadence nods. "I know."

I dip my head to kiss her just as a chill passes through her body. "Alright, Sunflower, let's get this tent put up so we can get you warm again."

"Is that your excuse to get me naked in nature?" She laughs pushing off of me and moving to the opposite side of the tent to help me get the poles up.

I flash her a wolfish grin. "Would you blame me if I said yes?"

"Not at all." She grins. "I had the same plan."

"Did you now?"

Kadence shrugs and helps me with the second pole. Our small home for the night finally comes to life. All it needs is the rain guard but the sky is clear, and I doubt it'll rain between now and tomorrow. The only thing on my mind is seeing her breathless beneath me. The spot we chose is tucked back into a small cove, trees separate us from the rest of the few campers around. Plenty of privacy for what I have planned for her.

I watch as she moves into the tent with our bedrolls, rolling them out for when we're ready to sleep. There isn't much I plan to do with her tomorrow for our time together. I mainly want to focus on just her. Everything feels heavy and the weight on my chest only grows with all the club bullshit that is coming to light. I know we still have to worry about Jeremy, that he is still a very real threat to my girl, but for now all I want is to spend time with her without the dark clouds hanging over us.

"Baby, do you think this is gonna be warm enough?" She asks, turning towards me. "Is it supposed to be cold?"

I smile at how domestic her question feels and how much I don't hate it. "We'll be fine darlin', besides," I reach out for her, tugging her to my chest again, "we'll make our own heat."

Kadence laughs, wrapping her arms around my waist. "Will we now?"

I nod with a soft hum.

"You're gonna have to feed me first," she coos, looking up at me. "I'm starving."

"Well it's a good thing I thought ahead now isn't it?" I give her a sly smile and walk over to the bike to grab the bag of food I bought from the saddlebag. None of it is fancy, some snacks, a couple of pop-tarts for the morning, and chocolate. I grin at her as we both move to the picnic table and I dump the contents of the bag onto the table. "Sit," I tilt my chin towards the bench. She listens and starts to go through the stash.

"You eat like a teenager," she laughs, holding up a bag of Cheetos and a Hershey's chocolate bar.

I smirk at her. "Hey now, we were a little busy doing other things, I didn't think of stopping."

Blush creeps over her features, only making me smile harder than I have in a while. I watch as she opens the bag of Cheetos and pops one into her mouth. "I haven't had these since I was on the road."

My smile falters for a moment. She hasn't really talked about her time between Miami and here. "How long were you out there for?"

Kadence glances up at me, those green eyes meeting my own. "For a couple of weeks," she admits softly. "I felt so trapped in that house for so long that I just wanted to feel.."

"Free." I finish for her.

She nods, her smile softening for me. "For the first time in years, I didn't have to answer to anyone except myself. I lived on this shit though." She picks up the bag of cheese puffs and gently waves them around. "These and powdered donuts."

I smile at her, grabbing the bag and popping a few of the puffs into my mouth. "What brought you out this direction?"

She lets out a sigh. "It was the furthest away from everyone I knew. All of the rumors, the death threats," her voice trails off with a soft shake of her head. "I just wanted to get away from it all."

I nod regarding her words. She packed up everything she ever knew to get away from her life. To build something new for herself. I have nothing but respect for that but...sometimes I still wonder if leaving her home that quickly called her back. "Would you ever go back?"

"Fuck no," she blurts with a laugh. "I'd have to be dragged back there." Kade's smile fades for a moment. "I would go back just to visit my dad though. If the car can't be fixed then I'd like to see him again."

"The car was your dad's?" I ask, taking in the new information.

"He had one just like it when I was a kid. Up until he died it was his favorite thing in the world." A haunted look flickers in her eyes for a moment. "My mother sold it right after he died. Called it an eyesore. It was the one thing of his I had left. She claimed she needed the money to take care of me, of the house... but I knew it was a lie when she came home with new clothes and shoes." She shakes her head as if she was trying to rid herself of the memories.

"You said his name was George?" I ask softly, tilting my head to catch her gaze and remembering that it was the name she wanted for her baby.

Kadence nods and smiles up at me. "He used to let me skip school on Wednesdays, twice a month we'd go to this little beach just outside of town. There was this ice cream stand there that had the best Oreo ice cream."

I smile, the warmth in my chest has spread to my limbs and it's only brought there by her. I can tell that her dad was a staple in her life. That even talking about him still shows the residual pain in her eyes from losing him. Though the more she talks openly about him and the soft smiles that flicker over her features when she remembers something only make me fall harder for her.

"Well, I don't know if I can beat Oreo ice cream," I say gently, reaching across the table to link my hands with hers, "but I know a spot we can go to tomorrow."

"Really?" She asks with so much hopefulness in her voice that it sends an ache straight through me.

"I don't want to replace your dad, Sunflower, but I want to give you that same happiness."

A sigh falls from her lips and it makes me smile. "C'mere." I tug her hands gently, pulling her up from her side of the table. She stands, moving towards me, and I turn so she can sit on my lap, just where I want her.

"I know we have to go back," she whispers, tucking her face into the crook of my neck as she sits down on me, "but I really wish we didn't."

"We'll do it again, as many times as you want after this shit settles." I promise. "Lord knows I could use the break every once in a while." I nudge her gently back a little so I can cup her face. "I know you do too."

"I don't need it all the time," she breathes, wrapping her arms around my neck. "Things just get overwhelming with all the testosterone." A ghost of a smile flickers over her face.

I lean forward, pressing my lips to her cheek and leaving a trail of kisses along her cheeks and down her jaw. "Well, I'm all yours whenever you want me."

Kadence sighs again, though this time it's almost dreamy as she leans into my touch. "Whenever I want?" Her hips roll against mine as she moves to straddle me. The wood beneath us creaks softly under the shift of our weight and it only makes me grin.

I nod. "Whenever."

She leans in, dragging her tongue along my bottom lip before pressing her lips to mine in a kiss that sends a jolt of lust straight to my cock. "Now," she breathes against me. "I want you now."

"As you wish, Sunflower," I say just as breathlessly before picking her up.

Her legs wrap around my waist as she continues to kiss me and I make a few steps to the tent, laying her down on the bedrolls before zipping the door shut.

Four times I lose myself in her tonight and she loses herself in me just the same if not more. It's hard to keep track but the sun starts to shine through the mesh roof of our tent and I can't help but stare at her. I barely got any sleep, but seeing her next to me, still sleeping and lying on her stomach, has me hard again and wanting more. The bedroll blanket is draped just over her hips giving me plenty of milky soft skin to trace my fingers on.

I can't help myself and move down to pepper her bare shoulder with featherlight kisses. When I feel her move beneath me, my lips quirk against her skin. A soft moan leaves her and the noise goes straight to my groin.

"How long have you been up?" She asks, though her eyes are still closed and her voice still heavy with sleep.

"For a while," I rasp back, propping myself up on my elbow and resting my head on my hand. "I was going to let you sleep a little longer, but we've got to get going."

Kadence groans softly, turning her head away from me. "A few more minutes."

I chuckle, sliding my hand down her back and under the blanket, taking a handful of her ass, not hard enough to hurt but enough that her hips lift softly and her back arches towards me a bit. A wicked smile forms on my lips as I lean down and kiss her shoulder again. "I promise to make it worth your while."

"How's that?" She asks breathlessly as my hand trails from her ass over her hip. I pull her towards me, rolling her onto her side to give me better access to her core.

"I have a few ideas," I whisper against the shell of her ear, "but this is the first one."

My fingers dive between her legs, sliding between her slit and finding her already wet. A triumphant smile takes over the wicked one as I explore her. A moan falls from her lips and her back arches even more. Her ass is pressed against my cock now, grinding just enough that the friction feels more like teasing.

"This is cheating," she sighs, turning her head to capture my lips.

I waste no time delving into her mouth, my tongue tangling with hers while my thumb works her clit. She moans into my mouth, craving this as much as I do. I take my time working her over, slipping two fingers within her as my knee slides between her legs. She takes the hint and hooks it over my hip.

"You can sleep when we're home, baby," I breathe against her neck, curling my fingers within her until she lets out a ragged moan and her body shudders with her release.

Her eyes are closed when I lift my head and her cheeks have the faintest bit of flush to them. I gently remove my hand, thrusting into her in one go. We both hiss at the feeling of her stretching around me and in this moment I know this is exactly where I would die happily. If it is nothing else but the sounds she makes and the way she feels clenched around me, I'd gladly give my last breath to this world.

Kade's body is still jelly, her legs shuddering gently as I rock in and out of her, both of us chasing release once more even after we spent all night barrelling towards it. I can feel the cord in my stomach winding up, that tightness in my lower back that tells me my release is creeping around the corner.

"I need you to come, Sunflower," I rasp against her neck, nipping and sucking at her skin.

As if on command her head rolls back onto my shoulder and soft curses fly from her lips into the morning sky. She clenches around me, sending me over the edge as I pulse within her and my own moans fill the tent. My hips stutter and I shudder as I fill her.

We both turn into puddles on the hard ground. The bedrolls doing nothing to help the rocks and dirt prodding into my back.

"I love you," she says in a whisper, rolling over and tucking herself against me, "way more than I care to admit."

I chuckle and press a kiss into her head. Knowing just exactly how she feels. "I love you too."

I never thought in a million years it would be so easy to say those words to someone. Especially not a woman I've known for a little over two months but with Kadence, it feels right. There's a naturalness to it that makes it feel like we've been saying it for fifty years to one another. My only wish is that we would have found each other sooner. That none of the bullshit we had to go through to get to this moment would have had to happen but maybe that's just it... Maybe fate has a fucked up way of bringing two people like us together.

She presses a kiss to my chest before sitting up and stretching her arms out in front of her. The marks I left on her shoulder and neck shine in the morning light, sending a wave of possessiveness through me knowing she's mine. She glances back at me with a grin.

"You wanted me up, cowboy, let's get going."

I laugh, sitting up with her, and cup the back of her neck, pulling her to me.

"If I would have known that's all it takes to get you outta bed, I would have tried that weeks ago." I smirk, kissing her quickly before letting her go.

"You'll have plenty of time to try it now," she remarks, grinning as she stands up in the tent in search of her discarded clothes.

I laugh tossing her shirt at her. "Is that a promise?"

"It is," she says, turning towards me with a smile on her face as she straightens out her clothes and I get dressed. My eyes catch hers with a grin but I pause seeing her smile fall for a moment. "I want this, Nash." Her voice is so soft I almost miss what she says. "Even with all the shit going on, I want a real shot at you and me."

I'm taken aback by her words for a moment and every nerve in my body feels like a livewire staring at her. "Baby, I thought that's what we were already doing?"

"We are." She takes a step towards me, her voice is high-pitched and her hands fall to my forearms. "We are," Kade repeats more confidently. "I just want to put it out there into the universe. Say it out loud because if we do that, then it makes it real."

"What about what we were doing before wasn't real?" I ask, my brows furrowing while looking down at her.

"Nothing," she sighs, "everything has been real." Her cheeks turn a soft shade of pink, "I'm not explaining this very well am I?"

"I want to say you are, but babe..." I shake my head still confused.

Kadence closes the distance between us. "I haven't put myself out there like this in a long time. Even before it was done for me. I don't want to hide from the fact that I'm falling for you, I don't want it to scare me into not doing things with you that I was too scared to do before."

"Like what?"

"Like get married," she says softly, glancing away from me for a brief moment, "and build a real family. Not one that bases love on ultimatums and guilt trips, but one that loves unconditionally. I've had the former and I don't ever want to go back to that again."

My heart feels like it's going to pound out of my chest. The thundering rhythm against my ribcage is almost too much, but when she looks back at me, I see just how genuine her feelings are. In the flecks of gray and gold in her eyes I do what always felt impossible until now.

I picture that life with her at the forefront.

I reach for her, wrapping my arms around her waist. "I never thought I'd ever get the chance to have any of that," I admit openly. "I saw how it turned out for my parents and it wasn't something I ever thought I'd want."

Her brows knit as she looks up at me.

"But I can't see a future without you by my side, Sunflower." I smile as soon as her brows relax and the corners of her mouth turn upward. I'm silent for another moment before kissing her. "You sure you wanna spend your life with me?" I rasp against her lips.

Without hesitation, she nods and whispers a yes that buries itself so deep in my soul that I feel myself sink everything I have into that one word just for her.

"I want to take you somewhere today."

"Where?" She whispers against my lips.

"It's a surprise," I grin, "but first, we need to get all this packed up and get you fed."

She smiles and every time I see it I swear she shoots sunlight from my head to my toes. "Deal, but..." she bites down on her bottom lip, "please don't make me eat from your teenager stash again."

I laugh and pepper her face with kisses. "Pancakes?"

Her eyes widen and her smile widens. "Pancakes."

KADENCE

The next few days after Santa Barbara fly by as the guys prepare for their run. I've barely seen Holden and despite the shit he and Cole are going through, they've spent most of that time together planning.

Even though we spend every night and morning together, I miss him. Something shifted between us during our time away and I know that we both feel it. Saying I love you isn't the only thing that has changed between us but now the shared glances, the lingering touches they all feel deeper.

Today though, I'm curled up in bed. Blake's lying next to me, flipping through random channels on the TV while my mind wanders to Holden. My eyes are closed when I hear the door open and close.

"How do you even watch anything on this TV? There's nothing good to watch." Blake's voice rings through the room.

"I have better things to watch than the TV, Porter," he chuckles, and it makes the corners of my mouth turn up. I open my eyes to glance at him as he wraps his arms around me and slides into the bed next to me.

"I'm going to ignore the fact that you tried making a dirty joke and go get us dinner." She slides off the other side of the bed. "Tell her to eat, or I'm forcing food down her throat."

"I'd like to see you try, Blake," I quip, glancing at her with a grin on my face. We've grown closer since the meeting with the Skulls.

Blake laughs as she heads towards the door. "I honestly would love to see you try and fight me."

"We both know I'd win!"

"Whatever you say, Andrews!" She yells as the door closes behind her.

Holden grins down at me. "You seem to be feeling better." His lips brush over my forehead. It's sweet and soft but I know he's checking for a fever again.

"It's hard not to feel happy around Blake." I admit pressing a soft kiss to his jawline, "and I haven't eaten, so no more puking. I just feel exhausted."

"Probably because you haven't eaten anything, Sunflower." He grabs my chin gently, lifting my gaze to his. "Promise me you'll try to eat something and drink water while I'm gone."

My heart rate picks up when I realize what day it is. "You guys are headed out?"

The look on his face turns somber. "Yeah, I was coming to say goodbye but..."

"I'll be fine. Blake will be here with me." I try to smile but the anxiety about them doing this run starts to seep in again. Heightened by the exhaustion, my body feels it leaves a sinking feeling in my gut. His brows furrow. "You have to go, Holden. If you don't it'll just make things worse between the club and the Skulls."

"I should have never told you what was going on," he sighs. "I hate that you're worried."

"I'd rather worry than be kept in the dark," I counter, moving to sit up. It takes more effort than it should for me to slide up and sit against the headboard. The dull throb in my head heightens for a moment as I move and my eyes slide closed to get my bearings.

"Baby," he whispers, his hand combing through my tangled hair. "I'll stay. The guys can do this without me."

I shake my head, opening my eyes to look at him because now the worry in his own voice is doing nothing to shake my nerves. "No, I'll be fine."

"Maybe we should call Lang?" He suggests with furrowed brows. Those ice blue eyes scan me as if he's looking for other injuries though everything I'm feeling is internal.

"Holden," I chuckle softly. "I'll be okay. It's just the flu or something. It'll go away." My eyes meet his and it takes everything I have to put on a brave face for him. We both know he has to go on this run with the guys. It's their only chance to not start a war with the other clubs. They can't afford it. "Go," I nudge him with my foot and smile, "I'll be fine."

"You're killin' me, Sunflower." He chuckles softly, pressing his lips to my forehead. "You'll call me if you need anything, yeah?"

I nod. "I will only if it's an emergency."

He frowns. "I'm going to go before this turns into a fight."

I laugh and shake my head. "I don't want to fight with you, Nash. I'll be fine, you're worried for no reason."

His brow raises as he shoots me a glare. The corner of my mouth turns upwards. I've never had someone who cares so much about me. Who worries about me. It's a strange feeling but it's not one that I'm afraid to indulge in with him.

The apartment door swings open and Blake strides back in with Cole on her heels. Her hand is covering her eyes. "You two decent?"

I chuckle as Cole rolls his eyes. "Nash, we gotta go."

"Don't let him do anything stupid," I say, glancing up at Cole.

"I won't."

"Can I get a little bit more credit than that please?" Holden says standing up off of the bed. "He's the one who does stupid shit."

Blake plops down on the bed next to me with a mystery bag of food and laughs. "You both do stupid shit and you get Wyatt to do it with you."

"On that note," Cole says, smacking his hand over Holden's shoulder. "Let's go."

Holden leans down and kisses me again, lingering for a moment before pulling back. "Anything at all," he murmurs, searching my eyes, "you call me. Got it?"

"Yes, sir," I whisper, pecking his lips once more before pushing against his chest. "Now go."

Holden stands straight and glances down at me before looking at Blake. "Blake."

"We've been over this a million times, Nash. I got her." Blake doesn't even glance up from the TV. "We'll be fine. Kadence *will* eat and I'll be here."

"Can we please stop forcing food down my throat?" I ask, glancing between the three of them.

Both Holden and Blake shoot me a look. "No."

"Get out, all of you," I laugh.

With one more kiss to the top of my head, Holden and Cole head out of the room. A few minutes later, I can hear the roar of their motorcycles fade off into the distance. My heart pounds as I silently begin the countdown of when they'll be back.

"They'll be fine," Blake says, nudging me softly. "You sure you'll be fine? You're looking a little green again." She winces.

"I'll be fine. What did you bring for food?"

"The boys grabbed burgers and fries. I may have swindled a couple from Scottie." She grins. "He folded like a cheap lawn chair when I said they were for you."

"I doubt that," I laugh as I grab the bag of food. My stomach turns at the smell of the grease and burnt meat and even with nothing in my stomach I freeze to fight off the bile creeping up my throat. "Oh God," I groan, fighting with the sheets as I crawl out of the bed and run to the bathroom.

"Hey, whoa!" Blake hollers after me.

I dry heave into the toilet, my chest clenching and throat already sore and raw. I hear the bathroom sink turn on while my head is still buried in the toilet and a moment later as I sink to the floor, a glass of water appears in front of me. "Are you sure this is just the flu?" Blake asks.

I take the glass from Blake and glare up at her. "What else would it be?"

"How long have you and Nash been... you know," she says, wiggling her eyebrows.

"Having sex?"

Blake nods.

"I mean... a few weeks." I look up at her. My head is still foggy and now pounding harder than before.

"Protected?"

"Blake!" I groan, trying to get up off the floor. Blake wraps a hand around my arm and helps me up.

"I'm serious, Kade. What if you're pregnant?" Blake says in a hushed whisper as if anyone else could hear us.

I look at Blake.

"I'm not pregnant. I can't be." I shake my head, denial setting in. There's no way I can be pregnant. Holden and I haven't been together that long and with everything that's happened before I'm not even sure if I can have kids again, let alone want them.

Blake's brows furrow but she doesn't say anything.

"I'm not," I say again. But what if I am? Blake's right, we haven't been using protection and lately, have been extremely reckless with our sex life. "*Fuck*. I can't be pregnant Blake. I can't." It feels like my heart is beating out of my chest as the realization hits me.

"Okay," Blake breathes. "It's going to be okay. We don't know for sure if you are."

"What if I am though?" I ask. "What if..." I know Holden loves me and I love him but our relationship is just starting, our life together is just starting. How the hell are we going to survive if a baby gets thrown into the mix and into the shit that's still unresolved?

"Hey." Blake cups her hands around my cheeks, holding my face. "No matter what happens, you will be okay. You and Holden *will* be okay."

My face crumples as I stare at my friend. "What do I do?" I ask in a soft broken whisper.

"We'll get a test and find out. Then we can freak out together." She flashes me a warm smile. "And try something other than burgers for you to eat because he will *kill* me if he finds out you're pregnant and I didn't force feed you."

"That's not funny," I say with a ghost of a smile. "He loves you too much to kill you."

"Yeah, but he loves you a hell of a lot more and I know for a fact that if you are pregnant, he'll love the shit out of that kid."

Tears prick at the corners of my eyes. Deep down I know that. Holden is a great man with a fucked up past, but I know we're one and the same.

"No," Blake says suddenly. "Don't you start crying because if you start, I'm going to start." Her eyes gloss over with tears as we look at each other. I bite my bottom lip. "Stop it, Andrews!" Blake whines, letting me go. "I'm going to run to the clubhouse, the girl's room has to have a pregnancy test in there somewhere."

"Oh God." I turn and leave the bathroom, falling onto the bed.

Blake follows me, slipping into her shoes. "I'll be back."

I groan, covering my face. "Okay."

The door to the apartment closes and another groan leaves me. The nausea I had ten minutes ago has moved aside in my stomach to make way for a pit of anxiety. Even as I wonder what life with Holden would be like I can't help but think back to the first time I got pregnant. When I found out I was terrified. Jeremy wasn't happy at first but the minute he figured out it was just another way to control me, his tune changed. In all honesty, I wasn't happy either until the flutters and the first ultrasound.

I had gone to that ultrasound alone. I wanted one thing for myself. One memory that wasn't tainted by the man who haunted my home.

An image of Holden looming over my shoulder while he tries to figure out what the images on the ultrasound screen are flashes in my mind. A huge grin spread over his face and his hand tangled in mine as we anxiously wait to find out if it's true. It makes my heart flutter with excitement and anxiety. The terrifying feelings I had the first time feel a lifetime away now.

Blake throws the door open, forcing me to sit up. She grins, waving a pink box in the air. "Found it and it terrifies me how many they have stashed in that room." Blake cringes before tearing the box open and handing me the wrapped test.

"I don't even want to know why that is," I mutter, standing up staring at the test. With a deep breath I look up at Blake who gives me a smile.

"You can do this."

"I can do this," I repeat as I move into the bathroom and tear the test open. Within a few minutes, I'm going to know whether or not our lives are about to change.

"I just wanna say, I'm really happy you're letting me be a part of this." Blake's voice comes through the door.

"If you're trying to make me cry, you're going to succeed," I respond as I wash my hands, setting the test upside down.

"I mean I'm not trying to." she says through the wood. After a few moments her voice floats through again. "Anything?"

I take a deep breath and pick up the test. Enough time has passed that the test should be ready. I look down at it and my heart stops.

"Kade?" Reaching over, I open the door. Tears fall down my cheeks as I show Blake the test. Her eyes go wide before looking back up at me. "Oh, honey," she says softly, throwing her arms around my neck and hugging me tightly.

Our lives are about to change and our world just got a little bigger.

KADENCE

"Kade, sweetheart, what are you doing?" Marlowe's voice echoes from behind me in the doorway of the small kitchen.

I spin around, sighing. "I *was* trying to make dinner for the guys but I'm failing pretty hard right now." I'm trying to make my father's chili. Something I haven't had since I was a kid and something I'm trying to make from memory. A feeling of defeat washes over me as Marlowe steps into the kitchen, wrapping an arm around my waist.

"I'm sure whatever you're going to make them, they'll eat just fine." She smiles. "Do you mind me asking why you decided to do this?"

"I wanted to give them something in return for taking care of me." I sound like a child when I say it. I've never had anyone do as much as the club has for me and it's a weird feeling to finally feel cared for. My hand slides over my stomach, a soft smile playing on my lips as I think about the child growing within me.

"You know they'd do it even without the chili." Marlowe laughs softly, picking up the wooden spoon I'm cooking with and stirs the pot once more before taking a taste. I watch her with a quiet nervousness hoping it doesn't taste nearly as bad as I think it does. "Needs some more cumin and it'll be perfect," she finally says after a moment and it makes me smile.

"I knew it," I laugh softly searching the pile of spices I've collected.

Marlowe leans against the counter next to the stove, watching me. My stomach flips as I add a few dashes of cumin to the chili again. Both of us are silent as I work. Other than Blake, no one else knows about the pregnancy and I'm not sure if I'm going to tell anyone other than Blake until Holden gets back. There's a lingering sense of dread that fills me every time I think about telling him. I have no idea how he's going to react. We promised everything to each other, and even though we're moving at the speed of a freight train, this feels too soon. Despite that, I already called the doctor who saw me at the hospital to make an appointment once Holden is home. I want to experience those first moments with him. The ultrasounds, the check-ups, all of it. Knowing how much he cares about me is the only thing keeping me grounded and able to sleep at night.

"You're good for them," Marlowe finally says after a few moments. "Holden and Cole," she clarifies.

"That's what I keep hearing," I say softly looking over at her. "I don't want to be a wedge between them but they're both probably two of the most stubborn men I've ever met."

Marlowe laughs. "You should have seen them when they were boys." A warm smile passes over her features as if she's remembering something from their past.

"How long have you known them?" I glance over at Marlowe, stirring the chili again.

"Most of their lives. Cole came to Tony and me when he was four, but Tony knew Holden's father from the club. Came up in the military together, started the club together." Marlowe sighs, "It was a different lifetime then."

"Cole came to you?" I ask, setting down the spoon.

Marlowe nods softly. "I couldn't have children. Tony and I adopted Cole when he turned five. No one really knows what happened to his parents."

"Did you know his parents?"

"Sort of? They were a couple who had moved into town, a little cabin not far from my home. One day Cole wandered into our back-yard. Tony found him huddled up in the gazebo and when we tried to take him back home his parents were..." Her voice trails off and she shakes her head as if to rid herself of the memory. "We took him in after that. No one really questioned it, no one really wanted the responsibility of a child, but Cole and Holden made quick friends and the fact that we practically fell in love with him, it was an easy decision to make."

I realize that's the reason Cole calls her 'Ma'.

A twinge of pain aches through my heart. The idea of a small Cole scared and alone wrenches at my heartstrings. "That must have been horrible for him."

"It helped that he was so young when it all happened. For a while he didn't understand that his parents had passed, but pretty soon he latched onto us." She smiles again, glancing over at me.

"Holden hasn't really talked a whole lot about his family. Other than Becca," I say softly, wrapping my arms around myself.

"I can't imagine why he would. His father, although a great club member, wasn't the best father. We were all relieved when that bastard died." Marlowe says.

"That's a little harsh, don't you think?"

"If you knew half of the things he put Holden and Becca through, you wouldn't think that." Marlowe shakes her head again and moves to taste the chili. I get the feeling that the conversation is over as soon as the spoon hits Marlowe's lips and she smiles. "It's perfect."

I nod, but it's sullen.

"He'll tell you everything when he's ready, sweetheart. Some of those wounds are still fresh," she says, setting down the spoon. "I have to say, I'm happy he's found love in you. I didn't think he'd ever settle down with someone."

My eyes land on Marlowe. "What do you mean?"

"He just never seemed interested in settling down, marriage, kids, all of that." She shrugs as if the last thing she said isn't a straight arrow through my heart.

"I don't know what to say to that," I say softly. The doubts I shooed away at every sharp turn the two of us encountered slowly start to creep back in.

"You don't have to say anything," Marlowe says. "He's different with you. He may not have been thinking of it then, but I can tell he is now. He told Cole he wants to clean up Becca's house."

"He did?" My brows furrow slightly.

"Cole asked if I could help him. He wants to make a life for himself, and that's more than I've seen from him in a long time."

Once again my hands fall to my belly, holding it as I absentmindedly run my right index finger over my left ring finger. He wants to be better, he wants a life for the two of us, and he's willing to face one of the hardest things he's had to go through head-on for me. A smile forms on my face as the doubts crawl back into their dark corners.

"What are you two doing in here?" Dex steps into the kitchen heading straight for the pot of stewing liquid. He leans over the stove, closing his eyes as he takes in the smell. For the first time in a long time I see a smile form on his face. "You cook this?" He glances over at me as I nod.

"Figured y'all would like to eat something other than the same burgers and fries you've had for the past week." A sly grin forms over my face as he picks up a new spoon and takes a bite. He groans the second he tastes it and drops his head.

"Fuck that's good." He chuckles. "Thanks, Kade."

"It's about done if you want to gather the guys," I say, moving to grab a stack of bowls from the cupboard.

"I'll do it, Dexter." Marlowe smiles. "They tend to listen to me when the feeding bell has rung more than they do the guys."

"That's cause they know if they don't come now, they won't eat," Dex chuckles, pecking her cheek as she moves past to leave. Marlowe flashes a smile at us before she leaves. Dex turns back to me, folding his arms across his chest. "How are you doing?"

"Are we going to ignore the fact that she just called you Dexter?" I grin.

Wolfe shoots me a look that could kill but immediately softens. "Yes, we are." He nudges me gently. "Seriously, how are you?"

I take a deep breath and let it out slowly. "Honestly? I'm okay, terrified because I haven't heard from Holden or Cole yet, but I have to trust they're okay."

"They are." He nods. "Cole sent word this morning the drop was successful."

I can't help but feel relieved. "So they're on their way back?"

"They'll be here tomorrow morning." He grins. "Why? Missing him already?"

"Am I that transparent?" I laugh.

"No," he says quietly, a soft smile on his face. "Just in love."

I'm taken by surprise at his words. We haven't really spoken all that much after my fall, just pleasant hellos, and I feel like Dex has pulled away from the relationship we were building especially after Holden saw us together in the club.

"Are we okay?" I ask nudging him with my elbow.

Dex glances at me again and after a moment he smiles. "Yeah. We're good."

"You'd tell me if we weren't?" I raise a brow at him.

"You bet." He nods, taking a deep breath. "Need any help with this?" Dex jerks his head towards the bowls and the chili.

I grab the stack of bowls and a handful of spoons. "Grab the pot if you don't mind?" I say, not quite believing him that we're fine, but deciding to leave it be when he nods and grabs it from the stove with pot holders. We make our way into the main room of the clubhouse, setting up a little area for everyone to gather around and grab food.

Wyatt storms through the swinging door of the clubhouse, Blake on his heels. "We have an issue," he says out of breath, pointing at the CCTV above the bar.

"What is it?" I ask, glancing towards the monitors.

"Stokes and Watson," Blake says, moving to my side.

"Shit," Dex curses as we watch a group of deputies in tactical gear storm past the gates, shoving members to the ground as Stokes makes his way to the door to the clubhouse with three officers on his flank, Watson following closely behind.

My stomach drops as I watch the men in Tac gear parade through the compound. A glimpse of Marlowe lying on the ground with a deputy straddling her from behind, holding her arms behind her back, doesn't do anything to quell the bile growing in my throat. Falcone is in the same position next to her. "What the hell do we do?"

Dex is as still as stone while his eyes are glued to the CCTV. A dark look passes over his features and his hands clench into fists at his side. "Do as he says." The words come out rough and strained as his jaw tightens.

"Dex," I hiss under my breath. "He can't just walk in–"

The door swings open, and Stokes steps inside with a shit-eating grin on his face. The air in the room goes deathly still as we all stare at each other. Blake's hand tightens around mine, and it gives me a miniscule of comfort to know I'm not alone.

"Do as he says," Dex repeats, this time quiet enough for only us to hear. He pins his shoulders back, lifting his chin as he stares at the man hell bent on ruining their lives. "What do you want, Stokes?"

My eyes land on Watson as he steps through the doorway. A menacing shadow to Stokes's pudgy face. My heart almost stops as soon as his beady eyes land on mine and a wicked grin spreads across his face.

"Just doing my job as Sheriff," he says wrapping his fingers around his belt loops. "I'd really like it if you'd make my job easy and get on the floor, hands behind your head." His eyes travel along the four of us standing there. When none of us move, his eyes narrow briefly. A flicker in the mask he so desperately tries to hide behind. "*Now.*"

A calloused hand wraps around my arm and instantly I know it's Dex, without even looking down. We all slowly lower to the ground, following his instructions. Even in doing so, I can feel the anger vibrating off of Wolfe next to me. It's overwhelming and I know that he's a ticking time bomb right now. My heart hammers in my chest as I lay against the cold ground. The wood smells of stale beer and cigarette smoke. Something I didn't notice until now and it only eggs on the nausea building within me.

"You know." Stokes doesn't move but his lackeys spread out from his flank, tossing tables over, kicking chairs and smashing glasses behind the bar. "This all could have been avoided if O'Neil would have just stayed on his own course. Followed orders like a good little soldier," he mocks, pulling out a chair and sliding his slimy body into it as Watson's eyes stay glued to me. "He's made things quite difficult for me and I'm starting to feel like I don't have the support of the Hounds anymore."

The man has the nerve to tsk in Dex's direction forcing a low growl out of him. "You never had the support of the Hounds," Dex says in a dangerous tone that sends chills up my spine.

"Is that so?" Stokes's brow raises as he glances over between Blake and me. "Well, I might have to start branching out then." He looks over Blake briefly before his eyes finally land on me. "Maybe different states might offer their... *support* for my cause."

As if my stomach wasn't sinking before, I feel it in my toes now. A sickening feeling washes over me as the realization hits.

"Ms. Andrews, right?" Stokes grins. "I've heard quite a lot about you in the past few weeks. Watson's been...obsessed, is one word." He rubs his hands over his thighs before folding them in his lap. "I wonder what would happen if Miami-Dade County found out their biggest missing person's case was right here in my own backyard."

"You *son of a bitch*," Dex curses, moving to get up off of the floor but Watson is quicker. Moving faster than I can register before a large boot lands on the back of Dex's neck digging him into the dirty floor.

"I wouldn't do that if I were you," Watson hisses. "You'd just give me one good reason to finally get rid of you, Wolfe." His head cocks to the side. "On second thought, maybe I'll just remove my foot and give you a fighting chance."

"Time and fucking place," Dex growls again.

Tears prick at the corners of my eyes. I can feel Blake's hand find mine, entangling our fingers as the entire room is destroyed around us. Glass is shattered everywhere. The pot of still-steaming chili lands on a wall somewhere behind us as the deputies turn into a swarm of tornadoes, wreaking havoc over the clubhouse.

"Now, now, gentlemen," Stokes says as he stands, kicking over the chair he was just in. "You two will have your chance but for now, I think I've made my point."

"And what's that?" I snap, surprising myself.

"Oh! She speaks!" Stokes claps his hands together in mock enjoyment. "My point is that O'Neil's little club wouldn't be anything without me. This club will *die* at my hands if he doesn't fall back into line." He kneels down in front of me, pushing the tendrils of hair out of my face with his fingertips until his hand wraps around my jaw tightly. "Because if he doesn't, I won't just destroy his clubhouse next time. I will take down every *goddamn* member myself until he is the only one left standing." Stokes leans his face in closer, heated breath fanning across my face and forcing me to swallow back bile again from the smell of it. "And then I will destroy him."

There's a pause, a moment where I forget that I need to breathe before he stands up again. With a snap of his fingers, the deputies file out of the door leaving Watson and himself last. "Tell your fearless leader I want to meet with him."

Stokes turns to leave but Watson remains still and I can hear the sole of his boot straining against the back of Dex's neck.

"Jake, quit playing with your food," Stokes snaps. In an instant his boot is gone and I see Dex take a subtle breath in. "Till next time, Wolfe."

As soon as the door to the clubhouse slams closed and the four of us are left, Dex is on his feet again. His face red with a look of pure malice I've never seen from him before plastered over his features. He reaches down to help me and Blake off of the floor as West stands, surveying the room.

"You okay?" Dex's voice is low as he stares at me. My hands rest over my lower stomach as worry and fear sets deep into my bones. I know

I have to be strong, not only for myself now but for Holden and our baby. With a steeled breath in, I nod.

He finally takes a deep breath and I feel Blake's arms wrap around me from the side. My eyes meet hers and I can tell she wants to ask me again if I'm fine. Her golden eyes flicker down to my stomach and all I can do to answer her is squeeze her arm in reassurance that we're fine. Marlowe and a few of the other members file their way in, all of them freezing as soon as the chaos of the room comes into view.

Moments pass where everyone is silent and the only thing that's clear when my eyes land on Dex's is that we're fucked.

HOLDEN

"West, slow down!" I yell into my phone. "What the hell are you talking about?"

We're pulled over into a clearing on the side of the highway. I can feel Cole's eyes boring into the back of my head as I try to understand what Wyatt is yelling about. I can make out Stokes's name and then I hear Wolfe cursing in the background. My heart sinks when Wyatt takes a breath.

"They destroyed the clubhouse, Nash."

"Kadence?" I ask instantly, my heart threatening to escape my chest as her name leaves my lips.

"She's okay, everyone is. Holden, listen to me." Wyatt pauses for a moment. *"Stokes knows about Kade. He threatened to call Miami and turn her in."*

"Where is she now?" I ask, my voice tight and hoarse from forcing myself to keep calm.

"Inside, cleaning up with Marlowe."

My gut sinks and my eyes close. On one hand I'm happy she's safe, on the other hand the guilt that starts to form a rock in my belly feels heavy.

"Tell her I'm on my way." I hang up and turn to look at Cole. We haven't spoken much on this trip. I'm still angry and Cole's still keeping his distance. But right now, Kadence is right. We have to put aside our bullshit for the good of the club. "Stokes and Watson raided the clubhouse." As soon as the words fall from my mouth, Cole's hackles rise. His jaw tightens and I watch as that familiar temper curls itself in his fists at his side.

"He's looking for a reason for me to kill him," Cole growls. He swings his leg over his bike and tosses me a pointed look silently telling me to do the same.

I climb onto my bike, anger and guilt tangling together in my chest like some fucked up version of barbed wire. "He threatened Kadence."

I can feel Cole's glare shoot over to me again as the sound of our engines come to life. We've been so focused on making things right with the Rollin' Skulls, buying ourselves what little time we can to keep the peace and meanwhile everything has fallen to shit back home. Again. And this time, Kadence has been in the center of it all.

The barbed wire around my heart wrenches again until it feels like I'm bleeding from the inside out. My hands ache with the grip I have on my handlebars but nothing is going to stop me from getting back to my girl. Not even the threatening "E" on my gas tank. We weren't far from the compound when we got the call from Wyatt and yet it still doesn't feel close enough.

Light fades from the sky as the gates open, granting Cole and me access to the club once again. I barely kick down the stand on my bike before I'm already off it and storming towards the clubhouse.

Tunnel vision takes over as everything around me fades away. The only thing on my mind is seeing her. Feeling her. Kissing those lips and confirming for myself and with these hands that she's alive and unharmed.

I can feel Cole hot on my heels, but as Wyatt and Dex step in front of us, a low growl emits from my chest. "Move, both of you."

"We need to talk," Dex snaps back.

"No," I say, turning my glare onto the man who was supposed to keep them safe. It's unwarranted anger towards Dex, I know that, but it's either that or I storm my way into Stokes's office and slam his face through his desk.

"Let him go," Cole says from behind me.

I glance back at him. A silent understanding passes between us as Cole gives me a nod. I turn back to Wyatt who's brows look to be permanently furrowed. "Where is she?"

"Inside with Ma," Wyatt says pinning back his shoulders and putting on a brave face between the four of us. He's the softest out of all the members. His heart is large and he willingly takes on the role of the club's brains. But now, he looks like that high school kid in a man's body. Terrified and hiding it the best he can.

"Thanks," I say moving past the members.

My legs move into a jog until I reach the clubhouse door, shoving it open hard enough the wood slams against the neighboring wall. For a moment I don't even recognize the place. Piles of swept-up glass and debris litter the floor. Chairs are tipped over and broken and every bottle of alcohol that was displayed on the wall behind the bar has been shattered. The doors to the Church are torn off and in disarray.

Standing in the middle of it all is Kade. Her hair is pulled up in a messy bun, her cheeks are flushed, and the bags under her eyes suggest that even though she spent the night at Marlowe's, she barely slept. My stomach sinks as I take a few steps towards her. The sound of my boots causes her to whip around, our eyes meeting for the first time in days.

"Sunflower," I exhale with a shaky breath.

Her shoulders drop before her hands loosen their grip on the broom she's holding. I reach for her, her face crumpling as I wrap my arms around her shoulders and her familiar sweet scent washes over me. "I'm so sorry," I whisper. "I'm so fucking sorry I left you here."

Kadence slips her arms around my waist, under my cut as she holds onto me. Her fingers tangle into the back of my shirt as she buries her face into my chest. A shuddering breath leaves her before she looks up at me.

"Stokes would have found a way in no matter what," she says and it breaks my heart. That she doesn't blame me but that she almost expected it.

"Are you okay?" I ask pulling back to inspect her for any injuries. She's wearing my sweatshirt and her legs are wrapped in soft black tights that hide her body from me.
"I'm okay," she says but something in her tone makes my eyes flicker to hers. I lift her chin with my thumb and forefinger as tears prick at the corners of her eyes.

"No, you aren't," I whisper, pressing my lips to hers with a soft kiss. One that lingers but that's filled with heartache. I break the kiss to look at her again. "How are you really?"

Kadence lets out a soft hollow laugh that stings every inch of my skin. "Terrified, exhausted, worried." She shrugs in my arms. "Take your pick." Her green eyes glisten as we stare at each other for a moment. Her lip worries between her teeth. "He threatened to call Jeremy, actually, he threatened to let Watson call Jeremy. Stokes said he's been obsessed with me and that if Cole didn't meet with him and didn't get in line with what Stokes wanted, he was going to call Miami and turn me in."

Her body shakes as she nervously rambles. No wonder she's fucking terrified. Her worst nightmare is closer than ever and I wasn't here to stop it and yet the thing that scares me the most is the feeling that Jeremy is going to get what he wants.

"Cole won't let that happen," I say trying to reassure her but it only deepens the crease between her brows.

"Then he gives up control of the club, Holden,"

"Let the club worry about that, baby, I can't–" my voice cracks seeing her wound up and that terrified look in her eye I haven't seen since the first time we met. "I can't let you get in the middle of this."

"Holden," she whines. "I'm already in the middle of it! Stokes knows about me and if he knows about me there's a good chance that Jeremy knows where I am!"

My hands rest on either side of her face, doing what I can to slow down her rapid breaths. "I won't let anything happen to you, Kadence, I made you that promise."

It breaks my heart to see the disbelief in her eyes. For her to second guess that I won't die trying to save her. It isn't the first time that thought has crossed my mind. I've lost enough sleep wondering when the other shoe is going to drop on our relationship. I have no doubt that she's in this as much as I am, but it feels like everything and everyone is trying to tear us apart. Nature, Jeremy, hell for a while I felt like Cole hated the fact that we're together. But my heart has never beat harder than when she's in the room. When she smiles at me it's like a ray of sunshine on our darkest days.

I'll give anything to have that smile back right now.

"That's not the only reason I'm scared," she admits softly backing away from me. Her hands worry at the hem of my sweatshirt she's wearing. Picking at the frayed ends of where I've worn it down. I let her move from my touch, giving her the space to process whatever gears are working overtime in her mind. "I have to tell you something." Kade's voice drops to barely a whisper.

"What is it?"

She takes in a shuddering breath, steeling her nerves for whatever she's about to tell me and every fear I have races to the forefront of my mind. My fingers itch to reach out and touch her. To ground myself to her in case all of this is too much and, while I'm dealing with club shit, she decides to leave, to hide away from everything trying to hurt her.

"I'm pregnant."

Those thoughts die as quickly as the words race from her lips.

"What?" I ask, not because I didn't hear her but because I can't believe it.

Kadence lets out an almost frustrated huff. "I'm pregnant."

"You are?" I breathe, taking a step towards her as the tears that prick at the corner of her eyes match mine. She nods with her bottom lip back between her teeth. "When?"

"The day you left," she says and my heart drops again, that I wasn't here. That she had to do it alone, had to find out alone. "Blake was there," Kadence whispers like she can sense the dread that fills me, battling the overwhelming sense of thrill that thrums through me.

My hands cup her face again and this time I can't help the wide smile that slowly grows over my features. "You're really pregnant?" I whisper and once again she nods.

"I wanted to wait until you got back to make an appointment, but the four tests Blake made me take says I am." She lets out a laugh and this time, it's full and sweet.

"Thank you," I whisper, kissing her again and wrapping my arms around her.

She rests her chin on my chest as she looks up at me. "You aren't upset."

I look down at her. She doesn't say it like a question but more of an observation. It hits me then that this is the second time she's had to go through this. Telling someone that she's pregnant and the underlying tone of her words makes me think that the last time went exactly the opposite.

"No, Sunflower," I lean in to kiss her softly. "I'm happy."

"It's soon," She whispers against my lips.

"Stop," I say gently. "I'm not him." I curl my fingers into the collar of her shirt, wrapping a hand around the side of her neck. "I don't care if it's too soon, hell I don't even care if I'm ready. I'm fucking happy."

The tears that have been threatening to fall down her cheeks finally break. She almost looks pained but I know it has nothing to do with me. It's everything to do with the asshole who broke her. Who tore down everything she loved to the point that she lost it all. I silently make myself a promise that I will never do that to her. That I will protect her and our child with every fiber of my being. "I'll die before something happens to you and this baby."

"That's what I'm afraid of," she whispers. "You have a tendency to be my white knight."

My eyes search hers. "It'll take a lot more than your ex to kill me, baby."

She falls silent and buries her face into my chest again. Holding on as if at any moment I'll disappear. Fuck that. I'm not going anywhere and neither is she.

"We're going to be okay," I whisper into the crown of her hair. Pressing my lips there for a moment. "All of us."

She nods and pulls back to look at me again, the tears gone and replaced by that soft smile. "At least we did things in the right order."

I let out a soft laugh and nod. "At least we have that."

KADENCE

"No, you aren't going." Holden folds his arms across his chest glaring down at me.

"It's just the store, Nash," I say, slipping his sweatshirt over my head.

It desperately needs a wash, but for some reason I can't bring myself to let it mix with my other clothes. It still faintly smells of leather and motor oil, of him, and it quickly became my safety blanket. I'm thankful that the morning sickness hasn't ruined his lingering scent.

He shakes his head. "First it'll be the store, next it'll be the diner and then Blake will want to go on some shopping spree for the baby." Holden groans before taking a step towards me, wrapping his strong arms around my waist. "You aren't supposed to leave the compound."

"And you promised not to be a helicopter," I counter back, raising a brow at him. "I can't stay cooped up here for the rest of my life, Nash."

"I'm also not going to put you or our baby in danger by letting you do something the prospects are capable of doing."

He has a point, but it's been a week since Holden returned home and no one has seen any signs of Stokes or Watson. It's comforting and yet not at the same time. Cole has been on edge all week, pulling the guys into Church every night to come up with a plan to get rid of our problems. Holden and I decided to keep the pregnancy to ourselves...and Blake until after everything dies down. Even with it being a tiny sliver of happiness that we all so desperately need, I don't want it to distract from what we need to do.

My heart flutters though when he mentions the baby. When we're alone, he finds every excuse to bring he or she up in conversation. His fingers dance across my stomach and it's like I can see the images he plays over and over in his mind of us as a family.

"You said our baby," I say softly with a smile, looking up at him.

"Because it is." Holden's lips press to the tip of my nose. "Don't distract me with our child." He chuckles, dipping his head to kiss my cheek and jaw. "What is at the store that you need so badly I can't send a member for it?"

"I wanted to try remaking the dinner I was going to make for the guys while you and Cole were gone." I smile, the words coming out more sheepishly than I meant. I haven't admitted to making dinner and things have been so busy it seems like everyone has forgotten.

He drops his forehead to mine and sighs. "We don't deserve your heart, Sunflower."

"Does that mean I can go?" I grin, peppering his jawline with soft kisses. "I'll make it up to you tonight." I waggle my eyebrows at him, forcing a chuckle from his lips as he tilts his head back and laughs. "*Please,*" I groan, dragging out the word.

"Alright, alright." He laughs. "Just take Wyatt with you. Cole needs me." The last few words trail off and I can see the guilt flicker in his eyes as his arms tighten around my body for a moment.

"I know, Holden." I smile, cupping his face. "You both need to be focused on finding Stokes and Watson. It doesn't mean you love me any less if you need to take care of club business and you don't have to feel guilty for it."

He sighs and drops his head to kiss me. A soft lingering kiss that makes my toes curl in the fuzzy socks I'm wearing. He always seems to do that, with one kiss showing me how much he truly cares. Pouring every ounce of love he can into each one. It's a testament of how different this relationship feels. How all of our dark shadows are outshined with every touch and kiss we share.

"Go," he whispers softly, his warm breath tickling my skin as he moves to bury his face into the crook of my neck, "before I change my mind and keep you in bed for the rest of the day."

"If I hadn't already promised Wolfe a remake of the chili I made, it'd be a very tempting offer." I laugh.

"I'm going to ignore the fact that you're leaving me to do a favor for him and pretend I didn't hear that," he grumbles, pressing a kiss to my temple as he grabs his cut off the bed.

I slip into my combat boots and shoot him a look. "He's a friend, Holden, and he took the brunt of Watson's torment the other night protecting me and Blake. It's a thanks, not an offer."

"I'm pretty sure he's in love with you," Holden mutters, shaking his head, slipping his old worn baseball cap over his buzzed hair.

I let out a soft laugh. "He's not in love with me."

Our eyes meet and the look in his eyes gives me pause. "You didn't see the way he looked at you the night--"

Raising a brow I stand and wrap my arms around him. "The night of the bridge?" I ask gently knowing it's still a touchy subject for both of us.

He swallows hard and nods. "He looked just as scared as I was that we'd lose you."

My hands slide to his chest, gripping the edges of his cut. "He's the one that told me not to give up on you, not to walk away from us."

His brows furrow.

"I'm not going anywhere, Holden. I'm in this with you, even more so now than ever." My fingers find his own as I slide his hand over my stomach. A silent reassurance that my world is now his, that we belong together and that it was us against it. "Do you love me?"

"More than you know," he says, dipping his head to kiss me again, his fingers digging into the softness of my belly.

I smile against his mouth. "I love you too."

Wyatt looked terrified when we climbed into the tow truck. His hands were glued to the steering wheel and he hadn't once taken his eyes off of the road as we drove to the town's general market. Even while we were in the store he seemed distracted. Stuck to my side and carrying the basket for me, but distracted.

The ride back is no different. It's driving me mad that the normally chipper and light-hearted West seems on edge.

"Okay, spill." I finally break the tension filling the cab and switch off the radio. "What the hell did Holden say to you?"

Wyatt's brown eyes flicker over to mine briefly before looking back at the road. I watch his hands curl over the steering wheel again. The leather whining under his white knuckles. "He didn't say anything."

"Bullshit." I laugh. "Wyatt, you're acting like someone put the fear of God into you."

He groans in that boyish way that makes me remember just how young he still is. One of the youngest prospects the Hounds have and still more of a member than most. "It wasn't Holden, okay?"

That shocks me. I raise a brow and turn towards him in the seat waiting for him to finish.

"It was Blake," he grumbles.

My brows shoot to my hairline as I try to stifle a laugh. "Blake?" I fail instantly to hold back my laughter.

Wyatt frowns and glances over at me. "She told me that if I didn't bring you back safely and stay stuck to you like glue then she'd burn my entire comic book collection." His eyes have turned back to the road, but the disdain in his voice is evident.

I chuckle and shake my head. My heart is full and warm at Blake's use of Holden's words.

"Sounds like an expensive collection," I say gently with a grin glancing over at him. The smile beams across his cheeks as he nods.

"It really is, I've been collecting them for years." Wyatt rambles on for the next few minutes as we make our way through a stretch of road that sits between the main part of town and the clubhouse. I smile to myself as he talks about something he loves so much. There isn't a weight on either of our shoulders as he explains the differences between Marvel and DC to me.

We're just about to the clubhouse when a siren sounds from behind us. Everything in my stomach drops when I look back and see a squad car trailing behind the truck.

"Fuck," Wyatt curses under his breath, shifting in his seat like he's debating on pulling over or racing back to the compound where we have defense in numbers.

I know how this works though. If he stops we have a chance of getting by on our own, but if he keeps going all hell will break loose and the fight the club has been preparing for would show up on their doorstep unannounced. I'm not ready for that. Not with so much more on the line now.

My hand slides over my belly, holding my sweatshirt there in my fingers as I look back to Wyatt. "Pull over."

His head shoots to the side looking at me with wide eyes. "Kadence, I can't."

"Yes you can, Wyatt. It'll be worse if you don't." My voice is soft and pleading as he stares at me for another moment before shaking his head.

"This is a bad idea," He mutters, pulling the wheel to the right and stopping on the shoulder.

"I know," I whisper as the sirens shut off. We both sit in silence for what feels like hours until a tap rings against Wyatt's window. I look only to meet the beady blue eyes of Watson. A wicked grin is spread across his face.

Wyatt rolls the window down, shifting nervously again as he glares up at the man who destroyed their clubhouse a week ago. "What's the problem?"

"Get out of the truck, West," Watson says firmly, tugging on the door and pulling it open.

Wyatt glances back at me and, like a freight train, I realize we made the wrong decision. He climbs from the truck only for Watson to slam the door closed behind him causing me to jump. Within seconds Wyatt is thrown into the side of the cab, still standing upright but with Watson's hands around his neck. I see Watson lean in, whispering something harshly to Wyatt but I can't make out any words.

My heart hammers in my chest as I watch the two of them exchange words. Wyatt's brows knit together as he glances back at the truck, our eyes meeting through the back window. He mouths something to me that looks an awfully lot like *I'm sorry*, just before Watson lands a punch straight into Wyatt's gut. The kid keels over, coughing and tries to catch his breath and before I even know what I'm doing, I'm opening the door.

"Wyatt!" I yell, my heart aching with how hard it's thundering and my knees shaking. How the fuck am I going to stop this? My feet hit the gravel and as I look up my heart stops. Dark, dangerous brown eyes stare back at me. He looks older, worn down, and almost manic.

I back into the open door of the tow truck, cornering myself as his boots crunch in the gravel beneath him. Menacingly, taunting.

"It's been a while," his voice echoes through me over the sound of Wyatt's blood filled sputters and Watson's hate filled blows.

Jeremy grins. The same grin I saw every time he became eerily quiet, every time just before he hurt me. All of the air expels out of my lungs as fear like I've never known creeps up my spine in twisted thorned claw like vines.

"Did you miss me, *Princess*?"

HOLDEN

The guys are becoming restless. Every meeting we have, every vote we put to pass, no one can seem to agree on a way to get rid of Stokes. Trey hates the idea of becoming Sheriff. In fact he seems to hate every idea that comes out of mine or Cole's mouth.

Cole smacks the gavel against the wooden table, pulling me back from my thoughts. Kadence should have been back by now, and even though I know she would never interrupt one of our Churches, I almost wanted her to. Just so I knew she was fine.

"That was pointless," Wolfe mutters, leaning back into his chair. The other members have filed out, leaving the three of us at the table. "We need a new fucking VP."

"No, the fuck we don't." Cole snaps, tossing the gavel onto the table. "Trey is..."

"Trey is an idiot," Wolfe counters, leaning over the table. "He's the only one out of all of us that doesn't have a fucking record, Cole. He's the only one that could take over the department and he's not willing to do it. What the hell do we do now?"

I let out a sigh, dragging a hand over my face. "You're forgetting the fact that Stokes is still in office, dipshit. And the fact that the fucker is in the wind."

"He can't hide out forever," Cole barks. "So we wait until he climbs out of his hole."

"I thought he wanted to meet you," Wolfe pipes up, shooting a look at him. "What the hell happened to that?"

"I reached out, same way I always do and he hasn't responded," Cole grits.

"Something has changed then," I say looking between the two of them. "Stokes wants power, he'd love to see you crawling back to him on hands and knees and begging him not to hurt the club. He wouldn't ignore the chance to see that."

"He's right," Wolfe grumbles, agreeing with me.

I watch as my words finally click in Cole's head. "Fuck. I'll reach out to the neighboring clubs and see if they've heard anything. Havoc would have called by now or sent a message if it had anything to do with him."

"Would he?" I fire. "Because the last time we were there you almost put one of his guys through a fucking table."

"And we did the run just fine without any issues," Cole counters, jamming his index finger against the table. "You know him. If something went wrong, we would have heard about it and no less would have gotten some fucking dark and twisty message."

"So what is it then?" Dex sighs.

The doors to the Church slam against the wall as Blake barges in, her face pale and eyes wide. Everything in the room stops when I see the look on her face.

"Wyatt," she breathes, her chest heaving and his name comes out like a sob.

Kadence.

The baby.

I'm on my feet so fast my vision tunnels. "Where is she?" I boom, scaring Porter. She shakes her head as tears fill her eyes and her brows furrow as she tries to steel her own nerves.

"She's not with him."

All three of us crowd through the doorway and out into the lot of the compound. Scottie is already on Wyatt, holding him up as he drags him towards the clubhouse. He's barely recognizable. His left eye is swollen shut, the opposite cheek is red and raised from his skin in an unnatural way and the white shirt he wore when he left is stained with dirt and blood. Every inch of him is covered in some gash or cut and the more I see, the more my heart sinks further in my chest.

"He needs a fucking doctor!" Wolfe barks shoving Cole to the side as he follows Scottie and Wyatt inside. I follow hearing that Cole is already on the phone with Lang.

"What the fuck happened?" I yell shoving between Scottie and Dex to get a look at West. Blake knelt on one side of him, doing her best to catch her breath and wipe away some of the dirt and debris stuck in his wounds.

"Watson," Wyatt groans.

I growl under my breath trying to keep calm to get whatever information I can before the doc shows up. "What happened?" I ask again.

Wyatt's one good eye lands on me, his brows knit together as much as they can with how swollen his face is. "I'm sorry," he whines.

"Wyatt." My voice is lower trying a different approach. "I don't need the apology, you can apologize when she's safe." I kneel down next to him. "What the fuck happened?" I ask again, my tone dangerous.

"Ambush," he rasps. "Watson pulled us over and made me get out of the truck. I–" he shifts again, his face crumpling in pain. "I didn't know what else to do. Kade told me to stop, I shouldn't have stopped, Nash."

I take a deep breath, shaky as all get out, but a breath nonetheless. "What else? Why did he take Kadence?"

"He didn't," Wyatt says, looking at me. "He had help."

"Who?" Dex says from behind me.

"I don't know, he didn't look familiar." Wyatt sounds pained, his voice is tight like he is doing everything he can to keep his shit together. I glance over my shoulder at Dex who swears under his breath. He pulls his phone from his pocket and hands it to me. My own worst nightmare on the screen.

"Was this him?" I ask, swallowing hard, showing Wyatt the screen.

Silence hangs in the air as Wyatt tries to sit up, leaning closer to the phone. "Who is that?" he asks.

"West," I snap my patience running thin, "Is this who was with Watson?"

Wyatt looks up at me and nods.

"Son of a bitch," Dex swears again, tearing the phone out of my hand. I stand, pushing between Scottie and Dex, pacing back and forth. Rage bubbles up in my chest, my heart racing with my fists clenching at my side.

"God damnit!" I finally yell snatching up a chair and tossing it to the side into another table cracking the wood. "Fuck!"

"Who is that?" I hear Wyatt ask again.

I feel someone grab the back of my cut, tugging me backward. I'm so blinded by the guilt and rage flowing through me that my fist cocks back as I spin around. Expecting to throw a blow at one of the guys but the moment I see Blake standing behind me I freeze. Her scowl firm and eyes red-rimmed.

"Get it together," she warns me. "She doesn't need your fucking anger right now. She needs you to find her and bring her back. Where she belongs."

"You don't think I fucking know that?" I roar. "This is my fucking fault, Blake! I should have never let her leave the compound!"

Blake pins back her shoulders, lifting her chin in defiance as she stares me down. "Blaming yourself is a waste of time." *It wasn't.* I know that. Her smile had blinded me this morning, letting me give in to her. Blake punches my arm hard. "Get out of that fucking head of yours, Nash, and get it the fuck together. For our girl."

Our girl.

I glance up looking around the room to see every member staring at the both of us, scowls are planted on Cole and Wolfe's faces.

"I'm going to kill him." I promise. "I'm done waiting. Stokes, Wats on..." My voice trails off in a breathless rage. "Jeremy. They all fucking die."

I notice that Trey has filed in at some point, seeing the carnage with wide eyes and in just enough reach that I can grab him by the collar of his cut and slam him against a neighboring wall. My voice drops dangerously low. "You better get the fuck ready to be Sheriff of this *god-forsaken* town. You don't get a fucking choice anymore."

KADENCE

*D*id you miss me, Princess?

I jerk with a gasp. Jeremy's voice rings in my head alongside the dull thud of a headache. A wave of nausea rolls through me as the musty smell of the room begins to take hold of my senses. It's dark aside from the table I'm sitting at and a bowl of what looks like day old oatmeal sits in front of me, doing nothing to quell my turning stomach. I feel a trickle of warm sticky liquid against my skin as I reach up to touch the gash on my temple. *That explains the headache.*

"You look different."

My eyes flick up to where his voice lurks in the dark. Squinting slightly only able to make out the silhouette of his figure hiding in the corner.

"What happened to you, Princess?" He sounds hurt, feigning pain in his voice as he takes a step forward, still shrouded by the darkness. I know it's not real. I know that the hurt he's pretending to feel is just that. Pretend.

I'm silent as he slowly creeps his way into the light. A tired yet dark look is in his eyes as he slams a hand on the table.

"Answer me!"

My eyes draw closed when I jump with the sound that echoes against the walls around us. "What are you doing here?"

"I came for you, baby," he sings, arms wide. "You've been missing for a very long time." Jeremy leans over the table and it's then I see the truly manic look in his eyes. "I wasted a lot of resources looking for you. Only to find you in some shithole town." He spits the words like venom and it takes everything in me not to wipe away the spit that lands on my cheek.

Deep down, I'm scared to say anything. Even the simplest of statements could set him off. For a moment I'm that same scared woman cowering in her kitchen corner. Until my mind wanders to the baby I'm carrying, to the man who hopefully knows by now I'm missing. Something wrenches in my heart, something so entangled within me that I narrow my eyes at him. Steeling myself against the power his gaze used to have.

"This shit hole town has been more of a home than Miami ever was," I taunt daringly.

He laughs and it sends a chill down my spine. "God, you were always so easily fooled." His eyes land on mine again as he pushes the bowl towards me. "Take a bite, baby, I made it."

I glance down at the bowl of slop and glare up at him. "I'm not eating it."

His jaw ticks as I sit back in the chair I'm surprised I'm not bound to. My eyes flick past him for a moment seeing something move in the shadows and I do my best to hide the racing of my heart.

"That's too bad." He shrugs, picking up the bowl and staring into it for a moment. "I was hoping you'd eat before our flight." In a flash Jeremy chucks the bowl to the side, sending it flying across the open space and shattering against what sounds like a concrete wall.

"Flight?" I ask and swallow back the rising bile.

Watson steps out into the light, glaring at Jeremy as he makes his way to the table. "Do you really need to make a mess?" He curses, staring at where the bowl crashed.

Jeremy rolls his eyes and glances over at him. "It was proving a point."

"Yeah that you're an asshole."

"What flight?" I all but yell bringing the two of them back. Two pairs of terrifying eyes hone in on me.

"We're going home, sweetheart!" Jeremy smiles though it doesn't reach his eyes. "Watson just got himself a promotion! It's time to cele-brate." He pats Watson's chest before turning away from me, grabbing something from the dark.

"You see, my darling," Jeremy drones on. "It's time we make this official. We're getting married." He says the words like they're the most obvious statement in the world with his back still to me, and when he turns around, my eyes flick down to where he's got a handful of zip ties. "And then, you're going to give me back the child *you* killed."

HOLDEN

"I want eyes on Stokes," Cole barks, gaining the attention of every member standing in the room. "I don't give a shit if we have to turn over every goddamn boulder in this town. I want his location within the hour."

The room hums with everyone's agreement as members begin to file out of Church. I glance over at Cole. That furious glare stuck behind his blue eyes matches my own. Blake took Wyatt to his room once Lang arrived with a reminder that he better get his shit together.

"We're wasting time not looking for Watson," I say as I make my way to the door. Even if we did get Stokes there was no guarantee that he would give up Watson. Hell at this point I wouldn't blame Stokes for it. That doesn't mean I won't do whatever it takes to get Kadence back.

"Let them do their job. We've got large enough targets on our backs without us running around town on a wild goose chase, Nash," Cole counters, and the rage that begins to bubble in my chest has me spinning on my heels and my fists twisting in Cole's shirt.

"This isn't some wild good chase," I hiss between my teeth. My eyes flash with anger as I glare at my best friend or whatever the fuck he is at this point. "This is *Kadence* we're talking about."

"I know that." Cole shoves me off.

"Do you?"

"What the fuck does that mean?" He says and I can hear the offense in his voice.

I shake my head. "It means that, just this once, I need you to be on my side. I need you to realize that this—" I pause almost close to telling him about the baby, "that she is worth whatever risk we have to take. Every bullet, every punch. Whatever the fuck it is, Kadence is worth that and more."

Cole's hands find his hips as he stares at me. The unresolved tension between the two of us bleeds out into the space. "I know that." He repeats. "I'm on your side, Nash."

"She's pregnant, Cole." I finally say after a moment and the weight I thought would be lifted by that only feels heavier. My eyes meet Cole's. There's an unreadable look on his face, something between sadness and anger.

"You didn't think to tell us that 'til now? How long have you two known?" He asks with disdain in his voice.

"A week or so. She found out before Stokes wrecked the club-house."

Cole lets out a long drawn out sigh, like somehow this has turned into an inconvenience for him. It takes everything I have not to toss him through the Church window. "Say what you're gonna say, Cole." My voice rumbles low as I get ready to leave the room.

"You happy about it?" Cole asks after a moment. "You ready for it?"

I glance over to my friend and shake my head. "Ready, fuck no." I pause. "Happy? More than I have been in a long time." It's the most honest we've been with each other in a minute. The tension between us has still been heavy but now is the time to put that shit aside. We could figure out what was left of our relationship after Kadence was back and after both her and the baby were safe.

"Good," Cole says.

I nod, unsure of how to move forward now. In other circumstances Cole may have been happy for me. We'd share a couple of beers and laugh about how I would be getting the kid I deserved. A troublemaker just like me. But this...dancing around the cracks in our friendship, it tarnished what should have been a good thing.

I feel my phone vibrate in my pocket and grab it. I glance down to see Scottie's name on the screen. Answering it, "Tell me you found him."

"Fucker's at home." Scottie's voice comes over the line. "Curled up in bed with one of Marlowe's girls."

That anger wraps around my core once more. "Send her back to Moon so Ma can deal with her. Give her the heads up."

"Alright," he responds. "What should we do with Stokes?"

I glance over at Cole. "Bring him here, string him up in the garage."

"You sure about that? Watson gets any hint that–"

"Just fucking do it, Scottie." I bark before hanging up. Without another word I leave the room, Cole hot on my heels as we make our way out to the lot.

I take a long drag off of my cigarette. A taste I've missed and a vice I didn't rely on once I pulled Kadence from that water. A lot of my vices haven't seen the light of day since Kadence has been around and it doesn't take an idiot to realize that she's at the core of it all.

The sound of Stokes's grunts echo against the garage door. Dex has been working him over for the past twenty minutes, trying to get whatever information out of him that he could. But my hands itch to get Stokes' blood on them. I'm tired of waiting. A full day of not knowing where Kadence is or even if she is still in the state.

Cole pushes the side door open and nods. "Better get in here before Wolfe gets the best of him."

With a nod I toss my cigarette to the ground, stomping out the ember before following Cole back inside.

Just as I had asked, Stokes is hanging by his wrists from the middle bay car lift. Wolfe's already done his work. Stokes looks almost unrecognizable with two swollen eyes, blood dripping from the smirk painted on his face. "Can he still talk?" I ask glancing over at where Dex is wiping his hands on a shop rag.

"Let's hope," Dex grumbles.

"You are all a bunch of idiots," Stokes mutters, spitting blood onto the ground.

I raise a brow. There's no chance in hell that Stokes doesn't have an idea of what's going on. "Where's your lap dog, Stokes?"

"What the hell are you talking about, Nash?"

"Watson, the tall blonde who has a knack for kidnapping women," I snap, kicking the back of Stokes's knee and forcing his feet out from under him. "Where is he?"

He starts to laugh, shaking his head. "You think I know what the hell he's up to?"

I glance up at Cole and Dex. "You came into our club, you put my woman on the ground and threatened to sick him on her. So yeah, I do think you know what he's up to." I lean down to meet Stokes eye to eye. "Where the fuck is Kadence?"

"*I don't know*," Stokes hisses.

"And I don't believe you." I stand and take a step back from Stokes. "Higher," I bark. In seconds Stokes is hoisted further into the air. His toes barely scrape the ground. "Where is she Stokes?"

He grunts as he tries to gain traction with his feet. My patience is wearing thin now. My fists clench at my side before I toss one into Stokes's gut. "Where is she!"

A rush of air leaves Stokes followed by a series of ragged coughs. I stare at him waiting for an answer. I can feel both Cole and Dex watching me. It's been a long time since we've had to do anything like this and the air is thick with a tension that makes it hard to control my breathing. All of the pent-up anger, the rage that I've shoved down, starts to rise in my chest. "I'm tired of waiting."

"Your fathers would be disgusted with you both," Stokes finally hisses through a rasp. "Turning to gun running and whore trading." A sinister laugh leaves him. "Do you know how many girls I pulled off the street for you? For Moon?"

"What the hell are you talking about?" Cole barks.

"All those broken girls I found." He grins with a bloody smile. "They had families, parents who loved them, and you turned them into dancers. Promising a better life."

"And you threatened them," I snap filling in the blanks. "For what?"

"For the money." He rolls his head towards me. "For the pussy."

Cole tosses a toolbox over before grabbing Stokes by the chin. "You stole girls to feed the club?"

"You stupid boy," Stokes mumbles. Cole roars as he drops Stokes and paces the shop. "You've been playing with the cards *I* give you. The guns, the women, all of it is because of me and you stuck your hand in the cookie jar without any question."

"You threatened my club!" Cole yells.

Stokes laughs again. "You *let* me."

"I'm going to fucking kill you," Cole hisses, shaking his head.

"Hey!" I bark, grabbing Cole by the back of his collar. "Get your shit together," I rumble, looking O'Neil in the eye.

"Watson's been obsessed with your girl for a while now," Stokes continues on. "I really couldn't stop him from calling Miami. That boy's head hasn't been screwed on right since well..." He trails off and even before he finishes I know. My eyes flick to Cole to see the realization on his face. "Watson was first on the scene of your sister's horrible accident," He taunts. "Why do you think that is?"

"You son of a bitch," I growl, hitting him again. "You blamed me, convinced half this town that I killed Becca!"

"No," he rasps. "You did that on your own, Nash. All they had to do was see the destructive mess you'd become after prison."

"You know where Kade is don't you?" Dex says, circling around Stokes like a shark sniffing for blood. "You're dead anyway, Stokes, you ain't got nothing to lose."

"If you kill me," he taunts, "you'll never get her back. That Miami prick and Watson will disappear so fast you'll be chasing your tails."

"Will." I say after a moment, "You said will disappear which means they haven't left town yet." My eyes narrow in on the old man. "Where the fuck is she?"

"I'm shocked you haven't found her. She's hidden in plain fucking sight." He trips over his feet again, causing his arms to strain against the chains. "The warehouse you idiots," Stokes hisses, "it's where Watson goes to hide."

"Fuck!" Cole yells. I know it's the first place we should have looked. Or one of them but we had been so hellbent on locating Stokes, no one thought to look there.

"Thanks," I say bitterly as I step back into line next to Dex. I hold out my hand and Wolfe drops a pistol into it. "You know, Stokes, you deserve a hell of a lot worse than what you're going to get from us. You corrupt piece of shit."

Cole moves to stand next to me. All three of us stare at Stokes with hatred in our eyes. Dex moves to hand Cole a pistol behind my back.

"And you three aren't anything other than a couple of orphaned assholes. The three of you destroy everything you fucking touch–"

Cole, Wolfe, and I all simultaneously raise our weapons, firing off three shots each before Stokes can finish his thought. His body slumps against the chains as blood pools around his feet.

"One evil down," Dex mutters, "two more assholes to go."

I hand him back the pistol. "Get the prospects to clean this shit up." I turn to Cole as Scottie comes into the shop. His eyes wide as he surveys the mangled body in the middle of the room. I spare him a glance. "Get Falcone over to the Sheriff's office. Any deputy who isn't on board with him becoming head, is out. I don't give a fuck how it happens."

Scottie glances at Cole. Looking for confirmation from his President. I don't have to turn to Cole before he gives the go ahead and Scottie nods.

"What are you going to do?" He asks.

"I'm going to go get my girl back and kill the motherfuckers who put their hands on her."

KADENCE

Fighting them was never a good idea. Trying to run was an even worse one as soon as I found out about the flight. About his plan to steal me away from Pine River. Now, my hands are bound to the chair I woke up in, my feet bound to the legs and my head pounding from the second hit I took.

Everything still feels foggy but it isn't the time to give into my body's need to curl up into a ball and take it. I'm done with the abuse from a man who never deserved me in the first place. There has to be a way out of this.

The room is still pitch black other than the light above me. Jeremy and Watson had left hours ago, leaving me here in this dark hell hole with nothing but the sound of chirping rats. If I can just figure out something, a way to get out of the binds I can make a run for it and pray they aren't watching me.

I tug on the binds again. Zip-ties that dig into my wrists and ankles. The chair they tied me to is wood, if I can just get it to tip over, hard enough to break I can get out of this. My heart starts to race in my chest with the hope of being able to get out. I've got one chance.

Closing my eyes I take a deep steadying breath, letting every thought racing through my mind quiet down before picking out noises in the silence. Rats, water dripping, the distant sound of a train on tracks. But no sounds of footsteps, no rattle of anything human.

Slowly, I start to rock the chair, using my feet to wobble back and forth, the legs whine underneath my weight as I move. With one more final shove, I start to tip over faster than intended. My shoulder lands first into the concrete floor and the chair doesn't budge.

"Fuck!" I hiss as pain radiates through my shoulder and down to my fingers. Tugging on the binds again I can't help but let out a soft sob. None of them budge. I'm still strapped to this fucking thing only now, I'm on my side and my shoulder feels like it's popped out of place.

"Shit, shit, shit, shit." The words come out strained in a whine while holding back tears. My eyes slide close and any ounce of hope of saving myself, saving the baby, leaves my body.

I'm not sure how long I stay on the floor like that but my arm has gone numb and the musty smell of the room is worse down here. My stomach churns just as the door to the building slams closed. I can already tell it's Jeremy. The way his boots thud across the floor, like a ticking time bomb just waiting for the right moment to explode.

"What the fuck did you do?" Jeremy hisses coming into the light. His anger is quickly replaced with a cackle. "Did you think you could actually get away from me?" Long fingers tangle into the back of my hair, tugging my head back so I have to look at him. "You stupid bitch."

"Get off of me," I snap trying to pull away from him but it's no use. The grip he has on me tightens, pulling an involuntary yelp from me as he drags me back up onto all four legs on the chair. I suck in a breath as fire radiates through my shoulder blade and pins and needles start to prickle down my arm. "Why are you doing this?" I ask harshly. "Why the fuck do you still want me?"

"Because you're *mine* and you owe me the life I promised you," Jeremy's voice booms across empty space. "Don't you get it Kadie–"

"Don't fucking call me that!" I pull at the restraints, trying to lunge at him even though I know it's completely useless.

He freezes in front of me, the table is the only thing separating us. "I forgot. Your mother is the only one that gets to call you that." A sickening grin spreads across his face. "You know I reached out to her. To try and find you but, like the ungrateful bitch you are, not even your mother knew. Who does that?" Jeremy shakes his head. "Just up and leaves their family?"

I let out a huff of frustration. "My mother never cared about my whereabouts."

His head tilts as he regards me. "Are you sure about that, Princess? Janice was pretty upset to find out you'd gone missing." He rounds the table and sits on the edge of it. Getting closer to me. "I assume you got her text message?"

I look up at him with my brows furrowed. The look in his eye has a sinking feeling that starts to riddle my gut.

"Well, I mean the text message *I* sent you." That wolfish smirk finds his lips as all of his teeth show. "See, Janice was beside herself that you left. All *woe is me, I should have been a better mother.*" He makes a face of disgust. "Honestly, it was quite exhausting. After the third hour of that lunch I was tired of hearing it."

He shrugs like whatever he isn't saying is obvious. "All I wanted was to know where you ran off to. To know why my sweet sweet *obedient* princess would just leave me to rot in jail."

"What did you do?"

Jeremy continues like I haven't said anything. "When she had no idea where you went I had to end her blubbering." He crosses his arms and lets out a long drawn out sigh. "Messier than I would have liked, but it got the job done."

I stare at him, tears prick at the corners of my eyes as the realization that he killed my mother starts to set in. "You killed her?"

"Looks like your mother had a heart for you after all." Jeremy shakes his head. "Too bad she won't be around to share it with you."

"You son of a bitch!" I scream just as a large hand impacts my cheek. His fingers wrap around my chin, squeezing painfully as he pulls my face to his.

"Watch your tone with me, Kadence. My patience with you is already wearing extremely thin." He lets me go, shoving my head back as he does so. "We have six hours before Watson's plane will be ready and if you don't want to spend that time with a bag over your head, I suggest you shut the fuck up."

I glare at him, twisting my wrists against the plastic ties trying anything to stretch it enough in order to get free. He stares at me.

"I feel bad Maria got caught up in this as well," he says and that switch flips back off as he sits back down on the edge of the table. "She's a good friend. Keeping secrets for you. Helping you leave...it's too bad she was attacked." He tuts.

My eyes narrow at him, biting my tongue to keep myself from saying something that will send him over the edge. If I wasn't pregnant, I'd fight like hell. But with the baby, this had to be strategic. As much as I can figure out on my own. I won't do anything to lose this baby. Not like I did the first and I sure as hell would not give Jeremy the satisfaction of knowing he killed another one of my children. Even if he blames me.

"Don't worry though, sweetheart, I made sure she had the best room in the ICU." He leans into me again as he says the words. Those dark hateful eyes holding my own.

"I'm going to kill you," I spit.

"I'd like to see you fucking try," Jeremy says standing. The door slams closed and Watson walks in the room, glancing between the two of us. I notice another person standing behind Watson, just within the shadows.

"Did you get what you needed?" Jeremy asks, rounding the table.

Watson nods, tugging the person forward. Bright red hair and snake eyes come into view under the dim light as Layla stares back at me. A smug smile pulling at her poorly painted lips.

"You went back for this?" Jeremy barks glaring at the woman who has done nothing but try to get between Holden and I for weeks. Only now, her fingers are laced between Watson's and she stands just far enough behind him like he'll protect her if anything goes wrong.

Watson glances back at Layla, rolling his eyes. "Didn't have much of a choice. She's been burned."

"O'Neil and Nash are going to figure out I gave her up soon enough. Jake offered me protection to get to Miami." She smiles so sweetly that my teeth ache in the worst way possible. Everything starts to click together.

"You told Watson when the guys left. When it would be safe to raid the clubhouse," I say, shooting a look at Layla. "And when Wyatt and I left."

Those snake eyes turn to me with nothing but hatred flowing in them. "Fuckers are stupid enough to believe I wasn't fucking Watson outside of the club?" She cackles. "Every run they've had fucked up was because of me," She says proudly like she's actually done something good.

"For what reason?" I bite. "So you can claim your fame as Pine River's best cock sucker?"

Layla screeches and lunges towards me and in a flash is yanked back by Watson. His arm holds tight around her waist as Layla struggles against him. "You cunt!" Layla screeches. "Nash will never love you!"

My eyes turn to slits at Layla. "He never loved *you*, Layla. He used you to warm his dick, that's it." The words come out just as harsh as I mean them and only egg on Layla's struggles against Watson's arms.

"You're going to pay for that you bitch!" She screams.

"Ladies!" Jeremy barks. "Shut the fuck up both of you." He leans over the table and glares at Layla. "Get your shit together or you'll end up tied to a chair next to her." The threat lands because Layla's eyes go wide and her struggle stops. "Watson, what's the status on the plane?"

"We have five hours," he mutters, letting Layla go without care. She stumbles to gain balance as her eyes stay glued on me.

"Good, keep your whore on her leash," Jeremy bites.

HOLDEN

Barely any light emits from the warehouse. I have no idea if she's still in there but we have to try. I have to bank on the thread of hope that Jeremy and Watson haven't already taken her back to Miami.

Dex hands me a tactical vest that Trey stole from the Sheriff's office before passing one to Scottie and O'Neil. I slip it over my head under the shroud of darkness from the treeline just outside of the warehouse. Passing pistols back and forth between the four of us.

"What's the plan?" Scottie asks, loading a shotgun with shells and handing it over to Cole.

I glance between the three men. All of them stare at me, awaiting instructions and for a brief moment, it throws me back on the battlefield. It's a strange feeling I haven't had in a long time. "Scottie and Wolfe, you two watch the perimeter. Get eyes on the exits and if anyone leaves that isn't Kade or us, shoot them."

Wolfe nods but Scottie just stares at me for a moment. "You okay doin' this, brother?"

I narrow my eyes on him. "I would burn down the world for her." *So yeah, I'm okay putting a bullet between their eyes if it means she's fine.*

Cole claps my shoulder. "We're with you, brother."

It's the first moment we've had where I don't want to rip Cole's hand off of me. We share a look and he nods. I meet my gaze with every one of theirs and shift on my feet. "If anything goes wrong, you get Kadence out of there."

"Nash-" Dex starts, but I shake my head.

"I mean it. Kadence is the priority. No matter what, she lives through this." All three men nod at me. I check once again that my pistol is tucked in the waistband of my jeans, my vest is secured and the shotgun I'm holding is loaded.

Cole looks over at me, "Ready?"

"Yeah."

Scottie and Dex break off, each of them circling opposite sides of the building. Cole and I wait until they're in position, each flicking our flashlight on to signal to them before we move toward the side entrance.

The tension between the two of us permeates as we make our way to the door. Both taking a stance on either side of it and sharing a look. I nod giving Cole the go ahead to yank the door open.

The metal creaks as he does and we push forward into the darkness. I hear Watson curse and another male voice I'm not familiar with. Cole pushes forward next to me as we crouch behind a stack of boxes. There's a clatter that sounds like a metal table falling over and hitting the concrete floor.

"Get off of me!" Kadence's voice echoes against the bare walls and every hair on my body stands to attention. The grip I have on the shotgun tightens as I glance back to Cole checking if he's ready. He nods once and that's all I need to move out from behind the boxes with Cole on my heels.

"I was wondering when you might show up," Watson seethes, training his gun toward my chest.

I ignore him, my eyes are glued to Kadence. Those big green eyes stare back at me, glossy from tears that I know she's refusing to shed.

Movement behind her catches my eye as the man I recognize from the news junket appears, his hand tangling into her hair and ripping her head back while the other hand moves a knife to her neck. He presses it just enough that her skin indents from the pressure. Anger like I've never felt before courses through my veins as I try to keep control for as long as I can. For her.

"So you must be the asshole she's been screwing behind my back," he spits.

Again, I ignore him, my eyes flicking back to Kade's. "You okay, baby?"

Her brows furrow but she nods. A small fleck of relief falls off of my shoulders but her forehead is caked in dried blood and the nasty gash along her hairline is red and angry. I glance between Jeremy and Watson. I know Cole is near me, his own shotgun trained on Watson.

"You know, she told me you're horrible, but man did she leave out how much of an actual piece of shit you are," I bite looking at Jeremy.

"She's a lying whore," Jeremy laughs. "But she's mine. Can't have some low rate biker taking what's mine now can I."

I shift on my feet again. "I'm only going to tell you this once. Watch the way you talk about her." My shotgun is aimed at Jeremy but it's far too close to Kadence than I like. I'm going to need to switch to my pistol if I want a clearer shot with less spread and an even lesser chance of hitting her.

"I'll talk about her any fucking way I want to. She was riding my dick *long* before she was yours." He seethes. "Drop the shotgun or I'll cut her so deep she'll be dead in seconds."

"I'd listen to him," Watson chimes in. "You don't have a shot here, Nash. Take it or leave it."

"Shut the fuck up!" Cole barks, jerking his shotgun in Watson's direction. "I know what you did, Watson."

"Do you?" He grins at Cole. "Tell me, O'Neil, what do you know?"

Silence falls between everyone. Kade's ragged breathing is the only thing I can hear. *As long as she's breathing.* I have to remind myself that she's handled Jeremy before. She knows his triggers, his patterns. I also know that if Jeremy is desperate enough to fly across the country for her, he won't kill her. It's the only hope I have as his gaze moves to Watson.

"You killed Becca," Cole says lowly, his voice trembling between rage and sadness.

Watson barks out a laugh. "You've just now figured that out? Tell me what else you've figured out."

Cole's brows knit together and his eyes flick to me before moving back to Watson.

"You don't know do you?" Watson chuckles. "You gotta be more careful about who you let wander around your clubhouse, O'Neil." Once again, a shadow creeps forward in the darkness and Layla moves to stand at Watson's side. "Wonder why we've always been one step ahead of you? How we found Kadence unprotected?"

Layla has the audacity to wave her fingers in my direction. That smile I used to gain comfort in after a long night of drinking only makes my skin crawl now. We've had a rat under our roof this whole time and this time it's at the expense of Kadence's life.

"You fucking bitch," Cole hisses. "You've been working for them? For Watson!" He moves the shotgun from Watson to Layla. Watson doesn't even flinch to try and protect her.

"I wanted to be a part of the club!" Her shrill voice cuts through the racing thoughts. The millions of ways that this could go wrong. "I wanted him!" She points a finger at me. "But he wanted this road trash instead!"

My gaze flicks to Layla at her words. "You've been betraying this club long before Kadence showed up, you snake." Layla betraying us, Watson admitting to Becca's death, my mind won't quiet down. Doing as Jeremy says, I drop the shotgun, instantly reaching for the pistol behind my back and aiming it right at Layla. Before she can protest, I pull the trigger. Hitting home right between her eyes.

Kadence holds back a scream but I catch the strangled noise that comes from her direction.

"What the fuck!" Watson yells watching as Layla's limp body falls to the floor. Cole trains his shotgun back onto Watson.

"Are you four done?" Jeremy says impatiently. The knife is still firmly pressed against Kadence's neck and as she swallows, a drip of dark liquid runs down her skin and below the collar of my sweatshirt. "Watson, hurry up or we're going to miss the plane."

"You aren't going anywhere," I bark, taking a step towards him and lifting the barrel of my gun at Jeremy. I've got to get the knife away from Kadence. Even shooting him, I can't risk the slip of his wrist and it cutting into Kade's neck.

Jeremy shifts behind Kadence and narrows in on me. "What do you want with this bitch anyway?" He tugs on her head again, bringing her head back so far she has to look up at him. "The only thing she's good at is being a pain in my ass. At least with me I can keep her in line. Tell me, she talk back to you yet? She's got a mouth on her when she wants."

He leans into her, brushing his nose against her hair. "She smells sweet too, tell me, Nash. You taste her yet?"

My hand tightens around the pistol as Kade's eyes close. My control is splintering. The need to get her as far away from Jeremy as possible is the only thing I can think about, that and killing him. A low rumble comes from my chest as I take another step.

"Get your hands off of *my wife.*"

Time stops when I realize what I said. Then satisfaction rolls through me as realization crosses over Jeremy's face and Watson falters for a second. I can't look at Cole. I can already feel the betrayal burning from my friend's eyes and into the side of my own head. Kadence's eyes lock onto mine and the corner of her mouth turns upward ever so slightly. In this moment alone, I know that even burning down the world for her would never be enough.

KADENCE

We got married that day in Santa Barbara. Holden told me he wanted to surprise me with something, wanted to take me someplace special, and drove us both to the courthouse. At first, I had a sliver of panic roll through me. Was it too fast? What would everyone else think? But then he kissed me. Soft and slow in the way that makes my insides melt and I realized then that marrying him made the rest of the world melt away. It doesn't matter if it was too fast or if everyone thought we were crazy. It was the one good thing we could look back on and not regret. And now? If we both die in this warehouse at the hands of men who thrive on cruelty, then at least I would die married to a man who loved me with his whole being.

Whatever Holden meant to do to try and distract Jeremy works. His hand holding the knife against my throat drops to his side though the grip he has on my hair never relents. *"Your what?"* Jeremy seethes as his head cocks to the side with narrowed eyes.

"My wife," Holden repeats and my heart starts to race in my chest. We have kept it a secret for weeks and hearing him say it out loud felt like claiming a part of me that had been sitting in limbo.

His fingers tighten in my hair to the point that it feels like he's ripping my scalp as he yanks my head back again. Dark and stormy eyes glare down at me. "You *married* him!" Jeremy booms.

I know he catches the glint in my eye when I see his fist raise in my peripheral. Before there's even an impact I push back in the chair again, landing on my back and this time the chair breaks and splintered wood digs into my back as I roll to the side in an instant. I see Holden lunge for Jeremy landing on top of him and delivering blow after blow to his face. Jeremy grunts as he kicks and tries to shove Holden off of him but it's no use.

Every instinct in me screams to fight. I glance around looking for anything I can use to help him. More grunts and a howl of pain echo in the warehouse and when I look up Cole and Watson are trading blows back and forth. There's so much chaos going on with the sounds of bones breaking and men yelling that it's hard to tell who has the upper hand. Although deep down, I know no one wins in this situation. Everyone ends up hurt one way or another.

"You motherfucker!" I hear Cole growl, "Fuck you!" He throws his fist into Watson's nose, knocking him back a few steps.

I look back to Holden and Jeremy. Holden is on his back, scrambling backward out of Jeremy's reach. Our eyes meet and in that second Jeremy reaches down to his ankle, pulling out a small handgun and aiming it right at Holden. "I'm going to kill you and then I'm going to fucking kill her!"

My eyes widen and my heart stops as the sound of the men fighting behind me fade away when his finger pulls the trigger. I move to scramble towards Jeremy but the sound of gunfire has me frozen, my eyes slamming close and when I open them again Holden's flat on his back. "Nash!" I scream watching his chest heave as he tries to catch his breath but from here I can't tell if Jeremy missed or not.

I know Jeremy knows all the weaknesses of the vests that Holden and Cole are wearing. He knows where to aim and the thought of losing Holden to him has me scrambling to my feet. I push up off of my shoulder and yelp in pain as the fire spreads to my fingertips again but I manage to get up. I spot the shotgun Holden dropped and sprint after it hearing Jeremy boom behind me.

I hear another yelp of pain and glance back at Cole as my fingers wrap around the shotgun. He's on his back and a knife sticking from his own shoulder. "Watson!" He growls but he's no longer going after Cole. The door the men have all been coming through slams closed and I know he's gone.

"You think that just because she's here she's yours!" Jeremy yells, lifting Holden by the collar of his tactical vest, his face inches from Jeremy's. "Kadence will always be mine." His voice is strained and so dangerously low that I don't think. I stand, pulling back the forend of the shotgun, pin back my shoulders and steady myself for the fight I've been running from for months.

"I won't ever be yours Jeremy," I spit, aiming for the back of his knee and pulling the trigger. He screams out in pain and his right leg buckles out from under him. Jeremy rolls onto his back scrambling backwards away from Holden as his eyes narrow in on me.

"You bitch!" He yells, "What the fuck!"

A feeling that I've never felt before courses through me. Power and hatred so pure it burns my veins. I pull back the forend again, loading another round. My eyes flick to Holden and the pool of blood gathering around his left pec. His bright glossy blue eyes are focused on me as he gasps for air. "Cole!" I yell, "Get to Holden."

Cole groans in the background but the shuffling that follows tells me that he's moving. "You okay, baby?" I ask in the same way he did. He gives me a quick nod before I turn my attention back to Jeremy. I know what I have to do and the guilt, the shame I thought I would have in needing to do it, is nowhere to be found.

"That was for my mother," I hiss, pulling the trigger again and this time aiming at his left knee. "That? Was for Maria."

"What the fuck are you doing!" He screeches between a scream.

"Giving you back every ounce of pain and more that you gave me." I say through my teeth. "You never deserved me or our child." Tears burn in my eyes as I cock the shotgun again shooting his right hand. "That was for Holden." The words are clenched between my tightened jaw and I repeat the shot on his left hand. "That was for every time you put your hands on me."

Jeremy is screaming out in pain, over and over until the sound becomes strangulated. His skin has turned a ghastly shade as he watches me with shock and horror on his face. "Stop, stop, please, stop," he begs me.

"You want mercy?" I narrow my eyes on him. I know both Holden and Cole are watching me. I can feel the heat of their gaze on my back as I step over Jeremy's legs. "Do you think you deserve any mercy for what you've done to me? To my family?" I hiss looking down at him. "You're a pathetic excuse for a man. You use power like it's heroin, Jeremy. You had to know that it was going to end like this one way or another. One of us was going to die and you failed to kill me the first time."

I crouch over him, gripping his chin between my fingers. The scruff I once loved years ago now feels like coarse sandpaper under my touch. "Now it's my turn," I rasp before dropping his head and aiming for his chest. "This is for *my* child that *you killed*."

The last shot rings out and finally, the already barely there light dims behind his dark eyes. Blood sputters from between his lips and he's gone. I toss the now empty shotgun down and sprint to Holden's side.

"Hey!" I almost whine grabbing his face. His eyes are opening and closing lazily and blood is pooling at the base of his throat. "Where is it?" I ask, looking up at Cole, who has his hand pressed against his collarbone. His eyes are glued to Holden's paling face. "Cole!"

They flick to my gaze and he shakes his head. "We have to get him out of here," he says in a broken whisper. His own blood drips down his arm but he doesn't seem to care.

I look back to Holden, those blue eyes bore into mine and tears fill my own again only this time they're for him. "You better not die on me, Nash." I whisper, pressing my forehead to his. "Don't you leave me."

A ragged chuckle leaves him followed by a cough as his hand grabs my sweatshirt in a loose grip. It's a small sign that he's still in there, that the Holden I know is still fighting.

The door to the building slams and my eyes instantly flick up to see Dex and Scottie running towards us.

Dex skids to a stop when he sees Jeremy's body.

"Jesus, Mary, and Joseph," Scottie whispers under his breath as both men's eyes fix to me.

"We need an ambulance," I choke out as I feel Holden tug at my sweatshirt. I look back down at him and his eyes have grown heavier. "Hey, hey, hey, whoa," I panic, patting the side of his face, trying to keep him awake. "Holden? Holden, stay awake, okay? Okay, baby? Please, look at me."

He opens his eyes and smiles. The man actually smiles at me. "*Sunflower.*" The word comes out raspy as his eyes close again.

"Holden!" I yell, my voice is desperate and threaded this time. "Do something!" I screech at Cole who stares at me. "Cole!"

"Kade!" Dex booms. "911 is on the way. He's gonna be okay." I feel him crouch next to me and I look down at Holden again. His eyes are closed but I can feel his chest barely moving and as long as it's moving he'll be okay. I have to hold on to that. "We can't come this far just for him to die," I whisper.

"He won't," Dex whispers back, wrapping an arm around my shoulder. I wince in pain and pull away from him. The adrenaline is starting to wear off and I can feel just how bad my shoulder is.

"Did you guys get Watson?" I ask looking back at Dex and Scottie. The two men look at each other with brows furrowed.

"No. We thought he was still here with you," Dex says, looking at Cole. "He ran off?"

"We'll find him," Scottie chimes in. "We have to."

I look at Cole. His face has turned green as he sits back and drops his head into his hands. I want to comfort him but any energy I have is gone. I can't. Not until Holden is safe. Safe and alive.

HOLDEN

Everything hurts. My chest, my face, every muscle in my body feels like I was run over by a freight train. I recognize the methodical beeping of hospital machines even before my eyes open. The last thing I remember is Kadence standing over Jeremy's body. I wanted to be the one to put him down. To have that on my conscience and not hers but the way she stood over him. The look in those green eyes had turned beautifully dangerous.

My eyes slowly open, blinded by the incandescent hospital bulbs, I squint them trying to get my bearings. I know I'm not at the clubhouse based on the smell of bleach clinging to my nostrils but there's something else that lingers over it. Her scent. Lavender and vanilla bean forces my eyes to open further just to catch a glimpse of her.

Kadence's long dark hair is splayed over the thin blanket at my side. Her arm is tucked under her cheek and her eyes are closed. She looks exhausted. Even though she's asleep I can still see the dark bags under her eyes and the harsh smattering of bruises that litter her cheek. The sound of the heart rate machine starts to pick up again as anger swells in my chest. I should have gotten to her sooner, shouldn't have let her leave the clubhouse the way I did. If I hadn't, this would have never happened to her.

But Jeremy would still be haunting Kade.

We'd still be running from Stokes and Watson.

I lift my hand, running my fingers gingerly through her soft waves. "Sunflower," I rasp, feeling the evidence left from a breathing tube in the soreness of my throat.

She stirs softly. That familiar mewl she makes when she doesn't want to wake up makes me smile. My Kade is still here. My woman who fought like hell for herself, for our baby and for me. My Sunflower.

"Baby," I rasp again and this time her head lifts. That sleepy look in her gaze catches mine and those green eyes widen when she realizes I'm awake. "Hi." I say softly.

Kade's eyes glisten in the light as tears gather at the corners of them. "Hi," she whispers back so softly that if my focus wasn't on her I would have missed it.

She stands and that's when I see the shoulder sling on her other arm. A range of emotions flashes through me as I reach for her. My fingertips brush her stomach. "The baby?"

Kade lets out a small laugh and grabs my hand, pressing my palm gently to her stomach. "The baby is fine. Healthy as can be at six weeks."

A rush of air leaves me and relief settles in my bones. "And you?"

"Just a bruised shoulder," she says, moving to sit on the edge of the bed. Her eyes find mine and she knows I have a million questions but judging by the look on her face she's willing to answer them. "You scared the shit out of me."

"I'm alive, baby," I whisper, trying to reassure her although I don't know why. I'm talking and breathing and she can see that.

My words have her shoulders drop and a smile forms on her face. I reach for her again and this time she leans to me as my hand wraps around the curvature of her neck pulling her closer. Our foreheads meet before I nudge her nose with mine and kiss her. Every unsaid *I love you*, every emotion bubbling inside of us poured into this one kiss and despite my own sling and the overwhelming aches my body feels it's almost as if her kiss erases it all until it's just the two of us.

Kade pulls away first and it feels like a rubber band snapping me back to reality. "There's something you should know," she says, chewing on her bottom lip.

My brows furrow. "What?"

"Watson disappeared."

That familiar feeling of rage comes back when I realize what that means. That asshole is still out there somewhere, a monster hiding in plain sight. My eyes find hers and I can tell she's gauging my reaction. If it weren't for the drugs pumping through me, her worried eyes and our child—I would probably be off the handle right now. Gathering every man I can find in order to hunt Watson down and kill him myself. My mind wanders to Cole and images of the two of them on the ground fighting flicker through my mind.

"I can see those wheels turning," she whispers, tangling her fingers into mine. "Talk to me."

"Are the guys looking for him?" I ask.

Her eyes move from me and she shakes her head. "Scottie and Dex are doing patrols, but Cole gave up this morning."

"What the hell do you mean he *gave up*?" I snap tilting my head to catch her gaze again. "Why the hell—"

"Baby," she squeezes my hand and her eyes flicker to the heart rate machine that's rapidly beeping again. "He wanted to focus on the club. Trey's already taking over the Sheriff's office with most of the town backing him. He's doing his best and he was worried about you."

"He doesn't need to worry about me, he needs to worry about finding the asshole that killed Becca."

Kade lets go of my hand to cup my cheek, running her thumb along my cheekbone. "Cole can't lose another, Nash. He's already barely holding on as it is."

There's something in the words that she says where it sounds like there's more. Cole and I haven't been on the best terms. Butting heads every chance we get, keeping things from one another that as kids we wouldn't dare not share with the other one.

"He's hurting."

"We're all hurting," I bite and shake my head.

"And we all need a break from the heavy shit," She says firmly, catching my gaze. "Wyatt needs to heal, *you* need to heal." She starts and I can't help the upturn twitch of the corners of my mouth as she does. "We have a baby we have to prepare for. Dex and Scottie are on a hunting spree," Kade starts rambling and it only grows the smile on my face.

"Okay, okay," I whisper, conceding to her. If not focusing on the fact that Watson is gone will help ease the obvious nerves she has, I'll do it.

Becca was a huge part of my life. Closer than most siblings and been through ten lifetimes' worth of pain. Even now, her sass and the way she loves the club flows through me. If I ever get the chance to avenge her death, I'll do it with a smile on my face and a trigger finger that's happy to pull. I know Becca wouldn't want me to live in the past. My sister would most definitely kick my ass for acting the way I have over the past four months. My grief overwhelmed my need to live and be present in the life I have. It was time to change.

I need to start living for myself, for the things that make me happy and for the woman sitting on this bed who looks like she hasn't had a full night's sleep in days while she waited for me to wake up.

"You killed Jeremy," I rasp, "are you?"

"Glad he's dead?" Kadence finishes for me.

"I was going to say *okay*, but that works too."

"I'm glad he's dead," she says with conviction. "I'm glad I can be sure that chapter of my life is done. He won't be able to haunt me anymore and..." Her eyes fill with tears.

"What is it?"

"When he had me before you and Cole showed up. He told me he killed my mother." The words leave her lips in a strained tone. Soft and as if she's trying to be strong for me. "And that he attacked Maria."

"The woman who helped you?" I ask.

Kadence nods. I swipe a tear from her cheek. "I have to live with that. That I let this man into my life and he took almost everything away. *I* had to be the one."

"You didn't, Sunflower." I shake my head, "That's not a burden I would ever want for you."

"Killing Jeremy wasn't a burden." Her green eyes flicker to mine. "It was inevitable."

I stare at her for a moment while the words settle in my chest. She's a lot more like me than I realized. I know Kadence is strong, probably stronger than I would ever be, given what she's been through and she's still sitting here with me with her head on straight and not a broken shell.

"You're a strong woman, Kadence." I nod. "Stronger than I'll ever be and what you did to Jeremy...he deserved worse."

She lets out a sigh and curls her fingers around mine again. "I want to go back to Florida, even under the radar, just to see Maria and bury my mother."

"We can do that." I pull her into my uninjured side pressing my lips to the crown of her head. "Whatever you need to do, Kade, I'm there with you."

"I love you," she whispers after a moment. The words feel different now, not weighed down by everything chasing us. They feel lighter, happier than before and how they should feel.

"I love you too," I rasp into her hair. Kadence carefully wraps her arm around my waist, curling into my side, and for the first time since I woke up, makes herself small against me. There still isn't anything I won't do for her. I'll drag my ass through Mosul again if it means bringing me to this point. To have the only woman who ever truly saw me in my arms.

"Marry me," I whisper.

Kadence lifts her head to look at me with furrowed brows. "We're already married," she says with confusion in her voice.

"No, Sunflower. Marry me for real. With all our friends, our family. The cake, you in a giant dress." A smile creeps over my lips as my fingers comb through her hair. "I want it all with you, Kadence, and I don't want to wipe away what's happened the last few months, but I want to start my future with you by my side."

Tears prick at the corners of her eyes again. The weight of everything surrounding the reason we're here lifts as she sits up slightly. "How the hell am I supposed to say no to that?"

My hand tangles in her hair and tugs at her roots gently, pulling her lips closer to mine. "You aren't," I rasp and press my lips to hers. Kadence mewls softly, the vibration sending a tingle down my spine and straight to my toes. She pulls away breathlessly and grins.

"Us against the world?"

"Us against the world."

EPILOGUE

"I now pronounce you both husband and wife...again." Scottie grins at the two of us. I laugh as Holden's arms wrap around me. The once small bump, now more prominent, is almost squished between us as he embraces me. "Kiss that bride of yours, Nash."

Holden's blue eyes drag from Scottie to me with a smile so wide I can't help but match it.

"C'mere, Sunflower," he rasps as one hand slides up my back and around the back of my neck.

"It's wife to you," I whisper as his lips graze against mine.

Holden shakes his head and the corners of his mouth turn up again as my hands grip onto the edges of his cut.

"You're still my Sunflower." Holden closes the distance between us, taking my top lip first as he kisses me and our friends cheer around us. Getting lost in the first kiss we've shared in hours, I whimper against his lips, feeling him smile against my own.

The sun beams down against the raging water of the river below. It glitters against the soft pearls and stones on my dress, creating a disco-like effect over the brand new wood and metal of the bridge. When I first suggested it as the place we should get married, Holden shook his head and went into many, many reasons as to why we would never get married here.

Trey had spent time with the city planners to fix the bridge after Holden called it a death trap. He wasn't entirely wrong, I had almost died because of the state the bridge was in previously. Under Holden's guidance, Trey had the bridge rebuilt to almost new only leaving the initials carved into one restored piece of the wood.

Holden pulls back from the kiss as the crowd begins to file off of the bridge and back towards the pull off through the cut down trail lined with flowers that led us out here.

"I have something for you," he says, tucking a tendril of hair behind my ear.

"You do?" I raise a brow. "I thought we said no gifts."

He narrows his eyes and bobs his head. "We did, but we'll just call this perfect timing."

I shove against his chest. "Holden Nash, what did you do?"

"Nothin' darlin', it wasn't all totally me," he admits, glancing behind him.

I follow his eyeline to where Cole and Blake are bickering back and forth about something. Holden shakes his head as we continue walking with everyone else. His fingers intertwine with mine as we walk down the trail until he came to a stop just before the opening out to the pull off. He lets go of my hand and turns to me, curling his fingers around my cheeks.

"I told you once I never wanted to replace your father and I know he couldn't be here today, so I wanted to give you the next best thing."

My brows furrow softly. "What?"

He dips his head, looking out beyond the tree line, and points. I turn to look and through the trees I see shiny black metal.

"Is that?" I whisper looking back up at him, seeing that mischievous smile plastered on his face.

"Go look," he says softly, pressing his lips to my forehead before letting me go.

Excitement flows through me as I make my way through the brush, holding my hand out behind me for him to take, which of course he does. Stepping out from the trees, in between the rows of motor-cycles parked, was my Comet. My father's Comet as I remember it. White-walled wheels, cherry red steering wheel and brand new black paint that glitters under the afternoon sun.

Tears fill my eyes and a sense of warmth washes over me. Holden lets go of my hand for a moment, stepping over to where Dex and Scottie are as they pass something to him. My eyes are glued to the car as I slowly walk around it.

"I can't believe it," I whisper.

"The guys worked hard," Cole says from behind me. "I swear Wyatt polished it three times before he let any of us touch it."

A tearful laugh leaves me as I glance over at West. His attention is on me with his arms wrapped around Blake's middle. The two of them finally gave each other a chance. After Watson's attack on Wyatt, Blake wouldn't leave his side for weeks and in that time the feelings they tried so hard to hide finally spilled over. It was the happiest I had ever seen the two of them.

"I can't believe it," I whisper again as Holden steps back over to me, jangling the keys between his fingers.

"Give it a go." He grins and opens the driver's side door for me.

I start to climb in, lifting my dress and huffing softly as the space between me and the steering wheel has shortened with my growing belly. Holden climbs in on the passenger side, leaning against the seat, watching me as I stick the key into the ignition and give it a turn. The car roars to life, sending a thrill down my spine. I look up at him with tears in my eyes. I was sure that this car would have been gone forever.

"You still plannin' on leaving?" He dares to ask me with a sly grin on his face as he reaches up and swipes away a tear from my cheek with the pad of his thumb.

"Not a chance," I whisper before leaning into him, kissing him softly with him welcoming it as our friends cheer again.

I understand why it felt like God laughed at my plans before. My plan was shit, full of ultimatums and tainted love. Now, I have the exact opposite. A man who would literally do anything to protect me and our child, a man who shows me what it means to be loved without condition. My family may be gone, a child lost and a missed opportunity with my mother but Holden Nash and the Hounds slowly fill in each crack left in my heart, day by day.

Acknowledgements

To my family, thank you so much for showing the support you do. Showing up with sharing posts, asking me how things are going and learning the process with me. I am truly grateful to have the family and friends that surround me. To Mom, thank you for being the first one to pre-order everything and ordering an obscene amount of your own copies to give away, lol. Thank you for always being there. To Dad, Alex & Megan, you guys have been amazingly supportive and genuinely curious and happy for me not just with this project but with Huckleberry as well. To Paul, thank you for never not telling me how proud you are of me. The overwhelming support is something I will never forget. I love you all so much.

To my **Street team & Beta readers,** you all got the uncut, raw version of this story and the amount of love everyone showed Holden and Kadence was overwhelming in the best way. Please never underestimate how appreciative I am of you all for taking the chance on me. Thank you for sharing this book out into the world so that others can love it as much as we do.

To **Bec,** You have given me way too much confidence in my ability write a book with little to no recommendations for changes and I love you for that, lol. Even though I still question on when not to use a comma, you have never made me feel bad for it. Thank you for editing for me, thank you for understanding my love for Simon & Soap and truly thank you for just being you. I love you so much and I'm so excited to start this next journey with you. Forever and always, The Holy Trinity of Angry Lil Bats.

To Sam, my Joey, my Sammilamb, the Sweetlilraz to my Detrimentum-x-x, I love you more than words can say. You are truly the sweetest bean I have ever been privileged enough to call a best friend. Between 3AM voice notes, to cry sessions on Marco Polo, to having pretty much the same brain. I'm grateful for your energy, for the positivity you bring to every conversation no matter where you are, the understanding and love that you show the people in your life and strangers. We may not talk every day but no matter if it's one day or thirty we always pick up where we leave off. Thank you for hearing me, seeing me and loving me. Love you and miss you always.

Last and definitely not least. To Shicara, you threatened that if I made you cry that you'd beat my ass writing this so... challenge accepted. You are the Bucky to my Buck, the Stevie to my Rian, the Stink to my Twinkle Toes. You have been more than a rock for me not just with becoming an author but in pretty much every aspect of my life. Who knew that one invite to the Sugar Club and one conversation about Catch & Release would put us here almost three years later. Co-authors, best friends, chaos gremlins and pain train conductors. I know you hate it when I get sappy but I can't help it. You have done more for me than anyone knows and probably more than you should have but we'll agree to disagree on that because I know you'll fight me on it anyways. Thank you for pushing me to become an author, to be a better writer, to always writing down my ramblings because I never take notes on anything. To listening to my five minute voice messages in discord because creativity only comes to me when driving apparently. To knowing the exact time I get home every day and always making sure I'm safe in more ways than just one. (are you crying yet?

because I am.) Thank you for always telling me I deserve better and more and helping me see my worth. For telling me not to be so hard on myself and that it's okay to take breaks and for keeping me sane when I get overwhelmed with things. You have invested so much into me and somedays I still don't understand why but I am always grateful that you did. I love you so so so much and I promise one day I'll finally get my passport so you can beat my ass (with love, I'm assuming) in person for this. You can't see it, but I'm tapping two fingers to my heart right now.

About the author

Jessica Norton lives in Washington State. She's the ripe age of 31 years old. She's been writing since high school but never anything published. Just daydreams and poems mostly. She's a hopeless romantic that writes Romance novels with Happy Ever Afters. This girl is a HUGE sucker for a good HEA. She enjoys dipping her toes into dark themes as well with the perfect amount of Spice. She's currently working on the second book in the Whiskey River series with Aubrey Taylor & the second book in the Hell Hounds MC Series.

Current Works and Coming Soon:
Huckleberry (Whiskey River Series – Released Oct 2024
Second Whiskey River Book (Expected Winter of 2025)
Second Hell Hounds MC Book (TBA)